Winging IT

H. P. Oliver

MYSTERIES IN HISTORY

HPO Productions
8698 Elk Grove Boulevard
Suite 1-271
Elk Grove, California 95624

Cover art and design by Steve Eitzen

Printed in the United States of America

ISBN-10: 0988833166
ISBN-13: 978-0-9888331-6-6

DEDICATION

For Judy

ACKNOWLEDGMENTS

The author wishes to thank and/or acknowledge the following individuals and organizations for the information and support they provided: David Stenn, author of *Clara Bow – Running Wild*; James H. Farmer, author of *Celluloid Wings*; William Wellman, Jr., author of *The Man and His Wings*; Hollywood Heritage; San Diego Air and Space Museum; Ventura County Library and Museum; Director Tony Bill for his brilliant film, *Flyboys*; Wendy and Ty Hamby for their firearms expertise; Tim McCoy for his historical and aviation knowledge; and Director General Cecil B. DeMille for allowing me to have my photo made outside his office door.

PLEASE NOTE

This book occasionally refers to individuals and groups with terms that are considered inappropriate in today's society. These terms, however, were in common usage during the historical period in which this story is set and are included here solely for the purpose of accurately depicting the attitudes and customs of the era.

Regional Location Map

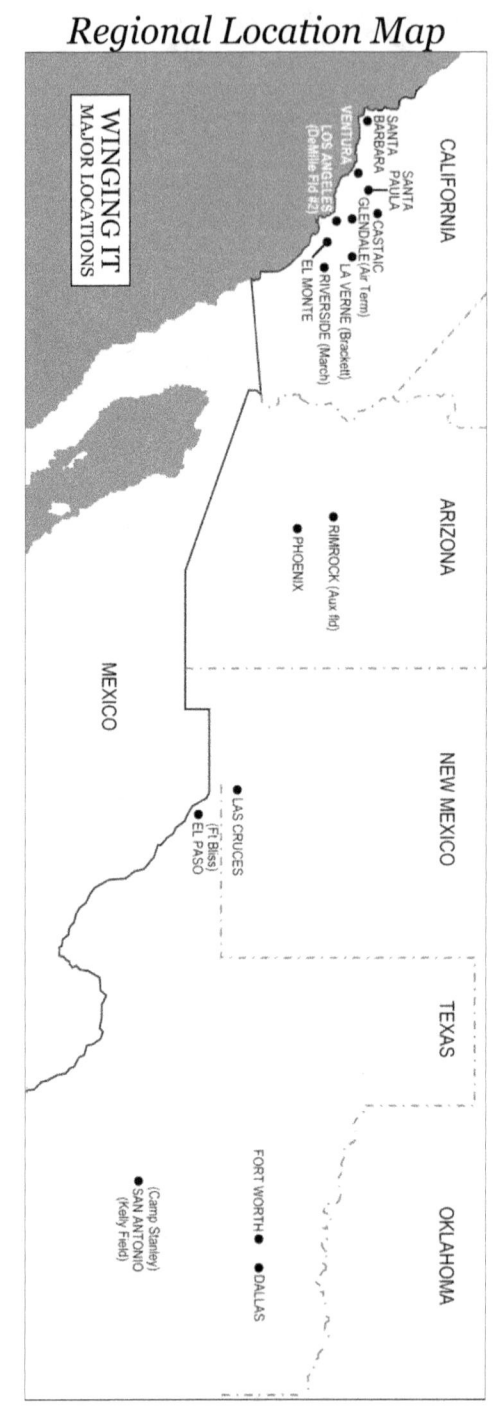

Metropolitan Location Map

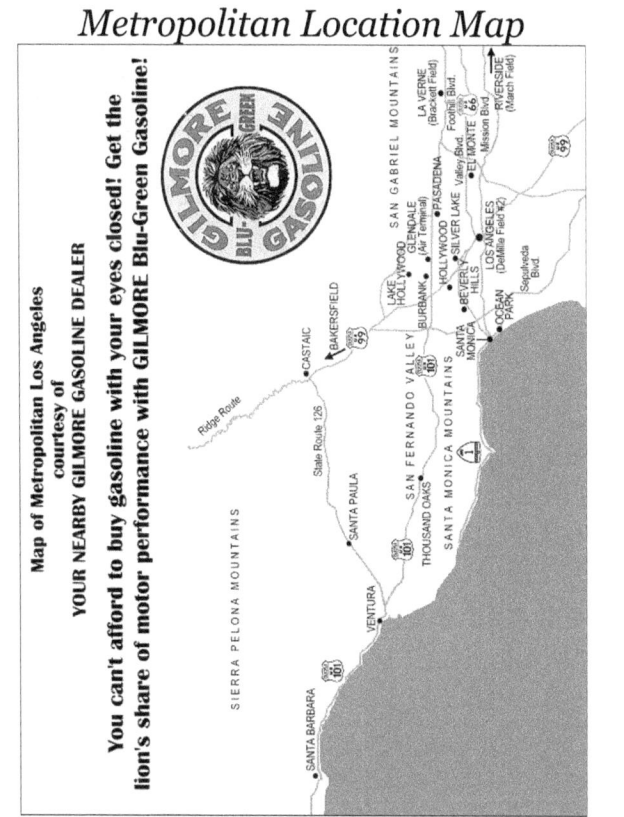

Winging IT

Author's Introduction

Dear Readers,

I feel I must begin *Winging IT* by confessing that most of the words in this novel are not mine. They are, rather, those of Edward J. Markham.

Markham first gained public notice during World War One as a pursuit (fighter) pilot, His wartime bravery earned him a Distinguished Service Cross with two oak leaf clusters and a Citation Star (equivalent of today's Silver Star). After the Great War he retuned to a career as a novelist and penned several popular novels during the 1920s.

The words I have borrowed from Edward Markham, however, come from another and quite different source—a journal he kept for a two month period during 1926. Markham's journal tells an incredible story that changed motion picture history, but the story of how I came by the document is nearly as interesting. That story begins early in 2014 when I received an email from a woman in Santa Barbara, California named Diane. (I have withheld her last name out of respect for her privacy.) Here are the first two paragraphs of that letter:

Dear Mr. Oliver,

*I am the grand niece of WWI aviator and 1920s author Edward Markham, and I am in possession of a unique piece of motion picture history. Specifically, I have a journal kept by Uncle Edward during the making of **Wings**, a motion picture on which he worked briefly as a consultant in 1926.*

I am bringing this to your attention because the journal relates an amazing and previously unknown piece of film history involving silent film actress Clara Bow. I believe this story needs to be told and I chose to offer you the opportunity of telling it because, after reading your novels, I am convinced you are the author who can best set the scene and make the story as real to readers today as it was to Uncle Edward almost 90 years ago.

The rest of Diane's email described the various sources she used to verify the authenticity of the journal and, to the extent possible, the accuracy of the story it tells. Then Diane extended an invitation for me to visit her in Santa Barbara to read the journal and discuss the project she proposed.

Even though I had no idea what secrets about Clara Bow were supposed to be lurking within the pages of Edward Markham's journal, the idea of exposing a ninety-year-old scandal fascinated me. On the other hand, folks often send me story ideas, but most of them turn out to be on subjects in which few have any interest. This was a little different, though, so I replied to Diane's email, scheduling an appointment with her during my next trip to the southern half of the state.

After doing a little homework of my own regarding her great uncle, I met with Diane and read Uncle Eddie's journal. Diane's description of the story it tells is an understatement. The events that occurred during those two months in 1926 did, indeed, change motion picture history.

To make, as they say, a long story short, I told Diane I was very interested in telling Uncle Eddie's story. We came to terms and agreed on how to approach the writing. Diane and I decided to write the story as a novel, making no claims to its authenticity and allowing me room to add dialogue based on the journal.

You hold the result in your hands. Enjoy the story. Whether you choose to believe it or not is up to you.

H. P. Oliver
October 30, 2014

Prologue

9:35 A.M. – Saturday – November 9, 1918
Above Northern France

From my assigned patrol altitude of 5,000 feet, the Albatross D-Three appeared as little more than a tiny black cross against the dark green farmland west of the German airfield at Ars-sur-Moselle. In fact, it was not the aircraft itself, but the dark shadow following along on the ground behind it that brought the Boche ship to my attention.

The Albatross was headed east at an altitude of about a thousand feet and at what seemed a leisurely speed. I speculated that the German flier might be completing his morning patrol and returning to one of the Jasta aerodromes around Labry. Such speculation, however, mattered little for, regardless of his reason for being on our side of the front lines, I intended to rid the sky of this Boche menace.

When I first saw the enemy pilot he was about a mile ahead of me and a mile to my right. Now, less than thirty seconds later we were abeam each other and I was watching him carefully for any sign that he had seen me. Seeing no such indication, I planned my attack.

Lowering the nose of my Spad S-Thirteen slightly to gain some airspeed and lose some altitude, I held my westerly course for another minute. I used that time to give the skies around me a thorough perusal. It was a common tactic of the Boche to send a lone flier out as bait while his comrades lurked nearby waiting to ambush the unwary French, British or American pilot who went for the bait like a big, stupid fish.

The skies on this particular morning, though, were clear and I put my plan of attack into motion by beginning a wide descending turn to the right. When I leveled my wings again, I was about three miles behind the Albatross and roughly two thousand feet above it. From the airspeed indicator attached to my port wing I calculated my speed at around 190 kilometers-per-hour—a speed of about 120 miles-per-hour in American terms. The Boche continued at his leisurely pace, oblivious to my presence. I would soon give him reason to regret his lack of vigilance.

During the next three or four minutes I continued to close the distance between us, all the while keeping a close watch on the sky above and behind me for other enemy aircraft. At the same time I made slight adjustments to my glide path so that I would end up slightly above the Albatross when the distance between us was reduced to one hundred yards—the perfect position from which to rake the Boche ship from nose to tail with deadly fire from my twin thirty-caliber Marlin machine guns.

When I reached the position from which I would begin my attack, I pulled the cocking lever to clear my guns and gave the sky around us one last look. Then, with my hand on the firing lever, I turned my attention back to my target and the Albatross had disappeared into thin air!

Mere seconds later I felt the impact of machinegun bullets slamming into the underside of my Spad and realized I had just fallen for one of the simplest and most effective tricks in the book. The Boche pilot had spotted me somewhere along the line, perhaps even before I saw him, and he had patiently waited for me to close into firing position. Then he had pulled his power completely off and lowered his nose, causing me to fly right over the top of his rapidly slowing ship. From that point he went to full power and raised his nose, putting my Spad directly in his gun sight.

Cursing the overconfidence that blinded me to the possibility that, by such a simple ruse, I could instantly become the hunted rather than the hunter, I did three things simultaneously. Slamming my throttle wide open, I stomped on my right rudder pedal and yanked the control stick back and to the right.

My Spad responded by instantly rolling into a tight, climbing turn to the right and, hopefully, out of my foe's line of fire. Feeling no more hits from the Boche's guns, I knew I had gained a momentary reprieve, but I fully expected the German to press his advantage by following me into my turn. When I turned to look back, however, the Albatross was again nowhere to be seen. Now what was he up to?

I lowered the nose my ship, but stayed in the right turn until I had completed a full three-hundred-sixty degree circle. Then, leveling my wings, I scanned the sky above and below for the Boche. I spotted him nearly a mile ahead of me and running to the east for all he was worth. He had also dropped to tree-top level, using the descent to increase his speed and make himself harder to see against the ground.

In level flight, my S-Thirteen had a speed advantage of about twenty miles-per-hour over the Albatross. I would add to this advantage during my descent. Thus, I knew I could overtake the Boche before he reached the front lines about ten miles to the east. Given the skill he had demonstrated by suckering me into his trap, however, getting the Albatross into my gun sight again might be another matter entirely.

With my throttle still wide open, I aimed my nose at the rapidly fleeing Albatross and began closing the distance between us again. I saw the German pilot look back at over his shoulder, and when I had closed to within firing range again, he took the only evasive action left to him. He pushed his left rudder pedal to the floor and the Albatross skidded left out of my gun sight.

I did exactly the same thing to bring my nose back on his tail. Just as that happened, he reversed the procedure and skidded to the right. Again, I followed his maneuver, but this time I kept my nose to the left of the Albatross so when he skidded back to the left a moment later, he flew directly into my line of fire.

Without hesitation, I fired both guns and watched tears appear in the fabric along the left side of the Boche ship. Almost instantly a thin line of black smoke streamed from his engine and the Albatross slowed. I had hit something critical and I knew I had him.

Reducing my speed, I centered the damaged Albatross in my aiming reticule and again opened fire. Pieces of the damaged machine flew off into the slipstream and I saw the D-Three's right wings sag. A split second later the Boche's nose came up and the ship shuddered on the verge of a stall.

To avoid a collision with the Albatross, I opened my throttle and pulled around into a climbing right turn. Suddenly my windscreen was filled with a long line of evergreen trees I had failed to notice while attacking the enemy ship. I pulled the stick back as far as it would go and my trusty Spad hopped over the tree tops with just a few feet to spare.

After clearing the trees, I resumed my turn to the right,

intending to set up another firing pass on the Albatross, but when I spotted the Boche ship, I knew the fight was over. My worthy foe and his ship were now a smoking pile of rubble on the ground alongside an east-west roadway that passed through the area. Even though I knew the German pilot would have gladly done the same thing to me had our positions been reversed, I felt a wave of sadness pass through me. A brave man had just lost his life in the service of his country. I wondered what he would say if I could ask him whether or not the honor of Germany was worth the price he had just paid for a small piece of it.

Looking down at the wreckage again, I saw two French farmers running toward the crashed Albatross with pitchforks in their hands to be used as weapons in the event the German pilot had survived the crash of his ship. They had no need of their makeshift weapons. The men waved enthusiastically as I passed over their heads. I am sure they felt no great loss at the death of a German pilot.

I climbed to about a thousand feet in a fairly tight spiral over the wreckage. From that altitude I could see that the road alongside which the German ship had crashed intersected a major north-south road about a mile further east. About five miles north along the north-south road lay a French village I recognized as Abaucourt. I made note of these landmarks so our ground troops could locate the Albatross's wreckage and confirm my sixth and, as the fates would have it be, final aerial victory of the Great War

Then also noting the position of the indicator on my ship's fuel gauge below the one-quarter mark, I turned southwest toward home, keeping a wary eye on the skies around me as I went. Home at that particular time was the airfield near Rembercourt where my unit—the First Pursuit Group of the Twenty-Seventh Aero Squadron—had been stationed for the past three months.

The next day, Sunday, 10 November, we awoke to a thick overcast of fog which kept our ships firmly anchored to the ground until mid-afternoon. Just as the sun appeared and patrols assignments were being made, however, we received a dispatch informing us that an armistice had been agreed to by all parties and the hostilities were to officially end at 1100 hours the following day—the eleventh hour of the eleventh day of the eleventh month of 1918. Since neither I nor any of my comrades were eager to tempt the fates and risk becoming our group's final fatality of the war, we flew only casual patrols close to home that afternoon and during the morning hours of Monday, 11 November.

As one might expect, news of the armistice raised hopes

throughout the squadron that we might be home for Christmas. That possibility grew increasingly doubtful as we waited through the rest of November for orders. Finally, on 5 December those orders arrived. We were sent southeast to the First Air Depot at Colombey-les-Belles Airdrome for the purpose of turning in our aircraft and maintenance equipment and to await our next posting.

The squadron sat around playing games of poker and grumbling at Colombey for two months until 2 February, when we were loaded aboard a train bound for the port town of Brest. Finally, after a month of delousing and paperwork, the members of the Twenty-Seventh Aero Squadron boarded the Navy cruiser USS Charleston and set sail for New York Harbor.

I arrived in New York on 18 March, 1919. There, most of my comrades were mustered out and gladly traveled on to their various hometowns across the country. I, however, was not to be so fortunate. My so-called "gallantry in the air" earned me a somewhat less desirable set of orders. Those orders said that I, First Lieutenant Edward J. Markham, was to report to the U.S. Air Service Pursuit Division at Rockwell Field, San Diego, California for temporary duty as an instructor of advanced pursuit tactics.

When I reported to Captain Clyde Balsley on Monday, 24 March, I learned that I was one of a handful of pilots who were selected as instructors for this specialized training program because of having demonstrated superior pursuit skills while serving in France. Simply stated, our assignment at Rockwell was to teach as many of those skills as possible to new, young pilots with no actual experience in air combat. Thus, along with a half-dozen other veteran fliers, I began conducting what would turn out to be three months of rigorous training exercises.

My fellow instructors were for the most part unknown to me with the exception of one familiar face, that of Lieutenant William Wellman, known to his close associates as "Wild Bill." That Wellman's face was a familiar one was purely a happenstance of war.

During my tour of duty in France I was returning from a solo patrol late one afternoon when my trusty Spad's Hispano-Suiza engine began wheezing and sputtering as if suddenly infected by a dire case of influenza. Along with this most undesirable behavior came rapid losses in both power and altitude. It was immediately clear to me that my ship would not make it back to my home field, so I turned around and made for an airfield over which I had flown a few minutes earlier.

With my intended landing spot in sight, I put my ship into a glide that, if my ailing engine held out long enough, would put me in position to land my Spad safely. Luck was with me that day for Hispano-Suiza breathed its last gasp and my prop came to an abrupt standstill just as I crossed the threshold of the field.

Relieved that both I and my ship were once again on solid terra firma and in more or less whole condition, all that remained was to find a mechanic who could repair my engine so that I might resume the trip back to my base at Rembercourt. As I rolled to a stop near one of the airfield's temporary hangars, two chaps in greasy coveralls trotted out to meet me—just the fellows I needed to see.

Hopping down from my cockpit, I spoke to the mechanics, and that was when I realized my difficulties were not yet over. It seemed I had landed at what I later learned was Luneville aerodrome, which at that particular point in the war was home to a squadron of Escadrille N.87 of the Aéronautique Militaire. That fact was particularly relevant to my situation because the two mechanics who had come out from their hangar to greet me spoke no English and I spoke no French.

As I endeavored to explain my situation to them I could see by their puzzled expressions that I was getting nowhere. Just as my frustration level was nearing the boiling point, a tall, lanky fellow in a blue uniform with French pilot wings over his left breast pocket strolled up. In perfect English he introduced himself as Corporal Bill Wellman and asked if he could be of some assistance.

Both surprised and relieved, I explained my circumstances to Wellman, and he in turn communicated them to the mechanics. This was rather interesting to watch because it turned out that Wellman parlez vous'd little more of the local lingo than I, but he had developed a sort of Pidgin-French that, in combination with a good deal of sign language, made it possible for him to communicate with his comrades.

Within moments the befuddled mechanics were grinning widely and nodding their understanding of the situation. They immediately turned their attention to my ailing engine and soon announced via Wellman that the engine could be repaired, but such repairs could not be completed until the next day.

Perversely, this news seemed to delight Wellman, and as he gave me a tour of the Luneville aerodrome, I came to understand why. Bill explained that he was the only American assigned to the squadron, and my remaining overnight there meant he would have the great pleasure of a fellow countryman with whom to share the evening. And share the evening we did, staying up half the night drinking the worst wine I have ever tasted while comparing our flying experiences and chatting about our plans for when the war ended.

As promised, my Spad was ready to fly by noon the following day, and with some reluctance, I bid my new friend adieu and made for home. Our paths were to cross a few more times before we left for home, and each time we met our friendship grew.

It is said that opposites attract one another and this was certainly the case with Wellman and me. To begin with, and as I have already noted, Wellman served in France as an American volunteer with the Lafayette Escadrille rather than as a member of the U.S. Army Air Service as I had.

Another difference between Wellman and I had to do with our methods of air combat. I believed my meager contributions to the allied victory in France were the result of cautiously and carefully thought out strategies, and flying with as much precision as I could muster. Wild Bill, on the other hand, earned his nickname flying with reckless abandon, relying more on skill and luck than planning and precision. While quite definitely not my way of doing things, I could not fault Wellman's methods for on his uniform blouse he wore the Croix de Guerre—the highly respected French medal of valor given to individuals who distinguished themselves by acts of heroism involving combat with enemy forces. What is more, his Croix de Guerre was decorated with two palm leaves, indicating he had earned the medal three times over. That is a feat not to be considered lightly.

Despite these and the many other differences between us, Wild Bill and I were good pals—a friendship that would last long beyond our respective tours of duty at Rockwell Field. In my case, that tour ended in mid-June, 1919, at which time I was mustered out of the Army. Having completed my service to my Uncle Sam, I returned home to Los Angeles and resumed a fledgling writing career I had barely begun before joining the Army Air Service two years earlier.

One

11:45 A.M. – Thursday – September 9, 1926
Hollywood, California

To describe my mood on this day, I will borrow a line or two from a popular Victrola recording performed by Al Jolson. I was "Sitting on top of the world, just rolling along. Just rolling along." The reasons for my sunny disposition were many, but they all had to do with the good fortune that had come my way during the seven years since the end of the Great War.

In addition to several of my short stories having been published in national magazines, the most notable of which being the widely-read *Saturday Evening Post*, two of my novels were proclaimed "top sellers" by the *New York Times* and *Los Angeles Times* newspapers. And the future of my literary career looked bright ahead as I had just sent my publisher a new manuscript I felt might have a very good chance of becoming yet another top seller.

What is more, a few years back, opportunity knocked loudly on my door in the form of a burgeoning motion picture industry hungry for new stories with which to meet the ever growing demand for the entertainments they manufactured. Writing scenarios, as motion picture stories are called, was proving to be extremely lucrative. I found I could turn out a good story in a matter of days and, once my scenarios had proven their worth, motion picture production companies were willing to pay handsomely for my work. I was now writing for the biggest studios in Los Angeles—the Universal Film Manufacturing Company, the Warner brothers and Famous Players-Lasky to name just three.

These good fortunes brought with them significant

10

improvements in my style of living. I now owned a small home in the prosperous Silver Lake district between Los Angeles proper and Hollywood, I was driving a spanking new roadster manufactured by the Stutz company, and my bank account balance was growing by leaps and bounds. And all of that before my twenty-eighth birthday! I was just rolling along, just rolling along.

At that particular moment I happened to be rolling along in the westbound direction on Sunset Boulevard toward a long-overdue luncheon with my old comrade-in-arms, Wild Bill Wellman. Our meeting place was to be a recently opened eatery called Greenblatt's Delicatessen at the western edge of Hollywood. Bill had suggested meeting there because the restaurant is already gaining a reputation as an outstanding place to eat and because it was not too great a distance from the newly acquired studio facilities of Famous Players-Lasky, where he was currently directing the production of a major motion picture. That Bill Wellman was thus employed gave strong testimony to his talent and skill, for few reached such a lofty rung on the motion picture career ladder. I knew from conversations and correspondence with Bill during the past seven years that attaining such success had been an arduous climb.

Upon leaving the service he tried his hand at acting, and though Bill cut a handsome figure on the motion picture screen, he did not care much for the work. He believed there were opportunities for which he was better suited on the other side of the camera. Bill chose becoming a director as his goal.

Lacking any sort of experience in that field, however, he was forced to start on the very bottom rung of the ladder—a position as messenger boy at the Goldwyn Studios. The job paid a mere twenty-two dollars per week. That was quite a comedown even from what we were paid by the U.S. Army. Bill's meager salary, along with the ending of a most unfortunate marriage to an actress by the name of Helene Chadwick, brought on tough times, and for a while he struggled along in nearly destitute straights.

After two years as a messenger boy, Bill reached the second rung of the ladder with the aid of a new found friend, comedian Will Rogers. Rogers was making films for Goldwyn then and, taking a liking to Bill, got him a promotion to the position of assistant property man on the sets where Rogers' films were being made. This new job brought with it both a slightly higher salary and the opportunity to observe the making of movies from a closer vantage point, thus adding considerably to his education in film making.

In my experience, one of Bill Wellman's strongest attributes is persistence. Once he sets his mind on something he sees it through. This trait ultimately brought Bill to yet a higher rung on the ladder when he was given a job as an assistant director. Working for many directors in this position gave Bill's education a great boost. Most of the films on which he worked were western melodramas and many of those were directed by the man Bill Wellman claims as his chief mentor, Bernard Durning.

It seems Durning saw promise in his assistant director and ultimately gave Bill an opportunity to fill in as the actual director of a Fox Film Corporation motion picture starring the cowboy actor, Dustin Farnum. Wellman's work on the film earned praise from the studio brass hats and more directing jobs were offered. During the next year or so Bill directed seven pictures, all of which were westerns, most featuring the popular cowboy actor Buck Jones in their leading roles. Figuring that the success of these films had earned him an increase in salary, Wild Bill went to William Fox and asked for a raise. Fox refused, a minor altercation ensued, and Wellman was fired.

Having by this time acquired the services of a talent agent, Bill figured his lack of employment would not last long. He had not, however, counted on the impact to his career the altercation with William Fox would have. Motion picture producers do not look kindly upon such goings on, so Wellman's enforced vacation lasted a good deal longer than expected. Ultimately, however, he was offered work by Harry Cohn, the head of production for the Columbia Pictures Corporation.

Success at Columbia led Bill to a position at Metro-Goldwyn-Mayer where he met and impressed producer B. P. Schulberg. Schulberg soon moved on to become head of production at Famous Players-Lasky and took with him two people—William Wellman and the popular actress Clara Bow, whose contracts Schulberg owned. In fact, some say the Bow and Wellman contracts were the only reasons Lasky hired Schulberg.

Greenblatt's Delicatessen was not difficult to find. The restaurant was located in a narrow storefront at the east end of a block-long, two-story building on the north side of Sunset Boulevard and a few blocks west of Fairfax Avenue. The interior of Greenblatt's was rather gloomy, being as it was paneled in dark woods. The wall extending back from the entrance was occupied by a traditional-style deli case stocked with every imaginable sort of prepared and smoked meats. Tables and chairs were arranged along the opposite wall.

Despite the gloom I quickly spotted Bill Wellman sitting at a table about one-third of the way back from the entrance. Looking up, Bill saw me approaching and stood to greet me. Offering his hand, he said enthusiastically, "Hello, Eddie! It's been far too long since we talked. How have you been?"

"Quite well, thank you, Bill. What about you?"

That question launched a long and animated conversation, the subjects of which alternated between reminiscences of the good old days and bringing each other up to date on the events of the several months that had passed since our last meeting. These discussions were held over large corned beef sandwiches slathered with spicy mustard. Little remained of our sandwiches but crumbs by the time I mentioned in passing that I had just sent my most recent manuscript to my publisher in New York City.

On hearing that piece of news, Bill said, "Wonderful, Eddie! Does that mean you have some time off?"

His question struck me as curious. Wondering what prompted it, I said, "Yes, in a manner of speaking. I expect it will be two or three weeks before we begin editing the book, so I plan to take a well deserved vacation."

Looking pleased, my old friend replied, "That's swell, but would you consider forgoing your vacation to consult with me on a project? You would be well paid for your time."

As I had begun to suspect, Bill had something on his mind besides discussing old times, and his question placed me in an awkward position. I was reluctant to turn down a job, especially one offered by an old pal, but at the same time I was really keen on the idea of getting away from it all for a few weeks. I said, "Gee, Bill, it's swell of you to think of me, but . . . ."

Wellman held up his hand, saying, "Wait, Eddie. Before you answer, let me tell you what this is about. It seems as if I have once again managed to get myself into something of a jam and I really need the help of someone I can rely on."

Bill's angular face took on an expression of concern and I took that to mean he really was in a pickle. Sensing that I was on the verge of giving up my planned vacation, I said, "All right, Bill, tell me what's going on."

Placing his elbows on the table, he leaned forward and said, "The project I've undertaken for B. P. Schulberg at Lasky-Paramount is a major motion picture of epic proportions—something a good deal grander and more complicated than anything I've attempted before. It seems a writer by the name of

John Saunders convinced Jesse Lasky that a film about World War One fliers would be profitable and Saunders just happened to have written such a story. Lasky bought the idea and had the story made into a film scenario by Louie Lighton and his wife . . . I forget her name."

"Hope Loring. Those two are at the top of the heap when it comes to writing for motion pictures."

"So I've been told. Anyway, the film is going to be called *Wings*, and Lasky wants his highest money-making star in the female lead."

"Would that be Clara Bow?"

Grimacing as he nodded, Bill said, "It would."

"That should be interesting."

"My feelings exactly, although 'interesting' isn't the word I would use. Besides Miss Bow, *Wings* will have a cast of thousands, including ground troops and fliers provided by the Army. The Army Air Corps is also providing hundreds of aircraft to reenact the flying scenes. We are quite literally recreating the air war over France!"

Shaking my head in amazement, I said, "Wow! That's some challenge."

Bill nodded and continued the description of his predicament. "What complicates matters even more is that much of the preparation for *Wings* was done before I came to the project, so I've been running like crazy to catch up and take charge. If this motion picture is to be successful, I have to direct it in my fashion, which means I must assert my authority at every step along the way. As you might imagine, I've got my hands full."

Nodding in appreciation of the situation as he described it, I said, "Yes, I can understand that. What I don't understand is how I can be of help to you. I'm a writer and you already have a scenario, and a well written one at that."

Wellman half-smiled and replied, "You know, Eddie, you are something else besides a writer."

Not seeing his point, I asked, "What else am I?"

"You are a decorated veteran flier of the Great War. You were there in the thick of the exact situation I am attempting to recreate in *Wings*."

Still not getting his point I said, "Sure, but so were you. In fact, you were there longer than I and saw more of the action first hand."

"That may be true, but you must picture what a director in my position is up against. In the combat scenes I will be responsible for the positioning of dozens of cameras and camera operators. I must also oversee the movement of aircraft, ground vehicles, artillery guns, explosive effects charges, and hundreds of troops. In many ways, my duties are almost the equal of those undertaken by General Black Jack Pershing during the real war.

"At the same time it is critical to the success of the picture that details be considered as important as the overall view. That, my good friend is where you come in." Bill paused, perhaps for effect, then continued. "I need someone at my side to observe those little details while I'm busy looking at the big picture—someone who was there during the real war and who can spot and alert me to mistakes in accuracy I might not see from my vantage point. I need you to help me avoid mistakes that could ruin what in all other ways would be an excellent motion picture."

To state it lightly, I was flabbergasted by the magnitude of what my friend expected of me. Intending to make that clear, I said, "Gosh almighty, Bill, that's an awful lot of responsibility! I'm not sure I'm up to . . . ."

"Of course you're up to it! I wouldn't ask you to do this if I wasn't absolutely sure you could handle the job. Besides that, the decisions as to what changes might be made would still be in my hands. All you have to do is observe and point out what you think are inaccuracies."

"I appreciate your faith in me, Bill, but surely there are military officers who are better equipped to do what you ask than I."

"Perhaps, but they lack one important quality. They would not have the nerve to kick me in the seat of my britches if it was needed. You, on the other hand, would do so with relish if the opportunity presented itself."

I could not help grinning at that statement. I could also not help being intrigued by the job Wellman was offering. Knowing full and well that I might be getting in well over my head, I decided then and there to rescue my old comrade in arms from his predicament, if that was truly within my ability, by accepting his offer.

With a sigh, I said, "Okay, Bill you've talked me into it. What do I have to do?"

Pulling some folded papers from his inside jacket pocket, Wellman said, "I knew you wouldn't let me down so I took the liberty of having a consultation contract prepared." Handing the papers to me across the table, he added, "Look it over, and if the terms are acceptable, sign it at the bottom. Then we can get down to the next step."

Unfolding the three-page contract, I saw that the first page was typed below the Famous Players-Lasky letterhead. The actual terms of the contract were not too different from those I had signed when writing scenarios. I let out an involuntary gasp, however, when I came to the daily consultation rate. I was to be paid an even one hundred dollars per day for my services. I had thought writing for the motion picture business was lucrative, but it was now clear that simply giving your opinion was even more rewarding. I stood to make between one thousand and fifteen-hundred dollars based on two to three five-day weeks!

I finished reading the contract then signed my name and entered the date in the spaces provided. Handing the papers back to Bill, I said, "Okay, what's next?"

Slipping the contract back into his pocket, he replied, "We have a production meeting scheduled for nine o'clock tomorrow morning. I'd like you to be there so I can introduce you to the cast and crew. Then we leave by train for San Antonio, Texas on Tuesday."

"San Antonio, Texas?" I exclaimed with surprise. "Why on earth are we going there?"

Wellman grinned at my shock and surprise. "For two very good reasons, my friend. First, San Antonio is expected by some to soon rival Hollywood as the motion picture production capital of the world. Several studios and production facilities have already set up shop in San Antonio. For us, that means film can be processed right there, rather than having to ship it back and forth to Hollywood or New York for processing.

"The second and even more important reason, is San Antonio's proximity to Kelly Field."

I interrupted, "You mean Camp Kelly? That's where I learned to fly pursuit ships!"

"Then you're already familiar with the area. Excellent! As I told you earlier, the Army is providing some of the fliers and aircraft for *Wings*. The pilots will fly out of Kelly Field. We've already recreated the front line trenches, a French village, and an aerodrome just outside of San Antonio, so everything will be quite convenient."

To my mind the words "San Antonio, Texas" and "convenient" seemed an unlikely combination. The ink, however, with which I had signed my name to Bill's contract was already dry and, come what may, I was now part of *Wings*.

Outside Greenblatt's Wellman gave me instructions for getting to the production meeting scheduled for the next day, after which we shook hands and I watched him drive away in a shiny blue Cadillac LaSalle roadster. Then I sat in my Stutz at the curb for several minutes contemplating the adventure on which I was about to embark. If nothing else, I thought, it would be interesting.

Two

7:45 A.M. – Friday – September 10, 1926
Edward Markham Residence, Silver Lake District

Buttoning the bottom button on my vest, I turned toward the mirror above my bureau. Some people, it seems, must stand on a set of scales to determine if they are gaining weight. I judge the same thing by the fit of my vests. The light brown one I had chosen for today fit perfectly with nary a bulge to be seen. This pleased me because it meant I weighed the same as I did when I left the Army Air Service seven years ago. Assuming I had not gotten shorter, I was six feet in height and 180 pounds in weight.

After slipping into my dark brown suit jacket, I consulted the mirror one last time to be sure the collar of my white dress shirt fit properly, that the knot in my light brown and green striped tie was secure, and that the part in my hair was straight. I also checked the shine on my brown oxford shoes. Lest I be thought a dandy, I should mention that I dressed-up a bit more than usual on this occasion so as to make a good impression when Bill Wellman introduced me to the cast and crew of *Wings*. I am a firm believer in the importance of first impressions.

Thus prepared, I backed my machine out of the garage under my house and set out for the Famous Players-Lasky motion picture company. I was allowing a little extra travel time because, while I had been to Lasky's Vine Street studio lot many times, this was my first visit to their new facilities on Marathon Street just off of Melrose Avenue.

To be absolutely accurate, I should point out that the Marathon lot was new to Lasky, but the studio facilities themselves have been in existence for some time. Until purchased by Famous Players-Lasky, the Marathon lot was known as the Brunton Studio and served as a rental facility for independent film producers in need of a place to make their motion pictures. The reason given by Lasky for the move was the need for more film stages and other buildings to meet their growing production schedule and they had already expanded as far as was possible on the old Vine Street property.

Such expansion speaks loudly of the success experienced by Famous Players-Lasky. Even though most of the company's films were now made in Hollywood, the company's headquarters were in New York City and they still maintained an east coast studio near that city. It would seem that Jesse Lasky of the Lasky Feature Play Company and Adolph Zukor of the Famous Players Film Company were doing quite well for themselves since the merger of their companies a decade ago. It was said that Famous Players-Lasky was now the largest and most successful motion picture manufacturer in the world.

Knowing something of Famous Players-Lasky's history ought to have prepared me for the sight that greeted my eyes as I completed the right turn from Melrose Avenue onto Bronson Avenue, but what I saw there was beyond any expectation I could have had. The scene a short block ahead, where Bronson met Marathon Street, was one verging on utter chaos. I had heard that Lasky planned to remodel the Brunton lot, but the term "remodel" hardly described the massive construction being undertaken there.

A literal army of workmen were amassed along the north side of Marathon Street. To the right a long, modern-looking structure was rising to a height of three floors. This, I thought, might be a new administration building. Adjacent to this structure and directly in line with Bronson Avenue was a nearly completed and elaborately ornate entrance arch featuring two spiraled columns on each side of the opening. Scaffolding was erected next to its crowning arch and several painters were busily adding the studio name above the opening. The sign said "Paramount Famous Lasky." Another name change?

Rumors—often the most reliable sources of news in the motion picture business—had it that, in an effort to cut out the middle man and increase the profits earned from their films, Lasky and Zukor had staged a coup d'état by secretly purchasing the company that distributed their films, Paramount Pictures. Judging by the sign, those rumors were quite true.

Slowly passing through the new entrance gate, I saw that the construction extended well beyond into the studio's interior. More workers, all manner of earthmoving equipment, and large cranes were rushing about the property like a busy colony of ants. Repeating what I said before, the term "remodel" comes nowhere close to describing the new and modern structures going up all around me.

Ironically, the nature of my destination on the lot was as far removed from new and modern as it could be. For some reason, perhaps nostalgia, Lasky had quite literally picked up and moved the first building the company occupied on their old Vine Street lot. Known by most as the "old barn" or the "DeMille barn," the structure began life as a horse barn and was still serving in that capacity in 1913 when a trainload of actors and technicians from the Lasky Feature Players Company landed in Hollywood in search of an authentic location for filming a western motion picture.

Believing they had found the ideal setting for their picture, the company rented half of the barn to serve as a production facility and office for Lasky's head of production and co-director of the film they had come west to make. His name was Cecil B. DeMille and the name of the motion picture they were making was *The Squaw Man*, an adaptation of a popular theatrical production.

Thus it was that *The Squaw Man* with actor Dustin Farnum in its leading role became the first motion picture produced entirely in Hollywood. When released, the film was successful beyond Jesse Lasky's wildest dreams, and the event of its production is thought by many to be the defining moment that led to a dusty little agricultural community on the outskirts of Los Angeles becoming the motion picture capital of the world.

Following Bill Wellman's somewhat complicated directions, I twisted and turned my way through the busy lot and eventually arrived at the spot where the old barn had been plopped down amidst the construction chaos. Aside from a few scratches in the white paint on its board siding, the two-story structure with its steeply pitched roof appeared to have suffered no undo indignities during the move from its original home.

Inside, the barn was divided into three main rooms—two smaller enclosures at the front and a large open area covering the rear three-quarters of the building. About two dozen wooden chairs were lined up in this larger area, and about half of them were occupied by men and a few women who were chatting amongst themselves. Being the new fellow on the block, I took up a position off toward the back of the room to observe the proceedings.

A steady trickle of arriving cast and crew members eventually filled the remaining chairs, with a few more standing as I was around the perimeter. At that point Bill Wellman hurried up to the front of the gathering with a sheaf of papers in his hand. He was accompanied by a man and a young redheaded woman. While I didn't recognize the man, I immediately identified the woman as the actress, Clara Bow.

From my vantage point at the back of the room, the most remarkable aspect of Miss Bow was her attire. She was in a simple, short-sleeved, silk blouse of a shade I can only describe as startlingly pink. At her throat was a double stand of rather large pearls. Below the pink blouse Miss Bow wore a knee-length, black, pleated skirt, and at her waist was a wide white belt that seemed to serve no purpose other than decorative. Her black high heeled shoes were of a practical height, but she wore them over a pair of white ankle socks. The outfit struck me as odd, but I must concede that women's fashions have always mystified me. For all I knew Miss Bow's costume was the latest style. If not, it might soon become such for the simple reason that Clara Bow was wearing it.

Upon seeing Miss Bow, one of the men sitting in the front row immediately stood and offered her his chair, which she accepted with a cheerful smile. Stepping behind a podium in front of the gathering, Wellman raised his hands and said, "Okay, folks, quiet down so we can get this show on the road. We'll start things off with some introductions. Many of you already know each other, but there are several new people here most of you probably haven't met before, including me. I'm Bill Wellman, your director.

"Since we're all going to be working together during the coming months, it's important we learn to recognize each other, so please stand up and let everyone get a look at you when I introduce you. First, I'll introduce the cast members who are here this morning, beginning with your leading lady, Clara Bow."

Standing, Miss Bow turned around, gave the group a wave, and said, "Hiya, everybody!" A young fellow in work clothes in the last row of chairs yelled, "Hiya, Clara!" That elicited a few chuckles from the group.

Wellman continued his introductions. "Next, meet one of the films two male leads, Charles 'Buddy' Rogers."

Rogers, who I knew by name only, was seated at the far end of the third row. He stood, threw everyone a casual salute, and sat down again.

"Our other male lead is Dick Arlen, but he couldn't be here this morning. You'll have a chance to meet him on the train Tuesday. Now, in addition to our leads, we have nine other credited plays in the cast. Those who will be going to San Antonio with us are El

Brendel, Richard Tucker, Gary Cooper, Gunboat Smith, Roscoe Karns, and Arlette Marchal."

Bill read the list at a fast pace and as he said their names, the actors popped up and down from their seats like jumping jacks. Then there was a brief pause in the proceedings. A woman who had just entered the room stepped up to the podium and handed Wellman a slip of paper. He read the note and they spoke for a few seconds, after which the woman nodded and hurried off to do whatever Bill had instructed her to do.

Wellman consulted his notes and resumed his presentation. "I want to take just a moment to give you some idea of the magnitude of this undertaking. In addition to the lead players and nine supporting actors, another twenty uncredited actors will appear in *Wings*, adding up to a total cast of twenty-nine.

"Add to that number more than a dozen stunt fliers, at least two dozen cinematographers and camera operators, along with assistant directors, editors, and other crew members, and the number of studio personnel involved in *Wings* jumps to nearly 120!"

A murmur of appreciation went through the assemblage. Clearly I was not the only person in the room who was impressed with the scope of this production.

Wellman looked around the room, and apparently pleased with the impact he was having, Bill continued, saying, "And that's just the tip of the iceberg. The Army Air Corps is supporting this project by providing us with close to two hundred airplanes and at least that many pilots to fly them. On top of that, five thousand troops from the Second Infantry Division at Fort Sam Houston will play the roles of the troops in the trenches. The Army is also providing all the military equipment—tanks, trucks, artillery, and even high explosives for special effects."

The "ooohs" and "aaahs" of the group grew in intensity with each new proof of *Wings'* magnitude Wellman threw out at them. He concluded this part of his presentation by saying, "Paramount has given us a budget of about two million dollars to make this film, and they are expecting an epic motion picture in return—one that will break box office records all over the country. Our job is to give them that epic film. What do you say? Can we do it?"

A rousing cheer that threatened to shake the ancient rafters of DeMille's barn went up from the crowd. Bill had set out to motivate his cast and crew and he had succeeded.

When the room quieted down again, Bill said, "Great! I knew I could count on you! Now, before we get down to the details of

Tuesday's trip to San Antonio, there are a couple more people I want to introduce so you'll know them when you see them. First, meet Charlie Barton. He's our property master and my right hand man on location. Stand up, Charlie, and let them get a look at you."

A handsome young man with a head full of dark hair and a cheerful expression stood up from a seat in the front row and waved. Wellman continued, "If we are successful with this film, much of the credit will go to the next two fellows I'm going to introduce. They are our chief cinematographer, Harry Perry, and his number one camera guy, Burton Steene. Between them these fellows have more experience with aerial photography than anyone else in the business. They're lurking at the back of the room, so take a look. You'll be seeing a lot of them during the coming weeks."

Perry and Steene were standing near me along the room's back wall. Dressed almost identically in black trousers and white shirts, they each gave the group a wave and Wellman looked in my direction, saying, "Okay, the last fellow I want you to know is an old comrade in arms of mine from the war in France. Eddie Markham flew pursuit ships for the Army Air Service over there and is a genuine hero. I asked Eddie as a personal favor to serve as a consultant on *Wings*. He's going to keep us honest and accurate to what really happened in the air war over France." Bill pointed in my direction and said, "Say hello, Eddie."

Feeling my face redden a little at Wellman's 'hero' comment, I threw him a casual salute as everyone in the room turned to stare at me. I will readily admit to feeling relief when everyone turned back to look at Wellman and he began to outline the details of the train trip to San Antonio. I have never thought of myself as a hero.

Bill explained that we would be taking the Southern Pacific's Sunset Limited from Los Angeles to San Antonio. The train was scheduled to depart from Central Station at nine o'clock Tuesday morning, arriving in San Antonio around three-fifteen in the morning on Thursday. Our marching orders were to be at the station no later than eight Tuesday morning.

While Wellman was explaining the itinerary, a movement in the front row of chairs caught my eye. The movement was Clara Bow turning in her seat to look at someone behind her. For a moment I had the idea that the someone at whom she was staring was me. Since I could think of no reason for America's motion picture sex goddess to have the slightest interest in me, I dismissed the incident and turned my attention back to Bill.

When the same thing happened again a few moments later, however, there was no doubt about who was attracting her attention. Our eyes locked and held for several seconds. During that time her expression was entirely noncommittal, giving me no clue as to why she found me so interesting. Perhaps I reminded her of someone she knew.

By this time Bill's account of our travel plans had reached San Antonio, where motor coaches would meet the train and transport us to our lodgings. Most of the cast and crew, he explained, would be staying at the Saint Anthony Hotel, but with a limited number of rooms available at that location some of us would be lodged at the nearby Menger Hotel.

Finally, Bill gave his notes one last look to see if he had missed any salient points. Apparently he had not because he then said, "Okay, that's the plan as it stands right now. If you have any production questions, see Charlie Barton. For questions or problems with the travel arrangements, stop by my office and talk with my secretary, Alice. And that's it, except to say see you all Tuesday morning at eight sharp and I'm counting on every one of you to help make *Wings* the best damned motion picture this studio ever produced!"

The assemblage erupted into enthusiastic applause and Bill Wellman gave us an acknowledging wave. The meeting over, some of the attendees left the barn in an apparent hurry to get on with whatever their assignments might be. The rest of us gathered into small groups and engaged in conversations that may or may not have had anything to do with our reason for being there. In my case, I was promptly approached by the man Bill had introduced as his right hand man.

With a smile, he offered his hand for a shake and said, "Hi, Mister Markham, I'm Charlie Barton."

Shaking the offered hand, I said, "Hello, Charlie, good to meet you. Call me Eddie."

"I just wanted to introduce myself, as I suspect our paths will cross frequently during the coming weeks. From what Bill tells me, we're lucky to have you with us. If you have any questions or need anything, just let me know."

"Thanks, Charlie. I'm sure I'll have many questions about the production end of things. These are uncharted waters for me."

He grinned. "Don't let that worry you. Even if you were an old hand at filmmaking, you'd have to forget most of what you know. Bill does things his own way and . . . ."

Charlie Barton was interrupted by the booming voice of Bill

Wellman. It came from somewhere across the room and said, "Charlie! Where are you? I need you here."

Barton gave me his ready smile again. "Oops, that's my master's voice. I'd better see what he wants." Offering his hand again, he said, "Just remember, whatever you need, let me know."

"Will do, Charlie. Thanks."

He trotted off to see what Wellman needed and, figuring it was time for me to get on with my day, I turned around and nearly ran over America's most popular sex symbol. She looked up at me with large brown eyes and a mischievous grin, said, "Hiya, Mista Markham, I'm Clara. I jus wanna intraduse myself an' meet the guy whoz s'posed to keep us honest."

Hoping I was translating her strong Brooklyn accent correctly, I said, "Hello, Clara. Please call me Eddie, and as for keeping anyone honest, that only applies to the authenticity of the film. Beyond that you're on your own."

"Well, dats good to hear 'cuz keepin' dis bunch a shmucks honest would be a tweny-foaw-ouwa a day job! Anyways, like I was sayin' . . . ."

Clara was looking beyond me toward the door, and whatever she saw there abruptly changed her expression to irritation. In a soft, almost inaudible voice she said, "Oh hell."

Before I could turn around to see what sight had brought about this sudden change in her demeanor, the rudest, most obnoxious man I have ever had the misfortune to encounter marched up and said harshly, "Clara, you and I need to talk."

"Sure, B. P. Jus lemme . . . ."

The man's hand shot out like a snake and grabbed her by the wrist in a grip that made Clara wince. He said, "Now!" and marched away, literally dragging her along behind him. Before they disappeared through the door, she looked back at me over her shoulder. Clara gave me a forced smile and rolled her eyes, as if to say, "The things I put up with!"

I shook my head in amazement at the rudeness I'd just witnessed and a hand gripped my shoulder from behind. Bill Wellman's voice said, "I see you've met our leading lady."

Turning, I said, "Yeah, and the most annoying character I've ever run into. Who the hell was that obnoxious so-and-so?"

Glancing toward the door, Bill said, "That, my friend, was Mister B. P. Schulberg."

Still angry, I spit back, "Wonderful. Just who the hell is B. P. Schulberg and what right does he have to treat a woman that way?"

Bill's grimaced as if what he was about to say caused him physical pain. "Unfortunately, Mister Schulberg is one of my bosses. Technically, he is the associate producer of *Wings*, and he can treat Miss Bow just about anyway he wants because he owns her."

Astonished, I said, "He owns her? Nobody can own someone else!"

"Perhaps it would be more accurate to say he owns her contract, but in this case it amounts to the same thing. He's made her the box office draw she's become, and she pretty much does what he says or else."

Shaking my head, I said, "I don't care what contracts he owns, he is a rude, inconsiderate jerk! What the hell does B. P. stand for, anyway?"

Bill almost grinned. "The initials stand for Benjamin Percival."

I muttered, "That figures."

The woman who had interrupted Bill's speech during the meeting came through the door in a hurry and made a beeline for Wellman. Seeing her, Bill said, "Looks like Alice has a problem, Eddie. See you Tuesday."

Wellman huddled with his secretary and I walked out to my automobile. On the way I looked around for Clara Bow and Schulberg, but they were nowhere to be seen. I climbed into the Stutz's leather driving seat and shook my head again. The movie business was a strange world, a world in which I was going to be immersed up to my neck for the next few weeks. I did not know whether to laugh or cry at that prospect, but whatever happened, it was not likely to be dull.

Three

7:05 A.M. (PT) – Tuesday – September 14, 1926
Edward Markham Residence, Silver Lake District

Awaiting the arrival of the taxicab I ordered, I stood on my front porch next to the suitcase and overnight bag I had packed for San Antonio and reviewed my preparations for the trip one more time to be sure I had not overlooked some crucial detail. Normally I am not such a nervous Nellie about traveling, but according to Bill Wellman, I might be away for as long as two weeks, a stay long enough to warrant additional preparations.

I had employed my next door neighbor's teenaged son, Jimmy Barker, to collect my mail, water the yard, and keep an eye on things in general. I had discussed the trip with my secretary, Elsie Johnson, and instructed her to keep an eye on the mail for word about the manuscript we sent to my publisher in New York. Finally, I had turned off the gas, made sure all the lights were out, and locked all the doors and windows.

As my taxicab pulled up to the curb, I decided I was as ready for the trip as I would ever be. The cabbie stowed my luggage in the trunk of his cab and we headed for the Los Angeles Central Station at Central and Fifth in the industrial area east of downtown.

The distance between Silver Lake and the station is not great and by seven-forty-five we were pulling up in front of the block-long, three-story, white stucco building with its five large arched windows rising above the entrance. I handed the cabdriver a dollar bill, telling him to keep the change and, luggage in hand, made for the nearest of the brass and glass double doors leading to the depot's waiting room.

From the experience of many rail trips I knew what lay beyond those doors. Below a ceiling soaring three full stories above the floor was cavernous space filled with row upon row of wooden benches, surrounded by ticket counters, shoeshine stands, news vendors, the ubiquitous Travelers Aid service stations, and the other purveyors of goods and services required by rail passengers. All of this was illuminated by two rows of large chandeliers hanging from the high ceiling. Each fixture was equipped with a circle of eight brightly glowing globes.

Not being well-schooled in the field of architecture, I cannot put a name to the waiting room's style of decor. It will have to suffice for me to say considerable attention must have been given to ornate details because they were everywhere. All in all, the scene must have been quite thrilling to the traveler who entered the space for the first time. It was a place befitting the beginning of an adventure.

That the Central Terminal had a huge waiting room was necessitated by the fact that it served as the arrival and departure points for the goodly number of Southern Pacific Railroad trains serving Los Angeles. Quite literally thousands of passengers passed through the terminal on a daily basis.

Even at that early hour the terminal was a-bustle with activity. Some, like myself, were travelers setting out on a trip. For others Central Terminal marked the ending point of a journey. Still others were there to welcome travelers to their destination or see them off on their adventures. Whatever their purposes for being there, several hundred people were milling around the waiting room and the sound of their voices echoed off the hard stone walls, creating quite a din.

Following instructions provided by Bill Wellman, I turned right just inside the entrance and made for the large clock on the wall ahead. It was in the area below the clock that we were instructed to meet. Halfway there, I located Charlie Barton. He and a few other crew members I vaguely recognized from Friday's meeting were standing near the wall.

As I approached, Charlie smiled his cheerful smile and said, "Good morning, Eddie! I see you're ahead of schedule."

"Hello, Charlie. Yes, I allowed a little extra time this morning to be on the safe side."

"That wasn't a bad idea. And being a little early will get you aboard the train ahead of the last minute rush."

Charlie removed a bulging stack of white envelopes from the side pocket of his jacket and quickly thumbed through them until he came to one bearing my name. He handed it to me, saying,

"Here's your ticket and car assignment. You can check your bags over there." Charlie pointed to a large "Baggage" sign near the doors that lead out to the trains. "The Sunset Limited will board in about fifteen minutes on Track Two. Just show your ticket to one of the conductors on the platform and he'll point you in the direction of your car."

"Thanks, Charlie. See you aboard."

I checked my suitcase with one of the redcaps at the baggage counter and slipped the claim check into the envelope with my ticket. I kept my overnight bag in hand because it contained the essential items needed for the nights I would spend aboard the Sunset Limited.

Next I wandered over to one of several newsstands scattered about the waiting room. There, I purchased the current edition of the Saturday Evening Post, the morning edition of the *Los Angeles Times*, a small box of Hershey Kisses, and one of my favorite candy bars, a Mister Goodbar. The total cost of my travel necessities came to twenty cents. Depositing the purchases in my overnight case, I looked around for a relatively quiet place to settle while I awaited the announcement that our train was ready for boarding.

I had just settled on an out-of-the-way bench when the deep, authoritative voice of the public address system came to life. Accompanied by an echo, the words it pronounced with perfect diction were "Your attention please. The Southern Pacific Sunset Limited bound for Phoenix, El Paso, Dallas, and New Orleans is now boarding on Track Two. Passengers holding tickets for the Sunset Limited may now board on Track Two."

That's when I felt it—the tingles I always experienced when I heard the boarding announcement for a train on which I was traveling. The adventure was about to begin!

I joined a small throng of passengers moving through a set of double doors in the back wall of the waiting room. The black letters on the white electric sign above the door said, "To Tracks 2 – 11." We descended a stairway to a brightly lit, yellow tiled tunnel running perpendicular to the tracks above us. The tunnel was interrupted at regular intervals by stairways leading up to the various boarding platforms. The first such stairway we came to was labeled, "Tracks 2 & 3." At the top of the stairs we stepped onto a long covered concrete platform between two sets of tracks. An arrow-shaped sign identified the track to our left as "Track Two," and on that track stood the dozen or so railroad cars making up Southern Pacific's most famous train.

The cars were painted a glossy dark olive green and each bore a line of formal gold letters below its windows proudly proclaiming, "SUNSET LIMITED." Below that and in smaller letters, most of the cars also wore a name taken from a locale along the route, such as Brazos, Pecos and El Norte.

We had come out on the platform at about the midpoint of the train. Without the slightest idea which way to turn, I approached a black-uniformed conductor and presented my ticket. He glanced at it and pointed to my right, toward the front half of the train, saying, "You're in the Tontos drawing room. That's two cars forward, just past the diner."

Having not taken the time to look at my ticket, the fact that Bill Wellman had booked me a drawing room reservation came as a pleasant surprise. Drawing rooms were considered to be far above compartments and standard Pullman sleepers as the epitome of luxury rail travel.

A white-coated Negro Pullman steward greeted me cheerfully at the rear entrance of the sleeping car identified as Tontos and, after looking at my ticket, said, "Yes, sir, your drawing room is in the rear section of the car. It will be the last door on your right just before you come to the standard sleeper section."

I stepped up onto the portable metal step placed on the platform to ease boarding, and from there climbed the vestibule stairs leading up to the car. Entering Tontos, I jogged left around the women's lavatory, at which point the aisle turned diagonally to the right. A door set in the angled wall on my right bore a plaque that said, "Drawing Room." I opened the door and stepped into my home away from home for the next few days.

To my immediate left as I entered the drawing room was a narrower door with a sign that said, "Toilet." Beyond that was the main area of the room. The outside wall featured two small sofas facing each other below a large window. On the inside wall were upper and lower berths. The upper berth was closed, that is, folded up and out of the way. The lower berth was made up and ready for use.

The entire drawing room space was paneled in a rich dark wood accented with gleaming brass fixtures. The seats were upholstered in a dark green cloth befitting the richness of the paneling and hardware. The accommodations were, indeed, luxurious.

I placed my overnight bag on the rear facing seat by the window, and because the drawing room was a trifle stuffy, I raised the window a couple of inches to let in some fresh air. Then I hung my jacket in a narrow hanging space on the back wall of the room and settled into the forward facing seat to watch my fellow passengers out on the platform.

Around eight-forty-five the bustle outside my window reached a crescendo with a steady stream of passengers hurrying along to their assigned cars. Then the activity gradually tapered off until, with only minutes left before our scheduled departure, there remained only members of the train crew and the final three passengers out on the platform.

One of those passengers was Clara Bow, who by her lethargic progress, I judged to be unaccustomed to arising so early in the day. Once again, her manner of dress was unusual. Miss Bow wore a full-length woolen coat that was much too heavy for the balmy morning air. The rest of her get-up consisted of large white-framed sunglasses and a pink scarf tied over her head in the fashion of a bandana. It occurred to me that Miss Bow's costume might be intended to disguise her from adoring fans. If so, it was much more likely to have the opposite effect.

The other two passengers were an older Negro woman who I thought might be Miss Bow's maid because she carried two overnight cases, and Charlie Barton who was doing his subtle best to hurry the studio's most popular player along the platform. At this, he was having little success.

At precisely one minute after eight I felt a slight lurch and we began to move. The Sunset Limited had begun its journey to San Antonio and points east. We passed through a complicated maze of tracks that alternately came together, split apart, and eventually became the single pair of rails that were the main eastbound line of the Southern Pacific Railroad.

Then the view outside my window became the same as those one sees on the outskirts of all large, metropolitan cities—a jumble of industrial activities taking place in and around a hodge-podge of large and small buildings. Trucks of all sizes and descriptions bustled about; delivering raw materials and carrying away finished products. Men in work clothes could be seen here and there going about the business of industry.

Knowing there would be little in the way of scenic views to look at for some time, I went to work at my own industry. After raising a small, folding writing desk from its stowage place below the window, I removed a thin sheaf of eight-and-a-half by eleven-inch newsprint paper from my overnight bag. The paper and a half-dozen freshly sharpened pencils were the result of a last-minute inspiration during a lull in my preparations for the trip. What finally occurred to me was that I would be missing a golden opportunity if I failed to write a feature article about the production of what from all indications promised to be an epic motion picture, particularly since I seemed to have become an integral part of that production.

I began the article by jotting down notes on my experiences since meeting Bill Wellman for lunch at Greenblatt's delicatessen last Thursday. That task completed, I began a fresh sheet of paper on which I composed what I hoped was an enticing lead-in for the article. Thus it was that I spent the first hour of my journey to San Antonio.

Just as I noticed the community of Pomona pass by my window, there came a knocking at the door of my drawing room. Upon opening the door, I found Charlie Barton in the passageway. He was swaying slightly with the movement of the train and his appearance was haggard. Charlie said, "Hello, Eddie. I just stopped by to make sure you have everything you need and that your accommodations are acceptable.

"The accommodations are swell and I can't think of a thing I need, but come on in and have a seat. You look like you've had a tough morning."

I think Charlie's first inclination was to decline my offer, probably because he still had a long list of things to do. Apparently, however, the opportunity to take a short break was too enticing to pass up. He said, "Thanks, Eddie, but just for a minute. I still have half of this train to check."

As Charlie flopped into the rear-facing seat by the window, I said, "I take it all the members of our happy little band made it aboard this morning?"

Nodding, he said, "Yes, everyone made it, but some only by a whisker."

"Including, I noticed, our leading lady."

With aggravation written all over his usually cheerful countenance, Charlie said, "I don't believe she was even fully awake when she arrived at the terminal. I wouldn't have been surprised to know she was still wearing her nightgown under that heavy coat."

"Apparently Miss Bow is not an early riser."

"Or she was hung over. I really hate to think what Bill would've said if she'd missed the train." After a brief pause, Charlie added, "Oh. Speaking of Bill, he would like you to stop by for a chat when you get a free moment this morning."

"Sure. Where will I find him?"

"Bill has the drawing room in the car just behind the dining car." Charlie gestured toward the rear of the train. "He said he'd be working there all morning."

On that note, Charlie Barton got to his feet and moved toward the door. "Remember, Eddie, if you need anything or have a problem, just let me know. I'm in Compartment A of Bill's car."

After seeing Charlie out, I packed up my writing paper, and stowed the little writing desk. Then, figuring there was no time like the present for a chat with the boss; I slipped my jacket on and headed off toward the rear of the train.

One aspect of rail travel I particularly enjoy is having my meals in the dining car, especially on Southern Pacific trains. They do it up brown.

The dining car wasn't yet open for meal service, and as I walked through, white-coated attendants were busy setting tables with implements from a cart they wheeled down the aisle. The tables they had completed were draped with immaculate white linen table cloths and set with dark green linen napkins, flatware embossed with the SP emblem, and pewter salvers also emblazoned with the railroad's emblem. At the center of each table was a small pewter bud vase in which was placed a cheerfully red carnation. I was already looking forward to lunch in the diner.

Bill Wellman's drawing room was in the same relative position of the train car as mine, but looking down the passageway, I could see that this car was different in that there were fewer standard Pullman sleeping accommodations and what I took to be two private compartments at the other end of the car.

I knocked on the drawing room door and was greeted by a hollered, "Yes. Come in!"

Bill obviously had plenty to occupy his time on the trip to San Antonio. He was in shirt-sleeves with his collar loosened, his tie akimbo, and a yellow wooden pencil stuck behind one ear. Every horizontal surface in the room was in use as makeshift office space. Stacks of neatly typewritten pages, hand-drawn diagrams, penciled lists, and other documents I couldn't begin to identify covered the seats, the little writing table, and both berths.

He looked up from a diagram in his hand and said, "Eddie, if anyone ever asks you to direct a film, turn around and run the other way as fast as you can!"

Grinning, I replied, "What, and miss out on all this fame and fortune?"

"Fame and fortune, my foot! This is insanity, plain and simple." Pausing to shove the papers on the rear facing seat to one side, Bill added, "Here, have a seat."

I sat gingerly so as not to disrupt any order that might have remained to the stack of papers he'd moved to make room and said, "I didn't mean to interrupt anything important, but Charlie said you wanted to see me and . . . ."

"Yes, I do. I have some things for you. Hang on while I find them."

He rummaged around in a large brown leather briefcase at his feet and came up with a sealed manila envelope on which my name had been typed. Handing it to me, Bill said, "You don't have to open this right now, but I want you to review some of the stuff in here before we get to San Antone tomorrow.

"What's in there is a copy of the final shooting scenario and diagrams of the Saint Mihiel battlefield. Our replica was built by the Army, so it's probably more authentic than it needs to be. Oh, and there's also a complete roster of the cast and crew in there with where they're staying in San Antone."

Accepting the bulging envelope, I said, "Thanks. I'll start getting familiar with all this stuff right away."

"Good. You don't have to memorize it or anything. I just want you to have the materials for reference. Now, your first assignment once we get settled is to visit the battlefield location—it's at Camp Stanley, about twenty miles north of town. Go out there and walk around. See how it compares to your memories of the war and let me know if you see anything that doesn't seem right."

"Okay, Bill. Will do. What are we using for transportation in San Antonio?"

"The Army is taking care of transportation to the various military camps we're using. They've set up a sort of motor pool with vehicles and drivers at the Saint Anthony Hotel. Just tell them who you are and where you want to go and they'll get you there."

The Sunset Limited had been gradually slowing for about ten minutes, but Bill didn't notice until we were almost stopped. He jerked his head up and said, "What the hell are we stopping for?"

I gestured toward the window. "This is Colton. It's a scheduled stop. We'll only be here for a few minutes."

Bill stared out the window as the Colton Southern Pacific depot slowly rolled into view. "Oh. Okay, I think that's all I have for you right now. Any questions?"

"No, sir, General Wellman. I have my marching orders."

He gave me a sour expression. "General, bah! I never made it past First Louie, and right now I feel more like a buck private stuck on permanent latrine duty."

I stood and threw Bill a casual salute. "And I'm sure you'll make those urinals sparkle, Private."

Feigning anger, Wellman threw his pencil at me. "Get the hell out of here and leave me to my misery."

Returning to my drawing room, I spent the rest of the morning buried in the materials Bill had given me. If I had not already gained an appreciation for the magnitude of our undertaking, reviewing the *Wings* shooting scenario and location preparations would have more than done the job. I began to understand the pressure Wellman had to be feeling.

Four

12:05 P.M. (PT) – Tuesday – September 14, 1926
The Sunset Limited – Near Redlands, California

A few minutes after noon, my stomach began demanding lunch, so I stowed my paperwork and made for the dining car. The diner was a beehive of activity and for a moment I thought I might have to wait for a seat, but then I spotted Charlie Barton signaling me from a table at the front of the car. There was an empty chair at the table he shared with actors Buddy Rogers and Gary Cooper.

Charlie introduced me to my table mates, two men who could not have been more different in personality. Rogers was gregarious and greeted me with an enthusiastic handshake. Cooper was reserved and said only "Call me Coop" as we shook hands.

Despite the lunch hour rush, a white-coated dining car attendant arrived promptly and cheerfully took my order for a green salad topped with Southern Pacific's unique French dressing, an Old Fashioned Chicken Pot Pie, and a glass of iced tea. The S.P.'s chicken pot pie was a long-time favorite of mine, particularly because it is topped with dumplings rather than the traditional pie crust.

With my lunch order placed, I turned my attention in full to the conversation at our table, which was centered around Roger's concern over the flying scenes in which he was to appear. It seemed he had innate fear of flying, and despite Charlie Barton's assurances that Wellman would be taking every precaution to insure his safety; the young actor was not at all convinced.

Rogers turned to me and said, "Eddie, am I remembering correctly that Bill said you were a pursuit pilot during the Great

War?"

"That's right; I was with the Army Air Service and flew in France."

"Okay," he replied, "As an expert on the subject, wouldn't you agree that flying is inherently dangerous?"

Hoping to bolster his confidence, I said, "Not at all. Flying is only really dangerous when someone is shooting at you. Otherwise, it's as safe as driving your automobile or riding aboard this railroad train."

Giving me a dubious look, Rogers said, "How can that be? If something goes wrong with an automobile or with this train, we simply step to the ground and we're out of danger. Stepping out of an airplane many thousands of feet in the air isn't quite as simple."

"True, but things seldom go wrong with a well-maintained airplane with an experienced pilot at the controls. You see, Buddy, airplanes by their very nature want to fly. They are designed for that purpose. Even in the rare event of a complete engine failure, the airplane will continue to fly, giving the pilot ample time to find a safe landing place so you can, as you put it, step to the ground."

Rogers said, "I'm not so sure that it's as simple a matter as you claim."

Cooper, who had been quietly taking in the conversation without comment, finally spoke up. "Buddy, when your time is up, it doesn't matter whether you're in an airplane or sitting on your front porch, your time is up and that's that."

As the conversation drifted along in that general direction, my lunch arrived and I dug into it with relish. I was nearly done when Miss Clara Bow made her entrance into the dining car. By this time the lunch rush was nearly over and there were empty tables to be had. Miss Bow and her escort chose one near the middle of the car.

Miss Bow was attired in a fashion similar to what she had worn at the DeMille barn meeting on Friday, except that her silk blouse was now a bright lime green and her pleated skirt was a darker shade of the same color. Her wide decorative belt and white ankle socks, however, were the same.

The young fellow with her wore a gray sweater over a white shirt with an open collar. He had a narrow angular face and thin lips slightly twisted into a permanent sneer. Atop his head was a shock of unruly blonde hair that somewhat resembled a haystack. The fellow was also sorely lacking in gentlemanly manners, for he plopped right into his seat at the table without holding Miss Bow's chair for her. Clara did not seem to notice this breach of etiquette, or if she did, it was unimportant to her.

A few minutes after Miss Bow's arrival, Buddy Rogers and Coop excused themselves from our table and left the diner in opposite directions. I was taking a last drink of my iced tea when I happened to glance in Clara Bow's direction over the rim of my glass. She was staring at me again, just as she had done at the meeting on Friday. Our eyes met for a moment during which time her expression changed to a blasé smile, as if she was saying, "Okay, you caught me staring at you. What of it?"

Her interest in me did not escape Charlie Barton's notice. With a grin he said, "Better watch out, Eddie. It looks like you might be Clara's next conquest."

I laughed. "That's not likely, Charlie. I'm hardly Miss Bow's type."

"I didn't know she had a type."

"Then let's just say she's not my type. I'm curious, though. Who's that fellow with her?"

"His name is Billy Blaylock. He's a stunt pilot Bill added to the crew roster over the weekend. According to Bill, that guy is the hottest flier in the business, second only to Dick Grace."

Nodding, I said, "In other words the guy is crazy as a loon."

Charlie chuckled. "Yeah, I guess that's a good way to put it."

"Well, Charlie, if you'll excuse me, I need to get back to the homework assignment Bill gave me."

"He's got you earning your keep already, huh? That's Bill for you."

Back in my drawing room, I removed a copy of the Saint Mihiel battlefield reconstruction plans and made an effort to recall my memories about what had happened at the real battlefield. What I remembered was that the battle had taken place over several days in the early autumn of 1918. The battle of Saint Mihiel stood out because it marked a turning point in the Great War.

The battle began when the American Expeditionary Force, along with British troops, began what was then called the "big push"—an all out attempt to break through the German lines in northeastern France and capture Metz, a city the Boche had fortified and were using as a stronghold. While the AEF did not achieve that objective until later, the offensive was successful in that it caught the enemy off guard and brought about a general retreat that would continue until the Germans agreed to the armistice that ended the war.

That much of the story could be found in any history book. My personal recollections of the battle were what I needed, and they came back to me in a flood of images that were still vivid after all these years. Our First Pursuit Group of the Twenty-Seventh Aero Squadron was flying out of Rembercourt, a few miles west of Saint Mihiel and because of our proximity to the battlefield, our role in the big push began a few weeks before the actual offensive.

Our initial assignment was to keep ships up at all times during the day to head off any Boche reconnaissance aircraft that attempted to cross the lines. The idea was to prevent the enemy from observing General Pershing's preparations for the big push, especially the ground troops he was amassing behind our lines.

At the same time we were charged with flying our own reconnaissance over enemy territory to keep the brass hats up to date on the locations of Boche troops and artillery. To help us accomplish these missions, we were supplied with hard-to-come-by high-octane aviation fuel that gave our ships greater performance at high altitudes. Also, some of our ships were equipped with new two-way radio equipment for up-to-the-moment observation reports.

The big push, itself, began with an early morning heavy artillery bombardment intended to reduce the enemy resistance. The bombardment lasted something like four hours, during which some reports claim a million shells were lobbed across the lines. Then, as American and British troops charged German lines, our mission changed to preventing Boche aircraft from interfering with the offensive and escorting our heavy bombers at high altitudes, from which they were to bomb enemy positions.

This latter part of the plan had to be scrapped, though, because the weather turned miserable, with heavy winds and rain storms preventing our ships from reaching their assigned bombing altitudes. Instead, the bombers were ordered to make low altitude bombing runs, flying below the heavy storm clouds. We pursuit pilots were also given permission to make strafing attacks on the retreating enemy ground troops once the bombers we escorted were safely back on our side of the lines.

I remember being in the air almost continuously for four days straight. We would take off before sunrise and fly until dark, returning to base only when necessary to refuel and rearm our ships. In one sense we were fortunate because enemy resistance in the air was light during the first two days because of the storms. During that time our greatest enemy was our grueling flying schedule. Tired pilots lose their edge and become less alert to the dangers around them. The fatalities our group suffered early the battle of Saint Mihiel were more often the result of ground fire and careless flying due to fatigue than encounters with Boche aircraft.

For my part, the worst of it was seeing the havoc we wreaked on the ground. Our bombs sent enemy body parts flying into the air along with other debris, and watching a dozen or more ground troops blasted to bits with every strafing pass we made with our twin machine guns turned my stomach. Yes, it was war and, yes, the Boche had killed thousands of our troops in the very same way, but when one is flying so low as to see the expressions of terror on men's faces split seconds before our bullets tore them apart, even the most hardened veterans of air combat could not fend off the sickening feeling of senseless slaughter.

I shook my head and looked out the window to erase the bloody images from my mind. If Bill Wellman was able to capture even to a small degree what we felt and experienced during the Battle of Saint Mihiel, he was one hell of a filmmaker.

The view out my window was now a desert scene beyond which lay a rather large body of water. The body of water had to be the Salton Sea, which meant we were well into the Imperial Valley and rapidly approaching the California-Arizona border.

I was still watching the barren countryside slide past my window a few moments later when I heard a light knock on my drawing room door. Upon opening the door I once again found myself looking into the big brown eyes of Clara Bow.

Surprised by her appearance on my threshold, I said the only thing I could think of to say, which was simply "Hello, Clara."

She, however, was not suffering from any such loss of words and immediately launched into a greeting that almost sounded rehearsed. "Hiya, Eddie. Sorry if I'm interruptin', but I need ta talk ta ya for a minute. Okay if I come in?"

I opened the door wide and stepped aside in the narrow entryway so she could pass. "Sure, Clara. Come on in."

She took short glances up and down the passageway before quickly stepping into my room. I gestured toward the window seats and said, "Have a seat and tell me what's on your mind."

Miss Bow settled into the rear-facing seat and, arranging herself into a schoolgirl posture with her knees pressed tightly together and her hands folded primly in her lap, waited while I took the opposite seat. When I was settled she said, "I wanna 'pologize for wha' happened las' Friday at the studio. It was an awful scene an . . . ."

"Clara," I interrupted, "You have no reason to apologize. That incident was entirely Schulberg's fault. His behavior was abominable!"

Frowning slightly, she cocked her head to one side. "His behavior was wha'?"

I immediately felt bad about using a word that obviously wasn't in her vocabulary, I said, "Abominable. It means something very bad . . . horrible."

Clara sounded the word out slowly, "A . . . bomb . . . in . . . a . . . bull." Then she grinned broadly. "Say, da's a really classy word. I gotta 'member it so I can say it nex' time somebody does somethin' horrible!"

Returning her smile, I said, "Yes, it's a word that comes in handy sometimes."

Frowning again, Clara asked, "How come ya know so many big words? Ya go ta college or somethin'?"

"Well, yes I did, but I'm a writer, so words are sort of my business."

Gleefully, she said, "You're a writer? Da's swell! I knew for sure you was a classy guy!"

"Why, thank you for saying so, Clara."

Still sitting in her prim and proper pose, she turned her head and looked out the window for a moment. That brought about an abrupt change of subject. Shaking her head, she said, "Dis is sure ugly country. Is dis wha' Texas looks like?"

"Most of the southwest looks something like this, but we're still a long way from Texas."

"I know. We don' get dare 'til Thursday. Da's what I don' like 'bout trains. They take so long ta get anywhere an' it's borin'."

I was about to offer her the reading material I bought at the depot, but before I could, she stood up, looked around the tiny compartment, and said, "On da other han', these drawin' rooms is pretty nice, kin'a cozy."

"Yes, the drawing rooms are nice, but . . . ."

Running her hand over the opened lower berth, she continued, "An' these beds look real comfy. Have ya tried it out yet?"

Getting an uncomfortable feeling, I replied, "No, I'll get around to that tonight. Now, ..."

Clara Bow turned, leaned a hip against my seat, and gently slid her hand over my shoulder. "Maybe we shoul' try it out together. Don' ya think?"

It suddenly struck me that Charlie Barton's prediction that I was to be Clara's next conquest had been dead on. I was in an awkward situation and I determined to end it as quickly as possible. I said, "I don't think that's such a good idea, Clara."

She pulled her hand away and took a quick, jerky step

backwards as if she'd been punched. With a surprised, almost shocked look on her face she said, "Why not? Don' ya like girls?"

Getting to my feet, I replied, "Sure, I like girls as much as the next fellow. I just happen to think intimate relations between a man and a woman should be more than fun and games. There should be some romance involved, maybe even a little love."

In an instant Clara's expression went from surprise to something I took to be mortification. In my eagerness to escape the uncomfortable situation in which I found myself, my rejection of Clara's uninvited advances had humiliated her.

Glaring at me, she shouted, "Ya think I'm a tramp, don' ya? Tha's wha' ya think, ain't it?" Suddenly tears welled up in her big brown eyes. "Well, I ain't wha' ya think, ya hear? An' 'scuse me all ta hell for the a-bomb-in-a-bull way I acted!"

Clara was nearly sobbing when she turned heel and ran from my drawing room. The door slammed loudly behind her and I was left feeling completely at loose ends. I had done the right thing, there was no doubt about that in my mind, but I felt I should have been more tactful in doing it. Instead, I had reduced Bill Wellman's star to tears and upset the applecart but good. Nice going, Eddie!

Five

6:00 P.M. (MT) – Tuesday – September 14, 1926
The Sunset Limited – East of Yuma, Arizona

I spent the rest of Tuesday afternoon going through the *Wings* scenario and making notes on the tentative filming schedule for San Antonio. My notations would give me a sequence in which to check locations for authenticity in the order they would be used.

Motion pictures, I long ago discovered, are not made in the chronological order of a film's scenario. Instead the scenes are filmed in an order that makes sense from a logistical point of view. In other words, all of the scenes involving certain actors in a certain location are shot at the same time, regardless of the order those scenes will appear in the final movie. This practice makes for much greater efficiency, but requires particular attention to detail so as to avoid continuity errors involving costumes, props and other considerations.

Finishing my notes, which in effect would become my marching orders for the first few days we were in San Antonio, I put the paperwork back into my overnight bag and consulted the Sunset Limited timetable. Since leaving Yuma about two hours earlier, the train had sped past numerous small towns and, according to the schedule, our next stop would occur in about an hour when we arrived in Phoenix.

When the train began slowing a few minutes later, however, I realized we were already arriving in Phoenix. I had forgotten to adjust my wristwatch for the Mountain Time zone when we entered Arizona. I corrected that oversight by advancing the hands of my watch one hour. A secondary effect of this adjustment was that it instantly became the dinner hour.

I was trying to decide whether or not I was hungry enough to make for the dining car when Charlie Barton knocked on my drawing room door. He said Bill Wellman had requested that I join him for dinner at six. I rolled down my shirt sleeves, slipped into my coat, and followed Charlie aft to the diner.

Bill was seated by himself at a table near the front of the dining car. I sat opposite him, facing the rear of the train and Charlie slid into the seat next to me. We ordered dinner—Roulades of Beef for Bill and Charlie, and Trout à la President for me—and then turned to the business at hand.

When Charlie informed me of Bill's dinner invitation, I had experienced a moment of concern, fearing that he had somehow heard about Clara Bow's visit to my drawing room that afternoon. I was, therefore, somewhat relieved when he launched into a discussion regarding the San Antonio filming schedule.

Consulting notes on a sheet of paper from his inside pocket, Bill said, "Our first location work will be with Clara in the French village. She's supposed to be driving an Army ambulance and arrives in the village just as a Heinie Gotham shows up and bombs the place to smithereens. We'll shoot the actual bombing scene last, after we've shot everything else that happens up to that point.

"Eddie, I'd like you to look the village set and battlefield over as early as you can Thursday morning. That way we'll have a little time to fix anything that needs fixing. That okay with you?"

"Sure. I'll head out there at the crack of dawn."

"Good. I'm anxious to hear what you think of the preparations, particularly since I haven't seen the finished layout yet. Charlie will arrive with me and the film crew around ten o'clock, so we can discuss your findings then. Also, I need you to take a look at the costumes—in this instance, British army uniforms—and the props so we don't run into any difficulties there."

I nodded. "Will do."

Our table conversation proceeded along those lines throughout dinner, after which Bill lapsed into a nostalgic mood, reminiscing about our time in France. "Ya know, Eddie, the American people have little idea of what it was like over there. One of the goals I'd like to accomplish with *Wings* is to enlighten them on the conditions, the people, and most of all the god-awful war itself. I want the people who see the film to come away with some idea of what it was really like—the carnage and destruction we saw over there. Does that seem like a realistic goal to you?"

"I had some thoughts along similar lines this afternoon, Bill. I did some remembering, and I didn't much care for what I remembered. Politicians and generals like to glorify war to boost civilian morale. They pinned medals on us and called us heroes, and that's what the American people saw of The Great War. Showing them how it really was will be a challenge, and if you succeed, a lot of people will be shocked."

Slamming his fist on the table for emphasis, Wellman said, "That's exactly what I'm looking for! I want to shock the hell out of 'em! If I could, I'd have them throwing up in the theater aisles just the way we puked our guts out after nearly every mission!"

Charlie Barton, who had concentrated on note-taking and said little during dinner, cleared his throat and made an over-the-shoulder gesture with his eyes. Bill looked around and realized that the volume level of his voice and the subject matter he spoke of was drawing disapproving looks from the diners seated nearby. Puking one's guts out was hardly the kind of chitchat that added to the enjoyment of the fine food served by the Southern Pacific Railroad.

Looking slightly abashed, Bill lowered his voice and apologized to Charlie and me. "I'm sorry, fellows. I got carried away. It's just that . . . well, I feel strongly about what we're doing here. Like Eddie said a minute ago, The Great War has been glorified to the American people, but there was absolutely nothing glorious about it. It was pure hell."

Glancing at the diners around us again, Bill said, "I guess I'd better get out of here before I get thrown off this train for conduct unbecoming." Standing, he added, "I'll see you fellows in the morning."

Barton and I both turned to watch Bill's progress to the rear of the dining car. He stopped at a few tables to chat briefly with cast and crew members, then he was gone.

Charlie breathed a sigh of relief. "Bill is decidedly passionate about *Wings*. I only hope we can pull it off as the film he wants it to be."

"I don't know much about the business of movie making, but if zeal counts for anything, *Wings* is destined for greatness."

"Sometimes it does count, especially if it rubs off on the cast and crew. The biggest problem Bill has is inexperience, both in his cast and in himself. Arlen and Rogers both seem dedicated to the project, but they're a long way from veteran actors."

Interested in Charlie's view of the situation, I prompted, "What about Clara Bow?"

He thought about my question for a moment before answering. "She's the wild card in the deck. Miss Bow is young and inexperienced too, but she has natural talent and a lot of box office appeal. Unfortunately, she's also unpredictable and her off-camera shenanigans can be distracting to others. If Bill can keep her in focus, Miss Bow could add a lot to *Wings*, but that's a very big 'if.'"

On the way back to my drawing room I considered Charlie Barton's observations of Clara Bow, particularly what he had said about her being a distraction to others. I knew that to be true from firsthand experience. It also occurred to me that I had not seen Clara in the dining car. I had no idea what that meant, if it meant anything at all.

In my compartment, I shrugged out of my jacket, loosened my collar, and poured about an inch of three-star Lucien Foucauld Cognac from a flask I spirited aboard in my overnight bag. I developed a taste for brandy while in France and prevailed upon the kindness of a wine merchant I had met there to keep me supplied since prohibition had became the law of the land over here.

I collapsed onto the forward-facing window seat and lit a Sanataella Centropolois cigar. Thus equipped, I settled in to read the now nearly day-old *Los Angeles Times* I had purchased before boarding the train.

The largest headline on the front page above the fold proclaimed, "U.S. Post Office railway clerks shoot to kill." The article reported, "Responding to an increasing number of railroad mail robberies, the Post Office Department dispatched a memo ordering its army of 25,000 railroad clerks to shoot to kill any bandits attempting to rob the mail." In an additional statement, the postal official threatened the use of Marines if railroad robberies continued. Maybe Jesse James has returned from the dead to seek revenge on modern day railroads.

The other lead story of the day was accompanied by a photograph that depicted row after row of hooded Ku Klux Klan members marching along Pennsylvania Avenue in Washington, D.C. The article described the parade as a demonstration of the Klan's political power. It sounded more to me like a demonstration of bigoted lunacy.

A doom and gloom story further along in the first section of the paper reported on the warning of a respected professor at the Massachusetts Institute of Technology that the U.S. would soon run out of fossil fuels, such as oil and gasoline. Doctor James Norris claimed it would soon be necessary for the country to turn either to solar energy from the sun or energy produced by burning vegetable matter. I questioned the Doctor's findings because it is widely known that Los Angeles sits above an ocean of crude oil, and southern California was only one of many such sources of fossil fuels scattered throughout the country. It seemed more likely that what the good professor had really discovered was the potential for publicity found in dire scientific predictions.

The lead story in the Metropolitan section summarized the progress of Los Angeles Police Department Chief James Davis since he took office earlier in the year. Davis had promised reform of the city's corruption-riddled police department, and thus far he was making a good show of keeping his promise. He had already fired more than 240 officers for bad conduct. He had also initiated a dragnet system for tracking down wanted criminals and instituted a program of using statistics for determining trends in crime.

His most noteworthy accomplishment, however, seemed to be the formation of a fifty-man "gun squad" for combating gun-toting criminals. The *Times* quoted Davis as saying he would "hold court on gunmen in the Los Angeles streets; I want them brought in dead, not alive and will reprimand any officer who shows the least mercy to a criminal." In some circles the new police chief was known as "two gun" Davis. The reason for that moniker was becoming increasingly apparent.

A somewhat related story on the next page reported that suspected L.A. crime family boss Joseph "Iron Man" Ardizzone and his right-hand man, Jack Dragna had avoided an indictment on racketeering charges by the Los Angeles County Grand Jury on grounds of insufficient evidence. Los Angeles District Attorney Asa Keyes had charged Ardizzone and Dragna with a long list of illegal activities, including prostitution, gambling, and numerous violations of the Volstead Act.

In combination, I found the Chief Davis story and the grand jury story particularly interesting because I recently penned a feature article on the L.A. mafia for W. R. Hearst's *Los Angeles Examiner*. I interviewed D.A. Keyes for the article, and while he spoke promisingly of an indictment against Ardizzone, he admitted off the record that he held little hope of success in that endeavor because of the mob's effectiveness at discouraging the testimony of witnesses against them.

The fact that the report on Chief Davis's efforts at police reform failed to make any mention of mob activities gave credence to the belief held by many that the LAPD had always turned a blind eye toward organized crime and continued to do so. There was, of course, only one reason for such behavior; department officials were still on the take just as they had been for years.

After refolding the *Times* and tossing it on the seat opposite me, I turned off the drawing room's overhead light so as to get a better look at the dark landscape rolling past my window. Aside from an occasional pair of automobile headlights on the highway paralleling the tracks, however, there was little to see.

The timetable indicated that, assuming the train was still on schedule, we were about an hour out of Tucson, Arizona. According to the timetable's miles column, the Sunset Limited had traveled roughly 420 miles since departing Central Station in Los Angeles a little more than twelve hours earlier. That distance represented about one-third of the total miles separating L.A. from San Antonio.

As an estimate of our progress, however, that figure was somewhat misleading. Now roaring through the vast nothingness of the southwestern desert, we were making much better time than we had in the densely populated areas behind us where more frequent stops were necessary.

I yawned, drained the last few drops of my Cognac, stubbed out my cigar, and prepared to retire for the night. As Clara Bow had predicted, the lower berth was quite comfortable, although I chose not to dwell on the conversation during which she had made that observation.

As the gentle swaying of the train and the rhythm of its wheels clacking along the track lulled me off to dreamland, I found myself attempting to decipher the whisper of an uneasy feeling somewhere in my subconscious mind. It seemed to be hinting that what started out as a capricious working vacation in the world of motion pictures was turning into something else—something with grave undertones.

As so often happens, though, my inner mind declined to offer further explanation. Perhaps it was nothing more than a lingering uneasiness from my unpleasant encounter with Miss Bow. Then again, maybe it was my subconscious mind's way of telling me it did not find the encounter nearly as unpleasant as my lofty moral values dictated it should. On that note, I cursed Sigmund Freud and rerouted my thoughts to the various options awaiting me for breakfast in the diner.

Six

6:30 A.M. (MT) – Wednesday – September 15, 1926
The Sunset Limited – Deming, New Mexico

In the unlikely event there happened to be chickens aboard the Sunset Limited Wednesday morning, I awoke before they did. Around six-thirty my eyes popped open and I knew they intended to stay open, so there was no sense lollygagging around in bed.

I climbed out of the berth, performed my morning ablutions, and set out on a quest for coffee. The dining car was open, but mostly empty at such an early hour, so I had my choice of tables. I took one near the entrance and ordered a hottle of coffee from one of the ever cheerful dining car attendants. I also ordered French toast in case I was hungry when the coffee woke me up.

I had just finished my first cup of coffee and was diving into the French toast when cinematographers Harry Perry and Burton Steene came through the dining car's front entrance. They stopped just inside while Steene explained something that required a lot of hand gestures and Perry paid rapt attention.

The explanation apparently completed, Perry looked up and noticed me. I threw him a casual salute and he pointed me out to Steene, saying, "There's just the guy who can help us out with this."

The two men stepped up to my table and Perry said, "Morning, Markham. Mind if we join you?"

"Not at all. Have a seat."

They sat in the chairs opposite me and Perry said, "Mister Markham, we have been attempting to work out a production problem and we've hit upon a possible solution. Since you were a flier in the war, you might be able tell us if it will work. Do you mind if we try the idea out on you?"

"Not at all. And call me Eddie."

"Thanks, Eddie. I'm Harry and this is Burt."

Burt Steene and I shook hands as Perry began his description of the problem they were facing. "Our problem concerns the matter of shooting close-ups of our actors in the cockpits of their planes. In the past these close-ups have generally been done at the studio with a mock cockpit in front of a painted backdrop. The mock cockpit is usually mounted on gimbals so it can be moved around to simulate the motion of a ship in the air.

"That technique, however, won't be used with *Wings* because one of the first things Wellman told me when I signed on was that he wanted realistic close-ups that were actually shot in the air. Now, Burt here, who has more experience with aerial photography than anyone else I know says, and I agree with him, there's no way to get what Wellman wants shooting plane to plane."

Steene chimed in, "You just can't get a camera ship close enough and in the right position to be a steady platform for close-ups. From the distances at which we have to work, you can't tell who the hell is flying the ship. That only leaves one option. We have to film the actor with a camera mounted on the plane itself. The problem is, without building a ship with some sort of special cockpit arrangement, there's no room for a camera operator in a single-seat pursuit ship like our actors are supposed to be flying."

Perry said, "But we think we've figured out a way to get what Wellman wants. Our idea is to use a motor-driven camera mounted in front of the cockpit and aimed at the pilot. Then we rig up a remote switch for starting and stopping the camera and mount it on the ship's control stick."

Steene picked up the description from there. "We do this on a two-seat ship with the camera positioned so it can't see the rear cockpit. Most people won't be able to tell it isn't a single-seat pursuit plane. We use a two-seater so we can put an experienced pilot in the rear cockpit to take the ship up to where the close-ups will be made, then he ducks down into his cockpit and the actor shoots the scene using the remote camera switch."

Perry again: "The thing is, this idea requires that the actor actually be flying the plane when the scenes are shot. He must be pilot, actor, director, and camera operator all at the same time, and we're debating whether or not Arlen, Rogers, and the others can pull that off. What do you think?"

I had to give them credit; they had devised a unique solution to the problem. From a pilot's point of view, however, I saw a couple of flies in the ointment. "My first thought is that you'll have a hell of a time positioning a camera in front of the cockpit. There isn't much room up there, especially with guns mounted."

Steene had an answer for that one. "We have a special camera for the job. It's called an Akeley and it was designed by a fellow who makes wildlife documentaries in remote places like the jungles of Africa. The Akeley camera was made to be portable so it's much smaller than studio cameras. Its only drawback is that it will only hold four-hundred feet of film, which is less than five minute's shooting time. A typical close-up shot burns up about a minute of film, so they'll only have a few tries to get the scene right before they run out of film. Hopefully that won't be too big a problem. The big issue is the actors."

Nodding my understanding, I said, "Well, I heard that Arlen flew with the Canadian Royal Flying Corps during the war. I don't think he saw any combat, but he should be able to handle a plane well enough to do what you need him to do. Rogers is another story.

"He was at our table for lunch yesterday, and during the conversation he made it very clear that he's nervous as hell about flying. Now, Rogers strikes me as a pretty sharp fellow, so I think he could learn enough about piloting to do what you need him to do. But first you'll have to get him over his fear of flying. That might not be easy."

Shrugging, Perry said, "If we can work out the technical details to make this idea work, and assuming Wellman approves of our idea, Rogers won't have any choice. He'll confront his fears or else."

Harry Perry did not specify what the "or else" amounted to and I didn't ask. Before long, the two cinematographers were knee-deep in another technical conversation involving momentary contact switches and vibration-free camera mounts that were well beyond my ken. By then I had finished my breakfast, so I excused myself and returned to my drawing room.

9:45 A.M. (CT) – Wednesday – September 15, 1926
The Sunset Limited – Arriving El Paso, Texas

Upon arriving in my drawing room, I discovered that the Pullman porter had already been there to remake my berth and tidy up. I had to hand it to Southern Pacific; they know how to keep their customers happy. Being thusly kept happy, I watched the proceedings outside my window for a few minutes.

While I was breakfasting the Sunset Limited had crossed the

New Mexico-Texas border and we were pulling into the El Paso depot. I consulted my wristwatch and the timetable and was reminded of the fact that the Lone Star State is in the Central Time Zone. Accordingly, I turned the hands of my watch forward another hour. The engineer braked the train to a stop at precisely nine-forty-five.

After watching the El Paso-bound passengers leave the train, I turned to the notes I had been making for a feature article on the production of *Wings* and added a few thoughts. I jotted down my recollections of the previous night's dinner conversation with Bill Wellman, particularly noting his impassioned comments about the horrors-of-war message he hoped to convey within the film. I then recorded the details of my breakfast conversation with Perry and Steene concerning the challenges involved in making realistic close-up shots of actors in the cockpits of pursuit ships. This was all fascinating stuff, or at least it would be if I could say it in non-technical terms readers would understand.

11:30 A.M. (CT) – Wednesday – September 15, 1926
The Sunset Limited – McNary, Texas

Having completed my writing chores for the morning, I consulted the Southern Pacific timetable. Nearly twenty-four hours had passed since the Sunset Limited left Los Angeles. During that time we had traveled more than 850 miles, which represented a little more than sixty percent of the 1,350-plus miles between Los Angeles and San Antonio. While I knew we were well past the halfway point of our journey, I also know that the last third of any rail trip, regardless of the distance, is the most tedious. Enduring the remaining sixteen hours would require patience and some creative time-killing.

There being little to see outside my window but sage brush and an occasional small town flashing by, I retrieved the copy of the *Saturday Evening Post* I purchased at Central Terminal. The cover featured a painting of some fellow in golfing togs and his young caddy staring in amazement at a lucky hole-in-one the golfer had just made.

Between its covers, the edition contained more than 250 pages on which I found several short stories, articles on a variety of subjects from Luther Burbank to women in sports, and of course, numerous advertisements for a wide variety of products from breakfast cereal to gasoline. While colorful and artfully worded, none of the advertisements convinced me that my wellbeing would be significantly improved by the purchase of the products they promoted.

12:50 P.M. (CT) – Wednesday – September 15, 1926
The Sunset Limited – Van Horn, Texas

A glance at my wristwatch informed me that the Central Time Zone lunch hour had arrived and was nearly passed by the time I read all of the stories and articles I found interesting in the *Saturday Evening Post*. My stomach, however, was in disagreement with my watch since only three hours had passed since the French toast I had for breakfast. This conflict was not at all uncommon in my travel experience. My internal clock always lagged behind the official local time on trips to the east. I referred to this phenomenon as train-lag.

I decided on a brisk hike to work up an appetite before partaking of lunch. Leaving my drawing room, I set out toward the front of the train. After passing through three sleeping cars— Pecos, Calaveras, and Brazos—I arrived at the baggage car, at which point I could go no further. Reversing my direction, I retraced my steps until I reached the dining car immediately behind the car in which my drawing room was located. Continuing on, I hiked through four additional sleeping cars—El Monte, El Norte, El Occidente, and El Oriente—before reaching the Sunset Limited's last car, a combination sleeper and observation car called the Sunset Beach. Since proceeding further would require a high-speed departure from the train, I once again reversed my direction.

Upon reaching the dining car again, I observed that it was nearly as empty as it had been during my early breakfast, with only a handful of the forty-some seats occupied. Since I saw no familiar faces among those taking a late lunch, I sat at an empty table and contemplated the menu choices for a light lunch. I settled on a Southern Pacific Salad Bowl, consisting of lettuce, tomatoes, cucumbers, radishes, bell peppers, and the S.P.'s tangy French dressing.

3:05 P.M. (CT) – Wednesday – September 15, 1926
The Sunset Limited – Alpine, Texas

Following lunch, I returned to my drawing room and reached for the thick envelope of *Wings* information Wellman gave me. I reviewed my notes on points of authenticity to check and updated my plans to include Bill's instructions to check the Saint Mihiel battlefield and the French village early on Thursday. I also read through the entire scenario for the second time because being familiar with the story-line seemed as if it would be helpful in performing my assignment.

Then I got out the *Saturday Evening Post* again, this time forcing myself to slog through the less interesting stories and articles I had skipped the first time. When I had absolutely drained the magazine of all the time-killing potential it had to offer, I rummaged around in my overnight bag for the Mr. Goodbar I purchased with my other last-minute travel supplies, and ate it; not because of hunger, but out of pure boredom.

The scenery beyond my window was doing little to accelerate the passage of time. There was absolutely nothing out there but a barren landscape of dry riverbeds, sagebrush, and a long, long highway connecting the few tiny communities that seem to have popped up where the highway happened to intersect another long, long highway going nowhere I could imagine wanting to be.

Judging by the timetable route map, we were running parallel to and slightly north of the Rio Grande River and the U.S.-Mexican border. If my memory of American history was correct, this landscape was part of the territory disputed during the Texas revolution back in the mid-1830s. While saying so out loud in this neck of the woods would probably have gotten me hung from the nearest cottonwood tree, I couldn't help thinking that the brave men who died defending the Alamo would have been much smarter to let the Mexicans have this godforsaken place.

The only positive aspect I could think of about this section of the Sunset Limited's route was that the train made no stops between El Paso and San Antonio. Despite this fact, we were still twelve hours from San Antonio.

5:15 P.M. (CT) – Wednesday – September 15, 1926
The Sunset Limited – Sanderson, Texas

I must have dozed off for a time because when I glanced out my window again we were roaring past another wide spot in the road where, for some reason that was entirely beyond my understanding, a few folks had erected the town of Sanderson. At least that was the name on the timetable that matched the time on my wristwatch, which was five-fifteen. Ten hours to go.

Feeling the need to rouse myself from my Texas-induced

stupor, I undertook another hike to the front of the train, and from there to the observation car at the rear of the train. The dining car was showing signs of life as I passed through on my return trip. Among the early diners were Charlie Barton and a fellow I did not recognize. They were just seating themselves at an empty table near the middle of the car. Charlie hailed me as I approached, saying, "Hey, Eddie, grab a seat and join us."

More from a need of conversation than a need for nourishment, I accepted his invitation. As we sat, Charlie gestured toward the third member of our party and said, "Eddie, meet Dick Grace, our chief stunt flier." Turning to Grace, Charlie completed his introduction. "Dick, this is Eddie Markham. Eddie flew in the Great War and he's with us as an authenticity consultant."

Grace was a shorter fellow with neatly-trimmed dark hair and the sharp-eyed look of a man who is constantly aware of his surroundings and everything happening within them. I had seen that same look on the faces of fliers I had known during the Great War—the ones who made it home from every mission with a fresh victory or two.

He grasped my hand in a strong grip and said, "Always happy to meet a fellow flier, Markham."

"Same here, Grace."

After the three of us dealt with the business of ordering dinner—I decided on the Southern Pacific Chicken Gumbo over rice—Grace looked at me, cocked his head to one side. "Ya know, Markham, I think I heard of you before. You were with the Army in France; won yourself a Citation Star, didn't ya?"

I nodded. "Yeah, they pinned a couple of medals on me, but I didn't do more than a lot of other guys who were never recognized for their efforts."

After considering this for a moment, the stunt pilot said, "I understand what you're sayin'. I was with the Navy in bombers. I got in on the Helgoland offensive."

"That was quite a show, a tough, well-defended target."

Grace shrugged. "No tougher than some of the others. Say, you still fly?"

"Yeah, I picked up a restored surplus Bristol F.2B from Fred Lewis a while back to keep my hand in."

"Would that be the British green and yellow one hangared down at DeMille Field off Wilshire?"

"That's my baby."

Dick Grace grinned widely. "Nice ship. You take good care of it."

"Thanks. You know what they say, 'Take good care of your airplane and . . . .'"

Grace joined in and we recited the last part of the often repeated flier's adage in unison, ". . . and it will take good care of you!"

Laughing, he said, "I think I've heard that one somewhere before!"

Throughout our meal Grace and I compared thoughts on a variety of airplanes and the state of private aviation today. I felt a little sorry for Charlie Barton because the conversation was quite literally over his head. Charlie was a good sport, though, and seemed to enjoy the banter.

Over coffee, the conversation shifted to the *Wings* aerial sequences to be filmed during the coming weeks, a subject in which Charlie was well-versed. Then Grace asked Barton a question I found interesting.

"Charlie, tell me something, how did this fellow Blaylock come to be signed on at the last minute?"

Barton said, "I'm not exactly sure, Dick. All I know is Wellman called late last Friday afternoon and told me Schulberg said Blaylock was a hot stunt pilot and we should sign him up before we left for San Antonio. Bill instructed me to take care of the details. What makes you ask?"

I found Grace's question interesting after witnessing Billy Blaylock's behavior with Clara Bow during lunch on Tuesday. I thought him a rather boorish fellow, thoroughly lacking in manners.

Not able to read Dick Grace's mind, I cannot say for sure what he was thinking, but his expression contradicted his answer to Barton's question. "No particular reason . . . just curious."

Grace was not enamored with Billy Blaylock, but he said nothing further on the subject. I could not help wondering what was behind his interest in the young stunt flier.

8:45 P.M. (CT) – Wednesday – September 15, 1926
The Sunset Limited – Spofford, Texas

Returning to my compartment after what turned out to be a most enjoyable dinner with Charlie Barton and Dick Grace, I poured a shot of Cognac, lit a cigar, and added a few thoughts to my *Wings* feature article notes. I was certain Grace's observations on the upcoming aerial stunt work would interest my readers. The article was shaping up quite nicely.

About quarter to nine the lights of another tiny community flashed past my window. My trusty Southern Pacific timetable advised me that the Sunset Limited had just blown through Spofford, Texas. That news in combination with some simple arithmetic alerted me to the fact that we were just six-and-a-half hours from our scheduled three-fifteen arrival in San Antonio.

It was long before my usual bedtime, but having arisen early, I thought I might be fatigued enough to sleep away some of those remaining six-plus hours. I made ready for bed and climbed into my berth. My mind was still busily anticipating the adventures awaiting me in San Antonio, but the swaying rhythm of the train soon rocked me into a sound sleep.

Seven

2:15 A.M. (MT) – Thursday – September 16, 1926
The Sunset Limited – San Antonio, Texas

As instructed, the Pullman porter awoke me at two-fifteen Thursday morning by rapping sharply on my drawing room door. I dragged myself out of the comfortable berth and, after washing my face with cold water to drive away the grogginess; I brushed my teeth, shaved, and combed my hair into some sort of order.

Back in the main part of the drawing room, I donned a clean white shirt, and my now badly wrinkled suit. Finally, I repacked my overnight bag and gave the compartment the once-over to be sure I wasn't leaving anything important behind.

My morning chores completed, I sat in the forward-facing window seat and stared out into the darkness for signs of San Antonio. A few minutes after three o'clock, when lights began appearing with greater frequency and the train slowed, I picked up my overnight bag, took one last look at the Tontos drawing room and headed for the rear vestibule of the car.

The Sunset Limited is indeed a crackerjack train and Wellman had treated me to the best accommodations available, but after forty-two hours of riding the rails, I was more than prepared to become a former passenger of the Limited. The thing for which I was not prepared, however, was the tide of warm air that flooded the vestibule when the train finally came to a stop and the conductor opened the outside door.

My recollections of the time I spent at nearby Kelly Field seemed quite clear, but time had dulled my memories of the miserable Texas heat. The dark night air outside the train, which was easily seventy-five degrees or more, brought those memories back into sharp focus.

My recollections of San Antonio's Southern Pacific depot, however, were accurate. Named for the Sunset Limited, Sunset Station is a more or less square two-story building in the Spanish mission style with an arched roof paralleling the station platform. Set in the arches at both ends of the roof are large circular stained glass windows. The one over the main entrance was a colorful depiction of the Southern Pacific emblem.

Crossing the covered platform, I entered the waiting room through a side entrance. As is the custom with Southern Pacific stations, the interior was one large space extending all the way up to the arched ceiling. The main entrance below the stained glass S.P. emblem was to my right, and to my left a grand staircase ascended to a second floor balcony surrounding the waiting area. Numerous doors opened off the balcony leading, I presumed, to the offices of the station's management. The arched ceiling was decorated with inlaid rectangular panels, each surrounded by a border of individual brightly illuminated light bulbs. The two rows of panels at the very peak of the arch were glass skylights. More light bulbs lined the underside of the balcony. In overall effect, the plethora of lights gave the station interior something of a sparkling holiday ambiance.

Aside from being about half the size of the Los Angeles Central Terminal, the San Antonio station was more modern and considerably less fussy than its overly ostentatious sister some thirteen-hundred miles to the west. It was also, at the hour of our arrival, considerably less crowded.

Ticket windows lined the street side of the waiting room, and opposite them along the wall closest to the platform was a long counter, over which signs read "Baggage Check-In" and "Baggage Claim." Knowing it would be a while before our bags arrived from the train; I stood next to an arched window overlooking the platform and watched my fellow passengers leave the Sunset Limited.

I saw Clara Bow step from the train, followed by her maid. Miss Bow was wearing the same long woolen overcoat she had worn when boarding the train in Los Angeles. I could not fathom why anyone would intentionally add that much heat to the warm San Antonio night. I also noted that her hair was somewhat undone and her general demeanor was that of someone who had just been awakened from a sound sleep.

Miss Bow was met halfway across the platform by a tall, distinguished-looking chap wearing knee boots, jodhpurs, and a white shirt with an open collar and rolled-up sleeves. He looked vaguely familiar, but I was not able to put a name with the face.

Clara and her mystery man embraced briefly and exchanged a few words, after which another man in chauffeur livery relieved Miss Bow's maid of the overnight bags she was carrying. Then Clara, her friend, and the chauffeur walked off toward the entrance end of the terminal building, while the maid entered the waiting room, apparently charged with retrieving the rest of her boss's luggage and somehow getting it to the hotel.

I also watched Buddy Rogers leave the train and take long, athletic strides across the platform. He entered the waiting room and joined the growing throng standing impatiently near the baggage claim counter. He was soon followed by Charlie Barton carrying another fat wad of what appeared to be white envelopes similar to those he had distributed at the station in Los Angeles.

Bill Wellman was one of the last to leave the Sunset Limited. Bill walked purposefully through the waiting room and out a side door on the street side of the building. Apparently the boss man was above such mundane chores as reclaiming his bags and transporting them to the hotel.

About that time the first cartload of suitcases arrived behind the baggage claim counter. I stayed back, preferring to wait until the crowd of impatient travelers thinned before venturing forth to claim my own bag. Finally, with bags in hand, I stepped out of the Sunset Station onto a sidewalk lined with a variety of motor coaches. Charlie Barton was out there distributing envelopes from the rapidly dwindling stack he carried. He looked rather harried and his usual cheerful smile was drooping some.

As I approached, Charlie quickly searched through his remaining envelopes until he found one with my name on it. My name was followed by the number 920. Handing me said envelope, he said, "You're on the first coach. Give this envelope and your bags to the bellboy next to the coach."

"Will do. Thanks, Charlie."

He looked up, gave me a brief look at the cheerful version of his smile, and said, "You're welcome, Eddie," giving me the impression I was one of the few who bothered to thank him for his efforts.

The bellboy standing alongside the first motor coach was dressed in a gray uniform with maroon piping and a cap worn at a jaunty angle. An emblem with the words "Hotel Saint Anthony" was embroidered on his uniform jacket. The young man opened my envelope, removed two cardboard string tags, and tied them to the carrying handles of my overnight bag and suitcase. Then he returned the envelope to me, saying, "That's your room number on the front of the envelope. You can go there straight away when you get to the hotel. The room will be open and your key will be on the bureau. Your bags will be delivered as soon as we can get them up there."

I tipped the boy a quarter, for which he seemed genuinely grateful, and climbed aboard the motor coach. The first seat behind the driver was vacant, so I took it. A moment later Charlie Barton stuck his head in the door and told the driver all of his passengers were aboard. Using a complicated linkage that ended in a handle near the coach's steering wheel, the driver closed the door, started his engine, and we were off to the Hotel Saint Anthony.

Only about a mile from Sunset Station, the Saint Anthony is a block-long, ten-story, brick edifice across East Travis Street from a tree-lined park in the heart of downtown San Antonio. Seeing the hotel again brought back more memories of my days at Camp Kelly. The Saint Anthony was much too swell for an air cadet's meager salary, but in town on a weekend pass, I once ventured into the hotel's lobby just to see how the rich people lived. I recall being quite impressed with the luxury of it all. Of course, that memory was from the perspective of a young man severely lacking in worldly experience.

Walking into the hotel for the first time since those days, I saw the place from a quite different point of view. The lobby was a long, narrow space extending to the left and right of the main entrance. The outside wall was lined with tall windows overlooking the park across Travis Street. Square columns topped with gilt filigree ran down the center of the space and supported a beamed ceiling decorated with deeply inset panels.

The walls, columns and ceiling were painted a shade of off-white and overstuffed chairs upholstered in beige material closely matching accents in the maroon carpet were set against the back wall and next to the columns. Sconces with elaborate brass mountings supporting illuminated white globes were affixed to the columns and walls to provide additional light. A large fireplace that I suspected seldom saw a fire was set into the back wall. The entire space was tidy and well-maintained, but seemed rather Spartan compared to its counterparts in more metropolitan cities, such as the new Biltmore Hotel in Los Angeles.

Noting the line already forming in front of the two elevators, I stopped the haggard bellman pushing a cartload of suitcases and asked where I might get a cup of coffee. He directed me to the hotel's all-night coffee shop at the other end of the lobby. The place was mostly empty, so I grabbed a table and ordered a cup of what turned out to be surprisingly good coffee.

After a second cup, I felt ready to take on the rest of the day and elevatored up to the ninth floor. Room 920 was located at the front of the building and its large window offered a pleasant view of the park across the street. While San Antonio was still at least an hour away from sunrise, I noticed that the sky to the east was a shade or two lighter than it had been when I looked in that direction from Sunrise Station.

The room itself was spacious and furnished with a loveseat, an overstuffed chair, an oak writing table, a large armoire, and a double-width bed. The attached bathroom was finished in gleaming white tile and was well-equipped with bars of soap and fluffy towels.

My bags had arrived while I had been getting my morning caffeine boost, so I unpacked my suitcase to the extent of hanging my shirts, trousers and jackets in a closet located next to the bathroom. My next steps were to strip down and take my first bath since leaving home Tuesday morning. Feeling clean again elevated my mood several notches.

I dressed in gray slacks and a pale blue dress shirt which I left open at the collar. I was planning on a day in the hot Texas sun and could see no reason for a tie and suit coat. Thus outfitted, I gathered up my wrinkled suit and the other garments I had worn on the train and stuffed them into the large paper bag provided by the hotel's laundry service. I filled in the blanks provided for cleaning instructions on a paper form clipped to the bag and placed the whole works in the hallway outside my room.

By quarter-to-six I had worked up an appetite for breakfast, so I locked my room and took the elevator down nine floors. Things had quieted down some in the Saint Anthony's lobby, although there were a few familiar faces from the *Wings* crew about. I guessed they were probably doing the same thing I was doing, killing the hour or so before it was time to go to work.

I noticed a fellow manning the hotel's concierge desk, so I asked if he had a map of the area. He did and was happy to give me one, complements of the Saint Anthony. With map in hand, I walked back through the lobby to the all-night coffee shop. It, too, was busier than it had been during my earlier visit, but there were still plenty of empty tables. I occupied one near the entrance and considered the limited options available on the all-night menu. The best choice for breakfast seemed to be eggs scrambled with

Cheddar cheese, served with a sausage patty and toast.

With my order placed and another cup of coffee in front of me, I unfolded my newly acquired map of San Antonio. Since it was intended for use by tourists, the map was sparsely detailed and included only major thoroughfares and locations of interest to vacationers. Fortunately, whoever published the map felt knowing the locations of the area's military installations would be useful to travelers.

Camp Kelly, now called Kelly Field, and Camp Stanley were clearly indicated, as were the locations of the Southern Pacific railroad station and the Saint Anthony hotel. Kelly Field, the old Army Air Service aerodrome where I learned to fly pursuit ships a decade ago was exactly where I remembered it; about seven miles southwest of San Antonio's downtown area. That would be seven miles as the crow or a Curtiss Jenney flies. The automobile route was a few miles further, as it involved going around some residential areas I did not recall being there when the advanced training instructors at Kelly were doing their best to make a decent pilot of me.

Camp Stanley, which I had only seen from the air during my training, looked to be about twenty miles due north of San Antonio, alongside U.S. Highway 87. I remembered the area as heavily wooded hill and gulley country over which our instructors insisted we practice our death-defying aerial maneuvers. We always figured that was because the region was largely unpopulated, reducing the likelihood of civilian injuries in the event one of us ham-fisted cadets lost control of our ship and augured it into the ground.

Having dawdled over breakfast and yet another cup of coffee for as long as I reasonably could, I set out to find the military vehicles Charlie Barton said would be available to transport us from the hotel to either Camp Stanley or Kelly Field as needed. It was just coming up on seven o'clock, and I hoped the Army still believed in getting things started at the crack of dawn.

The hotel concierge helpfully directed me to a rear exit that opened onto an alley behind the hotel, in which was parked a column of olive-drab Army transport vehicles. Among the half dozen or so automobiles and trucks were three Oshkosh one-and-a-quarter-ton troop transports equipped with canvas tarps over their beds to provide relief from the heat, which was now climbing into the low-80s.

The first vehicle in the line, however, was a three- or four-year-old Dodge Brothers Touring Car with a large white star and "U. S.

Army" painted on its olive-green doors. Standing next to the car were a spit-and-polish sergeant-major and a somewhat less polished corporal. The corporal was puffing a fag and the sergeant-major was organizing papers on his wooden clipboard. He looked up as I approached and said, "Good morning, Sergeant. I'm with the Lasky film company and I would sure appreciate a ride up to Camp Stanley."

Somewhat gruffly, as if he was not overly pleased about playing nursemaid to a bunch of Hollywood movie people, the sergeant said, "What's your name?"

"Eddie Markham."

The sergeant ran a forefinger down a list on his clipboard. When his finger stopped moving, he stiffened slightly and his demeanor changed noticeably. "Yes, sir, you're on the list."

Turning to the corporal, who appeared to be only mildly interested in the proceedings, the sergeant-major said, "Doyle, I'm assigning you and your vehicle to Lieutenant Markham here. Take him out to Camp Stanley and stay with him for as long as he needs you."

Corporal Doyle said, "Okay, Sarge." Then looking at me, he added, "Climb aboard and we'll be off, Lieutenant."

As I headed toward the passenger-side door of the corporal's staff car, I said, "Sergeant, I'm curious, how did you know I had been in the service?"

"Because you're listed on the roster as Lieutenant Markham, Edward, Army Air Corps, retired, sir."

I said, "I see. Thanks for your help, Sergeant," and thought to myself that Charlie Barton was well schooled in the art of getting cooperation from the military. It never would have occurred to me that under these circumstances a former Army flying officer would receive preferential treatment. That likelihood, however, had not escaped Charlie.

Setting the ignition advance and hand throttle, the corporal gave his Dodge Brothers touring car a crank and the engine started immediately. With its four-cylinder power plant ticking over like a fine Swiss watch, my driver climbed into his seat behind the steering wheel and we were off to Camp Stanley

Eight

8:00 A.M. (MT) – Thursday – September 16, 1926
Camp Stanley – San Antonio, Texas

The trip out to Camp Stanley took about forty-five minutes. Upon our arrival, Corporal Doyle braked to a stop at the camp's main entrance and exchanged words with a military police first sergeant who was on duty at the gate. While they spoke, the sergeant filled in blanks on a sheet of paper attached to his clipboard. Since my days in the service, wooden clipboards seemed to have replaced Enfield rifles as the Army's most critical item of equipment.

When the sergeant finished his paperwork, he looked me in the eye and, standing to attention, briskly raised his right hand to the brim of his campaign hat in a snappy salute. I automatically returned his salute, and then wondered in amazement at how quickly I had slipped back into military protocol. Old habits do indeed die hard.

After driving us through the gate, Corporal Doyle pulled to one side of the road and asked, "Where would you like to go first, Lieutenant?"

Looking at my wristwatch and realizing I still had a couple of hours before I was to meet Bill Wellman at the French village set, I said, "Let's take a look at the battlefield mock-up."

Doyle drove us past the offices, barracks, mess halls, and other buildings of Camp Stanley and continued a few miles through the hill and gulley country to the northeast. When we arrived at a large flat piece of terrain, he stopped and announced, "Here we are."

I stepped out onto the touring car's running board and, shielding my eyes from the sun in the eastern sky, I scanned the recreated battlefield. There wasn't much to see from the ground level, just two parallel lines of zig-zagging ditches with about sixty or seventy yards of empty space between them.

All told, Wellman's Saint Mihiel battlefield covered maybe a square mile, in which the most prominent features were a pair of what resembled wooden oil derricks—one located at each end of the battlefield. These had clearly been erected to facilitate filming, because such flimsy structures would not have lasted five minutes at the original battlefield. Pointing to the closer of the two derricks, I said, "Let's go over to that tower so we can get up higher for a better look."

Doyle put the touring car into first gear and I hung on as we bounced over two hundred or so feet of uneven terrain. I climbed a ladder attached to the side of the structure, which now appeared to be about a hundred feet in height and featured platforms at about twenty-foot intervals. I ascended to the second of these platforms and stepped onto it for a bird's-eye view of Bill Wellman's Saint Mihiel battlefield.

For those who may have missed the pleasure of serving in combat during The Great War, a few words of explanation might be helpful to understanding the scene before me. By the time the Germans invaded France, the science of war had advanced significantly, giving both sides weapons of far greater destructive power than those of past wars. Such weapons included rapid-fire machine guns and long-range artillery guns capable of accurately lobbing deadly shells great distances from safe positions far behind the front lines.

To defend against such advanced weapons, the ground war in France was fought from trenches. Typically these field works were six to eight feet deep and anywhere from four to ten feet in width. They were reinforced with dirt berms, rocks, sandbags, wooden beams, and anything else that was handy and might stop a bullet or the blast from an artillery shell.

Opposing soldiers dug these protective trenches parallel to each other, and as long as they remained in their trenches, infantrymen were relatively safe. The actual fighting occurred in the spaces between the trenches. These open areas were typically known as "no man's land," and they were the last places a soldier intent on surviving the war wanted to be because they offered little or no protection from enemy infantry fire or artillery barrages. What's more, these areas were often strung with barbed wire and other impediments intended to slow the advance of an infantry attack. An infantryman caught in no man's land was a dead duck.

Thus, the Germans and the allies reached something of a stalemate to which the only possible solutions were secret flanking attacks, which were extremely difficult to do effectively. In fact, if it had not been for the airplane, the combatants of The Great War might still be glaring at each other across no man's lands from the safety of their trenches.

Bombers and their escorting pursuit planes, along with scout ships and observation balloons added a new dimension to warfare. Men who had been relatively safe in their trenches were now subject to accurate and deadly fire from the open skies above their heads. The airplane changed the shape of all wars to come.

The most noticeable difference between Bill Wellman's mock-up and my memories of the actual Saint Mihiel battlefield was a matter of scale. The width of the no man's land was less than half that of the original, and of course the trenches themselves were shorter. The Saint Mihiel trenches went on for miles and miles.

I knew this discrepancy was intentional. The elements of the battlefield had been painstakingly positioned to suit the eye of the camera and it seemed unlikely that the smaller scale would be noticeable in the finished product.

Another obvious difference I noticed, however, would have to be dealt with before Bill's cameras could begin turning. The Army engineers had done a precise job of earthmoving in creating the scene, and therein was the problem. The results of their efforts were simply too pristine.

These trenches were dug with far more precision than was possible under actual war conditions. The trenches on both sides of the real Saint Mihiel battlefield were slapdash affairs to begin with, and countless rounds of artillery bombardment had caused cave-ins and other damage that had been repaired only to the extent necessary for protection of the infantrymen they sheltered. The too perfect mock battlefield was an issue that needed attention, but I was fairly certain I had a solution to offer.

I was so absorbed in the scene before me, I had not noticed Corporal Doyle standing beside me on the observation platform until he said, "They built quite a layout out here. I wonder if that's what it was really like."

"Besides being a good deal smaller than the original, it's not too far off, Corporal."

"You saw the real thing?"

It had not occurred to me that Doyle was too young to have served in France nearly a decade ago. Feeling a little ancient at age twenty-eight, I said, "Yes, I flew with the First Pursuit Group,

Twenty-Seventh Aero Squadron. We got in on the battle of Saint Mihiel."

"Gosh, that's something! It must have been exciting to be in the middle of a real war."

A little surprised, I looked at the young corporal beside me. He seemed to have some romantic notion of what it was like to be in a deadly fight for one's life. I was tempted to set him straight, but thought better of it. Chances were that nothing I could say would replace his fantasy with the stark reality of war and hopefully he would never have to learn the difference first hand.

"Exciting doesn't begin to describe it, Corporal. Let's climb down and take a drive around the battlefield so I can see it from some other angles. Then we can head over to the French village set."

We stopped a few times during our circumnavigation so I could scamper down into the trenches for a closer view. Looking out at no man's land from a well-protected trench on the German side, the thought struck me that the combatants on both sides of The Great War would have gladly exchanged their reality for Bill Wellman's superior version of the Saint Mihiel embattlements.

My first view of "Mervale," the fictional French village in *Wings* was from a distance of perhaps one-half of a mile, and it was impressive. My previous experience with outdoor motion picture sets had been on studio back lots where the buildings were little more than false fronts. That was all they needed to be because the fronts were all the camera would see. Here, though, the set would be shot from the ground and from the air, so Lasky's carpenters were required to construct somewhat complete buildings.

Mervale had been constructed against a hilly background at the junction of two unpaved roads. The village consisted of nearly twenty structures, including a church with a graveyard, a cafe, homes, and other buildings. Some of them had facades of stone or brick and some were simple wooden structures. All, however, were given a damaged patina to replicate the effects of war. It looked quite realistic.

Corporal Doyle parked his Dodge Brothers touring car on the village outskirts where it would not be in the way, and I walked through the set for a closer look. Even though I knew the buildings were shells, I would not have been surprised to see French villagers going about their daily business, just as I had seen in real French villages. Try as I might, I could not find any fault with the set's authenticity.

We were not alone in Mervale as we had been on the deserted

battlefield. For company we had about twenty extras in British "Tommy" uniforms and an even larger number of film crew members, some busily going about tasks and others just smoking cigarettes and chatting.

Tripod-mounted cameras were being set up on the dirt road a few hundred feet south of the village in readiness for the first scenes on the day's shooting schedule. I strolled over to that area to watch the proceedings. I had not been there for more than a few minutes when two more Dodge touring cars in Army livery came roaring up the dusty road and pulled to a stop. Bill Wellman and Charlie Barton climbed out of the first car, and Clara Bow, accompanied by two women I thought might be make-up and costume assistants, stepped down out of the second. Miss Bow was dressed in a costume that somewhat resembled a U.S. army uniform, with a Sam Brown belt, knee boots, and a narrow overseas cap, more commonly known to the troops as a go-to-hell cap.

According to the *Wings* scenario, Miss Bow's character, Mary, volunteers to serve in France as a driver, delivering truckloads of medical supplies wherever they were needed behind the allied lines. Since, in my experience, women serving in such capacities had been a rarity in France, I had little to go on with regard to the authenticity of her costume. Fortunately, the same would be true of most who would see the motion picture.

I had been so interested in Miss Bow's costume I failed to notice that Charlie Barton was also in uniform, that of a British Tommy. The only explanation I could think of for his being in costume was that he was to play some part in one of the scenes about to be shot. It was not uncommon for directors to use non-actors in bit parts just so crew members would have the fun of seeing themselves on the screen of their local movie houses.

Barton rushed off to take care of some urgent business and Bill Wellman, in knee boots, riding britches and a white shirt, just stood there surveying the scene before him. I walked over next to Bill, but said nothing because I thought he might be doing some director thing in his mind and I did not want to interrupt what ever that might be.

Eventually he noticed me and said, "Hello, Eddie. Whatcha think of our version of France?"

"Somebody did their homework well because the village looks very much like what I remember seeing over there. I found no authenticity issues with it. Your battlefield, however, is another matter."

Frowning, Wellman said, "What's wrong with my battlefield? It was replicated from aerial reconnaissance photos taken during the war, so it should be perfect."

"That's the problem, Bill. It's too perfect. The trenches and, especially no man's land, show no signs of battle damage. It's all perfectly pristine."

"I see your point. I'll see if I can get the Army to send in their bulldozers again to mess things up a little. That should go over real big with their engineers."

It was time for my clever solution to the problem. "I know a way to make it even more realistic."

"What's that?"

"There's an artillery unit stationed here, isn't there?"

Wellman nodded and by his expression I could tell he was already ahead of me. "Brilliant, Eddie! There's an artillery unit of the Second Division stationed right here on the base. I'll arrange for them to do a couple of training sessions with our no man's land as their target area. You can't get more authentic than that!"

Grinning back at him, I said, "You sure can't!"

Wellman shook my hand heartily. "Eddie, you just earned your keep and then some!"

"I'm glad I could add something worthwhile to the project. I wasn't so sure I could."

The rest of the morning was spent filming a sequence of scenes that would become one of the lighter moments in *Wings*. It began with Clara Bow driving her truck along a dirt road amidst a column of British Tommys. At one point she inadvertently bumps her truck into one of the soldiers, played by Charlie Barton.

The soldier is not hurt, but when he sees who is driving the truck, he feigns injury to get some attention from the pretty young driver. Clara's character, thinking she has injured the soldier, is devastated and runs to his aid. She lavishes her attentions on him and he is clearly enjoying the situation when a British staff sergeant who knows Barton is faking orders him back to the column in no uncertain terms. Clara, of course, is surprised when the soldier, obviously uninjured, jumps up and rejoins his comrades. The sequence ends with a medium shot of Clara having a good-natured laugh over the incident.

This being my first opportunity to watch the famous Clara Bow at work, I was quite impressed with her acting skills. She did exactly what Wellman told her to do, emoting dramatically when so directed, and then exuding a bubbling glee that was so contagious everyone on the set was smiling through the scene with her. Clearly, Miss Bow was a whole lot more than just a pretty face.

I also had to hand it to Charlie Barton. He portrayed the malingering Tommy with a subtle humor that made me think he must have had some acting experience somewhere along the line. I could not imagine how anyone might have played the scene any better.

Bill Wellman seemed quite pleased with the scenes as well, and was smiling broadly when he yelled "cut" for the final time and sent everyone off for a lunch break. The noon meal—bag lunches consisting of roast beef sandwiches, apples and coffee—arrived in an Army truck and was greeted with enthusiasm. As the extras and crew members searched out comfortable, shady spots to enjoy their lunches, Clara Bow and her entourage climbed aboard the car in which they had arrived and bounced off down the dusty road.

By this time the Texas sun had cooked up a temperature I felt must be past the ninety-degree mark. Sweating freely in my shirtsleeves, I had to feel sorry for the soldier extras in their heavy wool uniforms. They were a game bunch who, despite the heat, soldiered on with little complaint.

Our lunch break ended around one-thirty and the crew immediately went to work striking the morning set and moving the cameras and other equipment to a spot along the dirt road north of the village. The process took most of an hour and about two-thirty everything and everyone was in place for the next sequence of scenes. Everyone, that is, but the film's leading lady.

Wellman made no effort to hide his annoyance over Miss Bow's tardiness, pacing back and forth behind the waiting cameras and growling comments one would be ill advised to repeat in polite company. Charlie Barton, who had traded his Tommy uniform blouse for a much cooler white cotton shirt, also seemed dismayed by the situation, his attention continuously switching back and forth between Bill Wellman and the dirt road by which Clara Bow would arrive at the new filming location.

Then, just when it seemed Bill's exasperation had reached the boiling point, a cloud of dust on the horizon announced the return of his leading lady. I have no idea how he managed to keep his temper in check when Miss Bow cheerfully stepped down from her Army touring car, acting as if she was right on time and all was well with the world.

The next sequence of scenes involved a group of soldiers and townspeople, accompanied by Clara Bow's character, at the scene of a crashed German Gotha bomber that had just bombed the village. Most of these scenes were high shots made by a camera mounted atop a five-foot platform.

The scenario called for Clara and the extras to celebrate the enemy ship's demise with cheers and by gleefully waving at the U.S. pursuit ship that shot it down. In one scene a British soldier points out that the pilot was a flying fool they call the "Shooting Star." Clara's character recognizes the nickname as that of her hometown sweetheart, Jack, played by Buddy Rogers. She responds by joyously blowing kisses to her hero in the sky.

Once again the shooting went smoothly and required only a few retakes. This time I watched Wellman more closely, and observed the cool efficiency with which he worked. In what little experience I had observing directors, it seemed many of them became quite emotional, screaming at their actors and carrying on like madmen. Wellman, on the other hand, remained calm and businesslike, giving firm directions that seemed to motivate rather than intimidate his cast and crew. He showed no anger or frustration when something did not go to his liking, and he frequently complemented his cast when the scene played out well.

Despite Bill's efficiency, however, the sun was low in the western sky by the time the final scene was, as they say, "in the can." Since the remaining sequence of scenes was rather complex, Wellman gave the order to call it a day with instructions for everyone to be back bright and early Friday morning to resume filming.

The Texas dust and heat had taken their toll and no complaints were heard as the extras happily boarded the trucks that would transport them back to their barracks and the Lasky crew loaded their equipment onto other trucks. The whole process went quite quickly and soon Corporal Doyle and I were alone in the deserted French village.

Doyle had obviously enjoyed his lazy day of watching how Hollywood made movies. During the return trip to the hotel, he proudly held up a slip of paper on which he had surreptitiously acquired Clara Bow's autograph during a lull in the filming. In a tidy script, the message read, "Hugs and kisses to my Army pal, Ryan. –Clara Bow." He certainly had a fine trophy to show the boys back at his barracks.

Upon arriving in the alley behind the Saint Anthony Hotel, the corporal informed me he would be there promptly at seven-thirty the next morning to take me back to Camp Stanley. I thanked him and wearily made for the elevator that would carry me up to room

920. I felt as if I had been up for a solid week and I was not quite through yet.

I took my second bath of the day to wash away the sweat and Camp Stanley dust, after which I dressed for dinner. A few minutes after six I made my way down to the hotel dining room and dinner with Charlie Barton.

In the dining room I found the crew members who had made it downstairs for the evening meal buzzing with excitement over some monumental event. Charlie told me the story. Upon returning from the day's shooting, Clara Bow had met briefly with local newspaper reporters for the purpose of announcing her engagement to motion picture director Victor Fleming.

Fleming, it turned out, was the fellow who met Miss Bow at the San Antonio S.P. depot that morning. He was, supposedly by coincidence, in San Antonio directing another Lasky film at Camp Bullis, adjacent to Camp Stanley.

The celebrated director had been at Miss Bow's side during the announcement which, according to Charlie, came as no big surprise to anyone but a few of Clara's other beaus who would no doubt be devastated over her choice of Fleming as her future husband. His somewhat sarcastic account made me think Charlie was less than impressed with the big news. I asked him why that might be.

"Eddie, Clara Bow has been engaged so many times during the past few years she could open her own jewelry store with the diamond rings she's collected."

Since I seldom paid much attention to such things, this came as news to me. "Is that so?"

Charlie grinned his boyish grin and said, "Well, I might have exaggerated the situation a little, but if it weren't for Miss Bow's frequent romantic encounters, the gossip columns and film magazines would be hard pressed for anything to print. And there's been so much of that stuff reported that nobody puts much stock in it anymore except her fans who seem to thrive on the intimate details of Clara Bow's love life."

"So Miss Bow isn't really going to marry Fleming?"

"Oh, there's always a chance she'll go through with it. Clara and Fleming have been very palsy-walsy for a while now. Fleming has also become quite a thorn in the side of Lasky's executives, especially Schulberg. Word is that Fleming and his lawyer helped Clara negotiate a new contract, which will cost Lasky a bundle and nearly cuts Schulberg out of the picture entirely. So, if for no other reason than gratitude, Clara might marry him."

That Clara Bow was about to become engaged made her behavior in my Sunset Limited drawing room even more remarkable. Miss Bow, it seemed, was one very confused young woman.

At that moment Harry Perry and Burt Steene passed our table on their way out. Perry acknowledged our presence and Steene said, "Barton, get busy and find us some clouds. I'm tired of sittin' around with nothing to shoot!"

Charlie chuckled. "Weather isn't my department. Go find an Indian and get him to do a cloud dance for you."

Curious, I asked, "What do they want clouds for? The skies were clear all day."

"They want clouds because Wellman decided filming air-to-air with a clear sky is boring. He says the shots need clouds for depth and contrast."

Smiling, I said, "You'd better remind Bill where we are. I don't think Texas allows clouds across the state line."

"I hope you're wrong. Otherwise we're going to be here a long damned time!"

On that note I bid Charlie a goodnight and rode the Saint Anthony's elevator back up to the ninth floor. I am fairly certain I was asleep within seconds of the time my head hit the pillow.

Nine

The last of Clara Bow's scenes on the San Antonio shooting schedule was by far the most dramatic. In it, Clara's character drives her supply truck into Mervale minutes before a giant German bomber, accompanied by an escort of two smaller fighting ships, bombs the village. The British troops bivouacked in Mervale have received warning of the bomber's approach and have taken cover, but nobody has told Clara's character.

The first scenes to be filmed were medium shots and close-ups of Clara in her truck wondering where everybody is. She hollers out a few times trying to find someone, but there are no responses to her shouts. Once again Miss Bow demonstrated her skills as an actress and the scenes in the truck were quickly completed.

Bill Wellman yelled "Cut!" and the crew quickly went to work setting up the next scenes on the shooting schedule. These were to be medium-long shots of Miss Bow, still wondering where everyone is, climbing down from the truck and looking around the village.

I was standing near the camera watching Bill Wellman walk around making adjustments to the scene and consulting with various and sundry crew members when Harry Perry called me over to the camera. Asking his camera operator to stand aside for a moment, Perry invited me to take a squint through the camera's viewfinder.

Doing so, I received a lesson in the art of filmmaking. Through the camera, the scene resembled a picture postcard view of a typical French village. The tombstones of the church graveyard appeared in the immediate foreground. To the left of the frame was the front of the church itself. Miss Bow's supply truck was positioned just beyond the graveyard, and stretching off into the distance behind the truck were the other buildings of Mervale. The elements of the set-up were skillfully balanced to give the viewer a very realistic sense of actually standing in the village watching the drama unfold. Involving the viewer thusly in the motion picture is an important element in motion picture making art.

When Wellman was satisfied that all was in readiness, he instructed Miss Bow to climb back into her truck and the crew members vanished from the camera's view. Then, after taking one final look through the viewfinder, Wellman shouted, "Camera" and the operator began cranking. A second or two later, he shouted, "Action" and the scene went into motion just as if he had turned a switch.

Miss Bow climbed down from the cab of her truck and walked a short distance into the village. At the critical moment Bill Wellman gave a verbal command and a series of special effect explosives went off, destroying village buildings in the background.

Clara responded with alarm and ran back to her truck, diving under it to shelter herself from the supposed bombs falling all around her. Wellman yelled, "Cut!" and the crew magically materialized to prepare for the next scene. Charlie Barton helped Miss Bow from her hiding place under the truck and, from behind me, I heard the sound of a diesel engine.

Turning, I saw two Army truck-cranes rolling up. Hanging from the boom of the first crane was a replica of the church steeple. The second crane was equipped with a clamshell bucket loaded with dirt and debris. The cranes were positioned on either side of the camera with their booms extended out across the graveyard so their payloads were directly over the parked Army supply truck.

It was then that I heard another sound—a more distant one—I did not expect to hear. It was the sound of an aircraft engine, a big, inline power plant, if I was not mistaken. Scanning the sky, I finally spotted what appeared to be a single-seat pursuit plane at an altitude of five- to six-thousand feet. Its pilot was flying large, lazy circles over the French village set, and while I could not make out the ship's markings at that distance, I guessed it to be an Army pilot from Kelly Field up for a first-hand look at the making of a motion picture, although it was hard to imagine that he could see much from such an altitude. Glancing around at the crew busily making preparations for the next scene, it was apparent that no one else noticed the aerial intruder. I hoped for the pilot's sake he did not stray into the camera's view. Wellman would have the cadet's wings for sure were he to make that mistake.

Preparations for the next scene took longer because it involved the coordination of more special effects explosions, falling debris, and numerous other elements. A look at my wristwatch told me this would likely be the final scene shot before the lunch break. The time was eleven-seventeen.

Finally everything was in readiness. The camera had been repositioned in such a way so as hide the fact that Miss Bow was no longer under her truck. She was, in fact, standing some distance behind the camera, well out of harm's way.

Once again Wellman took a look through the camera viewfinder before yelling "Camera . . . action!" On that command all hell broke loose. More explosive charges placed in the village buildings were set off and showers of debris from the explosions landed on the dirt street. Amid the explosions, Wellman pointed his index finger at the operator of the first crane who released his load. A split-second later the church steeple landed with impressive impact atop the supply truck. Seconds later, Wellman gave a similar direction to the operator of the second crane, at which point he dumped the contents of his clamshell bucket on top of the now severely damaged truck. All the while the camera operator calmly turned his crank, recording the chaos and carnage on film.

When the explosions ended and, after waiting several seconds for the camera to capture the settling of the dust raised by the simulated bombing attack, Bill Wellman yelled, "Cut!"

I had just witnessed the filming of one of *Wing's* most dramatic moments. When interspersed with aerial photos of the Gotha bomber dropping its payload, the final product would become an amazingly accurate recreation of the German bombing of a French village. I could not help feeling a sense of awe over the scene's realism.

It was something of a shame the camera could not also record the deafening sounds of the explosions or capture their intense concussive impacts. During The Great War, it was the effect of that concussion on a soldier's body that struck more fear into his heart than any other aspect of an artillery or bombing attack. It was a feeling I had once hoped I would never encounter again, and even though I knew what I was witnessing was not really war, it still took great effort to still the panic I momentarily felt at the height of the explosive chaos in Mervale.

Bill Wellman gave an order to strike the set, and crew members again appeared to begin moving equipment and restoring order to the French village. I walked up the street to where Wellman was talking with Charlie Barton and some others. Standing there waiting to congratulate Bill on the effectiveness of the scene he had just recorded, I again became aware of the aircraft engine I heard earlier. It was much louder now and getting louder by the second.

Looking in the direction from which the sound was coming, I was surprised to see a pursuit ship done up in an allied war paint scheme roaring toward us at tree-top level, looking for all the world as if the pilot was setting up a strafing run down the central street of the village. Some Kelly Field cadet was sure to get his ears pinned back for this stunt!

From the corner of my eye I spotted Clara Bow. She was standing in the middle of the street staring up at the onrushing ship as if she was mesmerized by the sight of it. Then I heard the distinct chattering of two large caliber machineguns and two parallel lines of dust began moving down the street toward us at an alarming rate of speed. There were no cameras turning and this was no special effect. The pilot was really strafing the village!

Film crew members up and down the road scattered, but Miss Bow still did not move. She just stood there watching death approach at one hundred miles per hour. I, on the other hand, started running for all I was worth. Passing behind Clara, I threw out my right arm and grabbed her around the waist.

Then, quite literally dragging her with me, I continued to pump my legs for all they were worth. I made about another four yards before my feet got tangled up in some debris and we slammed face first to the ground. I rolled on top of Clara in the hope of shielding her and braced myself for the deadly impact of those big caliber slugs.

I did indeed feel their impact, but not on my body. What I felt was the impact of the rounds hitting the ground a yard or so behind us. They made a thudding sound and shook the earth. Next I heard the ship's engine scream as the pilot pushed his throttle to full power, and I knew he would be making a climbing turn to line up for another run at us. I had performed the same maneuver myself dozens of times.

Lifting myself off of Clara's limp body, I rolled her onto her side. Blood was pouring from a scrape on her right cheek and her wide-open eyes were staring up in me in utter terror. "Clara, are you hit?"

After a long moment during which she seemed to be trying to understand my question, she shook her head. I said, "Good! Come on, we have to get to cover before that guy gets back!"

I scrambled to my feet and held my hand out to her. Clara grabbed it and with the aid of my urgent pulling, she got to her feet. Once again I took off running, this time toward the space between the nearest of the village buildings. Clara stumbled along behind me, and once we were safely out of the line of fire, I propped her against a wall, and searched the sky for the flier who had very nearly killed America's most popular movie star seconds earlier.

The sound of his engine was distant again and I finally spotted the ship. It was a tiny speck climbing away to the northeast. I breathed a big sigh of relief. The pilot, apparently content with the damage he had already caused, was not returning for another pass.

I turned to Clara, saying, "Its okay. He's not coming back."

She responded without words, but by grabbing my arm with both hands and hanging on for dear life. That was when Bill Wellman, followed by Charlie Barton and a few other crew members, ran up to us. Looking with alarm at the blood on his leading lady's face he said, "Clara! Clara, are you all right?"

She looked at Bill for a moment and then looked up at me without saying a word. I answered Bill's question for her. "She got that scrape on her cheek when we hit the ground and I expect she'll have some nasty bruises, but other than that, I think she's okay."

Wellman's expression changed to relief, and turning to the gathering crowd behind us, he shouted, "Someone get a first aid kit!" After that Bill's thoughts automatically shifted to his next highest priority. To Charlie Barton he said, "Get over to Kelly Field and find out who the hell was flying that ship!"

Barton said, "Yes, sir" and turned to carry out his boss's instructions.

I stopped him in his tracks, saying, "That won't do any good, Bill. That ship wasn't one of ours."

Wellman spun back to face me. "What the hell do you mean it wasn't one of ours? How do you know that?"

"I know it for a couple of reasons. First, that was a Curtiss XP-Zero-A. They only built a few of them for testing, but the ship never went into production. The Air Corps never flew them."

Bill looked confused. "But it was done up in a U.S. paint scheme just like the ships we're using."

Nodding, I said, "Yes, it was, but did you notice the roundels?

From the outside in they were white-red-blue, the reverse of the U.S. insignia. That isn't a mistake the Army is very likely to make. Besides that, the pilot was heading northeast when I last saw him, in the opposite direction from Kelly Field."

Still trying to fathom what had just happened, Bill said, "Then who the hell was flying that ship?"

"Apparently, someone who wanted us to think it was one of ours. Beyond that, it's going to take the sheriff's department and probably the Texas Rangers to find the pilot because that ship could be hidden in any barn between here and the Oklahoma border."

That news caused an abrupt reversal of Wellman's thinking. "No. No cops. At least not until I talk with Lasky. He's for sure gonna want to keep this out of the newspapers."

At that point an Army corpsman with a dark green canvas medical bag slung over his shoulder arrived on the scene. Clara allowed him to clean and dress the scrape on her cheek, but she kept her two-handed grip on my arm the whole time he was doctoring her.

While that was going on, Bill Wellman gave the crew instructions to load their equipment. The filming of *Wings* was over for today. His final instruction was to Charlie Barton. "Charlie, send someone to the nearest telephone and arrange for a doctor to examine Miss Bow at the hotel, and then escort her back to the Saint Anthony."

That was when Clara spoke her first words since the strafing. "No! I'm stayin' with Eddie!"

Wellman looked at me and I gave him a raised-eyebrow expression that said I was as surprised at Miss Bow's outburst as he. Without comment Bill revised his instructions. "Okay, Charlie, you make the telephone call and, Eddie, you escort Miss Bow to the hotel. I'll meet you there later."

Having been given my marching orders, I guided Clara through the churchyard toward the spot where Corporal Doyle had been watching events unfold from a safe distance. When Doyle saw us heading in his direction, he started the touring car's engine and drove over to meet us.

Helping Clara into the front seat, I said, "Corporal, we need to get back to the hotel as fast as you can get there."

I climbed into the automobile after Miss Bow, and with her seated between Doyle and myself, he sped off up the dirt road that led back through the camp to the highway. Once we were on paved roads and the going was smoother, Clara leaned her head against my shoulder. She remained in that position until Doyle pulled into the alley behind the Saint Anthony at about one-thirty.

As I walked Clara into the hotel she was holding onto my arm again, but in a more relaxed grip. I hoped that meant she was calming down and recovering from the terrifying experience of nearly being gunned-down by an antique war plane in the middle of a fake French village.

Miss Bow's room was on the same floor as mine—the ninth— and when the elevator door opened, she directed me two doors past my room to number nine-sixteen. Her maid answered my knock and opened the door wide. A squat bearded man wearing thick glasses and a dark suit stood up from the overstuffed chair in which he had been seated. A black leather doctor's bag rested at his feet.

Room nine-sixteen was a full-fledged suite with a sitting room, separate bedroom, and bath. Clara reluctantly released my arm and went into the bedroom with her maid, who was tsk-tsking over the large white dressing on her boss's cheek. The bedroom door, I noted, remained open while the maid helped Clara out of her boots and uniform, under which she wore only a thin, ribbed cotton singlet and sensible white panties.

While this was going on, I introduced myself to the doctor and explained that I was a close friend of his patient. While that was not entirely true, it was the most expedient description I could think of for my role in the incident.

The doctor identified himself as Leopold Hires, MD, a private practitioner who also served in the capacity of the hotel's on call doctor. He then asked for a description of the incident in which Miss Bow had been injured.

Remembering Wellman's concern over publicity, I gave Doctor Hires a brief and highly inaccurate account of how Miss Bow had fallen and injured herself while filming a scene. The good doctor seemed satisfied with that explanation.

By that time Clara was undressed and stretched out on her bed. The doctor went in to perform his examination and I took a seat in the sitting room. The bed was visible through the open door and Clara kept her eyes fixed on me while Hires examined her, as if she was afraid I might suddenly disappear. I will readily admit to feeling somewhat unnerved by Miss Bow's attachment to me. She didn't strike me as a clinging vine sort of woman, not at all, and yet clinging she was; to me.

The doctor spent about half-an-hour giving Clara an extremely thorough examination before he snapped the latches on his medical bag and returned to gave me a full report on her condition. "Miss Bow's most serious physical injury appears to be the laceration on her cheek. I believe, however, that the wound will heal without any significant scarring. I also found numerous deep bruises on her arms and legs; no doubt the result of taking a hard fall on uneven ground."

I nodded and said, "That makes sense. There were rocks and other debris on the ground where she fell. Anything else?"

The doctor put on a thoughtful expression for a few moments, and then said, "No other physical damage that I could find, but she seems to be in a state of shock, far more so than I would expect from a woman who has simply taken a bad fall. Do you have any idea why that might be?"

Sticking with my lie, I said, "There were explosive charges being detonated during the scene. It was all rather loud and chaotic. That might explain the shock."

I thought Hires looked dubious about my explanation, but he continued his report without further comment on reasons Clara might be in shock. "I redressed the laceration on her cheek and I administered a mild sedative. Hopefully, Miss Bow will be feeling more like herself when she awakes in two or three hours.

"I will instruct the pharmacy to send more bandages, adhesive tape and peroxide for keeping the wound clean and properly dressed. I am also prescribing sleeping pills to be used in the event the patient remains in her current agitated state. I wrote down and explained the dosage instructions for Miss Bow's maid. She seems quite bright and I am confident she understands my instructions."

Removing a business card from his vest pocket, Doctor Hires offered it to me. "I will return tomorrow afternoon to check on Miss Bow, but if her condition should change before then, you are to call me at the telephone exchange printed on my card. I can be reached in that way day or night."

I accepted his card and said, "I understand. Thank you, Doctor."

He glanced back toward the bedroom and cleared his throat. "Ah, Mister Markham, may I inquire as to whom I should send my bill?"

Smiling at the doctor's apparent reluctance to mention his fee, I said, "Please address your bill to Lasky—that's L-A-S-K-Y—hyphen Paramount Pictures, and send it to the attention of Charles Barton here at the hotel. Mister Barton will see that your fee is paid promptly."

Hires wrote the information in a small pocket notebook and said, "Thank you Mister Markham." Then offering his hand, he added, "A good day to you, sir."

After seeing Doctor Hires out, I walked into the bedroom. America's favorite motion picture star still looked somewhat bedraggled, but better than she had been before seeing the doctor. Clara's eyes were drooping a little, presumably from the sedative, but they widened when she saw me. She held her hand out and I took it, sitting on the edge of the bed because there was nowhere else to sit. Clara's maid took note of this and gave me what I interpreted as a disapproving look.

Clara mumbled, "Stay close, will ya, Eddie?"

"Don't worry, Clara, I won't be far away. You just relax and get some rest. The doctor assures me you will be feeling better when you wake up again."

Her eyelids closed and in a drowsy voice she said something that sounded like, "Thanks for bein' my hero."

I told her it was my pleasure to be her hero, but I doubt if she heard me. A few seconds later her hand that had been holding mine went limp, and I stood up. Turning to Clara's maid, I said softly, "I'm going to get cleaned up and have some lunch. I'll check back in a few hours. If you should need me before then, I'm in room nine-twenty, just down the hall. If I'm not there, I'll be downstairs. Okay?"

I had the idea the woman was revising her opinion of me. Maybe I was not such a bad guy for sitting on her mistress's bed after all. She said, "Yes, sir, Mister Eddie. I will keep a close eye on Miss Bow and I will call if she needs you."

Ten

2:45 P.M. (MT) – Friday – September 17, 1926
Saint Anthony Hotel – San Antonio, Texas

I rode the elevator down to the Saint Anthony's lobby, walked to the front desk, and requested my room key. The desk clerk gave me an odd look before handing over the key to room 920.

Back upstairs, the bathroom mirror provided an explanation for the clerk's odd look. To put it mildly, I was a mess. There was a jagged hole in each knee of my trousers and large smears of blood on my shirt. Adding to my state of dishevelment were my face and hands, which were covered with Texas dirt. Deciding my pants were beyond repair, I stuffed them into the wastepaper basket. I considered doing the same with my shirt, but decided I might be able to bleach the blood out when I got back home.

Removing the stained shirt, I could not help wondering how much a man's shirt with Clara Bow's blood on it might be worth. It was exactly the sort of morbid artifact some extreme celebrity admirers would find irresistible. Shaking my head in disgust at that thought, I folded the shirt and placed it at the bottom of my suitcase.

Next, I went to work scrubbing the dirt off my face, hands, arms, and knees. It took some doing, but I finally got myself cleaned up sufficiently to avoid any further odd looks from desk clerks. Looking more closely, I saw that Miss Bow was not the only one who had acquired some nasty bruises during our close brush with death. I had a few colorful examples of my own, and I was gradually becoming aware of the aches and pains that went along with those bruises.

After donning a clean white shirt and a fresh pair of trousers, I decided the next order of business was lunch. My wristwatch, which came through the incident in better shape than I, said it was nearly three-thirty.

Stepping out of the elevator in the lobby, I came face to face with Charlie Barton. "Hey, Eddie, I was just comin' up to see you. How's our leading lady?"

"In better shape than my stomach. Let's go to the coffee shop so I can get some lunch, and I'll tell you what the doctor had to say."

I ordered a plate of spaghetti and meatballs and gave Charlie a thorough account of Doctor Hires' findings. I also handed over the business card Hires gave me and told Barton to expect a bill addressed to his attention at the hotel.

Then I dove into my spaghetti with considerable enthusiasm and Charlie said, "Damn, Eddie, you sure saved the day out there. If you hadn't gotten Clara out of the way, she'd be a dead duck for sure. You're genuine hero, you know that?"

Swallowing a mouthful of noodles and meatball, I replied, "Oh hell, Charlie, you'd have done the same thing if you'd seen the danger first."

Charlie Barton shook his head. "I'm not so sure about that. When I realized what was happening, I was frozen to the spot. I doubt if I could have even gotten myself out of harm's way. I just stood there watching it all happen. Bill did exactly the same thing. No, Eddie, you're the only one who had the guts to do something out there."

Twirling another forkful of spaghetti, I said, "Whatever you say, Charlie. Speaking of Wellman, where is he?"

"Bill went out to the part of the Army base where Victor Fleming is filming to tell him what happened." Barton glanced at his wristwatch and added, "By now I imagine Bill's up in his room making telephone calls to Hollywood. He hates talking to Jesse Lasky, but there was no way out of it this time."

"I don't know Lasky very well. Is he easily upset by bad news?"

Charlie grinned. "He does if the bad news has anything to do with money. And to him, Clara Bow is the same as money. I expect he's putting all the blame for this on Bill's shoulders."

"That's hogwash! How the hell was Bill supposed to know some deranged lunatic was going to shoot up the set?"

The grin disappeared from Barton's face. "Obviously, he couldn't know. The big questions are who did it and why."

"I'd say it was someone who doesn't much care for Clara Bow."

Charlie looked surprised. "You think that guy was really gunning for Clara?"

"There's no doubt about that. Didn't you see how he tried to follow us with his machinegun fire when I pulled Clara out of the way? If it hadn't been for the church, he'd have nailed us."

"The church?"

"Yeah. He came within a yard of hitting us as it was, but he couldn't get any closer to our side of the street because the church was in his way. He'd have hit it when he tried to climb out of his strafing run. Whoever he was, though, he's a crackerjack flier—maybe someone with a good deal of aerial combat experience."

Now Charlie looked downright shocked. "Holy cow! Who would want to kill Clara?"

"You are in a better position to offer possible answers to that question than I, but it did occur to me that killing off the film's leading lady is a surefire way to stop the production of *Wings*. It's a bit drastic, but it would get the job done."

Barton stood. "You'll have to excuse me, Eddie. I need to find Bill and tell him what you just told me."

I looked up at him. "Sure, but Wellman already knows Clara was the target of that attack. Bill is an experienced pursuit pilot. I'm sure he's already arrived at the same conclusion."

Charlie Barton walked briskly out of the coffee shop looking like a man who had a great deal on his mind. I finished my lunch and signed the check, but when I stood to leave, I was somewhat wobbly. The muscles in my legs were stiffening up—an indication that I was not as fit as I thought I was.

The cure for stiff muscles is to use them, so I strolled a couple of laps around the hotel's long lobby to loosen things up a little. By the time I pressed the elevator call button, I was moving more easily, if not less painfully.

In my room, I removed the notes on my *Wings* experiences I had been making for the past few days from my overnight bag. Seating myself at the writing table, I recorded my recollections of the morning's events. It was highly unlikely that I would ever be able to publish the account, but it seemed a good idea to jot them down.

Completing that chore, I was thinking about swallowing a couple of aspirin tablets and stretching out on the bed when someone knocked on the door. My visitors turned out to be Bill Wellman and the man who had met Clara Bow at the San Antonio Southern Pacific Depot upon our arrival yesterday morning—the man I thought might be Victor Fleming.

Fleming, if that's who he was, stood a little behind Wellman, who said, "Hello, Eddie. Do you mind if we come in? We need to have a conversation."

Opening the door wide, I said, "I don't mind at all, Bill. Come on in."

Once inside, Wellman gestured toward the man with him and said, "Eddie, I'd like you to meet Victor Fleming. Victor, this is Eddie Markham."

Fleming and I shook hands and, gesturing to the room's overstuffed chair and loveseat, I said, "Gentlemen, make yourselves comfortable."

Victor Fleming settled into the overstuffed chair and Wellman, carrying a square package wrapped in brown paper, went to the loveseat, but he did not look at all comfortable. Bill sat on the edge of the cushion, leaning forward with his forearms resting on his knees, looking for all the world like a man with big troubles. I returned to the wooden chair at the writing desk and waited for the conversation to begin.

Fleming got the ball rolling. "First, Mister Markham, I want to express my extreme gratitude to you for saving Clara's life this morning. Bill tells me she would no longer be with us if you had not pulled her to safety. Thank you for your quick thinking."

Getting a little tired of having the hero's role thrust on me, I made an offhand gesture and said, "Glad I was able to help."

I had the idea Bill sympathized with my distaste for the adoration I was receiving. Changing the subject, he said, "Eddie, I had a conversation with Jesse Lasky a while ago and we've just come from seeing Clara. It appears we are facing a dilemma to which you are apparently the only remedy."

I had an inkling of what was coming, but I kept that to myself. "What's the dilemma, Bill?"

"Lasky has ordered me to get Clara back to Hollywood immediately so he can have his studio cops protect her from any further attempts on her life."

What I had told Charlie Barton about Wellman knowing that Clara Bow was the intended target of the morning's incident had been accurate. He clearly had no doubts about that. I said, "Sounds like an excellent idea to me."

Bill glanced over at Fleming who said, "Part of the difficulty is that Clara has formed a rather strong attachment to you."

"So it would seem. Please believe me when I say I have done nothing to encourage that attachment."

Fleming nodded. "The thought that you might have done so never entered my mind. It's just the way Clara is. You see, for all her worldly behavior, Clara is in many ways an extremely insecure woman with a somewhat childish way of thinking. Knowing that about her makes the attachment she's formed to you a perfectly natural occurrence."

Relieved that Fleming held no grudges about his new fiancé's feelings toward me, I said, "I'm sure Miss Bow will get over it quickly as soon as she gets back to more familiar surroundings where she feels safe."

It was Bill's turn to advance the explanation of their dilemma. "The problem, Eddie, is getting her back to those more familiar surroundings. She absolutely refuses to go anywhere or do anything without you. It was all we could do to keep her from coming with us to see you. Even at that Clara made us promise we would send you to her room as soon as we finished our conversation."

I sighed. The dilemma facing Wellman and Fleming was just about what I had figured it to be. That they thought I was in some way the solution to that dilemma did nothing to alleviate the sense of foreboding I had with regard to what that solution might be.

When my response was nothing more than a nod, Bill was left with no choice but to finally reveal the purpose of their visit. "Eddie, I need to ask a tremendous favor. We need you to escort Clara safely back to Hollywood."

Now there was a thrilling thought. Given the unpleasant encounter I had with Clara Bow in my drawing room aboard the Sunset Limited, spending another three days on the train with Miss Bow, this time with her hanging onto my arm the entire time, was asking more than I felt obligated to do.

Bill's next comment, however, made his proposition slightly more tolerable. "Barton has talked the Army brass into flying you and Clara back to Los Angeles. You're scheduled to depart at oh-seven-hundred tomorrow morning. If all goes according to plan, you'll be landing at the Glendale Air Terminal before noon on Sunday. When you get there, you can turn Clara over to Lasky's people and fly right back here. What do ya say, Eddie? Will you do it?"

It was the part about everything going according to plan that was making me uneasy. There was no doubt in my mind that the Army would get us to California by noon on Sunday, but that's where my confidence in the scheme ended. "Bill, have you explained all this to Clara, especially the part about me leaving her in L.A. and flying back to Texas?"

After just a moment of hesitation, Wellman said, "Well, we thought things might go more easily if you explained that part to

Clara."

"In other words, you two brave gentlemen are sticking me with the job of breaking the news of this plan to her."

"Yeah. That seems like . . . ."

"And tell me, Bill, what if Clara doesn't want to be handed over to Lasky's people? What if she insists on me sticking around? That seems a likely possibility."

I glanced at Fleming, and by his expression, I got the feeling he thought it was a likely possibility, too. Bill cleared his throat and said, "Well, if that happens, you might need to spend a day or two in L.A. before returning to Texas. But we think, once she's home, Clara will feel less dependent on you."

Looking for some bright spot in my situation, I asked, "Is Clara's maid going back with us?"

Fleming answered that one. "Yes, I understand that arrangements have been made with the Army for three passengers, so Ruth will be traveling with you."

That news was an addition to the positive side of the equation in my mind. At least I would not be dealing with Clara all by myself.

Wellman and Fleming were now staring at me waiting for an answer to their question. The way things were, I really had little choice in the matter. Feeling rather put upon, I said, "I have some serious doubts about all this, but if we're going to get Clara safely back home, I guess I have to take her there."

Both of my visitors looked relieved. Fleming said, "Thanks, Markham. I know this is a hell of an imposition, but as you said, the only way we can get Clara to safety is if you take her there."

Wellman picked up the package he brought with him and walked over to where I was sitting. Handing it to me, he said, "This is a little extra insurance. I'm sure you know how to use it."

The brown paper package was heavy, and when I got it open, I saw why. It contained a Colt Model 1911 semi-automatic pistol and a cardboard box of the big forty-five caliber rounds it fired.

Looking up at Wellman, I said, "This is kind of drastic, isn't it? Or do you know something I don't know?"

"It's just a precaution, Eddie. If you and I are right about that flier being out to get Clara, you might find a use for that Colt before this is all over. I hope not, but better safe than sorry."

I sat there feeling the weight of the pistol in my hand and trying to decide if it made me feel better or worse. I decided on the latter.

Wellman, still standing next to my chair, pulled a thick, letter-sized envelope from his hip pocket and held it out to me. "Here's some extra cash for any expenses you might have along the way."

I opened the envelope and thumbed through the wad of twenty-dollar bills inside it. Apparently Bill was expecting me to have quite a few expenses—about five-hundred dollars' worth. Again, I got the distinct feeling I was getting much deeper into a situation in which I did not belong in the first place.

On that note, Fleming stood up and headed toward the door. "Good luck, Markham, and thanks again for your help."

Bill Wellman also turned toward the door. "Charlie Barton will have your transportation to Kelly Field here at six tomorrow morning. I'd appreciate it if you would call Charlie or me when you get back to L.A., just so we know you made it safely."

I was about to say, "If we make it safely," but missed my chance. Both Wellman and Fleming were out the door and gone. They made me think of rats deserting a sinking ship. Sitting there with that fat wad of cash in my hand and a howitzer-sized pistol on the writing table beside me, I said, "Markham, you are a first class chump!"

With those words ringing in my ears, I buried the cash, Colt and ammunition in my overnight bag and set out to tackle the first absurd task with which Wellman had saddled me—convincing Miss Clara Bow that flying back to California with me in the morning would be the most wonderful thing that ever happened to her.

I knocked on the door to room 916. When Clara's maid opened the door and let me in, I was surprised to see her mistress sitting on a loveseat similar to the one in my room. She was wearing a short, shocking pink terrycloth robe that provided modesty down to about mid-thigh. Her big brown eyes, one of which was slightly swollen, lit up when she saw me and she held out her hand. I sat next to her on the loveseat and she wrapped her arm around mine.

"Thanks for comin' back, Eddie. I was startin' ta get scared ya wouldn't."

I said, "How are you feelin', kiddo?"

She shrugged a little and said, "Not so bad."

I could not say whether her limited contributions to our conversation were due to lingering effects from the sedative or simply a lack of anything to say. Mostly Clara was just sitting there clinging to my arm as if I was her favorite stuffed animal doll. Figuring that any further conversation would have to come from me, I jumped in with both feet.

"Clara, how would you like to take an airplane ride tomorrow?"

She looked at me with trepidation in those big brown eyes and whispered, "Wit you?"

"Yes, with me. If it's okay with you, we're going to fly back to California tomorrow morning."

Clara nodded once, accepting my proposition without further discussion. Relieved to be past that hurdle, I turned to her maid, who was trying to appear inconspicuous just beyond the bedroom doorway. "You're invited, too, Ruth. Charlie Barton will be here about six tomorrow morning with transportation to the airfield."

The woman nodded. "I'll be sure we are all packed and ready to leave by then."

If the Negro maid had any fear of flying, she did not show it. Heck, for all I knew, she was a seasoned air traveler.

Clara's head was resting against my shoulder, and when I looked down again, I saw that her eyes were closed. Taking that as my exit cue, I said softly, "Clara, I have some details to take care of so we can leave in the morning and you look like you could do with some sleep. So why don't you hop back in bed and I'll be here bright and early in the morning to pick you up."

I was expecting resistance to my departure, and when she simply nodded again, I took it as a hopeful sign that her attachment to me was beginning to wear off. Disentangling her arm from mine, I stood up. Through half-closed eyes, Clara looked up at me for a second before her eyelids closed all the way.

I passed Ruth on my way to the door and she gave me a small nod I took as a sign that she approved of the way I was handling the situation. Outside room 916, I took a deep breath and hoped to hell Ruth was as wise as she seemed to be.

Eleven

6:40 A.M. (MT) – Saturday – September 18, 1926
Kelly Field – San Antonio, Texas

I immediately recognized the three-engined transport ship awaiting our arrival on the tarmac near the south end of Kelly Field's runway because it was quite possibly the ugliest aircraft I have ever seen. That the ship had been the subject of numerous articles appearing in *Aviation Week* magazine during the past year also made it recognizable.

"Ford's Aero Flivver," as the new AT-4 Trimotor was known by those who were less than enthralled by its design, was the result of Henry Ford's apparent desire to monopolize aircraft manufacturing in the same way he became the leading manufacturer of automobiles in the United States. Built by a Ford subsidiary, the Stout Metal Aircraft Company, Ford's futuristic ship was truly something to behold.

The Trimotor got its name from the fact that it had a radial engine hanging from its wing on each side of the fuselage and a third engine in its nose. It sat on a pair of conventional landing gear wheels—one below each wing-mounted engine—and a small tail wheel, all of which gave the ship a rather snooty, nose-in-the-air attitude. Another major contributor to the aircraft's ungainly appearance was also its most advanced feature; the entire ship was built of metal rather than the more typical wood and fabric construction. The fuselage was clad in corrugated aluminum that bore a strong resemblance to the sort of tin roof you would expect to see on a shed out behind the barn.

Still, according to all accounts, including that of Henry Ford, the Trimotor was the "safest ship around." I hoped those accounts were accurate because we were about to spend nearly fifteen hours covering about thirteen hundred miles in the thing.

An Army Air Corps captain with pilot's wings on his uniform blouse met us as we climbed down from the Saint Anthony's motor coach Charlie Barton had arranged as our transportation from the hotel to Kelly Field. While the captain and Charlie had a brief conversation, two enlisted men loaded all of our baggage aboard the Trimotor—all of our baggage, that is, except for my overnight case, which I carried because it contained the cash and the Colt pistol Bill Wellman gave me. I had no expectation of actually needing the blessed thing, but in the unlikely event I did, the pistol would be of little help if it wasn't handy, and it was too darn bulky to carry around comfortably in my jacket pocket.

Clara Bow, covered once again in her long, woolen coat was in her usual early morning drowsy state, but she still stuck close to my side while Ruth, her maid, stood off to one side watching the proceedings. The dressing on Clara's cheek looked fresh and she was moving somewhat gingerly as if in pain. Considering her previous day's experience, that was to be expected.

Even though the sun had just risen, the air was mild, verging on warm, so I was relieved when Charlie finished his conversation with the Air Corps captain and we trooped off to board the aircraft. The sooner we left Texas for cooler climes, the happier I would be.

The Trimotor's entrance hatch was located just behind the starboard wing, and after helping Clara and Ruth aboard, Charlie Barton turned to me. "Good luck. Keep your eyes open and get our gal back to Los Angeles in one piece."

"I'll do my best, Charlie."

"I know you will, Eddie. See you in a few days."

Despite my doubts as to how soon I would be seeing Charlie Barton again, I nodded. Then we shook hands and I climbed aboard the ship.

Inside, the narrow fuselage was equipped with two rows of six wicker chairs separated by a narrow aisle. Each seat had its own window and interior lighting was provided by small, dim bulbs located on decorative wooden panels above the windows. The seats looked more like those you would expect to see on a veranda than something that belonged in an airplane. While rather confining in comparison to a railroad passenger car, the cabin was almost cavernous by aircraft standards.

Clara had chosen a seat about halfway up the starboard side of the ship. I hoisted my overnight bag onto the rack above the seat opposite Clara's and made myself comfortable. Clara seemed a little more alert now and was looking around the cabin as if fascinated by its modern features. Ruth was sitting two seats behind us on Clara's side of the cabin.

The cockpit door in the bulkhead at the front of the cabin was open, and while the pilot and copilot seats were not visible from where I sat, I could see a lot of switch-flipping and knob-pushing going on up there as the Air Corps captain with whom Charlie had conversed and his copilot went through a lengthy checklist of preparations for our departure. There would be no kick-the-tires-and-light-the-fire takeoffs for these boys, no, siree. They were doing things the Army way—strictly by the book.

Several minutes later, the Trimotor's engines roared to life one at a time. When they were all up to full song, the copilot, a second lieutenant, stuck his head through the cockpit door and informed his three passengers that we were about to take off and that we should remain in our seats until the ship leveled off at our cruising altitude. As an afterthought, he added that there was a restroom at the rear of the cabin should we find ourselves in need of such facilities.

Immediately after he returned to his seat on the starboard side of the cockpit, the ship began rolling over the tarmac toward the runway. Once in position at the south end of the runway, the pilots revved the engines to a high pitch and performed yet another check of the ship's readiness for flight.

Then we were rolling down the runway, gaining speed at what seemed to me a surprising rate for such a heavy airplane. I felt the ship begin to shift its weight from the main gear wheels to its wings. I admired the pilot's skill as we completed the transition from ground to air smoothly and with a minimum of fuss and bother.

Glancing out the window to my right, I saw Kelly Field fall away below us as the pilot gradually raised the Trimotor's nose into a steeper angle of climb. I looked over to see how Clara was doing and saw that she was relaxed and seemed to be enjoying this new adventure. Two seats behind her, Ruth was looking out her window with a slightly apprehensive expression, but she kept whatever fears she might have in check.

Soon after we were airborne, our pilot executed a gradual left turn to a compass heading of roughly northwest, and we continued to climb for another six or seven minutes. When we reached an altitude I estimated to be about five-thousand feet, the pilot eased back on his throttles and the ship's nose lowered into an attitude of level flight. I could feel the Trimotor's speed increasing once it was no longer fighting gravity to climb.

Below us the countryside was all hills and gullies, just as it was around Camp Stanley. My flier's brain dutifully noted that this was not a landscape on which it would be easy to find a level, open space for an emergency landing, especially in a large ship like the Trimotor. This observation was not a cause for concern, but merely a point to keep in mind had I been at the controls.

I looked across the narrow aisle at Clara. Her attention was focused somewhere beyond the window. It was then that I realized we had not spoken since I had escorted her and Ruth down to the Saint Anthony's lobby more than an hour earlier. Thinking it might be a good idea to find out what was on her mind, I said, "How are you doing, Clara?"

She turned to look at me and replied, "Okay, I guess. I'm jus' kinda stiff an' sore from yes'erday."

I nodded. "I'm not at all surprised. We made a pretty hard landing on the set yesterday. I apologize for treating you so roughly."

"Eddie, you don' gotta 'pologize for nothin'. You saved my life, for cryin' out loud!"

"Well, just the same, I wish I could have done it without bouncing you around like that."

Clara did not reply immediately, but just kept looking at me with those big brown eyes. After several moments she said, "Eddie?"

"Yes."

"Do ya know wha' happened out there? I mean, do ya know why that airplane shot at us."

"No, I don't have the answer to that one. Wellman has Charlie Barton and others looking into the incident, so maybe they'll figure it out."

Frowning, Clara said, "It wasn' no accident, was it? The guy in tha' airplane meant to kill me, din' he?"

Hoping she could handle a straight answer, I said, "I might be wrong, but it sure looked that way to me."

Miss Clara Bow was no dummy. She had known the answer to her question before she asked it. Clara confirmed that, saying, "Tha's wha' I thought. I mus'a got somebody awful mad at me, but I sure don' know who."

"It would seem so, but try not to worry about it. A lot of people are making sure whoever that might be doesn't get another chance to hurt you."

She shook her head slightly. "I'm not afraid long as I'm wit' you." As if to emphasize that point, Clara reached across the aisle and put her hand on mine. "I don' got much faith in all those other people, but I got faith in you, Eddie. Ya know?"

There it was again in more or less plain English; that attachment I was hoping would become less important to her. Clearly, things were not going the way I was hoping, and that made me nervous. I was in no way qualified to be a knight in shining armor for America's most glamorous motion picture actress. Clara was still looking at me, apparently expecting an answer to her question, so I gave her the only answer I could. Nodding, I said, "I know, Clara. I'll do my best." Then I patted her hand and added, "I'm going up to chat with the pilot for a minute. I'll be right back."

Clara nodded and returned her attention to the window. I squeezed out of my seat into the aisle and made my way forward. The cabin height was barely six feet, so I had to bend forward at the waist a little to keep from bumping my noggin.

Leaning through the cockpit door, I asked, "How are we doing, Captain?"

Glancing over his shoulder and with a hint of southern accent, "Why, things are just hunky-dory up here. How are things back in the cabin?"

"We're enjoying a smooth flight. This Trimotor is quite a ship."

"It is, indeed. Ford gave this one to the Army Air Corps to test and we've been flyin' it all over creation. It took a little gettin' used to at first, but once we got the hang of how this big, ol' airplane handles, it's been a dream to fly."

"I was wondering how the Corps got their hands on one so quickly. I've been following articles about the ship's development in *Aviation Week*, and I figure this must be one of the first off the assembly line."

The Captain grinned at me. "Actually, you're ridin' aboard the very first AT-4 off the assembly line. You read *Aviation Week*? You a flier?"

"I'm an amateur flier these days. I was in the Army Air Service during The Great War. I flew pursuit ships in France."

"How 'bout that! See much action?"

Returning the captain's smile, I said, "More than enough to convince me combat flying ain't all it's cracked up to be."

"I'm sure you're right about that. Still, I can't help but be a little jealous of you fellows who actually flew in combat. The Corps spends a lot of time and money teachin' us skills we'll most likely never use. Seems sort of wasteful." The captain paused, then stuck his right hand out in my direction. "By the way, my name is

Arnie Miller."

I shook the hand he offered and said, "Eddie Markham."

"Pleased to know ya, Eddie. That fellow over there who's actually doin' all the work up here is Ronny Jones."

The copilot turned and nodded in my direction. I nodded back and said, "Well, I apologize for distracting you fellows from your job, but I came up here to get an idea of our route and itinerary."

Miller said, "Sure. We're making the trip to Los Angeles in three legs. Our first stop is Fort Bliss—that's up by El Paso and we should get there around eleven-hundred hours. Then we refuel and head for some little auxiliary field out in the middle of Arizona near Prescott called Rimrock. If we don't hit any bad weather, which we shouldn't, we'll drop in there around fifteen-thirty this afternoon. That's three-thirty civilian time."

Chuckling, I said, "You don't have to translate, Arnie. I still remember how the Army tells time."

"Glad to hear that. I know a couple of career sergeants who still haven't got it straight. Anyhow, we'll lay over there tonight and finish the trip off tomorrow morning. We'll take off at oh-eight-hundred and we ought to be at the Glendale Air Terminal before lunch. That all sound okay to you?"

"Sounds fine to me. I'm just glad you guys were available to get us back to L.A."

The captain gave me a conspiratorial grin. "Yeah, I was a little surprised about that. We don't usually provide taxi service for civilians unless they're high-falutin politicians. I figured you guys must have some pretty good clout with the brass, and then when you came aboard this morning I figured it out."

"You did?"

"Sure, Eddie. I go to enough movies to know Clara Bow when I see her, and I seen her right back there in the cabin. Say, you think there's a chance Ronny and I could get Miss Bow's autograph before this trip is over?"

Laughing, I said, "I think there's a real good chance of that, Arnie. In fact, I'll personally make sure you fellows each get a personalized autograph from Miss Bow. But, I'd appreciate it if you'd keep her being here just between us."

Captain Miller was also laughing when he said, "Damn! You mean I don't get to brag about how I flew the famous Clara Bow to Los Angeles?"

"Well, how 'bout holding off on the bragging for just a little while? We've got kind of a touchy situation going on right now and we're trying to keep Miss Bow's whereabouts under wraps until things blow over."

I'm not sure what the captain read into my reply, but he gave me a wink and said, "Sure, Eddie, mum's the word . . . for now."

Clara had a mild look of concern on her face when I got back to my seat. "You was gone a long time. Is everythin' okay?"

"Everything is just swell. We've got a sharp pilot who knows his onions, so I think we're in good hands."

"Good. When do we get home?"

"We layover at a little town in Arizona tonight, and then finish the trip tomorrow morning. We should be in Glendale about lunch time."

"Tomorrow! I thought these airplanes was s'posed to be fast!"

"They are. I'll take a day-and-a-half on an airplane over three days on a train anytime."

"Yeah, I guess. Sorry, I'm jus' anxious to get back."

I said I could certainly understand her being anxious to get home and that ended the conversation. A few moments later, Clara's eyelids got droopy and she drifted off to sleep. I felt as if I could use a snooze, too, but that seemed like it would be dereliction of duty. I was responsible for Clara and I find it difficult to be responsible for much of anything when I'm asleep. So I spent the rest of the morning watching the endless Texas countryside slide by below our wings.

We landed at Fort Bliss, Texas right on time, and Captain Arnie Miller informed us we would be there about an hour—just long enough to refuel the ship and get a bite of lunch. While he and Ronny Jones made preparations for fuel and whatever other maintenance the Trimotor required, Clara, Ruth and I walked across the tarmac toward the airfield operations building which, according to Captain Miller, also housed a small cafe for the convenience of maintenance crews and transient fliers.

Fort Bliss is one of the oldest US military establishments in the west, having been established before the Civil War. Since then it has grown into a military installation of impressive size, although the oppressive heat of the day made appreciation of this fact difficult. To my eyes, the place was just another collection of unimaginative government buildings laid out in a perfect grid and surrounded by flat terrain. There was, I should add in fairness, a fairly good-sized range of mountains visible some distance beyond the base.

The heat had caused Clara to shed her woolen coat, under which she was attired in one of her typical costumes—a dark blue pleated skirt, white silk blouse, and blue Mary Jane-style pumps with white ankle socks. For a prototypical flapper, Miss Bow was not an adventuresome dresser.

The only interesting event during our brief stay at Fort Bliss occurred as we entered the cafe. Ruth stopped at the door, saying she would wait in the lobby area and asking that we bring her a sandwich when we finished our lunch.

This, I concluded, was because of her race. While it saddened me that she felt this was necessary, I could understand her desire to avoid trouble by not entering a public eatery. Clara, however, was having none of it. Dragging Ruth by the hand, she marched into the cafe saying, "Tha's applesauce, Ruth. You're gonna have lunch wit' us and if anybody don' like it, they can go straight ta hell."

As things turned out, nobody seemed to care that a Negro woman was eating lunch in the cafe, although I sensed that Ruth was quite nervous the entire time we were there. The only reason I found this incident worthy of note is that it elevated my opinion of Clara Bow several notches. That she had the courage to treat her maid as an equal was not an attribute I would have guessed she possessed.

At precisely twelve-fifteen, we were back in our seats and the big Trimotor was accelerating down the Fort Bliss runway, stirring up great clouds of Texas dust along the edges of the tarmac in its wake. As soon as our wheels were clear of the ground and we had gained a few hundred feet of altitude, Captain Miller resumed a northwestly heading that put us on a diagonal course across the southwest corner of New Mexico, and from there, to the center of Arizona.

Despite the fact that we had finally left Texas behind us, there was little change in the landscape below. It still consisted largely of great open expanses of nothing. Clara had apparently lost all interest in the scenery, choosing instead to read a book she removed from her large handbag. Glancing across the aisle, I noted with some interest that the book she was reading was *Gentlemen Prefer Blondes*, a currently popular novel by a casual acquaintance of mine, fellow screen scenarist and author, Anita Loos.

I found this interesting for two reasons. First, Clara Bow did not impress me as someone who enjoyed reading as a pastime, and second, Miss Loos wrote about somewhat sophisticated subjects that I would have imagined were of little interest to Clara. America's ultimate flapper, it seemed, was full of surprises and I began to suspect I had done Miss Bow an injustice by taking her at face value. She was, I reminded myself, an accomplished actress, and I spent the rest of the flight contemplating just exactly where the actress ended and the real person began. I still had no answer to that question a few hours later when we began our descent for landing at Rimrock.

The Army Air Corps' auxiliary airfields were intended to be support facilities for nearby full-fledged bases, and are primarily for training purposes. As such, they seldom provided more than the most basic services. Rimrock Army Air Corps Auxiliary Airfield certainly fit that description.

I concluded that Rimrock started out as a civilian field because it was still serving in that capacity despite the Army Air Corps' presence there. What I saw from the air was a dirt runway with four small hangars and a couple of outbuildings. The few aircraft I could see on the ground were mostly civilian ships, although I spotted two Consolidated PT-1 primary trainers parked next to one of the hangars and what looked like another PT-1 on the other side of the runway.

Once on the ground, Captain Miller taxied the Trimotor over to the hangar where the training aircraft were parked and we all trooped out of the ship. It felt good to stretch my legs and move around without ducking my head to avoid colliding with a low ceiling.

After our pilots made arrangements with one of the Army Air Crops enlisted men lounging around the hangar to refuel the Trimotor, we addressed the matter of where we would spend the night. Needless to say, there were no military accommodations on the tiny auxiliary airfield. There was, however, a combination auto court and diner with the grand name of Rimrock Lodge across the highway.

We hiked over there and rented three of the Rimrock Lodge's four small cottages. Later, after dinner in the diner, during which Clara provided our delighted pilots with the promised personally autographed photos of herself, we retired to our rooms. I, however, ended up spending a good part of the night standing, or more accurately, sitting guard in the cottage occupied by Clara and Ruth.

Around midnight I decided it would be safe to get a few hours of sleep, so I went to my own cottage and hit the sack. When the loud rolling thunder claps of a storm passing through the area woke me a little before six Sunday morning, I gave up on the idea of any further sleep. Instead, I made myself presentable and went in search of coffee. Fortunately, the diner opened early and served a fairly decent cup of Java.

Sitting at a table next to one of the Rimrock Lodge's windows, I drank my coffee, watched bucketfuls of rain cascade down from the heavens, and contemplated the delay it would cause in our travel plans. By seven o' clock, however the storm subsided and I smiled at the thought of spending the night in my very own bed.

Twelve

8:00 A.M. (MT) – Sunday – September 19, 1926
Rimrock Auxiliary Airfield – Camp Verde, Arizona

For such a tiny airfield, Rimrock was a busy place at eight o' clock on a Sunday morning. Apparently word had gotten out that our Ford Trimotor had arrived the afternoon before, and what must have been most of the area's population turned out to see this modern marvel of the air and watch its departure.

When I realized the Trimotor was attracting a crowd, I hurried Clara and Ruth aboard to reduce the likelihood that Clara would be recognized. I doubted that my efforts were successful, though, because the mere fact of two women boarding an Army Air Corps transport in the middle of nowhere was, in itself, a remarkable event.

For that reason, I was relieved when our pilots finished their external preflight inspection of the ship—a process that was delayed by numerous questions from the curious onlookers—and boarded the Trimotor. After Ronny Jones secured the hatch and Captain Miller stowed their gear, including a stack of aeronautical charts and a thermos bottle of what I presumed to be coffee, in the cockpit, our pilots began their preflight checklist.

Finally the engines were started and, at precisely five minutes past eight o' clock by my wristwatch, the Trimotor taxied out to the west end of Rimrock's runway. The earlier thunderstorm had passed through the area from east to west, and the prevailing wind was still blowing in the same direction. That meant we would be taking off to the east, into the wind, before turning around to the westerly heading that would aim us toward Los Angeles. It also meant that the thunderstorm was now between us and our destination. That fact pretty much guaranteed a bumpy flight.

We began encountering rough air almost immediately after takeoff and I sensed that the constant jostling of the ship was making Clara and Ruth nervous. I assured them there was no cause for alarm, and that the ship was designed to take such bumps in stride. I added that the ride would smooth out once we got ahead of the storm.

I was watching the black clouds ahead grow larger in my narrow view through the cockpit windshield when I felt the ship bank to the left. That made sense. Captain Miller had decided to slip around the south end of the storm, avoiding the worst of the rain and turbulence. The detour would add some time to our trip, but would make for a much more pleasant flight.

It was about an hour later, after we skirted the storm and were back on our original course, that I sensed something was amiss in the cockpit. At one point I saw Arnie Miller reach across the cockpit toward his copilot a couple of times. Although I could not see exactly what Miller was doing, it appeared as if he was shaking Ronny Jones.

There was only one reason I could think of for Miller to be doing that, and I was just thinking of going forward to see if I could help with whatever might be wrong with our copilot when the Trimotor's nose pitched down sharply and we went into a dive. There was definitely something wrong up there!

I jumped out of my seat and ran down the sloping aisle. Poking my head into the cockpit, I immediately spotted the problem. Arnie Miller was out cold and, slumping forward, he was putting pressure on the control wheel. That explained the sudden dive. Glancing over to the right side of the cockpit, I saw that Ronny Jones was also unconscious. He was slumped against his side of the cockpit.

Grabbing Miller's shoulder, I pulled him back into his seat which released the forward pressure on the control wheel. The Trimotor's nose popped up like a cork in the water and we were back in a more or less level flight attitude. Miller had trimmed the ship to maintain level flight and, under the present circumstances, that was a definite plus because, being the only conscious flier aboard, I was now pilot in command of the airplane.

But there was one big obstacle to overcome before I could assume that role. Leaning back toward the cockpit door, I hollered, "Ruth, come up here quick! I need you!"

I chose Ruth over Clara because she was the heftier of the two, and getting Miller out of his seat so I could fly the ship was going to take all the muscle we could muster. Both women were looking a little panicky, but Ruth wasted no time in coming forward to the cockpit.

Ruth was a bright gal, and it didn't take her long to size up the situation. She cried, "Lord A' Mighty, we're all gonna die!"

Shouting to be heard over the engine racket, I tried to snap Ruth out of her panic. "No, we're not going to die. I'm a pilot. I can fly this ship, but I need your help to get the pilot out of his seat so I can reach the controls.

"I'll lift him out of his seat and push him toward the cockpit doorway. When I get him there, you help support his weight so we can get him out of here. Ready? Here we go."

Moving carefully in the cramped space so as to avoid bumping the control wheel or the throttles, I slid my arms under Miller's armpits and lifted. Fortunately, Arnie Miller was not a big man and I was able to slide his limp body up out of the pilot's seat and back against the cockpit bulkhead behind him. From there I slid him toward the doorway.

"Ruth, when I get him into the opening, you get a hold of him under his left arm and help support his weight while I step out of the cockpit. Then we'll slide him toward that passenger seat to your left."

I slid Miller into the opening and Ruth did exactly what I asked. With her helping to support Miller's weight, I stepped down into the cabin and we manhandled the unconscious pilot into the front passenger seat on the port side of the ship. As we did so, an extra pair of hands reached in to help. Clara had come forward to help out.

"Good work, Ruth. I've got to get busy flying this airplane. You gals see if you can do anything for him."

Not waiting for a reply, I stepped back into the cockpit and slid into the pilot's seat and stared at the complex instrument panel in front of me. The ships I was used to flying seldom had more than a couple of engine gauges and the most basic flight instruments—bank and turn indicator, altimeter and compass. The Trimotor's panel, on the other hand, had a dozen or more dials and gauges, many of which meant absolutely nothing to me. Since, however, the ship was behaving itself and most of the needles in front of me were pointing toward the centers of their arcs, I figured we had neither too much nor too little of anything at the moment and concentrated on the fundamentals of flying an airplane.

The most pressing concern was altitude. The altimeter was telling me we were flying at about 3,400 feet. Knowing there were mountains between us and our destination, I guessed that Miller had been flying high enough to avoid running into them, but we had lost some of that altitude when he collapsed against the control wheel and I needed to get us back up where we belonged. The question was how much altitude had we lost during the dive?

I made a guess of at least 1,500 feet, and decided to climb up to six-thousand feet just to give an extra margin of safety. Grasping the control wheel, which felt a lot like the steering wheel in my Stutz roadster, I gradually applied some back pressure. When the wheel hardly moved, I pulled harder. Eventually, after applying a lot more back pressure than I expected it would take, the ship's nose grudgingly lifted itself above the horizon. I had just learned something about the Trimotor: It was a darned heavy aircraft and a good deal of muscle was required to make it do what I wanted it to do.

Filing that lesson away for future reference, I kept the wheel back and watched the altimeter slowly move in a clockwise direction. I also kept an eye on the airspeed indicator. It had been pointing at about 90 miles per hour before I started to climb. Now it was showing about 75 MPH. It was natural for the ship to slow some when asked to climb, but I had to be sure it did not slow so much as to enter a stall.

A stall happens when the speed of the air moving over and under the wings slows to the point where it no longer provides enough lift to keep the ship in the air. All airplanes have what's known as a "stall speed." That number is one of the first things a pilot learns about a particular ship because stalls lead to spins and spins lead directly to terra firma.

Unfortunately, that particular piece of information was missing from my limited knowledge of the Trimotor. I figured we were still well above the ship's stall speed, though, because I felt none of the buffeting and other characteristics that usually precede a stall.

Sensing movement to my right, I turned and saw Ruth leaning into the cockpit. She said, "Mister Eddie, that man back there is in a bad way. His heartbeat is real weak and he's just barely breathing. I loosened his tie and collar, but I don't know anything else to do for him."

Returning my attention to the panel, I nodded and said, "Thanks, Ruth. Now take a look at this fellow in the copilot's seat."

She stepped into the cockpit and bent over Ronny Jones. After a couple of minutes, Ruth straightened and said, "Mister Eddie, I think this poor man is dead. I can't find no heartbeat and he ain't breathing at all that I can tell."

"Okay, Ruth, thanks for your help. Now you and Clara can sit down and relax. Everything is under control up here."

Ruth stepped down out of the cockpit, but leaned back in and said, "What are we going to do, Mister Eddie?"

"I'm going to figure out exactly where we are and then head for the nearest big city with an airport so we can get the pilot some medical help."

She said, "Okay, but that had best be soon."

Ruth disappeared back into the cabin and the altimeter needle finally reached the big white "6" on instrument's black face. I eased off on the control wheel and the Trimotor's nose slid back down to the horizon. A quick glance at the airspeed indicator showed that we were back to 90 MPH. Now the question was would the Trimotor hold itself at the new altitude without my having to keep pressure on the control wheel or retrimming the ship. Despite being heavy, the Trimotor is a stable ship and it was staying put, so I turned my attention to my next concern, namely, where the heck were we?

When over unfamiliar territory, pilots keep track of their location by comparing landmarks on the ground to those on an aeronautical chart. I remembered seeing Arnie Miller carry charts aboard back at Rimrock, so I looked around the cockpit for them. They were right where most fliers keep their charts, down along the left side of the pilot's seat.

My opinion that Arnie Miller was a darned good pilot was confirmed when I looked at the top chart in the stack. He had folded it to show a pencil line that began at Rimrock Auxiliary Airfield. Turning the chart over, I saw the pencil line continued to an airport symbol identified as Glendale Air Terminal. He had been doing it all correctly and by the book, for which I now had even more reason to be grateful.

The direction of the line he had drawn on the chart more or less matched our compass heading of 260 degrees, so I concluded we were still on course, although I reminded myself that the pencil line might not be a hundred percent accurate owing to the detour Miller had made around the thunderstorm. Still, I figured we were probably somewhere pretty close to that line, but where exactly?

I recalled noting that we had taxied out to the Rimrock runway at five minutes after eight. From that I figured we actually got into the air around eight-ten. The time was now nine-fifty-five. We had been airborne for one hour and forty-five minutes. Figuring the time and speed it would have taken us to reach six-thousand feet and calculating our speed at 90 MPH from that point, I estimated we had traveled about 116 miles. Using the chart's scale and my pencil as a measuring device, I penciled an X over Arnie Miller's course line and jotted down the time next to it.

Studying the chart, I determined that, if my calculations were anywhere near correct, we should be just west of the Colorado River. I turned and looked as far back as I could through the side window, and there it was, a major river with twists and turns that matched the Colorado as it was depicted on the chart.

I looked around for another landmark to verify my estimate of our position. There were damned few landmarks to be had in this godforsaken desert, but sunlight glinting off of a large body of water to the southwest gave me what I needed. According to the chart, I was looking at the Salton Sea and it was exactly where it should have been relative to the position I had fixed.

Now all I had to do was find a major city with an airport where we could land and get Captain Miller the urgent medical attention he needed. That would be no easy task because big cities are scarce in this part of the world. There was Las Vegas to the north, but it was more of a cow town than a city. Phoenix was some distance behind us and the sprawling metropolis of Los Angeles lay ahead. Then I noticed a symbol on the chart that was just what I was looking for.

Ahead and slightly south of our current heading was March Field, an Army Air Corps base near Riverside, California. March was a big base that was sure to have complete medical facilities, which was exactly what we needed.

I estimated a slight left turn to a heading of 245 degrees would take us directly to March. Applying pressure to the left rudder pedal, I turned the control wheel in the direction I wanted to go. Again, it took a lot of muscle to get the big Trimotor turned, and I felt the ship slide a little, indicating I wasn't using enough rudder, but pretty or not, I completed the turn and we took up our new course. A few more calculations told me we were just a little more than a hundred miles from March Field—slightly more than an hour's flying time from our destination.

Taking a deep breath, I relaxed a little and scanned the instruments again. As best I could tell, the three big radial engines were all happy and contented. We had, however, lost about two hundred feet of altitude. I studied the chart for the elevations of the mountains ahead and found that we still had plenty of height to avoid them. I would have been feeling pretty pleased with myself if it weren't for the fact that I still had to get a very heavy airplane I had never landed before on the ground in one piece at our destination.

Remembering that Arnie Miller and Ronny Jones did everything by the book, my next step was to search the cockpit for that book, or at least the takeoff and landing checklists they had used so diligently. I found the checklists attached to a wooden clipboard stowed alongside the copilot's seat. Making a concerted effort not to dwell on the fact that my copilot was a corpse, I reached across Ronny Jones' body and retrieved the clipboard.

Keeping one eye on our progress outside the cockpit, I thumbed through the checklists until I found the one labeled "Landing." There, printed in bold type across the top of the page, I found the most vital piece of information about the Trimotor I was missing. It said: "The minimum flying speed for this aircraft at gross weight (10,300 lbs) is 64 MPH indicated airspeed." In simple terms, that meant a fully loaded Trimotor would stall, or stop flying when its airspeed indicator dropped to 64 miles per hour. Since, with only five people aboard, we were a long way from being at the ship's gross weight, 64 was a safe number.

I went through the items on the landing checklist itself, locating the various knobs, switches and gauges I would need to be concerned with when the big moment arrived. That chore done, I looked around the cockpit trying to think of anything else I needed to know or do that was absolutely necessary to flying the ship.

When nothing came to mind, I realized I could not put off the inevitable any longer. As one of my old squadron mates frequently said, "It was time to fish or cut bait." In other words, it was time to plan my approach to March Air Field and put Mister Ford's tin goose on the ground, hopefully in one piece.

Thirteen

9:15 A.M. (PT) – Sunday – September 19, 1926
Over Twentynine Palms, California

If my estimate of our position was correct, the small town directly ahead was Twentynine Palms, which was about fifty miles from March Field. It was time to begin a descent that would take us down to an altitude of about a thousand feet when we got to the field. I put my hand on the three throttle levers just below the center of the instrument panel and gently—very gently—eased them back a little.

The Trimotor responded by lowering its nose a little below the horizon. That was the result I was expecting. The result I was not expecting was the corresponding increase in airspeed. A slight increase in our speed was normal, but a glance at the airspeed indicator showed that the Trimotor was now traveling through the air at 105 miles per hour. The jump in speed was a solid reminder that I was at the controls of a very heavy ship and I needed to pay close attention to our speed to avoid letting things get out of hand.

Ruth chose that moment to give me a report on Arnie Miller's condition. Leaning into the cockpit, she asked, "Are we getting close to our landing place, Mister Eddie?"

Keeping my eyes glued to the instrument panel, I said, "Yes, Ruth. We should be on the ground in about half an hour."

"I hope that's soon enough. This man out here is still breathing, but just barely."

"Okay, Ruth. I'm doing all I can to get us on the ground quickly. Thanks for the report."

When she made no reply, I was relieved. My hands were about to get very full and distractions were the last things I needed. Our descent had stabilized for the moment, so I took the opportunity for another look at the aeronautical chart. The thing I needed to find there was the radio frequency of the March Field tower. Military airfields take a dim view of folks who drop in unannounced.

Finding the numbers I needed, I reached over to the right side of the cockpit and turned the radio tuning dial to the March Field frequency. Then I reached back for the headphone set that was hanging on a hook behind my seat. I donned the phones and raised the radio volume until I heard a hissing sound. After a moment a voice came loud and clear through the static.

"Army niner-two-seven-zero from March tower, you are cleared to land."

The response from whoever the tower was talking to was weaker. "March . . . roger. Niner . . . seven . . . ."

That brief conversation confirmed I had dialed in the correct radio frequency and I was about to interject some excitement into the lives of the March Field tower operations crew. I removed the microphone from its clip next to the radio, took a deep breath, and pressed the small button on the side of the microphone.

"March Field tower, this is an inbound Army transport. March Field tower, this is an inbound Army transport. How do you read? How do you read? Over."

Assuming they heard my transmission, I could imagine the fellows in the tower shaking their heads over this yokel who was illiterate in military radio protocol. A moment later I knew for certain they were receiving me. Out of the static in my headphones a brusque voice said, "Inbound Army transport from March Field. Identify yourself. Repeat, identify yourself. Over."

I took another deep breath and said, "March Field, we are an AT-Four Trimotor inbound from the east and we are declaring an emergency. Repeat, we are declaring an emergency. Over."

Now the fellows on the ground were really shaking their heads. Since the Trimotor was a brand new ship, it even was possible they had never heard of it. After a slightly longer pause, the air operations officer replied, "AT-Four Trimotor state the nature of your emergency. Over."

"March tower, I am a civilian pilot who assumed control of this ship when both pilots became seriously ill. The copilot is dead and the pilot is unconscious. He needs immediate medical attention. Repeat, the pilot is unconscious and needs immediate medical attention. Over."

I had to give the fellow in the tower credit for knowing how to handle the unexpected. In a voice that was completely calm, he said, "Trimotor, understood. Say your location, altitude and heading. Over."

I took quick looks out the windshield and at the aeronautical chart. "March tower, we are just east of Desert Hot Springs . . . ." Glancing at the altimeter and compass, I added, "Descending through three-thousand feet on a heading of two-four-five degrees. Over."

"Trimotor, understood. Are you able to land the ship by yourself? Over."

That question struck me as funny and I was tempted to say no just to find out how they planned to send someone up to help me land the ship. Figuring, however, the air operations people probably would not see the humor in that, I keyed the microphone and gave them the straight dope. "March tower, I have never landed anything this size before, but at the moment, things seem to be under control. Over."

"Trimotor, understood. The current conditions at March Field are as follows: Wind four miles per hour out of the north. Ceiling and visibility unlimited. Runway three-three is active. Over."

"March Field, understand runway three-three is active. Over."

As most airports, military airfields assign numbers to runways based on compass headings. Therefore, runway three-three ran more or less north and south. That fit with the wind information he had given me.

"Trimotor, recommend approach directly over the airfield at one-thousand feet, then a turn to the south to line up for final approach. Complete turn to the runway heading before you reach the town of Perris, five miles south of the field. We are dispatching emergency vehicles to meet you. Report again when you have field in sight. Over."

Looking out beyond the Trimotor's nose I spotted a valley just beyond a low ridge of mountains, and at the west end of the valley was the very welcome sight of a large airfield. I pressed the microphone button and said, "March Field, I have you in sight. Over and thanks."

"Trimotor, we see you. Your position is good and you are cleared to land." After a momentary pause, he added, "Good luck, Trimotor. Over and out."

I tucked the microphone under my right thigh to keep it from getting lost in the event I needed it again. That was when I suddenly remembered I was not alone in this adventure. Turning toward the cabin door, I shouted, "We're approaching the field. Brace yourselves. This might be a bumpy landing!"

Then I suddenly remembered something else. Words my basic flight training instructor was quite fond of saying more than a dozen years ago popped into my head. "There are three constantly changing variables in the landing equation—location, altitude and speed. Keep them in balance with each other and you will make a good landing. Let them get out of balance and your Uncle Sam will be very displeased with you for breaking one of his airplanes."

Since those days, hundreds of landings had made the process more or less automatic for me, but the landing I was now attempting was quite different from any I had ever made before. Pay attention to your flight instructor, Markham!

As we crossed the low ridge at the east end of the valley the altimeter needle was rapidly closing in on one thousand feet. It was time to level off and lose some of my accumulated airspeed.

Applying steady back pressure to the control wheel, I lifted the Trimotor's nose back up to the horizon. At the lower power setting I used for our descent, the airspeed dropped off rapidly. I put my right hand on the throttles in case my speed dropped too much and I needed more power. The altimeter showed exactly one thousand feet and the airspeed settled at about 80 MPH. That seemed like a good speed because the turn I was about to make would cause our speed to drop even more. Keep the equation balanced.

This was the point in a landing when things begin happening quickly. March Field was almost under the Trimotor's nose. I took a quick look down to fix the layout in my mind and noticed several vehicles lined up on a taxiway just east of the runway. One of them was a bright red fire truck.

I held my course for another forty seconds or so, and then it was time to make my turn to the south. Keeping my right hand on the throttles again in case I needed to add power, I pushed down hard on the left rudder pedal while turning the control wheel to the left.

Almost grudgingly, the Trimotor lowered its left wing and began turning. I felt the ship getting heavier . . . airspeed dropping to 70 MPH . . . nearly through the turn . . . roll out level . . . airspeed 75 . . . better.

Heading south now . . . small town ahead . . . must be Perris. Altimeter slowly unwinding . . . 800 feet.

The controller's voice rang out in my earphones, "Trimotor, your position is good. I will call your next turn. Over."

Small town ahead growing larger in windshield . . . altitude 700 . . . airspeed 75.

"Trimotor, begin one-hundred-eighty degree left turn for final approach. Over."

Left rudder pedal . . . control wheel left . . . forward pressure to keep nose down and airspeed up. Turning . . . ship feels sluggish . . . flying through a sky full of mush. Slight buffeting . . . airspeed too low . . . close to stall . . . add power!

Still turning . . . airspeed 75 . . . altitude 500 . . . rolling out of turn. Runway straight ahead . . . altitude 400 . . . airspeed 75.

"Trimotor, your position is good, but you are below the approach slope. Slow your rate of descent. Over."

Adding power . . . altitude 300 . . . airspeed 80.

"Trimotor, you are still too low. Slow your descent. Repeat, slow your descent. Over."

More power . . . runway coming up fast . . . ship drifting right . . . kick left rudder to keep runway lined up . . . altitude 200 . . . descending more gradually now . . . airspeed 75.

"Trimotor, position and rate of descent good. Over."

Runway numbers flash by . . . altitude 100 . . . airspeed 75 . . . too fast . . . reduce power. Altitude 50 . . . airspeed 70 . . . still too fast . . . reduce power more.

Tires hit runway . . . screech . . . bounce . . . sinking back down . . . tires screech again . . . and stick . . . throttles full back.

Forward pressure on control wheel . . . keep tail up as long as possible . . . pushing hard on both rudder pedals to apply brakes . . . slowing . . . tail touches down . . . speed bleeding off quickly . . . lots of runway left.

"Trimotor, good job! Turn right off runway at next taxiway."

Going too slowly . . . release brakes . . . remember checklist instructions to taxi on center engine only . . . adding power to center engine.

Runway turnoff ahead . . . apply right rudder and brake . . . turning . . . release right brake . . . off the runway . . . pull center engine power . . . roll to stop . . . switches off . . . resume breathing.

Fourteen

As I lifted myself out of the Trimotor's pilot seat onto none too steady legs, the hatch at the rear of the fuselage swung open and an Army Captain carrying a doctor's bag scrambled into the cabin. In a clear, authoritative voice he asked, "Where is the injured man?"

Ruth and Clara, who were still in their seats and looking a little shell shocked after our harrowing landing, both pointed to the front of the cabin where Arnie Miller was slumped in a passenger seat. As the doctor hurried up the narrow aisle toward Miller's seat, two Army corpsmen struggled through the hatch behind him with a canvas stretcher.

Upon arriving at Miller's side, the doctor withdrew a stethoscope from his bag and set about examining the unconscious pilot. Several minutes later the doctor removed a small vial and a hypodermic syringe. After administering a shot, he turned to his two medics and said, "This man is alive, but he's hanging by a thread. Get him to the post hospital as fast as you can. Tell the emergency doctor on duty this fellow seems to be suffering from severe Anaphylaxis. Tell them I've administered a five milligram injection of adrenaline. Go!"

The two medics worked quickly in the cramped cabin, lifting Captain Miller onto their stretcher and carrying him out of the cabin. While they were doing that, the doctor looked at me and asked, "Where is the man reported as deceased?"

"Up here in the copilot's seat. Let me get out of your way."

I stepped down into the cabin and the doctor climbed up into the cockpit. This time his examination was brief. To no one in particular, he said, "There's nothing we can do for this man. He's long gone. I'll have him taken to the post hospital morgue as soon as this aircraft is cleared."

The doctor returned the stethoscope to his bag and stepped down out of the cockpit. As he did so, I asked, "What got them, doctor, food poisoning?"

He stopped, turned to face me, and tilted his head a little to one side. "I suppose that's a possibility. When did the pilots last eat?"

I thought back to the morning's departure from Rimrock and said, "It was probably between six-thirty and seven this morning, mountain time. They both seemed fine during their preflight inspection and when they boarded the ship a little before eight."

"And when did they start showing signs of being ill?"

"I sensed something was wrong in the cockpit around nine-fifteen. The copilot passed out first. The pilot lost consciousness about nine-thirty. That's when I took over the controls."

"And that was still mountain time?"

I nodded and the doctor said, "Well, the timing is about right, but I don't think we're dealing with a bacterial infection here. The symptoms are much too severe."

"What then? Some kind of contagious disease?"

The doctor shook his head. "No, not that either. We'll know more when an autopsy is performed on that fellow up in the cockpit, but if I had to hazard a guess right now, I'd say these men ingested a powerful, fast acting poison, such as strychnine, or more likely, some form of arsenic."

On that disconcerting note, the doctor walked briskly back to the cabin hatch and exited the ship while I stood there contemplating his diagnosis. It was definitely not what I wanted to hear because his guess as to what hit our pilots went a long way toward confirming a suspicion that had been lingering in my head since Arnie Miller passed out in the pilot's seat. If I was right, whoever had tried to kill Clara Bow in Texas had just tried again; only this time an innocent man was the victim. And if Captain Miller didn't pull through, the ante would be up to two innocent men.

As I turned to leave the ship, I saw that Ruth had already done so, but Clara was still standing in the aisle next to her seat. When I got to her, she threw her arms around me and pressed her head to my chest.

I gave her a couple of reassuring pats and said, "It's all right, Clara. We're safely on the ground and everything is going to be okay."

She looked up at me with her big brown eyes and said, "Eddie, you are wonderful, just wonderful."

Then she stood on tiptoes and planted a kiss square on my lips that did absolutely nothing to relieve my already wobbly legs. When the kiss ended, she smiled brightly at me and walked back toward the cabin hatch, where willing hands helped her to the ground.

I used my handkerchief to remove a fair amount of lip rouge from my mouth, after which I lifted my overnight case from the overhead rack and headed for the hatch. As I did so, I was struck with a feeling that something was slightly out of whack with what had just happened in the aisle, but I couldn't put my finger on exactly what it was.

As I hopped down from the ship a beefy Army sergeant with a black and white military police armband stepped up to me and said, "I have instructions to escort you and the other passengers to the base commander's office." He gestured to a four-door, olive drab staff car with big white stars on its front doors and added, "We'll take that automobile."

Clara and Ruth were already seated in the rear of the touring car, and the MP followed closely behind me as I walked toward the Dodge. For some reason I had the uneasy feeling his role was more that of a guard than an escort.

As the sergeant drove briskly away, I turned and looked back at the Trimotor sitting on the taxiway. The ship had a proud look about her, and with good reason. She had just survived a rough landing at the hands of a bumbling pilot who had no business being at her controls in the first place. My hat was off to the Stout Airplane Company's engineers.

Sitting as it does on the periphery of a desert, March Army Air Corps field was far from the most picturesque military base I had ever seen. Most of the buildings—barracks and the like—were of wood construction with the empty areas between them covered in weeds. The only exceptions to this were a long row of hangars lining the airstrip and the buildings surrounding the parade ground. The structures around this neatly manicured central area of the base were more permanent looking buildings constructed in the Spanish mission style.

Our destination turned out to be one of these. It was the post administration headquarters, a more imposing two-story structure with a tile roof. The MP escorted us to a first-floor outer office near the front of the building. As we entered, a pleasant-faced sergeant stood up behind a desk and invited the women to have a seat. I, on the other hand, was pointed toward a door bearing the words, "Private" and "Base Commander."

As I entered the inner office, a tall, slender bird-colonel with graying hair stood up from his desk, offered his hand, and said, "Good morning, I'm Colonel Efram Smythe."

Shaking the hand he offered, I said, "Good morning, sir. I'm Eddie Markham."

"Nice to meet you, Eddie. Please take a seat and make yourself comfortable."

Setting my overnight case on the floor next to one the two guest chairs facing the desk, I did as instructed. As Colonel Smythe reseated himself, I took stock of the emblems on his uniform jacket, which included a pair of gold pilot wings, indicating that the Colonel had not always flown a desk. Below his wings, Smythe wore three campaign ribbons: The victory medal received by all who served in the Great War, a 1914/1915 star indicating service in France or Belgium during the war, and a distinguished service medal. This latter decoration was not directly tied to combat and might have been awarded for any number of reasons, most of them not demanding heroism.

Colonel Smythe looked across his desk at me and said, "Our Air Operations people tell me you just made one hell of a fine landing in a new ship you've never flown before. You must be quite the experienced pilot."

Not being sure exactly where our conversation might be headed, I thought this might be an excellent time to interject some good old military esprit de corps into the proceedings. "I flew with the Twenty-seventh Aero Squadron's First Pursuit Group in France during the Great War, sir. Since then I've tried to keep my hand in by flying as often as I can."

The colonel looked sincerely impressed. "You flew pursuits in France? That explains how you were able to get that transport safely on the ground today."

"Thank you, sir, but in this instance, it was more a case of good luck than good piloting."

"I sincerely doubt that, Eddie. Now, if you don't mind, please tell me how this all came about. How did you as a civilian end up flying one of our transport ships?"

I began my answer to his question at the beginning, explaining how the Army Air Corps was working with the Paramount film crew in San Antonio, and how Charlie Barton had arranged for our flight back to Los Angeles aboard the Trimotor. I did not, however, tell Colonel Smythe that Clara Bow was one of the passengers on the flight, nor did I give him the specific reason for our hasty departure from Texas.

As I spoke, the colonel made copious notes. When I finished the story, he set his pencil down said, "All I can say is it was good providence that you were aboard that ship when our pilots took ill. Otherwise, we would have lost a valuable aircraft along with its crew and passengers."

I simply nodded. This did not seem like a good time to mention my suspicion that, had we not been on that aircraft, the pilots would not have been taken ill.

Colonel Smythe looked at his notes. "I think you'll understand that I must make some telephone calls to verify a few details you've given me. I hope you will not take offense at my need to do so."

"No offense taken, sir."

Smythe smiled in a manner that oozed sincerity. "Good! This shouldn't take very long. Perhaps you would like to go to the Officer's Club for a bite to eat while I make my telephone calls."

"That sounds fine, sir, but I have a request before we do that. I need to speak with my boss in San Antonio and tell him what's happened. Could you direct me to a public telephone?"

Smythe smiled again. "Nonsense, Eddie. You may use my desk phone to place your call. The Air Corps certainly owes you at least that much." Standing, he added, I'll have the post operator connect to an outside telephone line, and then I'll give you some privacy while I go out and introduce myself to your fellow passengers."

When the colonel handed me his telephone handset, a dial tone buzzed in my ear. I dialed "O" for an operator and Smythe strolled out of his office, closing the door behind him. I told the operator I wanted to make a person-to-person call to either William Wellman or Charles Barton at the Saint Anthony hotel in San Antonio, Texas.

Since it was Sunday and no filming was scheduled, I figured I had a reasonable chance of catching either Wellman or Barton at the hotel. I got Wellman.

"Hello, Eddie. Did you arrive in Los Angeles safely?"

"Not quite, Bill. We encountered a small problem on the way." I followed that with a short version of the small problem we encountered.

When I finished the story, Wellman said, "Hell! It sounds like you saved the day again! I'll have Charlie call Lasky and explain the situation. You want me to have the studio send someone out to pick you up at the base?"

"I'd rather you didn't do that, Bill."

"Oh? Why not?"

Choosing my words carefully because I had no idea who might be listening in to the conversation, I said, "Bill, I have a strong suspicion that all this might be related to the incident at Camp Stanley last Friday. On the off chance I'm right about that, it might be better if you let us handle things from this end. In fact, it would be best if you simply told them we landed at an alternate field in the desert without any further specifics."

I could tell from his tone that Bill suddenly had a lot of questions on his mind, but he seemed to understand the need for discretion. "All right, Eddie, I'll leave it up to you. I'll just have Barton tell the studio that you're on your way in and that you will contact them." Wellman paused for a moment, and then said, "Please call me again soon, though, and let me know what you're up to. Needless to say, I am concerned."

When I returned to the colonel's outer office, he was chatting with Clara. On seeing me, Smythe said, "Eddie, you've been holding out on me! You didn't tell me one of your passengers was a glamorous motion picture actress."

I smiled. "Well, Colonel, that detail sort of slipped my mind in all the excitement. Also, Miss Bow is sort of traveling incognito, so I'm sure her studio would appreciate it if you could keep her whereabouts under wraps, at least for right now.

Smythe smiled his cordial smile. "I certainly understand." Then, addressing his secretary and the MP, he said, "You heard Mister Markham. Consider Miss Bow's presence here classified information. Understood?"

Almost in unison, both men said, "Yes, sir."

To me, Smythe said, "I've instructed the sergeant here," he gestured toward the MP, "to escort you over to the Officer's Club. I'll join you there after I've taken care of the business I mentioned earlier."

Standing, Clara said, "If you don't mind, Colonel, Miss Brown says she isn't hungry and would prefer to wait here."

I thought I saw a little relief on Smythe's face as he replied, "That's quite all right." Turning to his secretary, the colonel said, "Sergeant, please see to Miss Brown's comfort and that she has anything she needs."

It was after hearing what she had just told Smythe that the light finally dawned and I figured out what it was that seemed strange to me about Clara as we were leaving the Trimotor. Miss Clara

Bow's thick Brooklyn accent had disappeared. Suddenly, her diction and pronunciation were nearly perfect. Staring at her in surprise, I thought, "You little phony," and I began to wonder how much of her public behavior, such as that I witnessed on the Sunset Limited, went along with the accent as part of her act.

Miss Bow was definitely not at all what she seemed to be. Somehow that revelation added to my respect for her in the same way her kindness toward Ruth had at the Fort Bliss airfield cafe.

Fifteen

11:00 A.M. (PT) – Sunday – September 19, 1926
March Army Air Corps Field – Near Riverside

Located on a large empty expanse of land several blocks from the parade ground, the March Field O Club could have passed for a desert oasis. The sprawling single story, stucco building in the Spanish mission style was surrounded by a carefully tended garden of hardy shrubs and miniature palm trees, all of which must have made it a welcome sight to the officers upon whom fate had bestowed a posting to this austere airfield.

Our MP escort shepherded Clara and me up the club's long walk, and once inside, he told the sergeant in a sharply-pressed uniform at the reception desk that we were to be the guests of Colonel Smythe, who would be joining us later. After saying his piece, the MP promptly turned and departed the club. I suspected he wasn't going far, though.

The receptionist/maitre d' showed us to a table next to a window at the front of a large dining room. I stashed my overnight bag under said table and spent a moment taking in our new surroundings.

I have seen more lavish officers' clubs in my day, but this one offered the distinct advantage of being a cool and quiet place to relax. The quiet was largely due to it being a Sunday and us being early for lunch. The only other customers in the dining room were three second lieutenants proudly wearing shiny new gold pilot wings on their chests. They were at a table near the back of the room drinking Coca-Cola and telling hangar stories.

After giving us time to study the menu, a Negro steward in a plum-colored mess jacket arrived to take our lunch orders. Clara said she was not very hungry and asked for a green salad with

Italian-style dressing. I, on the other hand, had worked up a healthy appetite since eating breakfast in Rimrock, Arizona, and ordered a cup of minestrone soup, a roast beef sandwich, and a Coke.

Our orders placed, I leaned back in my chair and studied the young redheaded woman seated across the table for a long moment. If this occasion had been a romantic date, a fellow could not ask for a prettier companion. Even with a two-inch square of gauze taped to her cheek, Clara was a beautiful woman full of life and energy. With a twinge of disappointment that surprised me a little, I reminded myself that this occasion was far from a romantic date, and that I was charged with the daunting responsibility for seeing that Miss Clara Bow remained full of life and energy.

Clara, who had also been looking around the dining room, noticed me watching her. She smiled a warm smile and tilted her head a little to one side. "Who are you staring at, mister?"

"Clara, we need to have a serious conversation."

Adopting a slightly more concerned expression, but one that was still warm and inviting, she said, "I know, Eddie."

"Before we have that conversation, though, I would like to ask you a personal question."

"Sure. Go ahead."

"What the heck happened to your Brooklyn accent?"

That brought a smile back to the Cupid's bow lips that had taken America by storm. "You noticed, huh?"

I just nodded and she said, "Well, I really talked like that when I first came to California and it bothered me that I sounded strange, so I went out and hired a speech teacher on my own. It took almost a year of hard work, but I finally got rid of the accent. Then, after all that, B. P.—Mister Schulberg—insisted that I go back to talking with the accent in public. He said it made me a more colorful character or something like that. He even got the newspapers to call me the Brooklyn Bombshell, for crying out loud. Thank goodness that didn't catch on a whole lot."

I nodded again and said, "So what made you suddenly decide to drop the accent today?"

Besides being very pleasant to look at, Clara's face was a constantly changing barometer of her moods. Her current expression hinted at embarrassment, not unlike the way a little girl might look if caught doing something naughty. In answer to my question, she said, "You did, silly."

Puzzled, I asked, "How did I do that?"

"By being you. Eddie, I admire and respect you, to say nothing of appreciating you having saved my life . . . twice. I want you to know the real me instead of the Clara Bow most people know. We're really two very different women."

"So I'm learning."

With a sincerity on her countenance I could not doubt, Clara said, "I really hope you will feel differently about the real me than you feel about the other Clara Bow."

I wasn't sure how I should respond to that, so I simply nodded. She was quite right, though. I was feeling a good deal more respect for the woman she was now than I had for the person I first met in Lasky's old barn.

The waiter brought our lunches and I found my minestrone to be delicious, but I had a good deal more to say, so I put my soup spoon down and said, "Clara, I don't know if you heard what the doctor told me after he examined the pilots, but the gist of his initial diagnosis is that our pilots were poisoned."

Solemnly, she said, "Yes, I heard that part."

"That diagnosis is important because it means we are in very big trouble."

Clara frowned. "I don't suppose there's any chance the pilots were poisoned by accident."

"Not on the heels of what happened at the French village in Texas Friday."

Shaking her head slowly, she said, "Eddie, I don't understand any of this. Who would want to kill me? What have I done?"

"I can't answer those questions yet, but there are a few things of which I am reasonably certain. Whoever is behind all this knows far too much about you, more than any outsider should know. For example, flying out of Texas on an Army transport ship was a last minute decision, yet if my suspicions are right, the killer somehow knew you were on that airplane."

With a look of surprise on her face, Clara said, "You mean it's someone at the studio?"

"Possibly, or someone with connections at the studio. It could even be somebody on the production crew in Texas."

Surprise turned to fear. "What are we going to do? They know everything about me!"

I shook my head. "Not quite everything. Based on my suspicion that whoever is out to get you is somehow connected to the studio, I did something I hope will break that connection, at least temporarily."

"What did you do?"

"I talked with Bill Wellman by telephone while I was in the

colonel's office, and I told him not to tell anyone at the studio where we landed. He'll tell Lasky there was a problem on the flight and that you survived, but he'll say we made an emergency landing out in the desert somewhere instead of telling them we're here at March Field.

"It won't take very long for the word to get out about where we actually landed, but that might be long enough for us to do some other things to throw them off the track. If you disagree with my decision to do that, it can be undone with one telephone call. That's up to you."

Clara looked thoughtful. "No. You did the right thing. I had already decided I wasn't going with Lasky's people when we got to Glendale. I don't trust any of them. The only one I trust is you."

Hoping her trust wasn't misplaced, I got back to my mental list of things we needed to talk about. "The other thing we know for certain about whoever is trying to kill you is that they are not at all concerned about who else might get hurt in the process. If things had worked out a little differently, four innocent people would have died with you on that airplane. As it is, one man did die and another may still die."

"I know that, Eddie, and I feel terrible about what happened to those men on my account. We have to keep anyone else from getting hurt."

"You're right, and that brings us to the here and now. In order to keep you safe we need to come up with a plan . . . ."

Interrupting, Clara said, "I already have a plan. I thought about it a lot since we got here, and there's only one thing I can do."

"Okay, what's that?"

"I have to disappear from the face of the earth until someone catches whoever is doing these awful things."

Since I was already thinking along similar lines, I said, "You could be right, but making you disappear will be difficult. Yours is not exactly an unknown face in the crowd."

"We can do it if you help me. I know we can. I've even figured out where I can disappear to."

I held up my hand in a motion to stop. "Don't say anymore until we're someplace where there's no chance of being overheard. And, of course, I'll help you. I promised Wellman and Victor Fleming I would keep you safe. But there's an additional problem you might not have taken into consideration."

She gave me another frown. "What additional problem?"

Leaning forward and speaking in lower tones, I said, "The Army Air Corps. As a matter of course, they are investigating what happened to their pilots, and once they find out for certain that Arnie Miller and Ronny Jones were deliberately poisoned, finding the culprit will become a priority of the highest order."

Still frowning, Clara said, "Yes, I'm sure it will, but how is that a problem for us?"

"At the very least, we are witnesses to murder, and in the minds of some, we may even be suspects. Colonel Smythe and his superiors are not going to let us just stroll off this post once the accident investigation becomes a murder investigation.

"Even now they're keeping a close eye on us. In case you didn't notice, our escort is an armed military policeman who is none too friendly. The point is, if we are detained here as part of a murder investigation, making you disappear will be impossible."

Clara was clearly surprised. "Can they do that? We're civilians!"

"I don't know how legal it would be in the civilian world, but legalities have never bothered the Army much in the past. They do pretty much whatever they want in their own bailiwick."

"Then what are we going to do?"

"We are going to do everything we can get off this post before the coroner or that doctor figure out for sure what really happened to Ronny Jones and Arnie Miller. Now, when Colonel Smythe joins us here, he probably won't have any details from the doctor yet, and certainly not from whoever is doing the autopsy on Jones. If I'm right about that, we need to convince Smythe you have to be somewhere in a hurry so he'll get us transportation off the post and in to Riverside."

Brightening a bit, Clara said, "Okay, leave the convincing to me. Good old Colonel Smythe thinks I'm the bee's knees."

"All right, Clara, but try not to appear overly anxious. We don't want to raise his suspicions."

She put on her grin again. "Hey, have you forgotten what I do for a living?"

That was a point for which I had no argument. Looking at my wristwatch, I said, "It's quarter to twelve and Smythe should be coming along soon. We had best finish our lunches so we'll be ready to go."

Clara said she didn't want any more of her salad, but she wouldn't mind having a little of my Coca-Cola. I told her to help herself and dug back into my soup and roast beef sandwich. I had just swallowed the last spoonful of minestrone when Smythe walked into the dining room.

Seating himself in one of the empty chairs at our table, he said,

"How are you enjoying our Officer's Club, Miss Bow?"

"It's lovely, Colonel, and the food is wonderful."

"Good! I'll pass your compliment on to our chef." Turning to me, Smythe changed both his tone and the subject. Sounding a little as if he was angry, the colonel said, "Lieutenant Markham, you were not entirely honest with me earlier. Besides forgetting to tell me about Miss Bow, you also failed to mention that you are a war hero."

I should have figured he would look into my service record while checking on the story I told him. That he was impressed with my accomplishments in the old Army Air Service could turn out to be an advantage. If nothing else, it gave him another reason to trust us.

"Sir, I didn't mention anything about my service record because I am no more a hero than a lot other guys, many of whom died performing their heroic deeds."

"That's not quite so, Lieutenant Markham. The Army does not hand out silver citation stars and distinguished service crosses without justification, and it seems you have both, plus two oak leaves for your distinguished service cross. That makes you a hero whether you like it or not."

I glanced at Clara, who looked somewhat star struck about the news that her protector was a decorated war hero. I said, "Thank you for saying so, Colonel Smythe." Then keeping my fingers crossed, I asked, "Colonel, were you able to confirm the details I gave you earlier?"

"Oh, yes. Everything you reported checks out with the people I talked with in San Antonio and at Fort Bliss. Your briefing was quite accurate in that regard."

Smiling, I said, "I'm glad to hear that. Now, may we prevail upon your hospitality once more for transportation to Riverside?"

"Certainly. I would be happy to arrange transportation for you, but I was hoping we could enjoy Miss Bow's company a little longer. We have very nice accommodations in our Visiting Officers' Quarters. I'm sure we could make you comfortable."

That was Clara's cue and she stepped smoothly into the scene without hesitation. "That would be wonderful, Colonel Smythe, but I'm afraid my people at the studio are anxious for me to return. They have already scheduled filming at several locations for tomorrow."

It wasn't so much what she said but how she said it that was so convincing. I could see real disappointment on Smythe's face as he said, "If that's how it must be, I'll arrange for a car to take you into town right away. I will admit, though, I am disappointed that you must leave so soon."

Clara beamed at him. "I'm disappointed, too, Colonel, but as soon as we get this film done, I will come back to see you." She paused for a moment with a thoughtful expression on her face, and then added, "I know! We'll arrange a special showing of Wings for your men. Do you think they would like that?"

Smythe was all smiles now. "I'm sure if you are there, they will love it, as will I. Thank you, Miss Bow. Now let's go round up your bags and get you on your way."

I gave Clara a hearty round of mental applause. She had played her part perfectly, and she'd even tossed Smythe a bone that left him smiling. Now our fate was in the hands of Lady Luck and I was holding my breath for the second time in one day.

As we left the Officer's Club, I noticed that our military police escort was nowhere to be seen. I took that as a positive sign, assuming Colonel Smythe had dismissed him after learning that my story checked out.

Back in Smythe's outer office, he instructed his secretary to call the motor pool and order a car for the purpose of transporting his guests to Riverside. In my nervous state it seemed to take hours for the car to arrive. In reality, it wasn't more than fifteen minutes, but I sweated out every one of those minutes with my heart jumping each time the telephone rang. Clara on the other hand seemed calm and perfectly at ease the entire time. There was something to be said for having acting skills.

Ever the gracious host, Colonel Smythe walked Clara, Ruth and me out to the waiting car, where we bid one another what I fervently hoped would remain a fond farewell. Once in the car, I was somewhat relieved that our driver was a Lieutenant from the motor pool rather than the less than friendly MP. Things were indeed looking up, which made me even more nervous.

Our first stop was the Air Operations building at the airfield, where our bags and other personal belongings had been stored after being removed from the Trimotor. The ship, I noted, had been taxied over to a nearby hangar. I also noted that several enlisted men seemed to be giving it a thorough going over. I hoped their great interest in the ship was simply due to it being a new aircraft they had not seen before, but doubted that was the case.

At long last we were rolled through the March Army Air Corps Airfield gate and turned north on Highway 395. Despite all indications that we were making good our getaway, I was still not convinced, and occasionally turned to look back, fully expecting to see a car full of MPs in hot pursuit.

Following a road sign pointing the direction to Riverside, our driver turned west on Alessandro Boulevard, and about thirty minutes later we pulled into the town's main business district. I asked the driver to drop us off at the Mission Inn because it was one of the few places in Riverside I knew. Lying through my teeth, I told him we were expecting to be met there by a car from Miss Bow's studio.

He dutifully pulled to the curb in front of the gaudy monstrosity of a hotel that seemed particularly out of place in a rural town like Riverside. After unloading our bags and until the Army car disappeared from view, we stood on the sidewalk looking as if we expected a studio limousine to pull up at any moment. I then hurried Clara and Ruth to a bench deep within the Mission Inn's lush gardens where we could not be seen from the street and relaxed for the first time since stepping off the Trimotor almost four hours earlier.

Sixteen

1:30 P.M. – Sunday – September 19, 1926
Mission Inn – Riverside

My next step was to find a way out of Riverside. Since Clara would be rather conspicuous on public transportation, we needed to find another means of travel, and I had spotted the solution to that problem driving into Riverside. About half a block down the street that ran along the east side of the Mission Inn I had seen the sign for a Hertz Drive-Ur-Self System automobile rental agency.

"Clara, there's an automobile rental agency less than a block away. If they're open on Sundays, I'm going to rent a car so we'll have some transportation. Do you think you'll be safe waiting here while I do that?"

After taking a look around at her surroundings, she said, "Sure. There are a few people around and I can scream like a banshee if I need to, so I think we'll be okay."

"All right, I'll make it as quick as I can."

Clara grinned her whimsical grin. "And pick us out something sassy!"

Thinking that a sassy automobile was the last thing we needed, I walked briskly off toward Orange Street, still toting my overnight case. Besides the need for keeping its contents handy, I figured the case would be something a business man who was in need of a rental auto might likely be carrying.

Crossing Orange Street mid-block, I was pleased to see that the Hertz Drive-Ur-Self System office was open for business. There were four nearly brand new automobiles parked in front of the agency office, and as I walked past them, I saw just what I was looking for. Clara would not think the dark blue Oldsmobile six-cylinder coupe fit her definition of sassy, but it had the definite advantages of being a sturdy car with plenty of get-up-and-go—qualities I suspected would come in handy before all was said and done.

The coupe would be a snug fit with all three of us on its single seat, but I had already decided that we would have to park Ruth somewhere safe once we were back in the Los Angeles area. I liked Ruth and she had already proven herself useful in an emergency, but having to conceal the identity of America's most popular motion picture actress was hard enough in itself without adding a Negro woman who would stick out like a sore thumb in many of the places we were likely to go.

A young man in a snappy sport coat came out of the agency office and greeted me. "Good afternoon, sir. Interested in renting a car?"

Pointing at the Oldsmobile coupe, I said, "Yes, that one."

He smiled broadly. "Certainly, sir. C'mon in inside and we'll have you in the driver's seat of that sporty little Olds in no time at all."

We sat at his desk and the fellow explained the terms to me. "That automobile rents for eleven-cents a mile. The only other requirements are that you have a valid driver's license, that you return it with a full tank of gasoline, just like it has now, and that you leave a fifty-dollar deposit which we will refund when you bring the automobile back in good condition."

"Do I have to return the car to this agency, or can I turn it in at another office, like in Los Angeles."

"One of the beauties of renting from the Hertz Drive-Ur-Self System is that you can return our cars to any of our locations within a hundred miles of where you rented it. We do charge a ten dollar fee for that convenience, though."

"All right, let's fill out the paperwork."

Reaching into a desk drawer, he pulled out a form that appeared to have four pages. From another drawer he brought out three sheets of carbon paper which he inserted between form's pages. Finally, he removed a fountain pen from his shirt pocket and said, "First, I'll need to see your driving license."

Opening my wallet, I handed him the white card I had been issued by the California Department of Motor Vehicles as proof of my ability to drive an automobile in accordance with the state's motor vehicle operation laws. From the information on the license, he entered my name, address, and physical description on his form.

That chore completed, he handed me back the license and

moved his pen down the form. "How long will you be needing the automobile for, sir?"

"At least a week, maybe longer."

Nodding, he filled in a blank on the form and said, "I'll put down two weeks, just to be on the safe side. And where will you be staying during that time?"

Several possible answers to that question occurred to me and I picked the least truthful of them. "I'll be right across the street at the Mission Inn for most of it."

"Very good, sir. Now I just need to fill in the information about the auto you're renting."

While he did that, I did a quick mental calculation of my finances. I had left Los Angeles with a little more than three-hundred dollars in my wallet. Of that I had spent about a hundred dollars on meals and incidentals during the trip to San Antonio and subsequent stay there. That left two-hundred, plus the five-hundred Bill Wellman gave me. So far, I had spent about fifty dollars of that on meals and two cottage rentals during our trip west. Subtracting the automobile rental deposit I would be left with about six-hundred dollars. Unless Clara's idea of how to disappear involved some very hefty expenses, I decided my finances were in pretty good shape.

The agent finished filling out lines and boxes on his form and turned it around so it faced me on the desk. "Now, sir, if you will just sign by the X there at the bottom, I'll take your deposit, and we'll be all set. Your copy of the form will serve as your deposit receipt."

I signed where he had indicated, thus agreeing to drive Mister Hertz's automobile safely and in compliance with all traffic laws, after which I handed over two twenties and a ten. The agent deposited the bills somewhere in his desk and signed the form on a line next to my signature.

He then handed me the second page of the form. "Here you go, sir. If you should encounter any difficulties with the car, or in the unlikely event you are involved in an accident, our telephone number is on the back of the form. You may call that number anytime, twenty-four hours a day. And, should the call be long distance, you may ask the operator to reverse the charges."

I nodded my understanding and the agent opened a cabinet on the wall that contained several automobile keys with small cardboard tags attached to them. He selected one and handed it to me. "Here you go, sir. Have a safe trip."

Out in the lot, I took a quick turn around the Oldsmobile to be sure there were no dents or other damage for which they might try to charge me when I returned the car. Finding none, I slipped my overnight bag into the narrow space behind the seat and climbed into the machine. The Oldsmobile's starting procedure was simple: Insert the key into its slot on the instrument panel and turn it a quarter turn, twist the ignition switch to the "ON" position, and engage the electric starter.

The powerful forty horsepower, six-cylinder engine started immediately, and I gave it a moment or two to warm up and get its oil flowing while I adjusted the driving mirrors. Then I pushed the transmission lever sprouting from the floorboard into first gear, released the handbrake, let out the clutch, and turned left onto Orange Avenue. The Mission Inn was now on my right, and near the end of the block I spotted an empty parking slot. I pulled in, locked the car doors, and went to find Clara and Ruth.

Leaving them alone had been necessary, but risky. I was relieved to see they were sitting on the bench, right where I had left them. Clara saw me coming and jumped up. "Hi, Eddie. Any luck?"

"Yes, we now have transportation. It's parked on the side street. Let's load up our luggage and get out of here."

Upon seeing the coupe, Clara said, "Gosh, couldn't you find anything larger?"

"I could have, but I picked this car for several reasons, two of which are that it's sturdy and fast."

With an expression that told me she was not entirely convinced I had made the best choice, Clara just said, "Okay, you're the boss."

The coupe's trunk was surprisingly large, but it still took some doing to get all of our bags stowed inside. That chore completed, we climbed in with Clara, the thinnest, sitting in the middle, her legs angled to the right so as not to be in the way of the gearshift lever.

I restarted the engine, backed out of the parking slot, and turned right onto the street that passed in front of the Mission Inn. After we had gone a few blocks, Clara asked, "Where are we going?"

"Right now, anywhere that isn't Riverside. We can work out the details once we're out of town."

Getting out of Riverside proved to be fairly simple. An auto club road sign informed me that the street we were on, Mission Boulevard, was also U.S. Route 60, the main road between where we were and Los Angeles. All I had to do was keep on going in the direction we were heading. With the matter of navigation now under control, it was time to move on to the next piece of business on my mental checklist.

"Ruth, do you have family in Los Angeles?"

Leaning forward and sounding a little leery, as if she knew what was coming, Ruth said, "Yes, sir, Mister Eddie. My older sister, Esther, and her family live in El Monte."

"Do you think Esther would be willing to put you up for a few days?"

"I know she would. They've got a big house with plenty of room, but why should I want to stay with her?"

"For a couple of reasons, Ruth. As you know all too well, someone has tried to kill Miss Bow twice in the past three days. She and I have decided that the best way to prevent another attempt on her life is for her to disappear for a while until we find out who's trying to kill her.

"This is very risky business and it will make my job of protecting Miss Bow easier if she is the only one I have to worry about. On top of that, there is no reason for you to be in danger any longer than absolutely necessary."

"I understand, Mister Eddie, but couldn't I just go home to Miss Clara's house?"

"That's not a good idea because you would still be in danger there. The killer seems to know a great deal about Miss Bow, and I'm sure that includes where she lives. If he went there looking for her and found you, he would try to make you tell him where she is. And even though you won't know where Miss Bow is, he isn't going to believe you don't know.

"On the other hand, I doubt very much that the killer knows you have a sister or where to find her. That makes staying with her one of the safest places you could be."

Ruth was quiet for a long moment before she said, "I see, Mister Eddie."

Clara piped up then, saying, "Ruth, I feel just awful that you've been caught up in all this trouble. I'll feel a lot better knowing you are in a safe place."

"I know, ma'am. Ain't none of this your fault. I just pray you will be safe and they figure out soon who is trying to hurt you."

The conversation ended with an agreement that we would go directly to El Monte and stop on the outskirts of town so Ruth could make a telephone call to let her sister know she was coming. That issue resolved, I concentrated on getting us to our new destination.

El Monte is located on the outskirts of Los Angeles and a little north of Route 60. Just after crossing the Santa Ana River on the western edge of Riverside, a mileage sign informed me the town of Pomona was twenty-four miles up the road and that we were forty-five miles from Los Angeles. From that I estimated we were about forty miles from El Monte. The time was two-fifteen, so at the posted speed limit of forty-five miles per hour, I estimated we would arrive around three-fifteen.

Despite the fact that I was born and raised in nearby Santa Barbara, I was driving through relatively unfamiliar territory. The metropolis of Los Angeles covers a huge area, and while I have been to Riverside a few times and know the main roads in the area, I had to pay close attention to our route lest we make an incorrect turn and waste precious time going in the wrong direction.

I also paid close attention to my driving mirrors so I would know if we were being followed. So far, it seemed as if we had slipped out of Riverside without the Army or the killer who was hunting Clara knowing about it. I hoped our luck in that regard continued.

Once out of town, U.S. Route 60 was a wide two-lane highway and with little traffic to contend with, so I was sorely tempted to step down a little more firmly on the gas. I resisted that temptation. The last thing we needed was to attract the attention of a gendarme.

In Pomona I followed highway signs pointing to El Monte and we ended up on Valley Boulevard, another very long, mostly east-west thoroughfare traversing the vast expanses of eastern Los Angeles County. Then, at three-twenty, we crossed the San Gabriel River and entered the outskirts of El Monte.

I saw a public telephone next to a Gilmore gasoline station on our right, and pulled up next to it. We all got out of the car to stretch our legs and I reminded Ruth to please get directions to her sister's house. Then, while she made her telephone call, I pulled the Oldsmobile over to the gasoline pumps and asked the attendant to fill our tank.

After he pumped a little less than four gallons into the Oldsmobile, the attendant checked our radiator water and oil levels and proclaimed them to be just fine. As I handed him a dollar bill for the gasoline, I asked if he had a map of the area. He came back with my four cents change and a spanking new roadmap of Los Angeles County which was free to customers, courtesy of the Gilmore Gasoline Company.

I arrived back at the telephone booth just as Ruth finished her call. The women squeezed back into the coupe and Ruth instructed me to continue on Valley Boulevard until I got to Mountain View Road, where I should turn to the left. Our next turn was another left onto a residential street called Magnolia. We were still in the first block of Magnolia when Ruth pointed to a tidy wood frame house on our left. I U-turned and pulled to the shoulder of the road next to the well maintained yard in front of Esther's home.

As we prepared to get out of the Oldsmobile, I said, "Ruth, I want you to take this," and held out my hand. She reached out hesitantly and I added, "It's forty dollars to help out with the extra expenses your family will have with you staying there."

She thanked me profusely, took the two twenty dollar bills, and handed me a small piece of paper in exchange. "This is my sister's number. Please call me on the telephone when this terrible thing is over and we can go back to Miss Clara's house."

"I will, Ruth."

"And please keep Miss Clara safe."

"I'll do the very best I can, I promise."

I stepped out of the Oldsmobile and turned toward Esther's house just as the front door burst open and the entire family poured out into the front yard. Leading the pack was a woman who bore a close resemblance to Ruth. Behind her came a man I thought might be Esther's husband and twin teenaged girls. Bringing up the rear was an elderly man who limped along behind the rest with the aid of a cane. When it came to welcoming Ruth, however, the older fellow was every bit as enthusiastic as everyone else in the family.

When the hugging and cheek-kissing finally ended, Ruth made introductions all around. The elderly man turned out to be Esther's father-in-law. The twins were so excited about meeting the famous motion picture actress, Clara Bow; they couldn't take their eyes off her. Then, as we removed Ruth's bags from the trunk, Esther invited us to stay for a fried chicken Sunday dinner that she was about to put on the table.

Clara thanked her kindly for the invitation, but explained that we wanted to get to where we were going before dark and we still had some distance to go. Finally Ruth and Clara gave each other long hugs and everyone waved as we drove away.

I was retracing our route back to Valley Boulevard when Clara said, "Eddie, pull over, I need to tell you something important."

"Go ahead. I can drive and listen at the same time."

"No, I want you to stop the car for a minute."

I said, "Okay," and turned into the nearly empty parking lot of a twenty-four hour cafe at the corner of Mountain View and a cross-street called Garvey. When we were parked and I set the handbrake, Clara put a gentle hand on my shoulder and took a deep breath as if she really did have something of great importance to say.

"First of all," she said, "I know the other reason you don't want Ruth with us—the reason you didn't say to her, and . . . ."

I started to speak, but Clara put the soft tips of her fingers over my lips. "Let me finish, Eddie." Then she took another deep breath and continued saying what she wanted to say. "I want you to know how much I appreciate the way you've treated Ruth. She's as much a friend to me as an employee, and the kindness you've shown her really means a lot to me."

Her speech apparently finished, Clara looked at me expectantly. Feeling a little embarrassed, I shrugged my shoulders. "I like Ruth. She's a good person. I don't know any other way to treat her."

Clara broke into a grin. "That you don't know any other way to treat Ruth but with kindness is one of the reasons I admire you so much. It's also one of the reasons I'm falling in love with you."

She leaned forward and kissed me softly on the mouth. The kiss lasted a long, sweet time, and when it was done, she looked at me again with tenderness showing in her big, brown eyes. It crossed my mind to ask Clara what her new fiancé, Victor Fleming, would have to say about all this, but I picked a gentler approach.

"Clara, I'm growing very fond of you, too, but right now we need to concentrate on keeping you alive. For that reason we have to set our emotions aside so they don't become a distraction until you're out of harm's way. Okay?"

She smiled softly and said, "Okay. Where to next?"

"I was about to ask you that question since you're the one with a plan. But first I could use a cup of coffee and this looks like a good place to get one. Would you like me to bring you some?"

Still smiling, Clara said, "Yes, please. With some sugar and cream, if you don't mind."

I left the Oldsmobile's engine idling and walked toward the cafe. As I did so, it occurred to me that the kiss Clara and I had just shared was the second of its kind today, although the first seemed more like six days ago than less than six hours ago. And this particular day still had a long way to go before it was over.

Seventeen

4:15 P.M. – Sunday – September 19, 1926
Cafe Parking Lot – El Monte

I returned to the Oldsmobile with two steaming cardboard containers of coffee and my trouser pocket sagging with the weight of five dollar's worth of quarters for a long distance telephone call I planned to make in a while. I handed the cup with cream and sugar to Clara and took a long drink from my own cup. The brew was fresh and strong, just exactly what I needed to keep my eyes open for the rest of an already eventful day that began a time zone to the east in Rimrock, Arizona.

After a few more swallows, I said, "Clara, while we were having lunch at the March Field Officer's Club, you said you knew how to make yourself disappear. Now's the time to tell me your plan."

"Well, it isn't so much a plan as a place."

"Okay, what place do you have in mind?"

"Do you know where San Buenaventura is?"

"Sure. It's a small town on the coast between Malibu and Santa Barbara. Most people just call it Ventura these days."

"Well, I was visiting friends there a year or so ago and saw a wonderful little auto court up on a hill above the town. It had beautiful gardens around individual bungalows with a view of the ocean. It looked like one of those garden court apartments they're building in the Hollywood hills.

"Anyway, I remembered the auto court last night, and thought it would be a good place to disappear to because it's kind of secluded." As an afterthought, she added, "It's the sort of quiet, cozy place newlyweds go on their honeymoons."

I gave Clara's idea some thought. It had possibilities, but from her description, the place had one big drawback. "It sounds good except for one thing. To keep you safe I need to be close by. In a hotel we could do that with adjoining rooms, but it would be much more difficult in an auto court with separate bungalows."

"We could stay in the same bungalow. You can't get any closer than that."

"And the gossip mongers would have a heyday with the news that Miss Clara Bow was spotted dallying in flagrante with a strange man in a secret hide-away."

"Eddie, the whole idea is to make Clara Bow disappear. Nobody will know it's me. Besides, there's a much greater chance of somebody recognizing me in a downtown hotel than in an out-of-the-way auto court."

"But if it came out later . . . ."

"Don't be such a worry wart. This sort of thing is done all the time." Then realizing the implication in what she'd just said, Clara blushed beet red and quickly added, "Not by me, but the newspapers and magazines don't know even half of what goes on in the motion picture business."

"Still, Clara, ..."

"Eddie, I think I know what's really bothering you about this, and I promise I won't . . . we won't do anything we have to be ashamed of later."

Clara obviously had her mind made up and nothing I could say was going to change it. I sighed and said, "All right, we'll risk the auto court. So far it looks like we slipped out of Riverside without anyone noticing and I know a back country route that will take us to Ventura without traipsing through Hollywood or anywhere else you're likely to be recognized. We'll just have to hope our luck holds."

Clara gave me another smile of the sort I was finding more and more attractive. "I'm glad you like my idea, Eddie. See, I'm not such a dumb bunny after all."

"Kiddo, a dumb bunny is just about the last thing I would think to call you."

She smiled at that and I finished off my coffee. When we got back to Valley Boulevard I turned left, the same direction we had been traveling before, and started looking for a main north-south thoroughfare. About four miles later I spotted Rosemead Boulevard and turned right. It would do just fine.

The community of El Monte is in the heart of a large agricultural area and is surrounded by farms and orchards stretching all the way to the San Gabriel Mountains several miles to the north. The terrain is generally flat and, with no obstacles in their way, the area's roads tend to be long and straight. This last feature was of particular importance to me because it meant I could see a long way behind us in my driving mirrors. As before, however, I saw no sign that anyone was following us.

After traveling about five miles north on Rosemead Boulevard we came to the east-west artery I was looking for, Foothill Boulevard. Foothill begins at its east end in Monrovia and runs west along the base of the mountains through Pasadena, until it eventually ends at U.S. Highway 99.

A much faster route to our destination would have been to remain on Valley Boulevard right into Los Angeles, where we could pick up U.S. Highway 101, which goes over to the coast and straight up to Ventura. I had chosen the long way around to avoid the more populated areas where it was more likely Clara would be recognized. That might have been an unnecessary precaution, but my watchwords had become "better safe than sorry."

We reached Pasadena a few minutes after five and I pulled into the parking lot of a grocery store with a "closed" sign in its window. The public telephone out in front of the store, however, was open for business. Clara gave me a questioning look and I said, "I need to make a long distance telephone call before we get any closer to Ventura."

"Who are you calling or is it none of my business?"

"It's very much your business. I'm going to call Bill Wellman. I didn't want to say too much on Colonel Smythe's telephone line because I couldn't be sure who might be listening in. Bill asked me to let him know how we were doing, so that's what I'm about to do."

Clara frowned. "Will you tell him where we're going?"

"No. I just want him to know you're okay and that we're disappearing for a few days until we figure out who's after you."

I walked over to the pay telephone and got a long distance operator on the line. After depositing most of the quarters in my pocket for a three-minute call, the operator got me connected to Bill Wellman's room at the Saint Anthony.

"Wellman here."

"Hi, Bill. Do you know who this is?"

It took him only a moment to shift mental gears. "Yes, I do."

"Good. I'm just calling to let you know I've hidden the package you sent me for safekeeping until we can find out who's trying to get their hands on it."

"I thought that might be what you intended to do."

"Is there any further word about last Friday from your end?"

"No, the powers that be have tied my hands on the matter."

"Then I'll just have to figure it out from this end."

"I should also tell you the powers that be are very upset over the disappearance of the package. They're making quite a fuss over it."

"Since I'm fairly certain someone in their bailiwick is at the heart of the problem, I think we should just let them stew about it. However, you might want to let your colleague there who has an interest in this matter know that the package is in good condition and I plan to keep it that way."

Wellman was pretty good at this talking in circles business. I was pretty sure he knew it was Victor Fleming to whom I was referring. He simply said, "Will do. Anything else?"

"Just one more thing. I strongly suspect the outfit that transported the package will also soon be interested in finding it as part of an investigation they will be conducting. That could make things difficult."

"Yes, it could. Be careful and let me know how things are going when you can."

"I will. Goodnight."

"Goodnight."

And that was it. By my wristwatch Wellman and I had used less than half the long distance time I was allotted, but we had said all that needed to be said. I slid back behind the Oldsmobile's steering wheel and got us back on the road.

Sounding anxious, Clara asked, "How did it go?"

"Fine. We talked in a sort of code because we didn't know who might be listening in at his end. I referred to you as the package he sent me and told him I had hidden the package until we found out who's trying to get their hands on it."

"I hope you didn't call me the package with a bow on it."

Chuckling, I said, "No, I didn't. I did ask Bill if he had any news about Friday's incident and he said the powers that be had tied his hands on the matter. I'm pretty sure that means Lasky has told him to keep the cops out of it to avoid publicity. Bill also said Lasky was quite upset over the disappearance of the package."

In a tone tinged with anger, Clara said, "That's just swell. The jerk is all upset because I'm missing, but he's more concerned about what the newspapers might say than he is with finding out who's trying to kill me."

"Well, I told Bill he could tell the powers that be their package is in good condition. I also suggested he pass that word onto Victor Fleming."

When she made no comment, I said, "Finally, I told him the Army would probably be looking for us as part of their investigation, and that might make things more difficult for us."

"Does Wellman know where you called from?"

"I didn't tell him, but I suppose anyone with a little authority who really wanted to know could get that information from telephone company records. That's why I called from Pasadena. Knowing where the call came from won't help anyone who's looking for us because we won't be anywhere near Pasadena."

Clara seemed to mull that over for a while. Then out of the blue she asked a very reasonable question. "Eddie, how do you know Bill Wellman isn't the one who's trying to kill me?"

It was my turn to do some mulling. The truth was I could not say with any certainty that Bill was not the culprit. For that matter I could not say I knew for sure Jesse Lasky or Schulberg or any of the other studio bigwigs was not trying to kill Clara. It just seemed darned unlikely that any of those men had a reason to kill the goose that laid golden eggs.

In answer to her question I said, "I don't know that Bill Wellman isn't trying to kill you, but a killer generally has a motive for what he does. Do you know of any reason Wellman would have for wanting you dead?"

"Well, besides the fact that I don't think he likes me very much, no. I guess I was just wondering why you trust Bill enough to make him the only one who knows what we're doing."

"It's not so much a matter of trust as a matter of responsibility. Bill is more or less my boss in this situation and he's the one who asked me to see that you got back to California safely. I figure I have a responsibility to keep him informed about our progress on the job he gave me to do. Besides that, it seems like a good idea for somebody to know what's going on."

Clara said, "Okay. I was just wondering," and that ended our conversation about Bill Wellman. It did not, however, end my thoughts about the situation. Mainly, I was thinking that hiding Clara would keep her safe for the time being, but she could not hide forever. Sooner or later we had to figure out who wanted her dead, and I had very few ideas of how to go about doing that.

It was nearly six o'clock and the sun was low enough in the western sky for the mountains around us to paint deep shadows across the road as I turned north on U.S. Highway 99. A dozen or so miles up ahead Highway 99 becomes what southern Californians commonly refer to as the "ridge route," a treacherous piece of road that was chiseled and blown out of sheer granite to become the main pathway from Los Angeles to Bakersfield, Fresno and points north in California's central valley.

According to a newspaper story I remembered reading when the road was completed just before I joined the Army Air Service, the ridge route was more than forty miles of paved road that twists and turns its way through nearly 700 curves as it traverses the Sierra Pelona mountain range. At the route's posted speed limit of fifteen miles-per-hour, the 112-mile drive from Los Angeles to Bakersfield typically takes at least twelve hours, which assumes the driver's radiator does not boil over in the summer heat or he is not trapped by a winter snowstorm.

Fortunately, my route to Ventura turned off Highway 99 onto State Route 126 in the little town of Castaic, the exact point at which the ridge route officially begins. We made that turn to the west about six-thirty and an auto club mileage sign informed us the town of Ventura was forty-five miles ahead. Another sign set the speed limit at forty-five miles per hour.

Based on that information one might assume we were only about an hour from our destination, but I had driven the road before and knew that the speed limit on Route 126 dropped to twenty-five miles per hour or less every time it passed through one of several small communities along the way. Realistically, we were more like an hour and a half from Ventura, assuming we made no stops, and I intended to make a couple of stops in one of those small communities to take care of some business that needed our attention before we arrived at our destination.

With the sun setting, the closer we got to the coast, the colder we got, and what was generously referred to as a heater in the Oldsmobile was doing little to take the chill off. By quarter past seven Clara was to the point of shivering in her thin silk blouse and she asked if we could stop long enough to get her wool coat out the trunk.

"Sure, but can you hold on for about ten minutes? We're almost into Santa Paula, the last little community before Ventura. We'll have some light there to see what we're doing."

Clara said she could wait and slid over closer to me on the seat to share some body heat. My time estimate turned out to be pretty close. I pulled to the curb under a street light provided by the town of Santa Paula a few minutes before seven-thirty.

I retrieved Clara's coat from the Oldsmobile's trunk and she got out of the car long enough to put it on. While she was doing that, I asked, "By any chance do you have a scarf handy?"

She fished around in the side pockets of her coat and came up with a dark blue scarf. I said, "It would be a good idea to put that on over your head and keep it close to your face so you aren't as recognizable."

Clara nodded, and as she tied the scarf around her face, I got us back on the road. As we drove along Santa Paula's main drag, I watched for a gasoline station that was open at seven-thirty on a Sunday night. The Oldsmobile's fuel gauge indicated we still had about half a tank left, but automobile gas gauges often suffer from severe cases of inaccuracy, and given our circumstances, I thought it better to err on the side of caution.

We passed two stations that were closed up tight, and I was running low on hope that we would find one open in this little community when a large, brightly-lit Texaco Gasoline sign appeared in the next block. The station was, in fact, open and I pulled up next to one of its pumps. I climbed down from the Oldsmobile as a young man in a white shirt with a red Texaco emblem on the pocket came out of the office to see what we wanted. I told him to "fill 'er up."

While the pump merrily dinged away at the rate of twenty-three cents per gallon, the fellow dutifully checked our radiator water, oil and tire pressures. He reported all to be just fine and asked if I would like the windshield cleaned. I told him not to bother. We had picked up a few bugs along the way, but I did not want him getting a good look at Clara through the glass as he removed the insect remains.

The pump finally stopped dinging at 6.8 gallons and I handed the attendant two one-dollar bills. When he returned with my forty-four cents in change, I asked him if he knew of a nearby cafe or restaurant that might be open.

Smiling, the young man said, "Yes, sir. Betty's stays open until nine o'clock every night. Her place is just up the street three blocks on your right." With a hint of pride in his voice, he added, "Betty is my mom."

I smiled back and thanked him for the information. Climbing back into the Oldsmobile, I made a mental note of the fact that its fuel gauge was remarkably accurate.

Eighteen

7:45 P.M. – Sunday – September 19, 1926
Betty's Cafe – Santa Paula

Betty's was a narrow little place sandwiched between a storefront real estate office and a two-story brick building that housed a bank and law offices. The space just inside Betty's front door was taken up by a few mismatched tables and chairs. Beyond them was a lunch counter with stools. Betty was a pleasant looking woman I placed in her forties. She was sitting on one of the stools at the counter chatting with her only other customers, an older couple seated at a table near the rear of the dining room.

When a little bell over the door announced our arrival, Betty welcomed us and said to sit wherever we liked. I picked a table off to one side at the front of the room and Betty brought us glasses of water and a pair of typewritten menus that were a little grimy from long use. Setting the menus before us, she cheerfully announced that the daily special was an especially good beef stew.

I looked at Clara and she nodded. To Betty I said, "The stew sounds good. We'll take two bowls and two cups of coffee."

Picking up the menus, Betty noticed the bandage on Clara's face and said, "Goodness, deary, what happened to your face?"

Clara smiled up at her and replied, "Oh, I was working out in the garden a few days ago and slipped on a muddy spot. I landed on some stones that scratched me a little. The bandage makes it look a lot worse than it really is."

Betty showed no sign that she knew she was talking to a famous motion picture star when she said, "Well, that's good," and went off to get our coffee and stew.

When Betty was out of earshot, I smiled at Clara. "That was quick thinking. Nice work."

"Actually it really wasn't quick thinking. I thought someone might ask about the bandage, so I made up that story to tell if they did."

Still smiling, I said, "Say, you're pretty good at this sneaky stuff."

With a twinkle in her eye, Clara said, "I'll take that as a compliment."

Betty returned with our orders and we dug into the stew with enthusiasm. It seemed like forever since we had last eaten and the stew tasted good—either that or I was just so hungry anything would have tasted good at that point.

As we ate, I brought up another piece of business. "I suppose you realize that we'll have to pretend to be married when we check into your auto court. Such establishments tend to frown on unmarried couples sharing rooms."

With a grin that struck me as more gleeful than the situation warranted, Clara said, "Yes, they do. Just so I don't mess up, what name are you going to use?"

"I thought I'd use Mister and Missus Allan Wilkinson. That's the name of a character in my current manuscript."

"What's my first name?"

I shrugged. "I guess it can be anything you want it to be."

"Can I be Mary? I've always thought Mary was a nice name."

"Okay, as of now you are Mary Wilkinson of . . . ah . . . let's make it San Diego."

Clara was clearly enjoying this game of recreating ourselves. Smiling, she said, "Okay. San Diego is a nice town to live in, but there's one thing we're missing that I'll bet you haven't thought of."

Frowning, I asked, "What?"

"Wedding rings, silly. Married people wear them, you know."

I grimaced and said, "You're right, I didn't think of that, but there's not much we can do about that now. We'll just have to make do without them and hope nobody notices."

Looking down at her hands, she said, "No we won't, at least, I won't."

Clara was wearing two rings, one on the ring finger of each hand. The one on her right hand was a simple wide gold band with an engraved geometric pattern and the ring on her left hand was a stylish diamond solitaire. She removed both rings and put them back on her left ring finger in the proper order for a wedding band and engagement ring.

Holding up her left hand so I could see the result, she said,

"There, now, Mister Wilkinson, see what good taste in jewelry you have?"

Nodding, I said, "Pretty clever. It should pass. I'll just keep my left hand in my pocket."

"You don't need to do that. A lot of men don't wear wedding rings." Then grinning, she added, "Usually men who are running around on their wives."

"I hope you don't think I'm that kind of man."

Her expression grew very serious. "No, Eddie, you are the last one in the world I would expect to be that kind of man."

With the details of our new personalities worked out, we dived back into our bowls of stew. Then Clara said, "It's my turn to ask you a personal question. Is that okay, Eddie?"

"Certainly. What's your question?"

"When Wellman introduced you in the meeting, he said you were a genuine war hero or something like that. I thought he might just be razzing you, but back at the airfield, that colonel sounded pretty impressed with the medals you won. He said the Army doesn't give medals like the ones you have without justification, so I was wondering what you got them for."

I shrugged my shoulders. "I guess the Army Air Service thought I did a good job of doing what they sent me to France to do, which was shooting down as many German bombers and fighting ships as I possibly could."

Clara studied my face for a brief time, then said, "Was it horrible? I mean, was the war awful?"

"Yes. Wars are fought by men trying to kill one another. That's horrible in my book, but I have to say we fliers had a lot easier time of it than the men fighting in the trenches. We had decent quarters and good food, and we were based safely behind the lines where enemy artillery couldn't reach us. The men in the trenches were cold and wet most of the time, and they were constantly being shelled and shot at. They were the real heroes."

"I'm sorry, Eddie. I should have realized the war was something you don't like to talk about. I just want to know all about you, and I think your experiences in the war are an important part of what makes you the person you are. I won't bring it up again."

I gave her a small smile. "That's okay, kiddo. I understand why you wanted to know. It's just that talking about those times brings back some painful memories, and sometime nightmares come along with the memories."

Clara nodded that she understood and we finished up our meal without much more conversation. After I paid the check—one dollar and twenty cents plus a fifteen-cent tip—Betty wished us a good night and we left her cafe.

Outside, I steered Clara over to a pay telephone in front of the real estate office next door. "We'd best call your auto court to make sure they have a vacancy and that they're still open. What's the name of the place?"

With an expression that made me think of a small child setting off for an amusement park with her parents, Clara said, "The Casa del Pacifico Motor Inn."

Since we did not have a telephone number for the place, I got an operator on the line who found the number and connected my call. After a couple of rings, a cheerful voice came over the wire. "Good evening, this is the Casa del Pacifico Motor Inn."

"Good evening. I'm calling to see if you have any vacancies tonight."

"Well, yes we do, but I was just about to close for the night. How soon would you be arriving?"

"You can probably answer that question better than I. We're in Santa Paula."

The fellow sounded relieved. "Oh. In that case you're only about twenty minutes away. I'll be happy to stay open until you get here. May I have your name, sir?"

Winking at Clara, I said, "Certainly, It's Allan Wilkinson."

Clara gave me an enthusiastic this-is-fun look and the fellow said, "Thank you, Mister Wilkinson. How many are in your party?"

"Two. Just my wife and myself."

"And how long will you be staying with us?"

That was a darned good question. I took a guess and said, "At least three nights, perhaps longer. We're on a driving vacation with no set itinerary. You might say we're just blowing along with the breeze."

The fellow sounded as if he thought blowing along with the breeze was a grand idea. "Good for you! As it happens, one of our nicest cottages is available. It's at the front of the court with a lovely view of the coast. It rents for three-dollars per night. Does that sound acceptable?"

"Yes, that sounds perfect."

"Good. I'll walk over and turn on the heat so the bungalow will be nice and cozy when you arrive. Do you know how to find us?"

"No, that was going to be my next question."

"Okay, we're at 327 Poli Street. It's very easy to find. Take

Route 126—it's also called Telegraph Road—west from Santa Paula and stay on it all the way into Ventura. When you cross Main Street, Telegraph Road turns into Thompson Boulevard, which is also U.S. Highway 101. Stay on Thompson until you get to Palm Street, where you make a right turn. Then just stay on Palm until it dead ends at Poli. Turn right and we're the first place on your left after you turn onto Poli. You can drive right into the court and park in front of the office, which will be on your left. Did you follow all of that?"

The fellow was right, the route was easy, especially since I had been to Ventura several times before and recognized the street names he gave me. I said, "Yes, I've got it. We'll see you in about twenty minutes then."

"I'll be watching for you."

I hung up the receiver earpiece and said, "Okay, Missus Wilkinson we have a cottage with an ocean view at a rate of three bucks a night—the best Casa del Pacifico has to offer."

"Gosh, the best they have? Let's go!"

The fellow's instructions were right on the money, as was his time estimate. We pulled up in front of Casa del Pacifico Motor Inn's office a few minutes past eight-thirty.

Like many modern auto courts, this one was laid out in a U-shape with a wide central driveway up the middle of the U. The office and three cottages were on the left side of the drive with four more on the right side. Two additional cottages were situated at the back across the closed end of the U. As you might expect from the place's Spanish name, the cottages and office were done up in the hacienda-style with red tile roofs, exposed beams, and adobe-like stucco finishes. Each cottage had its own attached carport.

What made the Casa del Pacifico different from most auto courts was the landscaping. Each cottage had its own garden out in front with lush shrubs and small palms, while baskets of hanging begonias decorated the small front porch in front of each cottage. More plants and trees were scattered around between and behind the cottages. Clara was right, the Casa del Pacifico was quite beautiful for an auto court.

While Clara waited in the Oldsmobile, I went into the office, which was essentially the same size and shape as the cottages, but the door opened into a small lobby furnished with comfortable-looking leather chairs and a counter. A debonair looking fellow wearing a handsomely tailored three-piece suit welcomed me.

"Good evening and welcome to the Casa del Pacifico Motor Inn. Would you be Mister Wilkinson?"

"I would."

"Wonderful. You made excellent time getting here." He offered his hand across the counter, saying, "My name is Ambrose DeBoyce. It was I who spoke with you on the telephone. My wife, Amanda and I are the proprietors of the Casa del Pacifico."

"Well, Mister DeBoyce, from what I can see in the dark, you have a lovely place here."

"Oh, thank you! I'll pass that along to Amanda. She oversees the grounds and plantings."

Then, turning a large leather bound registration book around to face me on the counter and opening it to the first page with an empty line, DeBoyce said, "Now, Mister Wilkinson, if you'll please sign the register, we'll get you and your wife to your cottage. You must be tired from driving."

I pulled the desk pen from its inkwell and filled in the information requested in three columns. Name: Mr. & Mrs. Alan Wilkinson. From: San Diego, Calif. Arrival Date: Sept. 19, '26."

Turning the registration book so he could see what I had written, our host said, "Thank you. Now, I believe you said you would be staying with us for at least three nights. Would you care to pay for those nights in advance?"

It was not a question. I guessed DeBoyce had been stiffed a few times by guests who stole away in the night, and he wanted his money up front. Considering the transitory nature of people who stay in auto courts, I could not blame him.

"Sure, that would be fine."

He looked relieved. Apparently some guests were not as agreeable as Mister Alan Wilkinson of San Diego. "Good. That will be nine dollars, please. That will pay you up through Tuesday night. If you should decide to stay longer, just let me know before then."

I counted out a five and four one-dollar bills on the counter and said, "There you are."

"Thank you, Mister Wilkerson. Just one moment while I write out a receipt for you."

The receipt completed, Ambrose DeBoyce handed me a carbon copy with a key that had a round brass tag attached. The number nine was engraved on the tag. He said, "You and your wife will be in cottage number nine. That is the one directly across from the office. You can pull your car directly across the driveway and into the carport.

"We typically close the office at eight each night and open again at six in the morning. Fresh complementary coffee is available for guests when we open the office. We also serve tea and cookies each afternoon at three.

"Should you need to make a telephone call, there is a public telephone just outside." He gestured to his left and added, "If you need a recommendation for a restaurant or directions, please do not hesitate to ask."

"Thank you, Mister DeBoyce. You've been most helpful. And thank you for staying open late so we could check in."

With a big smile, he said, "You are entirely welcome. I hope you and your wife enjoy your visit to the Casa del Pacifico Motor Inn, Mister Wilkinson."

Turning toward the office door, I said, "I'm sure we will. Goodnight, Mister DeBoyce."

As I climbed back into the Oldsmobile, Clara asked, "All set?"

"All set and looking forward to getting some sleep."

I backed the coupe in the carport attached to cottage number nine, figuring that parking nose out might give us a small advantage in the event we had to leave in a hurry. Then I toted our luggage into the cottage. Without Ruth's bags, we were down to Clara's two suitcases, my suitcase, and my overnight case. Seeing that it was going to take two trips to move the bags, Clara offered to help. I handed her the key and said, "Okay, kiddo, you can open the door."

With all the bags in and the Oldsmobile's doors and trunk locked, I took a minute to examine our new quarters. The room was surprisingly large and its decor continued the exterior's hacienda theme with textured lath and plaster walls, exposed ceiling beams, and roughhewn furniture made of a light wood I thought might be oak. The spacious room was illuminated by four bulbs in a black wrought iron fixture suspended a foot or so below the ceiling on a chain. It was turned on and off by a switch mounted next to the door.

The only door in or out was in the wall facing the office—if my mental compass was correct—the west wall. The bed, covered with a colorful spread that made me think of a Mexican serape, was against the north wall and flanked by two small nightstands. Each end of the wall was occupied by an armchair upholstered in the same colorful material as the bedspread.

The east wall, opposite the cottage door, offered two more doors to explore. The one on the left opened into a spacious bathroom equipped with a large claw-foot tub, a commode, a pedestal sink, and a set of shelves on which were stacked fresh towels. A one-foot-by-two-foot window was set high in the wall above the tub. On close examination, I discovered that only half of the window could be opened, making it too small for anyone to climb through.

The door at the right end of the east wall revealed a large built-in closet into which Clara was busily hanging blouses from the larger of her two suitcases. The bathroom and closet extended into the room creating a niche in which was set a dressing table with an attached mirror. A small ceiling fixture in the niche provided illumination for milady's grooming.

The room's south wall featured a large window, in front of which was a four-foot square table with four chairs. In the corner where the south wall met the west wall sat a good-sized chest of drawers.

Two smaller windows, one on each side of the door, were set into the west wall. These looked out on the planting area in front of the cottage, and beyond it, the driveway and office. Checking to be sure the door was securely bolted; I walked over to the large window in the south wall. It was covered by wooden-slatted Venetian blinds that could be tilted to allow light into the room or raised for an unobstructed view. At the moment, that view was mostly the twinkling lights of downtown Ventura.

The Casa del Pacifico was built on a shelf carved out of the hillside about ten feet above Poli Street, so there was a rather steep drop-off beyond the plantings outside our cottage. Unfortunately, there were no street lights in this residential area, which meant the large window was the most vulnerable to a break-in.

I was contemplating how to protect against that vulnerability when Clara joined me at the window. Leaning slightly against me, she said, "Aren't the lights beautiful?"

"They are, indeed. And during the day, we'll be able to see the ocean out there beyond the town."

Turning to look up at me, she said, "Well, was I right about this place? Do you like it?"

I looked down into those soft, brown eyes and felt feelings I didn't want to feel. "Yes, Clara, you were absolutely right. This is one of the nicest auto courts I've ever seen, but right now, I'm more interested in getting some shuteye than I am in the view."

She snorted in a most unladylike way and said, "Some romantic you are!" Changing the subject, she said, "I'd like to wash away the Texas and Arizona dust and soak in the tub for a few minutes before going to bed. Do you mind?"

"Not so long as you let me go in and brush my teeth first so I can climb into that bed over there."

"Fair enough."

As I brushed my teeth, I glanced at the scruffy looking guy in the mirror over the bathroom sink. He needed a shave, his hair could do with a washing, and he probably would have benefited greatly from a bath, but I decided those chores would have to wait until morning. All I wanted to do at that moment was sleep.

Finished with my tooth brushing and face washing chores, I swapped rooms with Clara. A moment later I heard water filling the bathtub. I dropped my toothbrush and tooth powder into my overnight case and stood there looking at Bill Wellman's forty-five caliber pistol. Finally, I came to the inescapable conclusion that, if actually needed, the darn thing would be absolutely worthless where it was. I lifted the pistol out of my case, worked the slide to chamber a round from the magazine, and set it on the nightstand closest to the door.

Then I stripped, put on my pajamas, turned off the light, and climbed into bed. Propping myself up, I spent minutes in a wasted effort to figure out how I was going to keep Clara safe and track down a killer at the same time. The effort was wasted because I could not get my tired brain to concentrate, so I gave up and stared off into space for a while. I was very near to dozing off when the bathroom door opened.

Clara was wearing a mint green, knee-length night gown made of some semi-transparent material. Backlit by the bathroom light, the gown left precious little to the imagination regarding the slim body it was intended to conceal. I looked away and was relieved when, after placing her toiletry articles on the dressing table, she turned off the bathroom light and climbed into bed.

As I slid down from my propped up position, Clara leaned over and kissed me gently on the cheek. "Goodnight, Eddie. Sweet dreams."

I said, "You, too, Clara," and we rolled over in opposite directions so we were each facing an opposite wall of the room. After a while I heard her breathing change to the slow easy rhythm of sleep. I was very near to the same state when I felt her move on the bed. The next thing I knew her back was pressed snugly against mine and I felt her warmth through my pajamas. Suddenly I was not as sleepy as I had been a moment before and I could feel my body responding naturally to the presence of America's sexiest motion picture star cuddling against me.

With no small amount of effort and a demonstration of superhuman willpower I battled my body's natural response into submission and, eventually, drifted off to sleep. The last conscious thought I remember was, "Markham, you aren't just a chump, you're the world's champion chump!"

Nineteen

7:15 A.M. – Monday – September 20, 1926
Casa del Pacifico Motor Inn – Ventura

A noise from somewhere in the room woke me with a start. My eyes popped open and it took a moment for the realization that it was no longer dark to sink in. Morning had arrived in the form of daylight filtered to a soft gray by an overcast sky. The source of the light seemed to be the large window across the room.

Blinking my eyes to clear away the sleep, I saw Clara, fully dressed, seated at the table next to the window drinking something from a white ceramic mug. I sat up on the edge of the bed and the movement caught her eye. She looked over at me and smiled. "Well, good morning, sleepyhead! I take it you slept well?"

Standing, I replied, "Yeah, too well. If an intruder had shown up last night, I would have slept right through it."

"Oh, don't be so hard on yourself. You had a long, rough day yesterday. You deserved a good sleep." Clara held up the mug in her hand. "Hey, they have coffee in the office and I got us some. It's fresh and strong."

Coffee sounded good, so I walked over and picked up the full mug from a metal Coca-Cola tray she had used to carry the coffee back from the office. Then, with my first swallow came the realization of how the coffee had gotten there. Angry with myself for not telling her to stay in the room unless I was with her, I blurted, "Clara, you are not to leave this room again without me! Do you understand?"

In an instant her expression changed from cheery to shock at my outburst, and from there to her little girl look. Now the little girl was near tears because she was being scolded for doing something she did not know was a bad thing to do.

Feeling like the meanest ogre there ever was, I sat in the chair next to Clara and put my hand on her arm. She cringed a little at my touch, almost as if she were expecting a beating. Softly, I said, "Clara, I'm sorry. I didn't mean to yell at you. I'm just angry with myself for not explaining that you shouldn't leave the room unless I'm with you. Forgive me?"

She put her hand gently on top of mine. "Of course I forgive you. It was my fault. I just wanted to have some coffee for you when you woke up, but I should have realized the danger, especially when I saw your gun on the nightstand. I can tell you that gave me quite a start."

"Actually, that's Bill Wellman's pistol. He loaned it to me before we left San Antonio just in case we ran into trouble. Let's make it a reminder to both of us that this is serious business and we have to keep our wits about us."

"I know, Eddie. I'm just so happy to be here and I feel so safe with you that it's hard for me to remember someone wants to hurt me. I'll be more careful, honest I will."

I took another swallow of the coffee. "I appreciate the coffee, though. I really need it this morning. I also need a bath and a shave and probably a lot of other stuff."

She was smiling again, but not quite as brightly as before. Standing, I said, "I guess I'd better get on with all that stuff."

After carrying my coffee into the bathroom, I returned and set my suitcase on the end of the bed. As I rummaged around for a clean shirt, trousers, underwear, and socks, Clara said brightly, "Say, Eddie, would you like me to put your things in the closet so the wrinkles hang out?"

I was about to say she didn't have to do that, but thought better of it. I had the idea Clara was looking for ways to carry more of her own weight in all of this, and hanging up my clothes for me was something she could do that would make her feel as if she was making a contribution. "Sure, kiddo that would be great. Thanks!"

I was feeling a whole lot more human when I finished my bath and washing my hair. A close shave with a fresh safety razor put the finishing touches on my humanization and I felt ready to take on the world again.

Looking at myself in the mirror, I shook my head. "No," I reminded myself, "Don't get cocky and complacent. You're dealing with a cold-blooded murderer determined to kill a woman who has suddenly become very important to you." Like Clara, it seemed I was just a little too happy about our current situation.

By the time I returned from the bathroom, Clara had finished hanging my clothes and was sitting at the table again. My suitcase was still open on the bed, and as I put my toiletry bag and pajamas into it, Clara said, "If that's my blood, I owe you a new shirt."

I looked down and saw the pale blue cotton shirt I had worn on Friday. Clara had uncovered it while hanging my things in the closet. The bloodstains had dried to a dark brown.

"Don't worry about it, kiddo. I thought I might be able to clean the stains off when I get home." I winked at her and added, "And, if I can't, one of your fans will probably pay me a hundred times what the shirt is worth just to get their hands on a bloody Clara Bow souvenir."

She laughed. "You know, you're probably right. I'll never understand people like that. I think they're nuts!"

"They're nuts all right, nuts about you. That's part of being a famous movie star."

Clara looked thoughtful. "You know, Eddie, sometimes I wonder if I really want to be a famous movie star. Once that was the most important thing in the world to me, but now . . . well, I'm discovering some other things I think might be more important."

I found myself really wanting to know what those things were, but that was all she had to say on the subject, so I gave her shoulder a squeeze and said, "How 'bout I go over to the office and see if I can talk them out more coffee? Cream and sugar, right?"

She said, "You remembered," as if she wasn't used to people caring enough about her to make note of things such as how she liked her coffee. She added, "I don't think you'll have any trouble getting refills. The man in the office seemed very nice."

After stowing my suitcase in the closet, I slipped into one of the sport coats Clara had carefully hung there for me. I dropped Wellman's Colt into my right coat pocket, picked up the tray with our empty coffee mugs, and headed for the door. The pistol felt heavy and pulled my coat out of shape. There had to be a better place to carry the darn thing.

On my way across the driveway to the office, I took a look around and saw nothing unusual or suspicious. I also got my first daylight look at the Casa del Pacifico. Even under an overcast sky, or maybe because of it, the colorful begonias and other blooms stood out vividly. I thought I might like to come back here sometime when I didn't have to keep my eyes open for a killer.

As I entered the little office lobby, Ambrose DeBoyce greeted me cheerfully. "Good morning, Mister Wilkinson. I trust your cottage is satisfactory?"

"It's very nice, Mister DeBoyce. We're thoroughly enjoying your hospitality."

"Wonderful! That's what we like to hear! How can I help you this morning?"

"I was hoping I might talk you out of a little more coffee."

"Of course! I just put out a fresh-brewed pot over there on the table. Help yourself."

I set the tray on a small table near the door and filled our cups from a shiny chromium pot with a black Bakelite handle. As I did so, DeBoyce said, "I had the delightful privilege of meeting your lovely wife earlier. She is certainly a bright, cheerful little ray of sunshine!"

Smiling back at him across the room, I said, "Yes, she certainly is. Mary is the joy of my life."

On my way back to cottage number nine, DeBoyce's "cheerful little ray of sunshine" comment kept going through my head. He was right, Clara was bright and cheerful this morning, which now struck me as odd because it was quite different from the way she had been on those previous occasions when I happened to see her in the morning. I could not help wondering what was different about this particular morning.

Clara and I were drinking our coffee and watching the overcast gradually burn away to reveal patches of clear, blue sky when curiosity finally got the better of me. "Clara, do you mind if I ask you another personal question?"

"Of course not. I'll tell you anything you want to know."

"The thing is you seem especially bright-eyed and cheerful this morning, and while I'm enjoying this side of you, it doesn't fit with the way you looked the other times I've seen you in the morning, like when you boarded the train in Los Angeles and when you got off in San Antonio. I'm just wondering about the change."

She gave me a small grimace and said, "Oh, that. Well, I have insomnia because of something that happened when I was a kid, so I don't sleep well. Most nights I stay up late and never get enough sleep. That makes my mornings kind of rough."

I nodded. "But what makes this morning so different?"

"I'm different this morning because I got the first good night's sleep I've had in months last night."

"After the long day we had yesterday, it's no wonder you slept well."

A tiny hint of coyness slipped into her expression, and she said, "Well, that's one reason."

Once again Clara had left me hanging with a mysterious comment. Well, if she did not want to tell me the other reasons she slept well, that was her business. I changed the subject.

"I guess we should get to planning our day while there's still some day left to plan for."

I thought I saw a little disappointment in her expression, but it was only there for a second. She said, "Okay, Eddie, tell me what you have in mind."

"Right now we have two priorities. The first is keeping you safe. The second is figuring out who wants to hurt you. I think we should concentrate on the first priority today by taking care of some things that will help insure your safety."

"Like what?"

"First, we need to get you some new clothes."

Putting on a hurt expression, she said, "What? Don't you like the way I dress?"

"What I think about the way you dress doesn't have anything to do with it. The idea is to make you less recognizable."

She turned her grin back up to full power. "To tell you the honest truth, I hate these outfits I wear. They're another one of B. P. Schulberg's brilliant ideas. He insisted I wear the pleated skirts, bright blouses, and wide belts because they make me stand out. He even thought I might start a new fashion style by wearing this stuff. I think it all looks ridiculous, especially the ankle socks."

"Okay, then, clothes shopping we will go."

Her excited little girl face was returning. "Where are we going to shop? Do you know the stores here?"

"I don't know all of them, but I do remember seeing a J. C. Penney store once when I was here before. That should . . . ."

"J. C. Penney? You're kidding me, right?"

"Why? What's wrong with J. C. Penney?"

"They sell frumpy clothes! They'll make me look like an old woman!"

"So long as you don't look like Clara Bow, that's fine. Plus, we're on a budget, so we have to watch our pennies, which we should be able to do at Penney's."

She gave me a mock glare. "Oh, that's cute. You're a regular W. C. Fields!" Then she put on a pouty expression and said, "Besides, I want to look pretty for you."

"Kiddo, you'd be gorgeous in an old pair of coveralls that were three sizes too big."

Clara jumped up and gave me a kiss on the cheek. "That's why I love you, Eddie. You say the nicest things to me!"

Then, trotting off toward the dressing table she said, "Give me just a minute to change this bandage and I'll be ready to go."

Standing behind her, I watched Clara in the mirror as she removed the old dressing. Doctor Hires had been right when he said the cuts on her face would heal nicely. They already looked much better than they had the last time I saw them.

Clara noticed this, too. "You know, I think I could put a smaller bandage on this now."

"I'd rather you put on another big one, at least until we get you into some new clothes."

Her expression in the mirror showed surprise. "Why?"

"Because it's a lot better if people look at the bandage than at the rest of your cute but highly recognizable face."

She smiled at my image in the mirror and just said, "Oh."

Looking back at her reflection, another reason she seemed so different this morning finally dawned on me: She wasn't wearing any make-up. Gone were the bright red lipstick and heavy, vampish shadows under her eyebrows. The result was an almost startling transition from exotic and sultry to a wholesome, almost childlike freshness. I wondered if she intended the change as a means of making herself less recognizable, or if it was another way of introducing me to the real Clara Bow. Whichever it was, I liked the change.

While Clara finished with the new dressing, I took Wellman's pistol out of my coat pocket and tried putting it in the only other place I could think to put it, inside my waistband at the small of my back. When I had it in place with the butt to the right so I could get hold of it quicker should that be necessary, I walked around and even jumped up and down a little to see if it would stay put. It was uncomfortable as heck, but the Colt stayed where I put it, so I left it there.

Next I picked up my overnight bag and hefted it. The case was not heavy, but I was darn tired of carrying it around everywhere I went. The problem was that, even though the Colt was now in my waistband, the bag still contained a box of ammunition and an envelope with five-hundred dollars of Bill Wellman's money in it, so I could not very well leave the bag in our room. By way of a compromise, I decided I would lock the bag inside the Oldsmobile while we were out.

Thinking about Bill Wellman's money reminded me that I was down to about sixty dollars in my wallet. Since we were about to go shopping for Clara's new wardrobe, I transferred five twenty dollar bills from the envelope to my wallet.

Having completed that chore, I was looking out the window closest to the bed when Clara presented herself. She had put on her wool coat and the dark blue scarf tied close around her face again without me reminding her to do so. I thought that maybe our little upset over her going for coffee might have had a positive effect after all.

She stood close and looked up into my face. Then we kissed as if it were the most natural thing in the world.

Since we hadn't eaten anything since the stew at Betty's Cafe in Santa Paula, and that seemed like days ago, I decided some breakfast was in order. I remembered the J. C. Penney's store being on Main Street, so I drove us in that general direction until we spotted a cafe attached to a small hotel called the American. Being late for breakfast and early for lunch, we had the American Cafe to ourselves, which was just dandy with me.

We sat at a table near the back of the small dining room and studied the menu. It did not require a great deal of study because there were only a half-dozen items from which to choose. Clara ordered oatmeal and a glass of orange juice. I chose corned beef hash with two poached eggs. What the cafe lacked in imagination, they made up for with fast service. Half an hour later we were properly fortified for a shopping expedition.

The Ventura J. C. Penney store was two blocks to the west and on the other side of Main Street. I pulled the Oldsmobile into an empty parking spot in front of the store, which was surprisingly large for a small town. Clara stared at the store through the car window for a moment, and then turned to look at me.

"Are you sure this is where you want me to shop, Eddie?"

I nodded. "I'm absolutely positive."

Clara grimaced. "Okay, but you're gonna have to help 'cuz I never shopped for frumpy clothes before."

With an evil grin, I said, "I wouldn't miss this for the world."

She rolled her eyes at me and hopped down out of the Oldsmobile. Inside the store, I was fearful that Clara was going to ask the first sales clerk she saw where the frumpy clothes department was, but she showed restraint and we found the missus department on our own.

Clara spent about thirty minutes browsing the racks and ended up with four outfits she deemed worthy of trying on. The first, and ultimately the one I liked best, was a knee-length Kelly green dress made of what Clara described as silk crepe. It had the sort of low waistline that seemed to be all the rage with a ribbon sash that tied at the back. What I liked about it was the way it kind of flowed with the movement of her body when she walked.

The second outfit she tried was a similar design in what I would call a peach color with four pale blue horizontal stripes at the low waist and a sort of built-scarf that tied at the collar. Her third choice was a little more complicated to describe. This one was off-white with pleats at the bottom and a wraparound top that resembled a jacket. Clara's final choice was a white pleated skirt and a long V-necked sweater with a geometric pattern in shades of green. Clara explained the sweater would be worn over some of the blouses she already had.

Each time Clara tried on one of the outfits, she emerged from the dressing room, performed a sort of twirl in front of the full-length mirror, and asked what I thought. This was a new experience for me and I will admit to finding the whole process rather enjoyable, especially since all of her choices struck me as stylish and appropriate to her shape and coloring.

To these selections we added three cloche hats—one each in dark green, off-white, and brown—with wide, turned down brims. Hats that partially concealed her face were ideal to our purpose.

The next item added to the growing stack on the clerk's counter was an off white, hip-length cotton jacket with big buttons and a belt that tied at the waist. The final items Clara selected were four pairs of hose in shades varying from "suntan" to "nude."

While I waited wallet in hand, Clara wrapped an arm through mine and the clerk added up the damage. The total was a whopping seventy-five dollars and some change. Even at J. C. Penney's fashion did not come cheap.

Loaded down with packages containing milady's new wardrobe, we passed through the men's department on our way out. I paused for a moment at a hat display, and Clara promptly picked up a dark brown fedora and placed it on my head at a rakish angle. As a general rule, I do not wear hats, but the whole idea of this exercise was to do things that were not according to the rules. The hat gave me jaunty and quite different appearance.

To the fedora Clara added a pale blue cotton shirt to replace the one stained with her blood, and I parted with another seven dollars. Thus, more than eighty dollars poorer, we loaded the Oldsmobile's trunk and headed back to the Casa del Pacifico.

Once all of our purchases were stored in the closet, Clara donned the green dress I liked and the green hat. I watched from one of the armchairs by the bed as she studied her reflection in the mirror over the dressing table. The changes in her look and, strangely, in her demeanor were remarkable. It was if little Clara

Bow had instantly grown up into a lovely sophisticated woman.

She pranced over and plopped down in my lap. "What do you think, sweetie? Am I frumpy enough to fool the public?"

"Kiddo, you missed frumpiness by a country mile. You are still the prettiest woman I ever laid eyes on and now you've got style to boot."

She gave me a big, wet smack on the lips and laid her head on my shoulder. "You know what I wish, Eddie?"

"No, tell me."

"I wish we could get on a boat and sail a million miles away from here to a place where they never even heard of motion pictures and Clara Bow. Someplace where people live in homey little cottages with gardens full of beautiful flowers and big back yards where kids grow up having fun and being loved by their moms and dads. That's what I wish."

I thought about the picture she had just painted. "That's a wonderful dream, Clara."

She sat up and looked at me with those big brown eyes. Her expression was soft and full of love. "Does it have to be just a dream, Eddie?"

I thought of words I had once written in a book. I recited them to Clara. "The things we want most in life always start out as dreams. Then, if we truly want them and work hard enough at it, we find ways to turn our dreams into reality."

A single tear rolled down her cheek before she buried her face in my neck and said softly, "Gosh, I love you so much it almost hurts."

Not having the slightest idea what to say next, I just held her close and wondered if those words I wrote had any honest truth to them. I found myself really hoping they did.

Twenty

Noon – Monday – September 20, 1926
Casa del Pacifico Motor Inn – Ventura

We spent a quiet afternoon in cottage number nine. Clara changed into her new skirt and sweater outfit, adding a bright green blouse from those she already had before our shopping expedition. She hung the pretty green dress in the closet to be saved, she said, for a special occasion, and settled into the armchair on the bathroom side of the bed with the book she was reading on the first day of our flight west, *Gentlemen Prefer Blondes*. I sat at the table by the window and did some writing and a lot of thinking.

The writing I did was in the form of additions to my article notes about the making of *Wings* I had begun on the train last Tuesday. That only a week had passed since I boarded the Sunset Limited for San Antonio was difficult to believe. So much had happened during those seven days it felt more like a month.

All that had happened during that time also changed the nature of the notes I was writing. Now I thought of them more as a journal because it seemed unlikely that the information in those notes would ever be seen by anyone other than me. Still, I felt a need to write it all down.

When I finished writing, I went back to the beginning of my notes and reread them carefully in hope of finding some small clue that would enlighten me as to who was trying to kill Clara. Finding nothing even remotely like that, I stacked the pages neatly and put them back into my overnight bag. It was time to do some serious thinking about how I was going to identify the man who was trying to kill Clara.

Because of Jesse Lasky's insistence on not reporting Friday's incident to the police so as to avoid the sensational newspaper headlines that would inevitably follow such a report, I had nothing beyond my own observations to go on. Given the interest the Army would surely have in finding out who poisoned their pilots, an investigation on their part was inevitable, but I could have no expectation of help from that quarter. So, in a very real sense, I was on my own and winging it.

I began by thinking about the two murder attempts and what they had in common. Both were planned by someone who knew precisely where Clara would be and precisely when she would be there. Both also involved aircraft. And both had failed only because I was there—the first time by coincidence and the second time by intention.

What, I wondered, did the killer think about that? I had certainly become a thorn in his side and a factor to be reckoned with in his next scheme to kill Clara. Would another attempt on her life be made? I was one-hundred percent sure there would be. The killer had already invested too much time, money, and effort into the enterprise to just give up.

It was then that I realized I was thinking of the man flying the Curtiss Oh-One in Texas as the killer, but was he the only killer? Assuming the same individual poisoned Arnie Miller and Ronny Jones, the smoking gun was most certainly in his hand, but that did not preclude the possibility that he was in cahoots with others, or even that he was no more than a lackey hired by some other person who wanted to end the life of Clara Bow.

The more I thought about those possibilities, the more stock I put in the paid lackey theory. What were the chances that someone who had access to Clara's schedule and to the last minute plan of flying her to California on an Army transport was also a skilled pursuit pilot and a clever assassin with the knowledge to kill by poison? It was possible, but not very darn likely.

So who in the inner circle of those associated with *Wings* would have a reason to kill Clara, and what could that reason be? From my point of view, that reason—the motive, as the police say it— would have to be the key to learning the identities of the killers. I did not have the resources to conduct a thorough investigation, to say nothing of tracking down a murderer with an aircraft at his disposal, so I would have to find his employer by figuring out who would profit from her demise.

Whoever said money was the root of all evil said a mouthful, so the better question would be who stood to make money, a great deal of it, if Clara died? No, that was still not exactly the right question. The right question was who would make a great deal of money if Clara died *and* had access to detailed inside information about her? That was the question I had to answer.

Unfortunately, knowing exactly the right question to ask did not put me one bit closer to whatever the answer might be. The problem was that I simply did not know enough about the people at Lasky and those involved with *Wings* to even make a start at seeking an answer. More than anything I wished I could pick up a telephone and have a conversation with Wellman or Charlie Barton.

Despite the fact that Clara said repeatedly she had no idea who would want to kill her, it might be that she actually did know, but did not know she knew. With that thought in mind, I decided my next step would be to sit down with her later tonight or first thing in the morning and ask every question I could think of in the hope one of them triggered an answer that would provide a clue as to who the killers might be. It was not much, but I felt a little better with even that meager plan of action to follow.

At that moment a loud squeaking sound from right outside our cottage door had me out of my seat and reaching for the pistol in my waistband. The squeaking was followed by a loud knock on the door. Startled, Clara looked up from her book in fear.

I shouted, "Who is it?"

A woman's voice answered. "Housekeeping, sir. I'm here to clean your room."

Stepping over to the window on the right side of the door I saw part of a wooden cart stacked with fresh towels, linens and cleaning supplies. I said, "Okay, just a minute."

Tucking the Colt back into my waistband, I turned to Clara and said, "Hey, kiddo, let's go for a walk."

A smile quickly replaced the fear that had been on her face a moment earlier. "That sounds wonderful!"

Clara put on one of her new hats while I grabbed my overnight case from the table and opened the door. A hefty woman with gray hair was standing out there holding a stack of towels. She stepped aside to let us by and I noticed that Clara had the good sense to be looking away from the maid as they passed each other.

After locking my overnight case in the Oldsmobile's trunk, we strolled hand in hand down to the far end of the Casa del Pacifico, making frequent stops so Clara could take a closer look at flowers that caught her eye. I never in a million years would have guessed that a gal from Brooklyn would be so fascinated by something as simple as a flower. Clara was just full of the unexpected.

While Clara smelled the flowers, I observed what I could about our fellow guests at the Casa del Pacifico. For one thing, there were not many of them. Only two cottage carports besides our were occupied, one by a bright yellow Cadillac open touring car with gleaming nickel plating around its radiator, and the other by an infinitely more plebian black Chevrolet four-door sedan.

Of course there might be other guests who were out taking in the sights, but this was Monday and it made sense that an auto court in a vacation spot would be quieter during the week. At the moment, that was to our advantage.

When Clara and I reached the closed end of the drive, we turned around and retraced our steps. As we approached the office end of the Casa del Pacifico, I saw that the maid's cart was still outside our cottage door, so I said, "Yesterday the owner of this place told me they serve tea and cookies every afternoon at three. It's a little past three right now, what do you say we attend the tea party?"

With a decidedly upper crust tone to her voice, Clara said, "Why, that sounds simply delightful." In a less haughty tone she added, "I wasn't hungry at lunchtime, but I could use a little something now. Cookies would be perfect."

So into the office lobby we went. Ambrose DeBoyce's usual place behind the counter had been usurped by an attractive middle-aged woman I guessed to be Missus DeBoyce—Amanda, if memory served me right. She said, "Good afternoon, Mister and Missus Wilkinson. You are right on time for tea. It's all set up on the table there, so please help yourselves.

Clara set about pouring tea into dainty teacups and I loaded a few sugar cookies onto a matching plate. As Clara poured, Amanda DeBoyce said, "Missus Wilkinson, that is a lovely sweater. That style is all the rage and the color is perfect for you!"

Keeping her attention on the teapot, Clara said, "Thank you. Allan is such a dear! He treated me to some new outfits while we were out this morning. He even took me to J. C. Penney's."

Missus DeBoyce said, "Well, you certainly have good taste in clothes, and it seems, in husbands as well."

The women had a chuckle over that remark before Clara and I took our tea and cookies out to one of the painted metal tables in front of the office. We had about the same view from there as we did from the big window in our cottage, and we sat there sipping, munching, and looking out over Ventura to the sea beyond it.

I am not much of a tea drinker, but the sugar cookies, home made and fresh, hit the spot. I was about to take a bite out of my second cookie when Clara said, "Eddie, could we do something special tonight?"

"What do you have in mind?"

Looking a trifle sheepish, she said, "Well, this will probably sound silly to you, but now that I don't look so much like me, could we go somewhere nice for dinner and maybe dancing tonight?"

"I don't think that sounds silly at all. The only problem is this is Monday and finding a nice place that has dancing in this little town might be difficult."

Clara sighed. "I didn't think of that, but maybe Missus DeBoyce knows of a place. It wouldn't hurt to ask."

"No, it wouldn't. I'll go in and do that."

I walked into the office and half turned at the counter so I could keep an eye on Clara. Missus DeBoyce came over from neatening up the tea table and said, "Yes, Mister Wilkinson, what can I do for you?"

"Well, my lovely wife just informed me she would like to go to a nice place for dinner and dancing tonight. Do you know of any place in town where we can do that on a Monday night?"

"Oh, my. Let me think."

She looked thoughtful for a long moment, then her face brightened. "I know! The Pierpont Inn! It's one of the nicest restaurants in town and they have a small orchestra that plays every night after the dinner hour."

"That's terrific! Thank you, Missus DeBoyce. We'll give it a try."

Outside the office I resumed my cookie eating and said, "We might be in luck. She thinks the Pierpont Inn has a small orchestra that plays every night in their dining room. She also said it's a nice place to eat."

Clara leaned over and kissed me on the cheek. "Thank you, Eddie. You're sweet to humor me."

Grinning, I said, "Don't be so sure my motives aren't selfish."

She winked at me. "I hope they are!"

Across the drive, the maid exited our cottage and closed the door. She was looking in our direction and I had the feeling she was studying us as she pushed her cart across the drive. I had no idea why she might have any interests in a couple of tourists from San Diego, but it was exactly the sort of attention I was trying to avoid. Plus, the woman had just spent an unsupervised thirty minutes in our cottage—plenty of time go through our possessions.

I cursed myself for not thinking of the possibility that someone might search our room. I had to start behaving more cautiously or

Clara was going to end up dead.

Okay, if someone did search the room, the damage was done, but what would such a search have disclosed? Everything of mine that might identify Clara was in my overnight case which was in the Oldsmobile's trunk, and she had taken her handbag with her when we left the room. However, I had no idea what might be in her luggage that would identify her. I thought it was a darned good idea to find out.

Returning to our cottage, I told Clara of my concern and we began going through her bags to find out what the maid or anyone else who had been in the room while we were out might have discovered. Right off the bat I noticed the monograms next to the carrying handles of her expensive matching suitcases. The gilt letters "C. B." didn't necessary mean the luggage belonged to Clara Bow, but they did mean the bags probably did not belong to someone named Mary Wilkinson.

The only other item of concern we turned up would have been a dead giveaway to Clara's identity. It was a diary or journal bound in high quality leather with her name embossed on the cover in an elaborate decorative script.

Clara was sitting on the end of the bed going through the larger of her two suitcases when she found it, and I heard her say, "Oh, oh."

I looked at the book she held in her hands and, fearing that we might be closing the barn door after the horse was long gone, I said, "That's definitely something we can't afford to leave in the room when we're not here."

"But where can we hide it? It's too big to fit in my handbag."

"There's room for it in my overnight bag."

Clara looked up at me for a moment, and then stared at the diary with a faraway expression on her face. Finally she seemed to make up her mind about something and held the book out to me. "Eddie, I never want to keep any secrets from you, but some of what I've written in here is real personal and I would be embarrassed to have anyone read it, especially you. Will you promise not to look in it?"

Accepting the diary, I said solemnly, "You have my word of honor."

She watched me place the book in my overnight case as if she was seeing something or someone special for the last time. Closing the overnight case, I said, "Don't worry, Clara. I'll respect your privacy and you can have it back anytime you want."

She closed the suitcase next to her on the bed and looked up at me with sincerity in her eyes. "There's no one on earth I trust more than you, Eddie."

Around five-thirty, Clara announced that it was time for her to dress for our big night on the town. She proceeded to disappear into the bathroom for quite a while. When Clara returned, she was wearing her new green dress with dark hose and her black pumps. With the addition of her new green hat, she was pretty as a picture and ready to go.

My preparations were somewhat less involved. I simply tied a dark brown tie around the collar of my white cotton shirt and slipped into my brown sport coat. I did not have to check on the location of the Colt pistol, because it was making its presence clearly known by poking me uncomfortably in the small of my back. After locking my overnight bag with its precious cargo in the Oldsmobile's trunk again for safekeeping, we set off for the Pierpont Inn.

The Inn—a rustic, rambling structure built in the craftsman style of architecture—was located on a bluff between downtown Ventura and the ocean. As the sun was close to setting, the parking area, located on the town side of the building, was fringed with deep shadows, so I took a slow drive through it to see what might be lurking in those shadows. Seeing nothing more sinister than an older couple taking a casual stroll with their cocker spaniel, I parked in front of the Pierpont Inn's main entrance and with Clara taking my arm, we walked through a lush planted area and into the Inn.

The dining room was situated on the ocean side of the building. It was a large comfortable sort of place with big windows overlooking the beach. The maitre d' seated us at a table for two next to one of the windows and alongside a parquet dance floor. A grand piano on the opposite side of the room bore a sign informing us that a musical group known as The Clippers was appearing nightly for our listening and dancing pleasure.

Given the small number of diners there, I was surprised the Inn was willing to pay for a band to entertain so few, but I was also grateful because dancing was part of Clara's wish for the evening. Our fellow diners numbered only eight—four couples all seated at tables near the windows.

The Inn's lengthy leather-bound menu offered a variety of seafood, the usual assortment of steaks and chops, and many accompaniments. We were still engrossed in the dinner decision making process when a swarthy fellow wearing a red vest and a thin moustache stepped up to our table and introduced himself as

Isaac, our waiter for the evening.

Isaac asked for our beverage choices and listed the options as coffee, tea, soft drinks, and a house specialty known as Planter's Punch. This last item, he explained with a conspiratorial wink, could be ordered with a little something extra blended in if we so desired.

I glanced at Clara. She gave me a grin and a nod, so I told Isaac we would have the Planter's Punch with the little something extra.

While our drinks were being prepared, we made our dinner choices; shrimp cocktails for openers, to be followed with a hearty cioppino and entrees of seared sea scallops in a tarragon-butter sauce. I conveyed this information to Isaac when he returned with our drinks and he commented on the excellence of our choices, something he no doubt told every diner regardless of their order. After Isaac set off to inform the kitchen of our excellent choices, I raised my glass and said, "Here's to a wonderful evening in the company of the loveliest and most delightful woman I have ever known."

Clara actually blushed a little as she said softly, "Thank you, Eddie."

We each took a sip of our punch and found it to be, as indirectly promised, a tasty blend of fruit juices and an excellent rum. Then we turned our attention to the particularly vivid sunset taking place outside our window. Iridescent shades of orange and yellow gradually transitioned to soft pinks and glowing purples as we watched.

At one point I glanced across the table at Clara. She was enthralled by the display of colors, her face aglow with the now muted tones coming through the window. For an instant my mind flashed back to the March Field Officer's Club where it had occurred to me that Clara was the ideal companion for a romantic date, but that our presence there was far from a romantic occasion. Now, only one day later, we were on what could not be construed as anything other than a romantic date and I was enjoying every second of it. That thought also reminded me that I must not get so wrapped up in Clara that I neglected my duty to keep her safe.

Having skipped lunch because of our late breakfast, our appetites were more than ready for a good meal, and the chef's creations met our needs and then some. Each course exceeded my expectations and I would have readily admitted to anyone who asked that the Pierpont Inn provided an outstanding dining experience.

About halfway through the meal Isaac noted that our glasses were empty and asked if we would like another round. Clara nodded eagerly, so I ordered another Planter's Punch for her and a cup of coffee for myself.

Clara cocked her head to one side with a questioning look, and I said, "The punch is great, but I have to keep my wits about me and not forget that your safety is in my hands."

She nodded her understanding and said, "Then I shouldn't have . . . ."

I interrupted her. "Just enjoy yourself. I'll take care of the rest."

With another of her soft smiles she said, "Eddie, I love you."

I returned her smile and said, "I seem to be getting pretty darned attached to you, too, kiddo."

A moment or two after the busboy cleared our dinner dishes away the room lights dimmed to a more romantic level and a piano arpeggio sounded from across the room. The fellow sitting at the piano said, "Good evening, ladies and gentlemen. We are the Clippers and we're here to play a little music for you. If you have any requests, let us know and we'll do our best to fill them.

"Now we'll get things started with a tune we're all hearing a lot on the radio, The Girl Friend." To his band, he said, "Ready fellows? Here we go . . . one, two, three . . . ."

And off they went with the piano leading and a bass and guitar providing the rhythm. For only three guys, they made a lot of music. Clara, moving her shoulders to the rhythm, looked over at me with bright-eyed expectation.

Standing, I said, "Okay, kiddo, but no tricky steps, I ain't no sheik."

I pulled Clara's chair out for her and we hit the dance floor with a sort of subdued Charleston. Apparently what we were doing must have looked like fun because two of the other couples joined us on the floor.

The Clippers followed their first number with another rouser, Yes, Sir, That's my Baby, only this time they added lyrics with all three musicians doing the singing. By the time they finished that one I was ready for break, even though Clara looked as if she could keep going all night.

Moments after we sat down at our table, Isaac showed up to inquire if the lady would care for another Planter's Punch. Clara said nothing but gave me a questioning look that said she was leaving the decision up to me. To Isaac I said, "Sure, one more for the lady."

As he went to fetch her third Planter's Punch of the evening, Clara said, "Hey, you're a pretty swell dancer. For some reason I had the idea you weren't much on dancing."

"I'm not. I was just sort of moving to the beat and letting you do all the work. I do better with the slow numbers."

"Then we'll just wait for them play some slow numbers. That's more what I had in mind, anyway."

Clara was about halfway through her drink and I had reached the bottom of my coffee cup when the fellow at the piano said, "All right, folks, we're going to slow things down a little with a set of songs for you love birds out there. Here's our rendition of Bye, Bye Blackbird."

I stood, saying, "Now this is a little more my speed."

A moment later I was holding Clara in my arms and we were fox-trotting our way around the dance floor. I kept my eyes busy searching the room for any sign of a threat, but it was darned difficult to keep my mind on that chore and off of my beautiful dance partner.

The song ended and we stopped moving, but Clara stayed right there in my arms waiting for the next song to begin. When the Clippers kicked off their next number, I recognized it as a very pretty new Gershwin tune called Someone To Watch Over Me.

As we began dancing again Clara pressed herself closer to me, resting her head on my chest. Then, as the second chorus began, I heard a soft, clear voice singing along with the music. It took me a moment to realize the voice belonged to Clara. She was singing so softly that no one else in the room could hear her, but I sure could.

There's a somebody I'm longing to see,
I hope that he turns out to be
Someone who'll watch over me.
I'm a little lamb who's lost in the wood.
I know I could always be good
To one who'll watch over me.

I held Clara a little closer and she looked up at me. She didn't say anything, she just looked up at my face with more love that I ever imagined could be expressed without words. I kissed her on the forehead and she snuggled back against my chest.

When the song ended and Clara looked up at me again there were tears streaming down both of her cheeks. Softly, she said, "Would you take me home now, Eddie?"

I paid the bill—twenty-two dollars, including a nice tip for

Isaac—and we walked out to the car, Clara hanging on tightly to my arm the whole way. Stepping out through the Pierpont Inn's main doors, I scanned the parking area. All was still peaceful and quiet.

Once we were back in the privacy of cottage number nine and I had locked the door, Clara threw her arms around me and the tears began to flow again. I was trying to figure out whether they were tears of joy or sorrow when she answered the question for me.

Between little sobs, Clara said, "I know I don't deserve anyone in my life as wonderful as you, but here you are. That's a miracle and I will thank God for it every day for the rest of my life."

Tilting her head up so I could see her face, I said, "Clara, I'm no miracle. I'm just . . . ."

"You are to me. Eddie, you don't know what my life has been like up until now, and I hope you will never know the worst parts, but for as long as I have been alive, this is the very first and only time I have ever felt completely loved and safe and respected. You've given me the one thing I've always wanted but could never find."

I could think of nothing to say in response, so I just held her, tight. We stood there like that for a long, long time, sharing the physical and emotional sensations of our love. Then we kissed the deepest, most intensely passionate kiss I had ever experienced and Clara whispered, "Let's go to bed, Eddie."

Twenty-One

7:00 A.M. – Tuesday – September 21, 1926
Casa del Pacífico Motor Inn – Ventura

Tuesday morning I awoke with Clara's back against my chest and my arm around her waist. Her skin was smooth and warm, and I spent the next five minutes trying to convince myself that there was no earthly reason to get out of bed.

Unfortunately, once I wake up I stay that way. I disentangled myself from Clara as gently as possible so as not to wake her. Then, after taking a look at the world through our windows and finding it peaceful, I ran a bath and prepared for the day ahead.

When I left the bathroom Clara's eyes were open. "G'morning, Eddie."

"Good morning, kiddo. How are you this morning?"

Stretching like a graceful cat waking from a nap, Clara said, "I'm wonderful, Eddie—more wonderful than I have ever been before."

I leaned over the bed and gave her a kiss on the forehead, but she didn't settle for that. Clara wrapped an arm around my neck and held me there while we kissed a warm and loving kiss. About the time my back was threatening to give out, she released me and I straightened.

"I'll go across the way and bring us some coffee. Be back in a minute."

Ambrose DeBoyce was at his usual station and a fresh pot of coffee sat on the table near the office door. As I poured two cups of coffee, DeBoyce said, "We have the first edition of the *Los Angeles Times*, if you're interested."

There was something about the tone of his voice that made me turn to look at him. DeBoyce's face gave nothing away, but I swapped him a nickel for a copy of the newspaper and tucked it under my arm as I carried our coffee back to cottage number nine.

When I walked in, the bed was empty and I could hear Clara moving around in the bathroom. I set the coffee tray down on the table by the window, took my first swallow of coffee, and unfolded the *Times*. The headline below the fold made my blood run cold.

In large, bold type spanning three columns, the headline said, "Motion picture actress sought in murder of Army officers." Filling two of the columns immediately below the headline was a photograph of Clara—an older publicity shot—captioned, "Popular Famous Players Lasky actress, Clara Bow."

The article, which carried no byline, read as follows:

The United States Army Air Corps is seeking the whereabouts of popular motion picture actress Clara Bow as a material witness in the strange murders of two officers.

Miss Bow, along with a former Army Air Corps pilot, Edgar Markley, and an unidentified colored woman were passengers aboard an Army transport aircraft that made an emergency landing at March Army Air Corps Base last Sunday morning. Upon boarding the ship, Army officials found the copilot, Second Lieutenant Ronald Jones, dead and the pilot, Captain Arnold Miller, near death.

An autopsy performed on Jones indicated that he had ingested a lethal amount of the poison known as arsenic. A thermos bottle of coffee discovered in the aircraft's cockpit was found to contain the same poison and is thought to be the means by which the pilot was murdered.

According to an Army spokesman, the fatal flight began at Kelley Field near San Antonio, Texas early on the morning of Saturday, September 18, when Miss Bow and her party boarded the transport ship for a courtesy flight scheduled to arrive at Glendale Air Terminal on the following day. Miss Bow had been in San Antonio filming a motion picture being produced by the Famous Players Lasky Company.

At first it was thought that the pilots were stricken by food poisoning, but when the autopsy results indicated foul play, the Army Air Corps immediately launched an investigation and began seeking the popular actress and the members of her party as material witnesses to the murders. The three were last seen in Riverside, California, but no further trace of them has been found.

When contacted for comment by the Times, a spokesman for Famous Players Lasky said they did not know where Miss Bow was at the moment and that they, too, were looking for her. Famous Players Lasky Company has pledged one-hundred percent cooperation with the Army's murder investigation.

I had just finished reading the article for a second time when Clara came out of the bathroom. She came over to the table and was reaching for her coffee when she spotted her photo and the headline.

"Oh, no! What's happened?"

"As I expected, the Army is searching for us as material witnesses in the murder of one or two of their pilots, although the article is unclear as to whether Arnie Miller is alive or dead."

"But . . . but why is my picture there?"

"That was probably the *Times'* idea. Front page photos of famous people sell newspapers. At least they got your name right. I'm now Edgar Markley."

"Well, they sure didn't do us any favor by printing my name or picture."

"No, they didn't. I anticipated the Army's murder investigation, but I did not expect a front page newspaper story to go with it." Pointing to the article, I said, "This might explain why DeBoyce made a point of telling me he had copies of the *Times* early edition available when I went over for coffee. He sounded a little strange to me, but I didn't know why. I think I do now."

"Well, we have to do something about this, don't we?"

Nodding, I said, "Yes, and the most logical something for us to do is to get the heck out of here in case DeBoyce has tumbled to who we are, or in case that housekeeping woman figured it out. The Army isn't offering a reward or anything, but if someone turns us in, they will probably get their name in the newspaper, and that alone might be more than enough incentive for somebody like the housekeeper."

There was a hint of panic in Clara's voice as she said, "Then shouldn't we be packing?"

"Sit down and finish your coffee while I think this through. We don't want to rush into something that will get us in deeper trouble than we've already got."

She sat and tried to drink some of her coffee, but her hand was shaking and she spilled a few drops on the table. Wiping up the coffee with a paper napkin, Clara said, "Damn it! Why can't they just leave us alone?"

I reached across the table and took her hand. "I know, kiddo. This is all pretty scary, but they haven't got us yet. The important thing now is to keep our wits about us so we can figure out how to turn this situation around. That business about the thermos bottle of coffee having the poison in it may have given me an idea about how to do that.

"I saw Captain Miller carrying the thermos bottle aboard the morning we left Rimrock, so we know how Miller and Jones were poisoned and something about how the poison got on the ship. That doesn't help with the 'who' part of this yet, but it's a start. Plus, it's information the Army probably doesn't have yet.

"I wish I knew if Miller was alive. If so, and he can talk, he could tell the investigators where the heck he got that coffee, and that might get us off the hook."

Clara's eyes grew wide. "You don't mean they think we had anything to do with it, do you?"

"It's hard to know what the Army is thinking."

"But why would we kill the pilots of a plane we were flying on? That would be a crazy thing to do!"

"Yes, it would be crazy . . . unless there was someone in our party who could fly that ship when the pilots conked out."

The panic was back in Clara's voice. "They DO think we had something to do with it!"

"Slow down, kiddo. Even if we had the opportunity and access to the poison, we had no reason—no motive—to kill those fellows. Why would we want to kill two strangers who were doing us a favor by giving us a lift to California?"

Holding the *Times* up, I said, "The biggest concern I have about this turn of events is it might help the Army find out where we are. The Army doesn't scare me much, but if they find us, they might lead whoever is trying to hurt you to us. That's why we've got to turn this thing around."

"Then what do we do, Eddie?"

I gave that a long moment of thought. The possibility that DeBoyce had us pegged for who we really were was the deciding factor. "It seems like the best first step really is to pack up and get out of here."

Clara jumped up, ready to begin packing, then she stopped. "But where will we go?"

"We can figure that out once we're on the road. Let's load up."

It took us no more than fifteen minutes to pack our bags. When they were stacked next to the door, Clara put her arms around me and said, "Eddie, I hate to leave here. It's been . . . a special place for us. I'm afraid if we leave . . . ."

I hugged her. "Clara, we're coming back when this is all over, and besides, we'll always have what we found here. Nobody can ever take that away from us."

There were tear streaks on her cheeks again when she looked up and nodded. I kissed her tears and said, "Sit tight for a minute while I go and talk to DeBoyce. I'd like to know what he intends to do. When I come back, we'll carry this stuff to the car and get on the road."

"Eddie, can I go with you? I don't want to stay in here by myself now."

"Sure. If we're going to do it that way, let's go ahead and carry our bags out. Then we'll be ready to go."

With our bags in the Oldsmobile's trunk and my overnight case behind its seat, we locked the car and walked hand-in-hand to the Casa del Pacifico office. Ambrose DeBoyce was still there and he didn't seem at all surprised that he had just seen us loading our bags into the car.

"I see you're leaving us, Mister Wilkinson. That means I owe you a refund for tonight's room rent."

"Don't worry about that, Mister DeBoyce. We had an agreement and I'll stick to that part of it. You don't owe us anything, but I would like a little information."

DeBoyce nodded. "You would like to know if I know who you really are."

"I kind of gathered that you do, and I apologize for misleading you. I assure you I would not have done so without a very good reason."

DeBoyce nodded again. "Mister Wilkinson, I have been in the hotel business for a good many years and I pride myself on my ability to judge the character of our guests. I believe you and Miss . . . Missus Wilkinson are good people who have found yourselves in a bad situation.

"Because I believe that, I have no intention of telling anyone you were here unless I am forced to. Amanda agrees with me on that point. We just wish you a safe journey and a quick resolution to the problems you face. I also hope you will come back and see us again under more pleasant circumstances."

Before I could think of a response, Clara said, "We will, Mister DeBoyce. You can count on that. We really appreciate your hospitality and friendship."

Five minutes later we were rolling out of Ventura on U.S. Route 101 in the southbound direction. After reading a highway sign that said Los Angeles was sixty-seven miles ahead, Clara said with surprise, "We're going back to Los Angeles?"

"We're going in that direction, but I haven't figured out what our final destination will be yet. We can talk about that, if you'd like."

"Okay. I have a question."

"Shoot."

"How would the Army find us if nobody tells them they've seen us?"

"That really wouldn't be very hard for them to do. We told Colonel Smythe a car from the studio was picking us up in Riverside. You can bet the first thing he did when he got the autopsy report was to call Lasky.

"The studio no doubt told him there were no arrangements made for a car to pick us up in Riverside. Upon learning that, Smythe's people would start checking public transportation—the train and bus depots—to find out if we left town by rail or coach.

"When they turn up nothing there, it will only be a matter of time before someone thinks to check the car rental agencies in Riverside, assuming there are more than one in town. Since I had to use my real name to rent this car, the Army knows or will soon know what kind of car we're driving right down to the license plate number.

"All they have to do is circulate that information to local police agencies and the California Highway Patrol and it's only a matter of time before some sharp-eyed cop spots us."

Clara frowned. "So we have to get rid of the car?"

"We have to do more than that. We can't just keep running and hiding because sooner or later we'll run out of places to hide. Besides that, hiding gets us no closer to finding out who wants to hurt you. It's high time we did something positive to give ourselves an advantage in this situation."

"How can we do that?"

"That's what I've been thinking about. Right now the Army is as much our enemy as the people who want to hurt you. I have an idea how we can turn things around and get the Army on our side. It's risky, but not as risky as doing nothing."

"What are you going to do?"

"Later I'm going to place a long-distance telephone call to Colonel Smythe and see if I can make a deal with him. We have valuable information that will help him find the people who poisoned his pilots, so I will offer to exchange that information for his promise to stop looking for us and to tell us what their investigation turns up."

"Oh, Eddie, do you think we can trust Smythe? He might agree just get us out of hiding, and then go back on his word."

"Smythe's situation is just as bad as ours in a different way. He's bound to be under a lot of pressure from his superiors to find out who poisoned two Army Air Corps officers. If he fails, it could mean the end of his Army career.

"He needs the information we have in the worst way, and I think he'll be willing to deal with us to get it, especially since I also have an idea about how to set it up so he'll have no choice but to do things our way if he wants the information."

I glanced over at Clara. Her expression told me this was another one of those times when she wasn't entirely convinced my idea was the right thing to do. I said, "Clara, if you disagree with my plan, we can try to come up with a better solution, but I really think dealing with Smythe is our best bet."

Clara reached across and put her hand on my leg. "Eddie, we'll do whatever you think we need to do. I'm just scared, that's all."

I patted her hand. "That makes two of us, kiddo, but we'll get through this, you'll see."

U.S. Route 101 heads inland from Ventura, winding its way over the low coastal hills that form the western end of the San Fernando Valley. Once over the hills, we were rolling past the valley's rich farms, ranches and orchards that grew out of the area's original Spanish land grants. When the City of Los Angeles brought water to the valley a dozen or so years ago, agriculture boomed and small farming towns—Thousand Oaks, Woodland Hills, Sherman Oaks, and Toluca, to name a few—sprang up and prospered along Ventura Road, the main east-west path through the San Fernando Valley.

Ventura Road was only recently designated U.S. Route 101, and the improved highway, along with the Southern Pacific Railroad, provides farmers with the means to move their produce to the markets of Los Angeles. Near the eastern end of the San Fernando Valley U.S. 101 turns south over the Cahuenga Pass and into Hollywood and Los Angeles proper.

As had been the case on our trip from El Monte to Ventura, Clara was fascinated with the countryside through which we drove. That fascination gave me the opportunity to take her mind off of our troubles. I was reciting what little I knew about the history of the San Fernando Valley when a Sheriff's motorcycle officer passed us, traveling in the westbound direction. I watched him in my rearview mirror, holding my breath and hoping he did not turn around to follow us. Luck, it seemed, was still with us because he showed absolutely no interest in the Oldsmobile.

When we reached the point where Route 101 turns south, I

continued east on Ventura Road, or Ventura Boulevard as it was named here, and at a few minutes past eleven o'clock, we arrived in the little municipality of Burbank, where I intended to make two stops. Turning north on San Fernando Road, we entered Burbank's business district, and a few blocks later, I pulled up in front of the first of my stops, the Security Bank at San Fernando Road and Olive Avenue.

While Clara waited in the Oldsmobile, I went into the bank and traded a five dollar bill for another pocketful of quarters, dimes and nickels. Then we drove a few blocks further on San Fernando Road to the outskirts of the downtown business district, where I pulled to the curb in front of an eatery called The Good Eats Cafe.

Lunch sounded good, but the thing that attracted me to the place was a small blue sign in the front window. Its white letters spelled out "Public Telephone Inside."

I turned to Clara. "Okay, kiddo, wish me luck. It's time to call Colonel Smythe."

She leaned over and gave me a kiss on the cheek. "You don't need luck, Eddie. You're gonna do just fine. Can I come with you?"

"That's what I had in mind. I can use the moral support."

Twenty-Two

11:30 A.M. – Tuesday – September 21, 1926
Good Eats Cafe – Burbank

The Good Eats Cafe's public telephone hung on a wall in a short hallway alongside the kitchen at the back of the restaurant. With Clara standing close by my side, I negotiated a long-distance person-to-person call to Colonel Efram Smythe in the office of the commandant at March Army Air Corp Field.

After reducing my pocketful of change by a goodly amount, the long distance operator completed the connection and a male voice answered, "Commandant's office."

The operator said, "I have a person-to-person long distance call for a Colonel Efram Smythe."

"One moment please. I'll connect you to his office."

I had been concerned that Smythe might be out his office, but it seemed we were in luck. A moment later Smythe's familiar bass voice came on the line. "Colonel Smythe speaking."

At that, the operator simply said, "Go ahead with your call, sir."

I said, "Hello, Colonel Smythe, this is Eddie Markham."

There was a long pause on the line, as if Smythe couldn't really believe I was calling him, or maybe he was deciding how best to give me a thorough chewing out. Finally, he said, "Markham, where the devil are you? We've been looking all over creation for you!"

"So I read in the *Times*."

Smythe cleared his throat. "Yes, well, the reporter chose to rewrite the information we gave him, but that's neither here nor there. You are wanted as material witnesses in a government murder case. Now, where the hell are you?"

"Smythe, it's the witness part that I'm calling you about. I have a proposition for you."

Smythe blustered, "Proposition? Lieutenant Markham you are hardly in a position to be making propositions!"

Colonel Smythe had used my former rank in the Army Air Service for intimidation purposes, but it didn't work. "That's MISTER Markham, Smythe, and I'm in a darn good position to be offering you a proposition because there's a whole lot more to this story than you know."

"Markham, I won't be making any deals with you. Just get your tail back here . . . ."

"Colonel Smythe, you'd be very smart to quiet down and listen to what I have to say before you decide that. You can always say no."

Another pause came down the line while Smythe calmed himself down. I glanced at Clara. She looked about as nervous as I felt. To my relief, Smythe said, "Okay, Markham, what's your proposition?"

"Colonel, some things happened before we boarded that Trimotor in San Antonio that have a bearing on all this. I am offering tell you everything I know about what happened up to and including the point at which Captain Miller and Lieutenant Jones were poisoned. That information will give you the motive for their poisoning as well as a good place to begin looking for the killers. You should also be aware that I'm the only one who knows the whole story and isn't sworn to secrecy or in fear of losing a good-paying job if I spill the beans. Now, in exchange for all that information I want two promises from you."

"What promises?"

"First, I want your word as an officer and a gentleman that you'll call off the manhunt for Miss Bow, Miss Bow's maid, and me. You'll have everything we know about the case, so there will no longer be any reason to bring us in, at least for the moment. And, second, I want your promise that you will pass along to me whatever progress you make in your murder investigation based on the information I give you.

"You'll understand why both of those promises are necessary to the deal when you hear the whole story of what's been going on, but suffice it to say we are dealing with cold-blooded killers and there are more lives at stake in this situation. What do you say?"

Clara held up both hands with fingers crossed while I waited for Smythe's answer. It took a moment for him to make up his mind, but when Smythe spoke again, I knew I had played my cards just exactly right.

"All right, Markham. It's against my better judgment, but I'll go along with your proposition, assuming that your information is really as important to this case as you say it is. When should I expect you here?"

"Well, that's the other part of this deal. I can't come to you, so you'll have to come to me."

"What?"

"Colonel, as I just said, there are other lives hanging in the balance here, and I am responsible for at least one of those lives. I can't risk showing up anywhere the killers might expect me to be."

"Okay, where do I meet you?"

"Are those wings on your chest just to impress the troops or are you still a qualified pilot?"

I said that in a joking way to lighten the mood of our conversation, but I could tell by the tone of his answer that I had hit on a matter of pride. "Except for that Ford Trimotor you brought in here, I am current in every type of ship on the base."

"Good. Here's what I would like you to do. Fly one of your single-seaters to Glendale Air Terminal. When you land, taxi over to the Kinner hangar. It's the largest one on the field and it's well marked.

"Park the ship alongside the hangar and walk about thirty yards to the Terminal Cafe at the eastern perimeter of the field. It's just a little lunch shop and most of their tables are outside. Sit at one of the tables and wait for me.

"I'll be watching, and if everything looks copasetic, I'll join you at the table. But if I see any hint of a trap or a trick, all bets are off. If that happens, we'll both be out a great deal."

There was another pause and I suspected Smythe was deciding how far he was going to let me push him. During this pause the long-distance operator's voice said, "Calling party, please stay on the line when you finish your call for additional charges."

The sound of the operator's voice seemed to jar a decision out of Smythe. He said, "Okay, Markham. When do you want to meet?"

I glanced at my watch. "It's eleven-thirty-five now and it shouldn't take you more than ninety minutes to get here from March, so let's make it a few minutes after one."

After yet another, shorter pause, I heard Smythe sigh into the telephone. He said, "Okay, Markham, I'll see you in ninety minutes at Glendale Air Terminal, but you'd damned well better be on the level with all these shenanigans!"

"I assure you I am, Colonel Smythe. In fact, I suggest you bring along a notebook. You'll want to write down a lot of the details I give you."

"All right. See you soon. Goodbye."

Smythe broke the connection without giving me a chance to say anything further, which was just fine with me because I was completely out of words. I clicked the receiver hook to signal the operator and she instructed me to deposit four more quarters for the additional time I had used. I did so and hung up the receiver.

Turning to Clara, I said, "Smythe went for the deal hook, line and sinker. We meet him at Glendale Air Terminal in ninety minutes."

Clara was staring at me wide-eyed. "We are? I thought sure you were making him so mad he'd tell you to go to hell. You keep amazing me!"

I grinned. "To be honest, I was a little worried about the same thing. What this proves is that I was right about the pressure Smythe's getting from his superiors. I offered him the only way out of this mess he can see, so he really didn't have any choice but to go along with the deal. It also tells me he doesn't have one more thing to go on than he had last Sunday."

Clara stood on tiptoes and gave me another kiss on the cheek. "Eddie, I can't tell you how much better I feel now. Thank you, darling."

I did not mention the possibility that Smythe might be playing a game of his own. That was why I had only given him ninety minutes to get to Glendale. If he intended to try something tricky, that didn't give him much time to set it up.

I said, "Come on, kiddo. Let's grab a quick bite of lunch before we have to get out to the field."

She thought that was a good idea and we found an empty table near the back of the Good Eats Cafe. Clara ordered the soup of the day, chicken noodle, and I ordered the blue plate special, lamb goulash over rice that turned out to be quite tasty. We made quick work of lunch, and by twelve-fifteen Clara and I were on our way to the airfield.

Glendale Air Terminal is located on the north bank of a bend in the Los Angeles River, opposite sprawling Griffith Park on the south side of the river. The field's single runway is paved and runs from the southeast to the northwest with the air services and hangars lined up along the eastern edge of the airfield's property.

We drove onto the field from an unpaved extension of Grandview Avenue and I slowly skirted the eastern perimeter of the field looking for any indication that things were not as they should be. I saw no official vehicles and nothing that seemed out of the ordinary for a weekday afternoon.

The Terminal Cafe at which we were to meet Colonel Smythe was a tiny building sitting in a gap between the field's two smaller hangars and the larger Kinner hangar. Looking for an inconspicuous location from which I could keep an eye on things, I pulled in alongside a few cars parked behind the small hangar closest to the cafe.

A mostly limp windsock atop the Kinner hangar told me there was a slight breeze out of the northwest, which meant arriving ships were landing from the southeast. Our parking spot gave me a clear view of the sky in that direction as well as the tables in front of the Terminal Cafe.

As we watched biplanes from the air services on the field take off and land—mostly student pilots I guessed—I briefed Clara on how I thought we ought to handle the meeting. "The most important thing is keeping an eye on what's going on around the field. If we see anything that looks out of place or unusual, we get out of here fast."

Clara put on her frown. "Do you think Colonel Smythe might try to catch us here or something?"

"I'm not too concerned about anything like that, but I want to have an emergency plan ready to go just in case."

"What should I do if everything looks okay when Smythe shows up?"

"Let's get one thing very clear. I'm not letting you out of my sight for any reason from here on out."

Clara smiled. "That's exactly where I want to be."

"If everything still looks all right when Smythe gets here, I'll pull the car up behind the cafe and turn around so we're pointed in the right direction if we should need to get out of here in a hurry. Then we'll walk around and meet Smythe together.

"I plan to give him the whole story from last Friday on, but I'm going to choose my words carefully because there are some things about all that he doesn't need to know. If Smythe should ask you a question, look at me before answering. I'll nod if I think it's okay to give him a straight answer. If I shake my head, it means don't answer his question directly. And if I think we're getting onto thin ice, I'll intervene. Okay?"

She nodded, but didn't say anything more. I looked at my wristwatch. It was about ten minutes to one. Despite the confidence I expressed to Clara, I was feeling the old, familiar tingles of trepidation I remembered feeling as we took off on a mission in our pursuit ships during the war. It wasn't exactly fear. The feeling was more like a healthy sense of caution.

The day was turning warm, so we rolled the Oldsmobile's side windows down to take advantage of the slight breezes. The ambient sounds of an airfield on a weekday afternoon drifted in on the breeze—the distinctive crackling of a rotary engine, the ringing clatter of a big wrench hitting a concrete hangar floor, the tinny tones of Whispering Jack Smith from a cheap radio in the cafe . . .

Who's wonderful, who's marvelous?
Miss Annabelle Lee.
Who's kissable, who's lovable?
Miss Annabelle Lee.

Suddenly another sound reached my ears—one that made my heart beat a little faster. It was the throaty growl of a mighty V-12 aircraft engine coming from somewhere to the southeast. I stared at the sky in that direction for a few seconds, and then I saw it—a tiny black speck that grew larger and eventually became a sleek Curtiss P-1 Hawk.

I kept my eyes on the ship and before long I could make out its black fuselage and the bright yellow paint on its upper and lower wings, the color scheme used by the Seventeenth Aero Squadron. Further verification of the ship's military identity came with the red and white horizontal stripes on its rudder and the big black letters spelling out U.-S.--A-R-M-Y across the underside of its lower wing. The letters were bracketed by the red, white and blue star roundels recently adopted by the United States armed forces.

Other people on the airfield were also now taking note of the approaching Hawk's unique growl. Two Kinner mechanics stepped outside their hangar and turned their eyes to the southeast. The sound caught Clara's attention, too. She was staring up at it as I said, "That is quite likely to be Colonel Smythe coming in, and he's right on time."

The engine's growl abruptly diminished as the pilot pulled the power off to let his ship settle on the runway. I missed the actual touchdown because the Kinner hangar was in the way, but a few seconds later the P-1 reappeared, turning from the runway to taxi in our direction. With the ship coming toward us head-on, I could clearly see the barrels of its synchronized thirty and fifty caliber machine guns mounted above the bulging engine fairing. Oh, what we would have given for a pursuit ship like the Hawk in France!

The P-1's pilot deftly maneuvered his ship to a point alongside the Kinner hangar and shut off the engine. I scanned the sky around the field, and then the field itself for anything that might hint at trouble. All appeared exactly as it should.

A tall, lanky form stepped out of the Hawk's cockpit onto its lower wing, and from there, to the ground. He chocked the tires using two pairs of bright yellow wooden blocks tied together with a hefty piece of rope. The pilot removed his leather helmet and donned an officer's cap, after which he took a quick look around and headed directly for the Terminal Cafe.

By now there was no doubt that the Hawk's pilot was Colonel Efram Smythe. From the shine of his highly polished knee-high boots to the careful alignment of the Sam Brown Belt over his uniform blouse, Smythe was every inch the personification of an Army Air Corps officer.

He seated himself facing the runway with his back to the cafe. I took one last cautious look around, and seeing nothing to indicate a trap, I started the Oldsmobile's engine and drove over to a spot behind the cafe. After turning the car around so it was pointed toward the field's only exit, I shut off the engine and said, "Okay, kiddo, let's go have our talk with the Colonel."

I walked around the Oldsmobile and opened its passenger door to help Clara out. As she stepped down, I was yet again struck by her beauty. Clara was wearing her new peach-colored dress with the pale blue stripes, and with her off-white cloche hat tipped at a jaunty angle that placed its brim low over her face, she looked absolutely fantastic. Clara took my arm and we set off for our chat with Colonel Smythe.

We were approaching him from behind, so when we were six or seven feet away, I said, "Good afternoon, Colonel Smythe."

He turned, and standing, said, "Hello, Markham."

I said, "You remember Miss Bow."

Making a gentlemanly half-bow in Clara's direction, he said, "I do, indeed. Hello, Miss Bow. I'm pleased to see you again, although I wish we were meeting under more pleasant circumstances."

Turning her irresistible charm up to full volume, Clara said, "I'm pleased to see you, too, Colonel Smythe. And I'm sorry for the inconvenience we've put you to, but I think you'll understand the necessity for our caution once you've heard what Eddie has to say."

Smythe muttered a quiet, "We'll see."

When we were all seated at the table, I kicked things off by saying, "Before we go any further, Colonel, how is Captain Miller doing? The *Times* was rather vague about his condition."

"It seems our Captain is made of stout stuff. He is alive, but still unconscious. The medics seem confident that, given time, he will recover."

"That's good news. I like Miller. Besides, when he is able to talk, he will vouch for some of what I'm about to tell you."

Again, Smythe said, "We'll see."

"Colonel, I think the best place to begin is on the Friday before we boarded your Trimotor to fly west. The whole thing started out at Camp Stanley, north of San Antonio. The motion picture crew had just finished filming scenes of Miss Bow arriving at a mock French village."

I spent the next forty-five minutes or so detailing everything that happened from the strafing attack on Friday to my landing of the Trimotor at March Field Sunday morning. There was no doubt that I had Smythe's attention. He made copious notes in a small notebook as I spoke, and I saw his eyebrows rise in surprise several times during my narration.

When I finished telling the tale, Smythe flipped back through several pages of notes he had made and shook his head. "That's one hell of a story, Markham. And since I have no reason to doubt any of it, I must assume for the moment it is the truth. I only wish you had been more forthcoming in my office Sunday morning."

I fibbed a little, saying, "I would have been, Colonel, but at the time we didn't know that Captain Miller and Lieutenant Jones had been poisoned. Once I learned that, I saw how all these incidents fit together and realized how important this information was to your investigation."

Smythe looked me in the eye for a long moment, as if trying to decide how much of the reason I had given him for not revealing everything I knew during our first conversation was hogwash. I kept a straight face and stared right back at him.

Finally he said, "Okay, Markham, I'll give you the benefit of the doubt on that point." Turning to Clara, he said, "Miss Bow, does what Markham here has told me fit with your recollections of the events?"

Clara glanced at me and I gave her a small nod. She said, "Yes, Colonel, although Eddie's memories are clearer than mine. I don't mind telling you I've been scared out of my wits ever since last Friday."

Smythe nodded. "I can certainly understand that. You've had a harrowing few days." After a momentary pause, he asked, "Can you think of anyone who might be behind all of this? Anyone who would stand to gain something from your . . . ah . . . death."

Again Clara gave me a glance and again I gave her the go-ahead nod. "No, I can't, and believe me; I've given that question a lot of thought. I must have made someone very angry with me, but I can't for the life of me think of what I did or to whom I did it. I wish I could."

"So do I, Miss Bow."

Smythe flipped through his notes again before saying, "Okay, Markham, I believe you've been on the level with me and I will make you the promises you asked for, although there will likely come a time when your testimony and that of Miss Bow will be required, probably in a federal court criminal proceeding."

"We understand that, Colonel, but by that time the danger to Miss Bow's life should be past and there will be no further reason for her to stay out of sight."

Smythe closed his notebook. "All right, in the meantime I'm counting on you to stay in touch. I plan to dispatch a pair of investigating officers to Rimrock first thing in the morning to see if they can learn anything about how that thermos bottle of coffee got laced with arsenic. I should have something on that for you by tomorrow night or Thursday morning.

"I also intend to initiate an inquiry with the Curtiss Aircraft Company into the whereabouts of that XP-Zero-A you think strafed you in Texas. That's a pretty rare bird, so it shouldn't be too difficult to find out what happened to the test models they built. I'm curious, though, what makes you so sure it was a Zero-A?"

"I'm certain that's what it was because I read an article about the ship's development in *Aviation Week* and I remember the ship has a unique box-shaped radiator sticking out from the starboard side of the engine fairing. I've never seen that design used before or since."

Smythe added that comment to his notes. "All right, Markham, unless you have anything else for me, I'll start back for March."

"No, Colonel, that's all I can think of right now. If I come up with anything else, I'll let you know."

Standing and slipping the notebook into his uniform breast pocket, Smythe made a small smile and said, "Miss Bow, I intend to hold you to the promise you made of a special viewing of your motion picture for us."

Clara looked up with a cheerful smile. "And I intend to keep that promise, Colonel."

I said, "Have a safe flight back to March."

He gave me a curt nod and walked briskly back to his Hawk. Clara and I were just leaving the airfield property when we saw Smythe leave the ground and roar into a near vertical climb. He was showing off and I could not blame him. Given the opportunity to fly a ship like that, I would be quite tempted to do the very same thing.

Twenty-Three

2:00 P.M. – Tuesday – September 21, 1926
Glendale

From the airfield we followed San Fernando Road south to Figueroa Street, where we turned right and headed downtown. I went through our meeting with Colonel Smythe in my mind and decided it had gone better than I had any right to expect.

It seemed Clara was not entirely sure of that. "What do you think, Eddie? Did we do the right thing by talking to Colonel Smythe?"

"I'm sure of it. Assuming he keeps his promise, the only ones looking for us at the moment are the killers, and I think we're still a few steps ahead of them. Plus, we have the U.S. Army on our side now, which should make finding out who wants to hurt you a good deal easier."

"So you think he believed what you told him?"

"I think so. He can verify some of it with long-distance telephone calls, so that ought to help our credibility."

Out of the corner of my eye, I noticed Clara was frowning. "What's bothering you, kiddo?"

"I'm not sure. I mean the Colonel was nice enough to me, but he didn't seem very friendly toward you."

"That isn't surprising. I pushed him around pretty hard when I set up our meeting. High-ranking military officers don't take kindly to that sort of thing, especially from civilians. Did you notice that razzle-dazzle takeoff he did? That was Smythe's way of getting a little revenge."

That confused Clara. "What do you mean?"

"He knows damned well that any former pursuit pilot would love to fly a hot ship like that Curtiss Hawk. Smythe was just reminding me that he can and I can't."

"Does that bother you?"

"Not in the least. We got what we wanted out of Smythe, and that is a major victory."

There was a softness in her tone as Clara said, "I'm glad what Smythe did doesn't bother you. I want you to be happy, even when times are tough like they are now. By the way, where are we going?"

"We're going to take care of some business, the first item of which is getting rid of this Oldsmobile."

Sounding puzzled again, Clara said, "How can we do that? Don't we need a car?"

"We definitely need a car, but we've been driving this one too long. I have an idea how we can make a change. I've been thinking about buying myself a fast little coupe to drive when I want something a little quieter and more comfortable than my Stutz roadster."

With surprise, Clara said, "You're going to buy a car?"

"Why not? It's something I've been thinking about for a while and now is as good a time as any. The first step is a stop at my bank to withdraw some cash. That will make the transaction go faster, but first I have to call the dealership to see what they've got and how much it's going to cost. I'll use one of the public telephones in the bank's lobby for that call."

My bank is the headquarters branch of the Security First National Bank in the five-hundred block of Spring Street. I took Figueroa south to Sixth Street, which I followed east to Spring. There I turned left and parked in the first empty spot I came to.

When Clara and I entered the bank, the gilt hands of the big clock on the lobby wall were pointing to two-fifteen. I steered Clara over to the row of public telephone booths against the wall to our right. A directory chained inside the booth provided a number for the Don Lee automobile dealership on Main Street. I dropped a nickel in the slot and dialed the number.

Don Lee owns dealerships all over the state because he is the exclusive Cadillac Motor Car distributor for the west coast. A few of Lee's dealerships also handle other automobile brands. The L.A. dealership, for example, sells Stutz automobiles in addition to Cadillacs, which is how I happened to know a fellow there named James Costello. He is the salesman who sold me my roadster.

The switchboard operator at the dealership put me through to Costello. "Hello, James. This is Eddie Markham. Remember me?"

Costello sounded happy to hear from me. "Of course, Mister Markham. How have you been?"

"Just swell, James, but I need you to help me find another car."

He sounded concerned. "Oh? I trust there's nothing wrong with your Stutz?"

"Oh, it's running fine. What I need is a second car—a fast, solid coupe. I need it in a hurry and I need it to be cheap."

"Does it have to be a new car or can it be something from our used car lot?"

"That will depend on what you've got, but a good used car would probably fit my budget better than a new one."

"Okay, Mister Markham, let me look through our used inventory. Hold on for just a moment."

Silence came over the line for about thirty seconds, and then Costello said, "I think I've got exactly what you're looking for here. It's a 1926 Cadillac 6430 two-passenger coupe. It's one we sold to a fellow when the new models came out during August of 1925.

"The fellow bought it for his son, and the boy only put a few hundred miles on it before he decided he wanted something larger so he could haul his pals around. We took the coupe in trade, and since it is a very low-mileage car and practically new, we use it as a demonstrator to show off the Cadillac V-8 when we have a performance-minded customer. The coupe is much lighter than the other closed Cadillacs, and with eighty-seven horses under the hood, it goes, if you'll pardon the expression, like a bat out of hell."

The car sounded right, so I asked, "How many miles on it now?"

"Less than five-hundred, more like around four-fifty. Does that sound like what you're looking for?"

"Maybe. What color is it? I don't want a car that attracts a lot of attention."

"It's a very conservative pale blue with a black top and fenders. The car also has the optional wire wheels."

"How much?"

Like most salesmen, Costello liked to beat around the bush a little when it came time to quote a price. The idea of the game is to find out what the buyer is willing to pay so the dealership gets the most money possible for the car. He said, "Well, what price range are you thinking of?"

I did not have time to play his game and I let him know it. "I'm in a hurry, James. Just give me the bottom dollar amount you'll take for the car and I'll tell you whether we have a deal or not."

A few more seconds of quiet passed over the line before

Costello said, "Well, Mister Markham, you being a good customer and all, I can let you have it for thirteen-hundred. That's less than half what the coupe sells for new."

Giving Clara a smile and a wink, I said, "I'll give you a grand for it out the door—cash—if you can have the car ready for me to pick up at three o'clock."

Costello took one final shot at increasing the size of his commission. "Gee, Mister Markham, that's an awfully low offer, I don't know if Mister Lee . . . ."

"James, I'm not gonna play this game with you. You know exactly what Lee will take for it because the lowest amount is written right there on the inventory card you're holding in your hand. Deal or not?"

"Okay, Mister Markham. Mister Lee will probably give me hell for this, but you've got a deal."

"Good, you tell Don Lee I said he's already got too much money anyway."

Costello chuckled. "I might have a problem with having it ready for you to pick up by three, though. We have to get your paperwork filled out and, of course, we want to wash the car before you take it."

"James, look in your files and use the information from when I bought the Stutz to fill out your paperwork. Nothing has changed. And don't worry about washing it, just fill up the tank and have it ready to roll as is."

"Okay, Mister Markham, you're the boss. I'll get the paperwork started right now and have a lot boy fill up the tank and check the oil, tires and radiator. See you in about half an hour."

"See you then, James. Goodbye."

Clara was grinning at me when I hung up the telephone receiver. "Wow, Eddie, you drive a hard bargain! For a minute there I thought you were gonna talk him into paying you for taking the car off his hands. What did you buy us?"

Taking Clara by the arm, I headed us toward one of the bank's cashier windows. "It's a slightly used 1926 Cadillac two-passenger coupe. It's a little larger than the Oldsmobile, but it doesn't weigh as much because the body is made of aluminum. Plus, it has more than twice the horsepower."

My favorite cashier at the bank is a young woman named Joyce. I almost always go to her window because she knows me and that usually speeds up whatever transaction I've come in for. Joyce already had a customer at her window.

As we stepped into line behind that customer, Clara asked,

"Yeah, but what about the important stuff? What color is it?"

"Pale blue with a black top and fenders."

"Gee, that sounds kinda dull, Eddie. Didn't they have a red one?"

"I'm sure they could have found something in red, but the idea here is to avoid attention, not attract it. Speaking of which, pull that hat brim down a little. I don't want Joyce recognizing you when we get up to her window."

Pulling her hat brim down, Clara said, "Oh, it's Joyce, is it. You two got somethin' going' on or what?"

"Yeah, we have something going on. She keeps my money safe for me and doles it out when I ask for it. Very sexy stuff."

"Okay, but if I catch her givin' you the eye, I'm gonna conk her one. I'm keepin' you all to myself!"

I smiled, and thinking how good it felt to have the prettiest, most exciting woman in America say she was keeping me all to herself, I said, "I'm gonna hold you to that. Now, when we get up to the window, keep an eye on the people in the bank behind us. If you see anything that doesn't look right, don't hesitate, give me a nudge."

Clara nodded and the fellow in front of us finished whatever business he was there to conduct. As we stepped up to Joyce's window, Clara half-turned and made a show of nonchalantly looking around the bank lobby and Joyce said, "Good afternoon, Mister Markham. How can I help you today?"

"Good afternoon, Joyce. I need to make a withdrawal from my savings account. I've got the book right here."

I handed her the little savings account book I kept in my billfold. She took it and asked, "How much would you want to withdraw?"

Since I had another purchase in mind I hoped to make in the not too distant future, I said, "I think two thousand will do it."

She filled out a withdrawal slip and slid it over for me to sign. "How would you like the money? Would twenty one-hundred-dollar bills be all right or do you need smaller denominations?"

"No, hundreds will be fine, and please slip them into an envelope for me, if you don't mind."

"I would be happy to do that, Mister Markham. I'll just take this over to the manager for approval. It shouldn't take but a minute. I'll be right back with your cash."

I watched as Joyce carried my savings book and the withdrawal slip over to the branch manager's desk and explained the transaction. He glanced up, smiled, and gave me a friendly wave.

We were old chums.

Then he initialed the withdrawal slip and accompanied Joyce into a small room next to the vault. When they came out, she was carrying a white business-sized envelope. Back at her window, she opened the envelope and counted out its contents, twenty one-hundred-dollar bills. After sliding the money back into the envelope, Joyce had me sign on another line of the withdrawal slip and handed the envelope to me. That done, she used one of those adjustable, self-inking gizmos to stamp the date in my savings account book and entered the amount of my withdrawal.

While she did that, I slipped the envelope into my inside coat pocket. Carrying around a large amount of cash like that gave me a second reason for putting up with the Colt pistol that was trying its darnedest to poke a hole in the small of my back.

Finally, Joyce handed me the updated savings account book and said, "After this withdrawal, your balance in this account is fourteen-thousand-three-hundred-and-twenty dollars. Is there anything else I can do for you, Mister Markham?"

Returning the savings book to my billfold, I said, "No, I think that will do it for today. Thanks for your help, Joyce."

She gave me a big, friendly smile. "You're welcome, Mister Markham. And thank you for being a customer of Security First National Bank."

I returned Joyce's smile and we left the bank. Back in the Oldsmobile, Clara asked, "Where to now?"

I looked at my watch. It was two-forty-five. I said, "Well, the dealership is at Twelfth and Main, and there's a Richfield station right where Spring turns into Main, so we'll make a quick stop there and fill the gas tank. We have to return this car with a full tank."

An attendant was already standing at the pump when I pulled into the Richfield station. I asked him to fill the tank, but not to bother with the oil and water. The total for the gas came to one dollar and thirty cents. I gave him the exact amount and pulled out of the station to continue south on Main.

As we drove, I told Clara how I thought we ought to handle picking up the new car and turning in the Oldsmobile. "At the dealership, I'll try to park at the curb instead of pulling into their car lot. When I get out, I want you to lock the doors and slide over behind the steering wheel.

"If James has the paperwork ready, we shouldn't be there for more than fifteen minutes. When I drive the new car off the lot, follow me. We'll drive a few blocks away and park so we can move the luggage and swap cars."

"Swap cars? You mean you're going to let me drive your new car?"

I looked over at Clara to see if she was trying to be funny. Her expression was entirely serious. "Why wouldn't I let you drive it?"

She shrugged a little. "I don't know. Some men are kind of strange about things like that. I promise I'll drive very carefully."

I reached over and gave her hand a squeeze. "Kiddo, I have no problem with you driving my car or anything else you might want to do, so forget about that nonsense."

Clara gave me a kiss on the cheek and I turned right onto Twelfth Street. The dealership was near the corner, but on the other side of the street. Since there wasn't much traffic, I made a U-turn and pulled up in front of a two-story brick building with a huge sign proclaiming that we had arrived at Don Lee Cadillac.

Twenty-Four

3:00 P.M. – Tuesday – September 21, 1926
Don Lee Cadillac Dealership – Los Angeles

On its left side, the Don Lee Cadillac dealership building was bordered by a large paved lot, and near the front of that lot sat a shiny pale blue and black coupe. I pulled the Oldsmobile forward and parked at the curb just opposite the Cadillac. Turning to Clara, I said, "I'll make this as quick as I can and I'll keep an eye on you the whole time we're here. Leave the engine running, and if you see anything that worries you, pull the car right onto the dealership lot and push the horn button long and hard. Okay?"

She took a nervous look around. "Okay, Eddie. Please hurry."

"What's wrong, honey?"

"I don't know. Suddenly I'm afraid to be more than three feet away from you. I was okay in Ventura, but here . . . I don't know, I guess I'm just a big fraidy-cat."

I took her hand. "I understand. I'd rather not leave you out here, but I'm trying to keep you out of sight as much as possible. At the bank, it was unavoidable, but here I can watch you from inside. Would you feel better if you came into the dealership with me?"

Clara shook her head emphatically. "No. We have to do this right. I can handle it, honest I can. Just hurry, okay?"

I looked into her big brown eyes and saw fear there. Seeing that fear made me want to hit whoever was putting it there very hard. I said, "Okay, kiddo. I'll be back before you know it."

After Clara locked the car doors and slid behind the steering wheel I turned and walked toward the dealership entrance. James Costello met me at the door, saying, "Good afternoon, Mister Markham. Your new car is all ready to go and so is the paperwork.

Would you like to take a look at the car?"

"Yes, James. I saw where it was parked in the lot. Why don't you bring the paperwork out while I look the car over. Then we can just complete our business right there."

Costello looked at me a little oddly, but said, "Okay, Mister Markham, however you'd like to do it. I'll get the papers and meet you out there in a minute."

I stepped back outside and walked down the sidewalk toward the lot. Passing Clara on the way, I gave her a wave. She waved back.

The Cadillac coupe looked brand new, despite having already been driven four or five hundred miles. Walking around it, I couldn't find so much as a scratch in the paint. I lifted one side of the hood and looked at the nearly four-hundred cubic inch V-8 engine. There wasn't an oil smudge anywhere on it. Don Lee's people knew how to prepare a car for delivery.

I was just closing the hood when Costello came out with a sheaf of papers in his left hand. "How does she look?"

"Looks like a brand new car."

"Would you like to take it for a spin before we sign the papers?"

"No, James, I don't have time for that. I'll take your word that it runs well."

"Okay, Mister Markham, let's get these forms signed so you can get on the road. Ah ... do you have the money?"

I slipped the Security First National Bank envelope from my inside coat pocket and counted out ten hundred dollar bills for him. "Here you go."

Costello counted the bills, and then slipped them into one of his side coat pockets. Handing me three pages labeled Automobile Purchase Contract, he said, "There are three copies of the purchase agreement. I've signed all three of them on behalf of the dealership. All you have to do is sign the top two. The third copy is yours to keep. Here's a pen."

I took the fountain pen he offered and quickly read the contract form. It described the car being purchased in detail, including its vehicle identification number. The form also described the terms of the purchase. The total price was shown as one thousand dollars. Below that, a down payment amount, also one thousand dollars, had been entered. At the bottom of the form there was a zero on the line for remaining balance owed.

After taking another quick glance to see that Clara was okay, I signed the top two copies and handed them back to Costello. I kept the pen in my hand because I knew there was more to come.

Next he handed me a three-part form entitled California Department of Motor Vehicles, Vehicle Ownership Transfer Request. Costello said, "Two copies of this one go to the DMV and we file one here for safekeeping. You need to sign all three copies."

After checking to be sure all the information was correct, I quickly signed the forms and returned them to Costello. Finally, he handed me a four-inch by five-inch card labeled, "Temporary Vehicle Registration." James said, "This is your temp registration. Carry it and the sales contract with you in the car until your permanent registration card arrives by mail.

"Since the car has already been registered, it has a license plate, so you aren't like to be stopped by the police for a registration question, but if you are, that card and your sales contract will prove you legally own the car. Do you have any questions about the forms we've signed?"

I said, "No," and handed Costello his pen.

He reached into his trouser pocket and brought out a gold key ring with two keys and a gold disk on it. The gold disk was inscribed with the famous Cadillac emblem. Costello handed me the key ring and said, "Congratulations, Mister Markham, you are now a Cadillac owner!"

I took the keys and said, "Thank you for taking care of all this promptly, James. I appreciate it and I'm sure you'll be seeing me again the next time I need an automobile."

He smiled broadly as we shook hands. "Thank you for your business, Mister Markham. Don Lee and I appreciate it."

Sliding onto the Cadillac's seat from the driver's side, I noted that the dashboard layout, though a good deal fancier, was essentially the same as that of the Oldsmobile. From this, I guessed the engine starting procedure might also be the same and gave it a try. My effort was rewarded by the healthy, but quiet, rumble of the Cadillac's big V-8 engine.

I threw James Costello a salute and pulled off Don Lee's lot, turning right onto Twelfth Street. In the rearview mirror I saw Clara pull out right behind me in the Oldsmobile. At the corner, I turned left on Main, and a block later, I made another left onto Eleventh Street.

The neighborhood through which we were driving was roughly half commercial and half residential. Up ahead I spotted a vacant lot and pulled to the curb next to it. Clara pulled in right behind me.

We both got out of our cars and Clara ran up and hugged me for all she was worth, saying, "I'm sorry I was so afraid back there, Eddie. I just . . . ."

"You have no reason to apologize, and you did just fine. Let's get the bags swapped so we can turn in the Oldsmobile and get on to other things. While I move the bags, would you please take a look around inside the passenger compartment and the trunk to be sure we aren't leaving anything behind? Oh, and give me the keys so I can unlock the trunk."

Clara said, "Sure," and dropped the Oldsmobile's keys into my hand.

While I carried our bags over and set them into the Cadillac's slightly roomier trunk, Clara did a thorough job of checking for items we might have forgotten. By the time I had the Cadillac trunk lid closed and locked, she had finished the task.

"Besides your overnight case, which is still behind the seat, the only thing I found was this."

She held up the Ventura County map I'd gotten at the gas station in Santa Paula. I didn't think we'd be needing it, but I saw no sense in leaving any clues behind as to where we had been. I pulled my overnight case out and set it on the Oldsmobile's driver seat. I dropped the map inside and removed another sixty dollars of Bill Wellman's money from the Hotel Saint Anthony envelope. Then I snapped the case closed and pushed it over to the passenger side of the seat.

Turning to Clara, I handed her the Cadillac's gold-plated key ring. She held it up and the late afternoon sun glinted off of the engraved fob. "Wow, snazzy!"

From her grin, I gathered she was pleased that we now had transportation that came closer to what she had referred to as "sassy" back in Riverside. Holding the keys tightly in her right hand, Clara said, "Okay, where do we have to go to turn in the car?"

"According to the directory in the bank's telephone booth, the nearest office of the Hertz Drive-Ur-Self System is on Figueroa between Sixth and Seventh Streets, so we can just continue out Eleventh until we hit Figueroa in about five blocks. Then we turn right and the car rental place should only be about four blocks further. Okay?"

Clara nodded. "Do you want to do it the same way we did it at the dealership? I mean, do you want me to wait for you in the car?"

"That would be the simplest way, if it's okay with you."

"I'll be fine, Eddie."

"Good. You can leave the engine idling and don't forget to lock the doors. Okay, kiddo, let's get this done."

I kept a close eye on the mirror again to make sure Clara wasn't having any trouble with the Cadillac. She wasn't. In fact, she drove it like a pro.

The Hertz office was right where it was supposed to be, and I drove directly onto the small lot in front. Then I removed the rental car agreement from my overnight case and stepped down from the Oldsmobile.

Clara was already at the curb. As I walked toward her, she slid over and unlocked the passenger side door. I handed her the overnight case, saying, "I won't need this in there, so please slip it behind the seat."

"Sure." She did as I requested, then locked the passenger door and slid back behind the wheel to wait for me.

I gave her a wave and turned toward the agency office. As I did so, a young fellow came out and said, "Good afternoon, how can I help you?"

Gesturing toward the Oldsmobile, I said, "I rented that coupe in Riverside a few days ago and I'd like to turn it in here, if I may."

"Certainly. Do you have your copy of the rental agreement with you?"

Handing him the paperwork and the car keys, I said, "Right here."

"Good. Go on inside the office and make yourself comfortable while I jot down the mileage on your form."

I waited for him at the office door, not wanting to get too far from Clara before I had to. The agent walked around the car, carefully examining it for damage. Finding none, he opened the driver-side door, read the mileage from the odometer, and wrote it on the rental agreement form.

Inside at his desk, the fellow did some arithmetic and entered the numbers on the rental agreement. When he was all done, he said, "You drove a total of two-hundred and twenty-eight miles. At eleven cents per mile, that comes to twenty-five dollars and eight cents. Then we add the ten dollar fee for returning the car here, and we get a total of thirty-five-oh-eight. We subtract that from your fifty dollar deposit and I owe you fourteen dollars and ninety-two cents."

I turned from watching Clara and said, "That sounds about right."

He removed a small tin money box from his desk drawer and began to count out my refund. I said, "If you have them, would you mind giving me three of those dollars in quarters? I have some long-distance telephone calls to make in a while."

Smiling, the fellow said, "I wouldn't mind at all." He gave me a ten dollar bill, a single, and three-dollars and ninety-two cents in coins. "Now I just need to enter all this information onto another form for the company copy. It will only take me a minute, and then I can give you your completed copy of the rental agreement back and you can be on your way."

"That's fine. Would you mind if I waited for you out in front?"

"Not at all. I'll be just a few minutes."

As I walked out to the Cadillac, Clara saw me coming and slid over to the passenger side of the seat. I rapped on the window and she rolled it down.

"We have to wait a minute or two for the guy to fill out another form, and then we can get out of here. And you might as well drive us to our next stop, which will be the nearest public telephone. I need to make a couple calls before we leave Los Angeles."

Clara grinned at me. "You really are living dangerously, letting me drive with you actually in the car!"

I winked at her. "I'm not worried. There should be a telephone someplace in the next few blocks. I don't think you can get us into too much trouble in that short distance."

She gave me an evil grin and said, "Don't be so sure. You'd be surprised what kind of trouble I can get into when I set my mind on it. Oh, oh, here comes your guy."

Handing me my copy of the rental agreement, the fellow said cheerfully, "Here you go, Mister Markham. Thank you for your business and for taking good care of our automobile. I hope you'll rent from the Hertz Drive-Ur-Self System again the next time you need a car."

Promising I would do just that, I climbed into the Caddy and closed the door. Clara slipped the transmission lever into low gear and pulled smoothly back into the light traffic on Figueroa Street.

Figueroa is a main north-south route that skirts the western edge of the downtown area. As such, it is home to several lower-priced hotels. There were two such hostelries in the next block, the Clinton and the Carlton. The Clinton was on our side of the street and had a convenient parking lot next door. Since hotels almost always have public telephones, I asked Clara to pull into the Clinton's lot. We parked the Cadillac and walked back to the hotel's street entrance. The Clinton had two telephone booths in its lobby. I stepped into one of them, dropped a nickel into the slot, and dialed my office number. I hadn't talked to Elsie, my secretary since leaving for Texas, and I was anxious to find out if she had heard from my New York publisher about the manuscript we had sent for his consideration.

The line rang six times with no answer. Glancing at my watch, I saw that it was already after four o'clock. With me away, Elsie had little to do, so I guessed she probably left the office a little early, perhaps to do some shopping.

I clicked the receiver hook to retrieve my nickel and reinserted it to make another call. This time I dialed my next door neighbor in Silver Lake. Jimmy, the boy I was paying to water my yard and keep an eye on things in my absence, answered the call. I said, "Hello, Jimmy, this is Eddie Markham."

"Oh, hello, Mister Markham. Are you back from Texas?"

"Not yet, Jimmy. I'll be gone a little longer. I just thought I would give you a call and see how things were at home."

"Everything is just fine here, Mister Markham. I've been watering your yard about every other day and I have all your mail in a cardboard box for you when you get back."

"Great. Anything else going on?"

Jimmy thought about the question for a moment and said, "Well, you did have a visitor yesterday while I was over watering. He said he was a friend of yours and was wondering if you were back from your trip yet. I told him you weren't and that I didn't know for sure when you would get back."

That somebody stopped by for a visit was unusual. Most of my friends call before they show up on my doorstep. I asked, "Did he give you his name?"

"No, sir. He just said he would check back in a few days."

"What did this fellow look like?"

"Well, he was a younger guy, kind of thin, and he had blonde hair that was kind of long and messed up. You know, not combed very neatly."

Staring absently through the hotel's front window, I mentally reviewed the list of friends who might stop by for a visit, and came up with no one matching that description. Faint alarm bells began going off somewhere in my head and I thought of another question to ask.

"Jimmy, what sort of car was this fellow driving?"

"Oh, it wasn't fancy or anything, just a four-door Chevrolet sedan. I think it was gray with black fenders."

It took my brain maybe three seconds to make the connection, but when the gears finally matched up and fell into place, the faint alarm bells I had been hearing went to full volume. Outside, parked at the curb in front of the Clinton Hotel, was a gray and black four-door Chevrolet sedan.

I couldn't see the driver, but I could see small clouds of exhaust smoke coming from the car's tailpipe. Whoever was in that car was waiting for someone. I had a bad feeling that I knew exactly who he was waiting for.

Jimmy's voice in the receiver said, "Mister Markham, are you still there?"

"Ah . . . yes, Jimmy, I'm still here. Sorry, something distracted me. It sounds as if you've got everything under control there. I'll give you a call in a few days and let you know when I'll be back."

"Okay, Mister Markham, that'll be fine. Have a safe trip home."

"Thanks, Jimmy, I will. Goodbye."

I replaced the receiver on its hook and distinctly heard my nickel fall into the telephone's coin box. Clara was sitting in a slightly threadbare armchair sandwiched in between the telephone booth and the lobby's front wall. I stepped out of the booth and said, "Clara, come over here."

She read something in my expression that put a frown on her face and quickly stepped to my side. "What's wrong, Eddie?"

"Turn around and take a look at that car out at the curb. Have you ever seen it before?"

Clara turned and stared out the front window. "You mean the gray and black one?"

"Yes."

She stared at the Chevrolet for another moment before turning back to me. "No, Eddie, I don't remember seeing that car before. Why?"

"I was talking to Jimmy, the next door neighbor's kid who is taking care of my yard while I'm gone, and he just told me I had a visitor yesterday—a fellow who didn't leave his name, but was driving a gray and black Chevrolet sedan just exactly like that one."

Clara's eyes were showing fear again. "Do you think that car is following us?"

"I'm sure there are many gray and black Chevrolet sedans in Los Angeles, but having one show up at my home and then here is an awfully big coincidence."

"What should we do?"

When we parked in the hotel parking lot I had noticed a side entrance to the hotel. Looking across the lobby, I spotted a narrow hallway I thought might end at that door. I said, "Come on, we're gonna get out of here by the side entrance."

Clara grabbed my arm and we quickly crossed the lobby to the hallway. I had been right about it leading to the side entrance, but when we stepped into the parking lot, the impromptu plan I had been counting on fell apart. I had hoped the parking lot went all the way through to the next block, or at least through to a service alley, but it did not. The only way in or out of the parking lot was the way we had come in from Figueroa Street.

The only advantage we had left was that the driver of the Chevrolet could not see us in the lot, but he would definitely see us leave. There was no way around that. I saw only two options open to us. One was to walk around and confront the guy in the Chevrolet. Doing that would allow me to see if he fit Jimmy's description of the visitor who had come by my house. That would be good to know, but confronting the guy could cause him to panic and do something rash.

The only other option was to drive out of the parking lot bold as brass and then try to lose the Chevrolet if it followed us. Clara was hanging onto my arm and watching me intently, waiting for me to tell her what to do. I said, "Come on, kiddo, let's get to the car."

She said nothing and trotted off ahead of me to the Cadillac's passenger door. I helped her in and went around to the other door. Once behind the wheel, I started the engine and said, "The only choice we've got is to drive out of here and see if the sedan follows us. If it does, we'll find a way to lose the guy. We've got plenty of horsepower on our side, so we should be able to leave him in our dust when we get out of the downtown traffic."

Again Clara said nothing. I could almost feel her fear and I wanted to make it go away. I backed out of the parking lot, pointed the Cadillac toward Figueroa Street, and took a deep breath.

Twenty-Five

4:15 P.M. – Tuesday – September 21, 1926
Figueroa Street – Los Angeles

Leaving the Clinton Hotel parking lot I turned right onto Figueroa. Before we got to the end of the block my rearview mirror showed the gray and black Chevrolet pulling away from the curb behind us.

As we crossed Fifth Street I said, "It looks like he's following us, all right."

Clara started to turn around for a look out the Cadillac's back window, but I stopped her. "Don't look back. I don't want him to know we're wise to him quite yet. If he thinks we don't know we're being followed, he might get careless and give us a chance to get a look at him."

With a strong note of concern in her voice, Clara said, "I thought you were going to try to lose him."

"Yes, we're going to lose him and I know just where to do it, but until we get there, I'm going to take it easy and see what he does."

Clara was quiet for a few blocks, but as we crossed First Street, she said, "What I want to know is how the devil did he find us?"

"That's a very good question, especially since he found us within the past twenty-four hours."

"How do you know that?"

"When he showed up at my place in Silver Lake about this time yesterday, the guy asked Jimmy questions like was I back from my trip yet? He didn't know where we were then, but he does now."

"Well, he didn't find us in this big city by accident! Who could have told him where we were? We haven't seen anybody who knows us since we left Ventura this morning, except . . . ."

"Colonel Smythe."

She sounded skeptical. "You think Colonel Smythe told him?"

"Probably not, but someone listening into our telephone conversation or whoever Smythe told he was meeting us in Glendale certainly could have passed the information on."

Clara was as much angry as she was afraid. "Oh, hell! This is getting worse and worse!"

Thinking back to my conversation with Jimmy, I said, "We do have a rough description of the fellow who showed up at my place. Jimmy said the guy was young, slender, and had longish blonde hair that was unkempt. Does that description fit anyone that you know?"

She looked thoughtful for a moment, and then said, "No, not that I can think of."

"It's possible that we've never laid eyes on whoever is in that Chevrolet back there, but given the fact that he or whoever he works for knows so much about you, I'd bet a buck we know him, or that we've at least seen him around."

Four blocks later we arrived at the intersection of Figueroa and Sunset and I turned left. The sedan was two cars behind us and got stuck in traffic at the intersection's four-way arterial stop. He was there long enough that I could have turned onto a side street and lost the guy right then and there, but I stayed on Sunset.

When he caught up again, he passed a couple of cars and moved right up behind us. The guy knew he had come close to losing us and he was not taking anymore chances. Now he was close enough that I could make out the shape of a face through his windshield, but I still could not see his features clearly enough to recognize him, assuming I had seen him somewhere before.

"Is he still back there?"

"He is, except now he's staying closer to us. Either he thinks we're not paying attention, or he just doesn't care whether we know he's behind us or not."

"I don't like this. How much further before you can lose him?"

"Not much."

We reached the Y-intersection where Sunset meets Hollywood Boulevard. I had a choice of veering right on Sunset or continuing straight on Hollywood Boulevard. I continued straight and the gray and black sedan followed along like an obedient puppy. We were now going through the central business district of Hollywood, and with all the jaywalking pedestrians, pokey streetcars, and impatient automobile drivers, we slowed to a crawl.

After crossing La Brea, though, the congestion thinned and we got moving again. In just a few more blocks Laurel Canyon

Boulevard would intersect Hollywood Boulevard, and that's where I intended to leave Mister Chevrolet in our dust.

When I saw the intersection coming up, I said, "Okay, kiddo, hang on. The ride is about to get bumpy."

Clara braced herself against the passenger door as I turned the steering wheel hard right and the Cadillac swung its nose onto Laurel Canyon. We were heading up into the Hollywood hills with roughly a quarter-mile of straight residential street ahead before Laurel Canyon Boulevard began zig-zagging its way up through the steep canyon for which it was named.

My plan was to use that quarter-mile to quickly put some distance between us and the Chevrolet. I pressed down more firmly on the throttle and the Caddy's V-8 responded with an immediate burst of acceleration. Unfortunately, the guy in the sedan anticipated my move and did the same thing, staying right on our tail.

I stomped down harder on the foot-feed and we began to pull away from the sedan. A quick glance in the rearview mirror as we approached the first curve, a ninety-degree right, showed a gap of at least fifty feet between us.

Then we were hard into the curve. I felt the Caddy's rear tires hop a little to the left midway through the turn. I was close to the limit of the tires' ability to maintain traction on the concrete roadway.

Coming out of the curve, I put the throttle down firmly and the big V-8 gave us a good burst of acceleration up the grade. We were now in a dense thicket of manzanita and oak which turned sunlight into shadows and made visibility difficult. When I saw the Chevrolet in my mirror again we had opened up the gap between us and the pursuing sedan to nearly a hundred feet. Progress!

The next curve was a wide sweeper to the left, as I positioned the Cadillac to take the turn, an after image of what I had just seen in the rearview mirror flashed in my mind. The guy had his left arm out the side window. I was pondering this strange behavior when a popping sound followed by a sharp "ping" solved the mystery.

I shouted, "Clara, get down on the floorboard! He's got a gun!"

She moved without hesitation, pushing herself off the seat and sliding down into the foot well. At nearly the precise moment she responded to my warning, I heard another "pop." This time the gunshot was followed by a flat "crunch."

The sweeping left turn was fairly well banked, but it was

immediately followed by a sharp turn to the right. The Caddy took the left turn like it was on rails and I stomped hard on the brake pedal to slow us down for the right turn.

I heard another pop, but I was too busy to worry about where that slug went. The Caddy's rear tires were screeching loudly on the concrete as we entered the right turn and I felt our rear end slide sharply to the left. The Cadillac was still surging forward with enough momentum to straighten us out again. With a swerve, we exited the turn onto a straight uphill section of road that looked to be about three-hundred feet long.

I pushed the throttle to the floor and chanced another glance into the rearview mirror. The first thing I saw there was a new spider web of cracks surrounding a neat hole in the passenger side of the back glass.

Beyond that I saw the nose of the Chevrolet sedan rounding the hard right turn, but it didn't look right. The sedan was in a sideways slide to the left—a slide that ended against the sturdy trunk of a large oak tree on the left shoulder of the road. In that moment I knew the chase was over. The tree trunk damned near folded the sedan in half.

Backing off the throttle, I said, "Clara, are you okay?"

A quiet "yes" came back from the foot well. I said, "It's okay now. He's done. You can get back onto the seat."

Clara pulled herself up out of the foot well and from the corner of my eye I watched her touch the hole in the back glass with a finger. That made me wonder where the slug had ended up. She showed me by next putting her finger against a tear in the gray cloth headliner up near the windshield.

My mind drew an imaginary line connecting the holes. That line went right through Clara's head. If she had been a split-second slower to move, the bullet would have hit her square in the back of the head. The guy had gotten off a very lucky shot, but our luck had been just a little better.

Clara placed a trembling hand on my right leg, and I held it whenever I could let go of the steering wheel for any length of time between curves. A few minutes later she turned in the seat and looked out the back window.

In an unsteady voice she said, "Are you sure he's not chasing us anymore?"

"I'm sure, honey. He tried to take that curve too fast and slid out of the turn into an oak tree trunk that nearly cut his car in half. We're okay now."

She made no reply, but I felt the trembling in her hand

gradually subside as we continued at a leisurely pace through the thick forests of foliage bordering on both sides of the road. Soon the brief flashes of sunlight that made it through gaps in the trees became longer and more frequent, and after a few more curves, we reached the top of the hill where Laurel Canyon Boulevard dead-ends at Mulholland Drive.

We had only gone a few hundred feet after I turned left onto Mulholland when Clara suddenly said, "Eddie, can we please stop for a minute?"

The tone of her voice sounded anxious, so I pulled off into a wide spot on the shoulder of the road and Clara quickly opened the door and jumped down from her seat. By the time I got around to her side of the car, she was on her hands and knees vomiting violently. I knelt next to Clara and put my arm around her waist to steady her. I could still feel her slim body shudder from the fierce spasms long after she had nothing left to vomit.

When her horrible gagging finally diminished, I handed Clara my handkerchief and helped her to her feet. She leaned against me and I held her close. After a time, Clara looked up at me.

"Eddie, I'm so sorry. I just couldn't . . . ."

I shushed her. "It's okay. We're all right."

Now sobs were shaking her body. "Eddie, I don't think I can take much more of this."

Stroking the back of her head, I said, "I know. You've shown a lot more courage than most women or men, for that matter, would have had in the same situation. I honestly believe we're very close to getting the answers that will bring all this to an end. Will you try to hang on a little longer?"

Clara looked up at me again. "I will if I can hang on to you."

"You can. We're in this together and we're going to get out of it together."

I helped her back into the Cadillac and walked around to the driver-side door. As I climbed behind the wheel, I looked off to the south and saw a panorama that stretched all the way to the Pacific Ocean. The sun was very near setting and lights in the buildings and along the roads below were beginning to twinkle in the gathering dusk. Under different circumstances it would have been pleasant to sit there and watch the sunset. Instead, I slipped the Caddy's shift lever into first gear and pulled back onto Mulholland Drive.

Mulholland runs east and west along the crest of the Santa Monica Mountains. It begins at the Cahuenga Pass above Hollywood and ends at the coast highway. In that distance,

Mulholland is intersected by only a few crossroads, the last of which was Sepulveda Boulevard, a main north-south artery carrying traffic in and out of the San Fernando Valley through a pass in the mountains.

When we got to Sepulveda I turned south and we drove down out of the Santa Monica Mountains. In an effort to take Clara's mind off of what had just happened and get her thinking about other things, I said, "I guess we should talk about where we go from here. First we need to find a safe place to stay for a night or two."

Sounding understandably glum, Clara's little girl voice said, "Where can we do that?"

"I have an idea. How would you like to go to Ocean Park?"

In a slightly brighter tone, she said, "Oh, I've been there. That's the place with the amusement piers and the ballrooms where they have those crazy dance marathon contests. But won't there be a lot of people there?"

"That's part of my idea. If we play like just another couple of tourists, we might fit right in and nobody will pay any attention to us. Besides, the summer season is almost over, so the place shouldn't be too crowded on a weekday night."

"Okay, maybe all the music and lights will cheer us up a little."

Ocean Park is squeezed into a narrow space along the beach between Santa Monica and Venice, and its primary reason for existence is fun. The attractions provided for that purpose include broad beaches and three or four long piers jammed packed with a variety of amusements, including carousels, roller coasters, whip rides, and every sort of concession imaginable, from skill games to an endless array of food stands. The area is also home to several large ballrooms where tourists dance the night away to the music of well-known orchestras.

During the summer months vast hoards of fun seekers drive, take streetcars, or ride Southern Pacific trains from all over southern California to bask in the sun and partake of the many pleasures available in Ocean Park. In short, the place is a highly profitable tourist Mecca.

As one might imagine, many of those tourists choose to spend entire weekends frolicking in Ocean Park, so there are numerous hotels and auto courts provided for their convenience. It was in one of those hostelries that I planned on us staying for the next night or two, hopefully camouflaged as fun-seekers enjoying one last fling before the summer came to an end.

We followed Sepulveda Boulevard south past Westwood and

into West Los Angeles, where I turned right onto Pico Boulevard. Pico took us right up to Ocean Avenue, the north-south thoroughfare that runs right along next to the beaches. I turned south on Ocean and a few blocks later we entered the carnival world of Ocean Beach.

By this time Clara had perked up considerably and she seemed to be delighting in the bright lights and colorful ambiance around us. With the Cadillac's windows down, a cacophony of shouted enticements from barkers along the sidewalk, the clatter of roller coasters, and gay music played by carousel calliopes washed over us. Along with the sights and sounds came a variety of interesting scents carried along by gentle sea breezes. The smells of popcorn, hot dogs and fried fish reminded me that dinner time was rapidly approaching. I decided, however, that finding safe lodgings for the night was our first priority.

With that in mind, I turned east on a main drag called Pier Street—a manmade canyon of hotels and auto courts. In the second block up from Ocean, I spotted what I thought might be our best choice, one of the classier auto courts with a cute name: The Tides Inn. After turning into their drive and stopping in front of an office with a brightly flashing "vacancy" sign, I told Clara to lock the car doors and sit tight for a minute while I made arrangements for our accommodations.

As I entered the office, a cuckoo clock on the wall behind the counter announced the hour by chirping six times. On the sixth chirp a blonde woman wearing a shiny red dress, dangling earrings that nearly brushed her shoulders, and too much makeup came through a door next to the cuckoo.

She smiled what was probably meant to be a welcoming smile and said, "Good evening, sir. How can I help you?"

"I'd like to rent a room."

"Certainly, sir. How many are in your party?"

"Just my wife and me."

"And how long will you be staying with us?"

"One or two nights. We haven't decided exactly how long we'll be here yet."

"Well, we'll make it just for tonight then, but there should be no problem if you decide to stay longer. This is the beginning of our off-season, so we have plenty of rooms available."

The woman picked up a map of The Tides Inn, and showing it to me, said, "Would you prefer a cottage nearer the back or one up front?"

The map showed a U-shaped layout very similar to the Casa del

Pacifico, except there appeared to be fifteen cottages instead of nine. I said, "I think up front would be better for us. In fact, if the cottage directly across from the office is available, that would work very nicely."

"Yes, sir. That's cottage number one and it's vacant. Our cottages rent for eight dollars a night, payable in advance."

"That's fine."

She pushed a slightly threadbare cloth-covered registration book across the counter and asked me to write down my information. Under the name column I wrote "Mr. & Mrs. Jerome Miller" and in the address column I wrote "Santa Barbara, Calif."

The woman in the red dress turned the registration book around and read what I had written. "From Santa Barbara? That's always been one of my favorite places."

Placing a five-dollar bill and three ones on the counter, I said, "Yes, we're fond of it."

The woman scooped up my eight dollars and filled out a receipt, which she handed me along with a brass key from which dangled a cardboard tag that identified the key as being for cottage number one. "Here's your receipt and your room key. I hope you enjoy your stay at The Tides Inn."

I pocketed the receipt and key. "Thank you, I'm sure we will."

Outside, Clara opened the driver-side door for me and I slid in. She asked, "All set?"

"We are." Pointing across the gravel drive, I added, "We're in number one over there. It will probably be noisier than one of the cottages at the back of the court, but being up close to the street makes it more difficult for anyone to bother us, and easier for us to leave in a hurry, if that became necessary."

Clara nodded. "Makes sense. Let's hurry and take our bags in so we can get something to eat. I'm hungry."

I started the Caddy and pulled across the drive, backing into a parking space alongside our cottage. The gravel drive and lack of a carport were more typical of most auto courts than the nicer arrangement at the Casa del Pacifico. The greenery was also sparser. There were, however, strings of festive colored bulbs hanging between poles lining the drive.

I handed Clara the key and my overnight case from behind the seat, and she trotted off to open the cottage door, while I got our bags out of the trunk. As I unlocked the trunk, I noticed a small groove of shiny aluminum in the trunk lid's paint. I now knew where the first bullet fired at us on Laurel Canyon Boulevard ended up. It had ricocheted off of the trunk lid. It was a dramatic reminder of how close we had come to a bad end.

Cottage number one was smaller than our bungalow at the Casa del Pacifico, and the furnishings were not nearly as nice. The room layout was nearly the same, though, except that there was no large window with a view, and instead of a closet, this room had a large armoire with double doors. The only other difference I noticed was an advantage from my point of view. The bathroom was equipped with a combination tub/shower. I much prefer showers over tub baths.

The cottage walls were painted a rather unattractive shade of pale green and the bedspread was a darker green that was not particularly in harmony with the walls. The curtains were either an off-white or filthy. I did not care to see which it was.

I set our suitcases on the bed next to my overnight case and locked the door. Clara was standing beside the bed looking rather forlorn. I put an arm around her waist and said, "What's bothering you, kiddo?"

Leaning against me, she answered, "Oh, nothing, really. I guess I'm just a little disappointed in this place after the Casa del Pacifico. But I would probably feel the same way about any room now. Our time in Ventura was so wonderful, and this place seems . . . well, just shabby and cheap."

"You're right, although, I must say the cheap part doesn't extend to the room rates here. This room is costing us five bucks a night more than the Casa del Pacifico."

Clara suddenly turned and threw her arms around me. "I'm sorry, darling. I love you with all my heart and I want everything to be wonderful and magical for us, but I can't make that happen. That's what's really bothering me."

I took her face between my hands and looked into her big brown eyes. They were full of love and tears. "Clara, I love you, too, and our magic is still there. It's just hiding from all of the bad things that have been happening to us."

With a sob, she said, "Do you really think so, Eddie?"

"I know so. And when we put an end to all those bad things once and for all, we'll find our magic still there, waiting for us. That's when we can start making those dreams we've been talking about come true."

"Oh, Eddie, I want that more than anything in the world!"

"Then that's exactly what we're going to do. So just keep remembering those dreams when things get tough like they were today. There are probably more of those tough times ahead, but together we'll make it through them."

Clara rested her head against my chest and I held her tight. In order to raise her spirits, I had just made a big promise, and it was a promise I was determined to keep.

Twenty-Six

6:15 P.M. – Tuesday – September 21, 1926
Ocean Park, Santa Monica

After helping Clara slip into her new off-white jacket with the belt, she adjusted my fedora at a rakish angle which, she assured me, would have all the gals swooning the moment they set eyes on it. Then we locked my overnight case in the Caddy's trunk and set off down Pier Street toward the bright lights of the amusement piers.

Pier Street dead-ends at the piers, which are spread out along a cross street called the Ocean Front Walk. We flipped a coin and turned left toward the southernmost of the three or four piers. On the way we passed Jones' Fun Palace, a roller skating rink, and two theaters.

Just beyond the theaters we turned right onto what a large sign told us was the Lick Pier. The beach on our left was mostly deserted, probably owing to the damp chill brought in by a fog bank that arrived just after sunset.

On our right was a string of small concession buildings, including a place called Alber's Waffle House. I was just thinking that a waffle smothered in maple syrup with a sausage or two might make a good dinner when Clara spotted another sign three doors down and said excitedly, "Oh, look! Chop suey! Have you ever had chop suey, Eddie?"

"No, that's one culinary delight I've managed to avoid."

Grabbing my hand she took off toward the chop suey joint. "Then come on! You're gonna love this!"

Thinking that was unlikely, I let her drag me along into a small restaurant with a dozen or so tables, about half of which were occupied. For atmosphere there were strings of faded paper lanterns hanging from the ceiling and a few cheap prints of scenes in China decorating the walls. So far I was not impressed.

A fellow who was decidedly not Chinese, but wore a high-collared black Chinese shirt with red trim bid us welcome and seated us at a table for two close to one of the front windows. After setting menus in front of us, he promised to return shortly with our tea. Apparently tea was served to all patrons, whether they ordered it or not.

Clara was grinning from ear to ear. "Ya know, chop suey isn't really Chinese. It was invented right near where I used to live in Brooklyn. You're gonna like this, it's swell stuff!"

I said I was sure she was right and picked up my menu. It seemed Clara's "swell stuff" was available in five flavors—beef, pork, shrimp, fish, and chicken. Or if one preferred, one could order the "House Combination," which included all of the above. There was also the option of having one's chop suey served the traditional way, on rice, or chow mein style with noodles.

Having very little idea what went into chop suey besides the aforementioned meats, I said, "Okay, kiddo, you got me into this. What do you recommend?"

Still excited about finding a favorite hometown dish right there in Ocean Park, Clara said, "Don't worry, honey, I'll do the ordering this time. Just get ready for somethin' really delicious."

Figuring she couldn't order anything that was worse than what I would have picked by flipping a coin, I said, "Okay. You're the boss."

A moment later our maitre d'/waiter arrived with two small teacups and a ceramic pitcher with steam spewing from its spout. "Be careful, the tea is really hot. Best let it sit for a few minutes." Then, pulling a pad of paper and a pencil from his hip pocket, he asked, "Have you decided what you'd like to eat?"

Clara spoke right up. "Yes, we'll have two big orders of your House Combination on rice. And lots of soy sauce."

Our waiter smiled at Clara's enthusiasm and said, "Yes, ma'am. Coming right up."

As he turned to leave our table, Clara added, "And don't forget the fortune cookies!"

He chuckled and said, "No, ma'am, I won't."

Our friendly waiter disappeared into the kitchen and I said, "Well, I see that you're an old hand at ordering this swell stuff."

"You bet! We have it all the time at home. Ruth gets it from a little joint in West Hollywood. Now, the next question is, do you want me to ask for a fork, or do you know how to use chopsticks?"

"Now, that's something I do know. I have a writer friend who insists on making his dinner guests use chopsticks, whether the food is Chinese or not. I think he does it just for the laughs he gets watching people trying to pick up things like peas with the sticks, but he took pity on me once and showed me how to use chopsticks properly. He also gave me a very detailed lesson in chopstick etiquette. So I am now well versed in the use of both Chinese and Japanese chopsticks."

Clara was pouring tea into our cups. "Well, how 'bout that! I figured you for a fork guy from the very beginning."

Feigning a Chinese accent, I said, "Young woman have many things yet to learn about honorable Eddie Markham."

Clara put a finger to the corner of each eye, and pushing up to give them a slant, she bowed and said, "Yes, oh learned master."

We both had a chuckle over that, and then I remembered something I had been meaning to tell Clara since I checked us into The Tides Inn. "By the way, kiddo, in case anyone asks, you are now Missus Jerome Miller. That's the name I used to register us at the auto court."

She tilted her head a little to one side, raised her eyebrows. "Jerome?"

"Yeah, well, it was the best I could do on short notice. Jerome is my dad's name and my middle name."

Clara's smile disappeared instantly. "Oh, Eddie, I'm sorry. I didn't mean to make fun of . . . ."

"Don't worry about it. I'm not a big fan of the name, either. I'm just grateful my folks didn't name me Jerome, Junior."

I took a sip of my tea and Clara said, "Are your folks still around?"

"Yes, they live up in Santa Barbara."

"I hope you don't mind me asking personal questions again. I just want to know everything about you."

"I don't mind at all. Ask me anything you'd like."

She grinned like a kid playing a fun game. "Okay, what's your mom's name?"

As always, Clara's smile was contagious and I found myself smiling back at her as I said, "Eloise."

"Eloise and Jerome. Those names kind of fit together. What does your father do, or is he retired?"

"No, dad is far from retired. He's an attorney and it seems he's a favorite of all those rich people who live up in Santa Barbara. They keep him quite busy doing whatever rich people need an attorney to do."

A hint of sadness passed over her face. "Then you come from a wealthy family."

"No. I mean my folks are doing well today, but when I was a kid we had very little money because dad was just getting started in his practice. We lived in a small rented house and mom gave piano lessons to bring in extra money. I even helped out when I got old enough to have an after school newspaper route."

The hint of sadness disappeared. "That's really swell, the whole family working together like that. Do you have any brothers or sisters?"

"Yes, I have a sister who is a few years younger than me."

"Oh? What's her name?"

"Well, on her birth certificate it's Mildred, but she goes by Millie."

"That's a pretty name."

"Yeah, but she didn't think much of it when I used to tease her all the time by calling her Silly Millie."

Clara looked stern. "Shame on you for teasing your little sister like that!"

"Oh, she got even—plenty of times."

Clara's happy face came back. "Good for her! What does Millie do now? Is she married?"

"No, she still lives with my folks. Millie is in her senior year at the state college up there. She's always been fascinated by Indian tribal cultures and that sort of thing, so she's studying to become an anthropologist."

Clara's sad face returned. "Wow, your family is really educated. If I ever meet them, they're gonna think I'm the original dumb Dora."

"Well, number one, you are definitely going to meet them, and soon. Number two, my family is going to love you to pieces, especially Millie. She's gonna think you're the duck's quack."

Clara frowned and cocked her head to the side again. "Why, for heaven's sake?"

"Because Millie is a big motion picture fan. Whenever a new film comes to one of the theaters in town, she's the first one in line to see it. When she finds out who you are, Millie is gonna drive you nuts with questions about how they make movies and what this actor or that actress is really like."

Clara's smile was back again. "Oh. Well, I'll gladly answer all of her questions, as long as she doesn't get too technical. I don't really know much about that side of it."

Our waiter showed up toting a big round tray from which he

distributed our dinners. First came two heaping plates of something on rice. Next, he placed a big bottle of soy sauce in the middle of the table and gave us each a pair of bamboo chopsticks in wax paper wrappers. Lastly, he set a bowl that must have contained half a dozen fortune cookies on the table.

"There you go, folks. Enjoy your dinners." Then, with a grin, he added, "Oh, and ma'am, if you need more fortune cookies, you just let me know."

Clara wasted no time unwrapping her chopsticks and digging into the heap on her plate. I, on the other hand, took my time with the same chore while examining the contents of my chop suey. Besides chunks of chicken, beef, shrimp, and the other meats, it seemed to consist mostly of vegetables—cabbage, celery, and bean sprouts, all in some sort of gluttonous sauce.

Thinking, "Here goes nothing," I picked up a morsel and popped it into my mouth. It was surprisingly tasty, somewhat like chow mein, but more flavorful. I tried some more. Maybe I was just hungry, but the stuff actually tasted quite good.

Between mouthfuls, Clara said, "This is delicious! What do you think? Did I steer you wrong."

"No, you were right, this really is swell stuff."

"Told you so!"

Enjoying the chop suey with nearly as much enthusiasm as Clara, I picked up our conversation where we had left off. "You know, kiddo, you and my sister are actually a lot alike in at least one way."

She looked puzzled. "What do you mean?"

"You both have lots of curiosity. Millie is always asking questions about things—how does it work or where did it come from? You're the same way. You asked a lot of questions about the places we saw during our travels the past few days."

Clara put on her serious face again. "Did I drive you crazy with all those questions?"

"Not at all. I think a healthy curiosity is one of the best personality traits a person can have."

"Well, I appreciate you being patient with me. It's just that even though I've been in California for a while, I haven't been anywhere except to a few filming locations. I've just been too darn busy to see the sights."

Changing the subject, I said, "Okay, I answered your questions about my family, now it's your turn. Are your folks still around?"

Clara's face dropped like someone had flipped a switch that shut off all of her energy. After a short hesitation, she said, "No, my mother passed on about three and a half years ago. Her name was Sara. She was sick a very long time."

"I'm sorry to hear that. What about your dad?"

"Yes, my father is still living. His name is Robert. He came out to California right after I did and he lived with me for a while. He doesn't anymore, though, because I bought him a place of his own."

"What does your father do?"

She made a face like a little girl might make after being given a dose of castor oil. "He says he's looking out for my interests, like a manager or an agent, but . . . ." Clara stopped mid-sentence, and for the first time since we had gotten to know each other, I could not read her expression. Her usually expressive face was completely blank, as if something had suddenly drained all the emotions out of her.

It was then I remembered Clara telling me that her life had been tough when she was a kid. Without thinking, I had just managed to drag up a lot of bad memories. Reaching across the table, I took her hand and said, "Let it go, kiddo. You don't have to tell me any more, now or ever."

Clara suddenly looked at me with a new expression I had never seen before—one filled with incredibly deep pain. "I want to tell you about it all, Eddie, I really do. It's just hard . . . it's hard because so many bad things have happened."

"I know. You told me that and I asked questions anyway. I promise I won't push you like that again. If and when you ever want to tell me more, I'll gladly listen, but if you never want to talk about it again, that's okay, too."

With moist eyes, she said, "Eddie, do you remember what I said to you when we got back from that Pierpont Inn place the other night . . . the part about the gift you've given me, the one I've always wanted but couldn't find? Do you remember that?"

"Yes, I remember it very clearly."

"Well, I meant that with all my heart. You've brought something new and clean and wonderful into my life. I want to protect that wonderful thing and keep it from ever becoming dirty and bad like so many other things in my life have been. Does that make any sense to you, Eddie?"

"It makes very good sense to me, Clara. I don't completely understand it all, but I understand what's in your heart, and that's enough for me."

The tears came then and she wiped at them with her napkin. "That's what makes you like a miracle to me. You never push me or make demands. You just let me be who I am and you watch over me and care for me in ways that make me feel loved for the first time in my life. I don't want that to ever end."

"It's not going to end, honey. We'll make sure of that."

"Oh, gosh, Eddie. Can we leave now? I want to be in a world with nobody but us in it for a while."

"Sure, but first we'd better at least eat up a couple of these fortune cookies after our waiter made a point of bringing you a whole bowl of them."

Clara managed a little smile. "Okay, you're right. I'll try one."

She cracked open the cookie and pulled out the little slip of paper with her fortune on it. "Okay, let's see what's in store for me."

As Clara read the fortune her eyes got wide. Then she grinned and said, "You'd better read this."

Holding Clara's fortune up to the light, I read it: "You have embarked on a wondrous and enchanted journey."

I said, "Well, how 'bout that?"

With something like awe in her voice, she said, "Yeah, how 'bout that? Now it's your turn. Let's see what you get."

I reached into the bowl and grabbed one of the folded cookies. Breaking it open, I popped half of it into my mouth and removed the fortune from the other half. The printing on the little slip of paper said, "Your powers of observation will serve you well."

Handing the fortune to Clara, I just said, "Not so far."

After reading it, she said, "Oh, you're wrong, Eddie. If you hadn't seen that sedan outside the hotel this afternoon, who knows what would have happened."

After paying our dinner bill, a whopping three dollars, including a four-bit tip for our friendly waiter, we walked out into the cool night air. As we stood outside the chop suey joint taking in the view, I noticed a flash of phosphorescence in the surf. Thinking the glowing surf might be a new experience for Clara, I said, "Come on, kiddo, I want to show you something."

With my arm around her waist, we walked further out on the pier where we could see the phosphorescence better. Along the way we passed the Bon Ton Ballroom and I was rather surprised to see Ben Pollack's name on the marquee. Pollack's orchestra was nationally known, and for them to be appearing here this late in the season was a pretty sure indication that a ballroom in Ocean Park could be a profitable venture.

When we reached a point on the pier where we could see the breakers up close, I stopped and pointed to the blue-green glow in the surf. "Have you ever seen anything like that before?"

She watched where I was pointing for a moment and then she saw the glow. "Oh, it's beautiful! What is it?"

"Well, the technical name is phosphorescence, although most people just call it glowing surf or something like that."

Clara was clearly captivated by the beautiful phenomenon. "It's so pretty! What makes the water glow like that?"

"I'm no expert on the subject, but I once read that the glow is caused by tiny, tiny marine creatures, I think they're called plankton. When the water they're in is agitated, like in the wake of a ship or in the surf, they glow. The creatures are so small it takes a microscope to see one of them, but there are millions of them in the ocean, and when a bunch of them get agitated, they make the water light up like that."

"What happens to them when they land on the beach?"

"Well, I guess some of them get washed back out to sea, but it's pretty much the end for those that are stuck on the beach."

Clara watched the glowing surf for a few more minutes in silence. Then she said, "Those little sea creatures are a lot like movie actors, aren't they?"

"Are they?"

"Yes. They put on a show that makes people happy for a little while, but doing it eventually kills them."

"Is movie acting that strenuous?"

"It can be, depending on the people in charge, but I'm not going to let that happen to me. I've already decided I'm getting out of the movie racket before I end up on the beach like those little sea creatures."

I was thinking about that analogy when a ruckus suddenly broke out somewhere on the pier behind us. Somebody shouted and I acted instinctively. Spinning around to face the noise, I stepped in front of Clara and reached for the pistol in the waistband of my trousers. I already had my hand on the Colt's butt when I realized the fuss had nothing to do with us.

What I saw was two brawny fellows escorting a smaller guy out of the Bon Ton Ballroom. The little guy must have smuggled some bootleg hooch in because he was very inebriated. Shouting curses, he struggled and kicked at his escorts.

We watched while they half-dragged him toward the street end of the pier. I relaxed and let the tension flow out of my muscles.

Beside me, Clara said, "Gosh, Eddie, you have reflexes like a cat! I never saw anyone move so fast!"

"Sorry. I guess I'm still a little on edge from our experience this afternoon."

"You didn't do anything to be sorry for. You were watching over me, like I was saying before. That's one of the reasons I love you so darn much."

I turned to face her, and when I saw the love in her eyes, I reacted instinctively again. Grabbing Clara and pulling her close, I kissed her long and hard on the lips. After the kiss, she put her arms around me, pressed her face to my shoulder. "Wow! That was quite a kiss! And you know what?"

"What?"

"That's the first time you ever kissed first. All the other times we really kissed, I kissed you, but this time you started it. It felt wonderful!"

We stood there holding each other for a few moments longer until Clara said, "Let's go home, darling."

The two fellows from the ballroom were walking back up the pier and the drunk was still shouting at them from the street. Clara said, "That fellow's behavior is abominable!" Then she grinned up at me. "Did I say it right, Eddie?"

"You did, indeed. That fellow just gave us an excellent example of abominable behavior."

Clara's use of the word I had taught her triggered a whole bunch of memories from that first day on the Sunset Limited. As we walked, my mind began showing me pictures from that day, but it seemed so long ago, I felt like I was looking at photographs in an old family album.

Then suddenly one picture flashed in my brain like lightening and I jumped as if I had gotten an electric shock. In that moment, I knew for certain who had strafed us in the French village, who had poisoned two Army pilots, and who had damned near killed us in Laurel Canyon a few hours earlier.

That revelation came as such a surprise, it made me stop in my tracks right there on the pier. Alarmed, Clara turned and said, "What's wrong, Eddie?"

I looked her in the eye and felt a small smile tug at my lips. "I know who it is."

Frowning, she said, "Who who is?"

"The guy who's trying to kill you."

Clara's eyes opened wide. "Who is it?"

"Billy Blaylock."

"Who's he?"

"He was a last minute addition to the stunt pilot crew for *Wings*, and he was on the Sunset Limited with us. In fact, you had lunch with him in the dining car on our first day out."

Looking astonished, she said, "That guy? How do you know it's him?"

"I know it has to be him for several reasons. First, he matches Jimmy's description of the guy who showed up at my place. Second, as an experienced stunt pilot he is perfectly capable of strafing us in Texas. Third, his knowledge of flying would have made planning the crash of that Army transport we were on easy for him.

"Plus, Charlie Barton told me Blaylock had been signed on to the crew at the insistence of B. P. Schulberg, which means he has connections within the Lasky organization that could give him all the information he has about you. See? It all fits!"

Clara shook her head in amazement. "It does! That is scary! What are we going to do about him?"

Feeling myself smile again, I said, "Tomorrow we stop being the hunted and become the hunters. We're going to find Mister Billy Blaylock."

Back at The Tides Inn we stretched out on the bed and I held Clara in my arms until she fell asleep. Finally I gently woke her and said, "Come on, kiddo, let's get you ready for bed."

She started to get up, and then stopped. "Aren't you coming to bed, darling?"

"Maybe later. I don't think anyone knows where we are, but that's what I thought when Blaylock showed up this afternoon. I just don't think I should be sleeping right now."

"Okay, if that's what you want."

Clara turned to get off the bed and this time I stopped her. "Kiddo, that's not even close to what I want. It's what I feel I have to do."

Her eyes softened. "I know, Eddie. You're just watching over me, but I sure will be glad when . . . well, you know what I mean."

I smiled and said, "I sure do."

Clara went into the bathroom to get ready for bed and I removed what I was now thinking of as a journal from my overnight case and began recording the day's events. When she returned, I put down my pencil and tucked her into bed with a kiss.

Then I turned out all the lights except for the desk lamp on the small table where I was writing. From the sound of her breathing, Clara fell asleep fairly quickly, but after a while it became a fitful sleep. I could hear her tossing and turning, and at one point, she cried out.

I went over to make sure she was okay. Clara was still asleep, but frowning and making small whimpering sounds. Guessing she was having nightmares, I sat on the edge of the bed and gently put my hand on her shoulder.

Her eyes opened with a start, but when she saw it was me touching her, she laid her cheek against my hand and dozed off again. When I finished bringing my notes up to date, I slipped the now rather thick stack of paper back into my overnight case. My next chore was figuring out how to accomplish what I had told Clara we were going to do next.

I had two ideas about how to find Billy Blaylock. The first was to talk with some of my flying buddies. Fliers are a close-knit community and we keep tabs on each other. I was fairly certain somebody I knew would also know Blaylock. They might even know where he lives or hangs out. A drive out to the airfield where I kept my ship seemed the best first step toward finding Clara's would-be killer.

My second idea was riskier. Charlie Barton told me that Blaylock was added to the *Wings* stunt pilot crew at B. P. Schulberg's urging, so there had to be some connection between the two men. If I got Schulberg to tell me about that connection, it could lead me to Blaylock. He might also give me some insight as to who the flier was working for.

What made confronting Schulberg risky was that I was beginning to suspect he was somehow involved in the scheme to kill Clara. If that suspicion proved correct, he was certainly not going to volunteer any incriminating information, and asking questions would tip him off to the fact that I knew who the killer was. If Schulberg told Blaylock the jig was up, I might never track him down.

I had another reason for not being overly enthusiastic about talking to Schulberg. After witnessing the way he treated Clara, I had developed an intense dislike for the man. It would require a great deal of restraint to keep from taking a poke at him.

All things considered, I decided it would be best to go ahead with plan number one and hold plan number two in abeyance to be used only if necessary. My thoughts continued to meander along these general lines until around midnight when Clara had another nightmare. This one ended with her sitting straight up in bed and sobbing hysterically. After putting the Colt on the nightstand, I stripped down to my shorts and slipped into bed next to her. She immediately slid into my arms and I held her close until the sobs died away. She was sleeping again, so I stayed right where I was and dozed off and on until the gray light of dawn showed around the edges of the curtains.

Twenty-Seven

6:30 A.M. – Wednesday – September 22, 1926
The Tides Inn – Ocean Park, Santa Monica

By the time I finished making myself ready for the day ahead; Clara was awake and sitting on the edge of the bed. Her eyes were puffy and she looked groggy. It occurred to me that a journalist seeing her in this state would assume Clara Bow was hung over, which is exactly how deceptive appearances lead to false rumors.

Seeing me come out of the bathroom, she stood and I gave her a hug. As I held her, Clara said, "Eddie, do we have to stay here again tonight?"

"No, we can stay anywhere we want."

"Good. I don't like it here."

"Fair enough. You get yourself ready to go and we'll be on our way."

My suitcase and overnight bag were on the bed ready to go when Clara finished getting ready. The outfit she had chosen for the day was her white skirt and the sweater with the green patterns over a white blouse. She had removed the bandage from her cheek and the wound was still healing nicely.

Clara put her toiletry items in her suitcase and said, "I'll be ready in just a minute. I need to put a new dressing on. I'm almost out of bandages, so is it okay if I cut one in half today?"

I knew we could always stop and pick up more gauze bandages, but I also sensed she was growing tired of walking around with a big white blotch on her face. "Sure. You need some help?"

She turned and looked at me for a moment. Then she ran over and put her arms around me. "Eddie, are we gonna be okay? Really?"

Holding her close, I said, "We're going to be fine, kiddo. In fact, things are going to start changing for the better today. You'll see."

"I sure hope so."

It was seven-forty-five when I carried our bags out to the Cadillac. The air outside was still chilly, so when Clara put on her green cloche hat, she also donned her short jacket. Then, after I checked us out of The Tides Inn, we departed Ocean Park.

As I drove north along the western edge of Santa Monica on Ocean Avenue, Clara asked where we were going. I said, "Our first stop is going to be a little ham and egg joint on Wilshire Boulevard. I think we could both use some coffee and a little breakfast. After that we'll go into downtown Los Angeles and make a couple of telephone calls."

"Who are you going to call?"

"First I'm going to check in with my secretary. I haven't talked to her since I left for Texas and she's probably wondering if I've disappeared from the face of the earth. After that, I thought you might like to call Ruth. I promised her we would let her know how things were going."

There was a little more life in Clara's voice when she said, "Can we do that? I've really missed Ruth."

"We can."

Clara put her hand on my arm. "Thanks, Eddie. You always seem to know what I need and want."

Paraphrasing a Texaco Oil Company advertising slogan, I said, "It's all part of my new and better service at no extra price."

For some reason that tickled her funny bone. She giggled and said, "Oh, you goof. I was being serious."

"I know it, kiddo, but I got a smile out of you, and this morning those are rare."

Clara gave me another smile. "You always make me smile, if not on the outside, then on the inside. What are we going to do after making those telephone calls?"

"We're going to the airfield where I keep my airplane to ask some of my flier friends if they know where we can find Billy Blaylock."

"Do you think they'll know where he is?"

"Fliers keep pretty good track of each other. I'm fairly certain someone will be able to tell us about Blaylock."

I turned right on Wilshire Boulevard and we were heading northeast toward downtown. As we drove, I kept a close eye on my rearview mirror. I saw no indication that we were being followed, but each time I glanced in the mirror, my eye was drawn to the bullet hole in the Cadillac's back window. It was a constant reminder to keep my wits about me.

A few blocks past Sepulveda I pulled over and parked in front of the Westside Diner, a tiny hole in the wall restaurant with a big reputation for turning out great breakfasts. I was definitely in need of a great breakfast.

Before we went in, though, we walked two doors down Wilshire to a newsstand where I bought a copy of the *L. A. Times*. It was nearly nine o'clock when we entered the diner and the breakfast rush was pretty much over. Despite this, the place had a busy, crowded feeling about it. The proprietor had crammed as many tables into the small dining room as possible to keep up with his growing clientele and a constant clatter of restaurant sounds—dishes being bussed and chairs scraping on the tile floor—echoed off the walls.

We had our choice of tables, so I steered Clara to a booth near the back of the dining room and helped her out of her coat. By the time we were seated, a tall, slender waitress in a white dress with a black apron that said "Connie" over her left breast arrived carrying two ceramic mugs in her left hand, a coffee pot in her right hand, and two paper menus tucked under her arm.

"You folks want coffee this morning?"

I answered in the affirmative and after filling our mugs; Connie gave us each a menu and said, "I'll be right back to take your breakfast orders."

While Clara stirred cream and sugar into her coffee from a little ceramic pitcher and a matching sugar bowl, I wasted no time in getting some of the strong, dark liquid into my system. After Clara had taken a few swallows of her coffee, I asked, "Whatcha gonna have for breakfast?"

She gave the menu an unenthusiastic look. "I'm not very hungry."

"It could turn out to be a long time before we get lunch, so how 'bout having at least a small bowl of oatmeal?"

"Okay."

Since I had been to the Westside Diner many times, I had no need to look at the menu. I knew exactly what I wanted. When Connie returned with an order pad and pencil in her hand, I ordered oatmeal with honey and fresh fruit for Clara, and ham and eggs sunny side up with fried potatoes and wheat toast for myself.

When Connie went off to put in our orders, I opened the *Times* to the local news section and scanned the headlines. Clara asked, "What are you looking for?"

"A story about a car crash on Laurel Canyon Boulevard

yesterday afternoon. And here it is."

The article was down in the lower right corner of the second page. It was short and to the point, reporting that an out of control sedan had gone off the road and crashed into a tree near the top of Laurel Canyon. The story said the accident occurred late in the afternoon and that the driver and any passengers who might have been riding in the black and gray Chevrolet sedan had left the scene by the time Los Angeles Police officers arrived. The L.A.P.D. was looking for the owner of the vehicle, but that task would be complicated by the fact that someone had removed its license plates and registration certificate.

I read the article to Clara and said, "Well, that tells us a couple of things."

"Like what?"

"First, if Blaylock was able to leave the accident scene, he wasn't too badly injured in the crash. Second, it tells us he was smart enough to remove anything from the car that would immediately identify him as the owner, assuming he is the owner and the car wasn't stolen. The cops will trace the owner eventually, but it will take some time."

Clara said, "So he's still out there somewhere trying to kill me. That's just wonderful."

"Maybe he's still out there trying to kill you. After failing three times, however, he might have also decided to give it up."

"That would be nice, but it isn't how my luck usually goes."

Connie returned with our breakfasts. I wolfed mine down while Clara picked at her oatmeal. When I was done, Connie removed my empty plate and refilled our coffee mugs.

"Clara, tell me about B. P. Schulberg."

"What do you want to know about him?"

"For starters, how did he end up owning your contract?"

In flat tones, as if she was reciting a story for the hundredth time, Clara said, "He saw me in a film I made in New York called *Down to the Sea in Ships* and offered me a three-month trial contract to come out to California to make a movie at his studio, Preferred Pictures. He gave me the second lead in *Maytime*, and it turned out pretty good, so he extended my contract for more money and loaned me out to other studios to get experience."

"So he got you your start in Hollywood. What kind of a man is he?"

Clara hesitated a moment, then said, "At first I liked him 'cuz he treated me nice and got me into lots of movies, but then things weren't so nice anymore."

"What things?"

She gave me a sort of grimace. Then with resignation in her voice, Clara said, "Well, you're gonna hear about it anyway, so you might as well hear it from me. It turned out B. P. expected more than just acting for what he was paying me, and if I wanted to keep making movies, I had to go along with it."

Sensing there was more to the story; I nodded solemnly and said, "What else?"

Clara sighed. "My contract said I got paid two-hundred a week, but when B. P. loaned me out to other studios, they were paying him five-hundred and more a week for me to be in their movies. He was putting the difference in his pocket."

I had already figured Schulberg for a jerk before our conversation started and I was liking him even less now. "Anything else?"

"Yes. After a while Mister Lasky offered B. P. a job at Famous Lasky, so B. P. kind of pulled a fast one by saying Preferred Pictures was bankrupt and closing the studio. Then he went to work for Lasky the next darn day. The people working at the studio lost their jobs and some investors lost money, but that didn't bother B. P. in the slightest."

"Charlie Barton told me Victor Fleming recently helped you negotiate a new contract with Lasky. He said the new contract cuts Schulberg out of the picture entirely. Is that right?"

Clara nodded. "Yeah, and I can tell you B. P. is madder than a hornet. That's what the fuss was about that day when I met you at the *Wings* production meeting. The rumor is that Lasky is going to fire B. P. because the only reason he hired him in the first place was because I was part of the deal. Now that I have a contract directly with Lasky, he doesn't need B. P. anymore. At first I felt kind of bad about that, but now I sort of feel like B. P. is finally gonna get what's comin' to him."

"Okay, thanks. That gives me a better idea of how Schulberg fits into all of this."

She reached across the table and put her hand on mine. With a worried frown, Clara said, "Eddie, I sure hope you don't feel any different about me now that you know I . . . well, now that you know how things were with B. P. Do you?"

"No, Clara, I don't feel any differently about you, except kind of sorry for all you had to go through to become an actress. Men like Schulberg disgust me."

Clara looked at me softly with love showing in her eyes. "Thank you, darling. I'm just glad he's out of my life now."

I wasn't so sure Schulberg was really out of Clara's life quite yet, but I did not say so. Instead, I said, "Okay, kiddo, let's get on with our day."

We continued driving toward downtown on Wilshire until we came to La Cienega Boulevard. I turned right on La Cienega and parked in the first empty parking spot we came to.

Clara asked, "What are we going to do here?"

"We're going into the O' Connor Building over there to make our telephone calls. I used to visit a friend who had an office in the building, so I know the lobby is quiet and has several public telephone booths."

The lobby of the five-story O' Connor Building was just as I remembered it, a moderate-sized space with polished granite walls off of which footsteps on the marble floor tiles bounced and echoed loudly. The telephones were lined up along the wall to our right. I said, "I'm going to call my office first, then you can place a call to Ruth. That okay with you?"

"Sure, that's fine."

I stepped into the booth closest to the street, dropped a nickel into the slot, and dialed my office number. Elsie answered on the second ring.

"Good morning, Edward Markham's office."

"Hi, Elsie, this is Eddie."

"Mister Markham! Where in heaven's name are you? I've been trying to reach you for two days, but that hotel in San Antonio said you had . . . ."

"I had to make a little change in plans, Elsie. I'll tell you all about when I see you. Have we heard from New York about the manuscript?"

"Yes, that's why I was trying to find you. A letter came from them on Monday. They love your manuscript and want to proceed with the book immediately. They enclosed a publishing contract with the letter."

"Great! Reply to their letter and tell them I'll be out of town for a few more days, but that I will sign the contract and we'll send it on to them as soon as I get back. Anything else?"

I could tell from Elsie's tone that there were questions on her mind, like where was I and what was I up to, but she also knew if I wanted her to know where I was, I would tell her. After a momentary hesitation, Elsie said, "Yes, a wire arrived for you from Texas yesterday. I think in might be something important. Do you want me to read it to you?"

"Yes please."

"It says, 'Arriving L.A. by air Wednesday night /STOP/ Urgent we talk /STOP/ Call my home after six /STOP/' It's signed C. Barton and it was sent from San Antonio, Texas yesterday at two p.m., mountain time."

So Charlie Barton was flying to Los Angeles and he wanted to talk to us. That was convenient, because there were some things I wanted to discuss with Charlie, too. But there was something about the wire that set off more of those faint alarm bells in my head. I liked Charlie because he seemed to be an all right kind of fellow so I could think of no specific reason for my uneasiness. All the same, it was there and I have learned not to ignore that feeling.

"Elsie, please do me a favor. Check the L.A. telephone directory for a Charles Barton."

"Will do. Hang on."

The sound of telephone directory pages being turned came over the line for a moment, and then Elsie said, "You're in luck, Mister Markham. There's only one Charles Barton in the book. If it's your guy, he lives on Delano Street in Toluca. You want the telephone number?"

I said I did and Elsie read off a number in the Poplar exchange. I wrote it down on the back of The Tides Inn hotel receipt, which happened to be the first piece of paper I found in my pocket.

"Thanks, Elsie. Anything else?"

"No, but I wouldn't mind knowing when you expect to return."

"With luck I should be back in the office next Monday. If that changes, I'll give you another call."

Elsie sounded a little exasperated with me. "All right, Mister Markham. Be careful and I'll see you Monday."

I returned the receiver to its hook and stepped out of the booth. "Well, that was a worthwhile call. Elsie had some news for me."

Clara said, "Good news, I hope."

"Yes, good news. Just before I left for Texas we sent a new manuscript to a publisher in New York. They read it and sent back a letter saying they want to publish it right away."

"That IS good news. Congratulations!"

"Thanks, kiddo. The other piece of news was a wire from Charlie Barton. He's arriving by air from Texas tonight and he wants to talk with us. We're supposed to call him at his home in Toluca after six o'clock."

Frowning, Clara said, "I wonder what he wants to talk about."

"Well, this is just a guess, but I suspect all hell has broken loose in Texas since we talked to Colonel Smythe yesterday. I'm sure he wasted no time in confirming what we told him, so Wellman is probably sitting between a rock and a hard place right now."

"What do you mean?"

"Remember that Lasky ordered Wellman not to tell authorities about the incident last Friday because he doesn't want any bad publicity. If I know Smythe, though, he's told Wellman all of the Army cooperation on *Wings* will come to an immediate halt if Bill doesn't give him the straight dope about the French village strafing."

Clara put on a mischievous grin. "Good for Smythe! That'll teach Lasky to take better care of his people."

The alarm bells in my head started their faint clanging again. There was something out of whack about what I had just told Clara I thought was the reason behind Barton's wire. What was it? When I still could not put my finger on it, I said, "You want to call Ruth now?"

"Yes please."

I handed Clara the change left in my pocket and the slip of paper Ruth gave me with her sister's number on it. "Just be careful not to say anything specific about where we've been, where we are, or where we're going, just in case someone is listening in on the line. Okay?"

"I'll be careful, Eddie."

"Good. I'll wait right over there where I can watch the street."

I walked about five paces toward the middle of the lobby where I could see the traffic on La Cienega through the O'Connor Building's double glass doors. I had moved away from the telephone booths as much to give Clara privacy as for the reason I had given her.

All I could hear of Clara's conversation was an occasional word that echoed off the lobby walls, but I could see her face as it went through a range of expressions from sadness to something that was almost joy. She had a lot to tell Ruth and it occurred to me that Clara's maid might be her only real friend in the world.

Telephone calls made, I turned back onto Wilshire and continued driving toward town. Our destination was at the corner of Wilshire and Crescent, a small airfield known as DeMille, Number Two. I turned left on Crescent, and from there onto the field itself. Then I drove along the backsides of a row of hangars and buildings that lined the Crescent side of the airfield.

When I came to the small hangar I rented for my ship, I pulled up alongside it and said, "You want to see what I spend all my money on?"

"Sure!"

I unlocked the hangar's side door, reached inside to turn on the light switch, and ushered Clara inside. She took about four steps, stopped, and stared up open-mouthed at the Bristol biplane sitting in the middle of the concrete floor. "Oh, Eddie, it's beautiful!"

"I think so. She's a Bristol F.2B, a British combination pursuit and observation plane. That's why she has two cockpits. Pursuit ships only have one. Ships like this were flown by both British and American fliers during the war."

"Gosh, is it really an old-timer?"

"Not too old. She was built near the end of the war, so that would make her about eight years old, but I bought her about a year ago from a fellow who specializes in converting military ships for civilian use. He takes his airplanes completely apart, then rebuilds them, replacing any worn parts with new ones. So, in a way, she's almost brand new."

"The green and yellow colors are really pretty together."

"Those are almost the same colors she was born with. The green on the fuselage is a little brighter than the original color, but the yellow wings are the same. Of course, during the war she had British or American roundels on her wings and a lot of other emblems and such."

Clara was standing on her tiptoes trying to see the upper half of the fuselage. I said, "Would you like to climb up so you can see inside her cockpits?"

"Yes, can I?"

"Sure, but there's a little trick to it. I'll show you."

I picked up the wooden step I built to making climbing aboard easier for people whose legs are shorter than mine and set it on the hangar floor behind the lower wing on the port side. Pointing to it, I said, "First, step up there. Next, put your left foot on that black area at the back of the wing and reach up with both hands so you can grab the edge of the rear cockpit. Then lift yourself up and put your right foot into that half-round opening in the side of the fuselage. Just be careful not to step anywhere else on the wing. The black area is re-enforced so you can stand on it. If you step anywhere else on the wing your foot might poke a hole in the fabric wing covering. Okay? Give it a try."

I was standing close by, ready to give her a hand, but Clara followed my instructions exactly, and even in high-heeled shoes, she had no trouble climbing aboard. I walked around to the starboard side of the fuselage and stepped up onto the wing so I could tell her what she was looking at.

"That post sticking up out of the floor in the front cockpit is the control stick. It's used to raise or lower the nose and bank the ship. The rudder pedals are right in front of it. Stepping down on them makes the ship yaw, or turn, left or right. That lever on your side of the cockpit is the throttle. You push it forward to increase engine speed or pull it back to decrease engine speed."

"How fast can it go?"

"Around a hundred-and-twenty."

"Wow! Is it fun to go a hundred-and-twenty miles an hour?"

Grinning, I said, "It sure is, especially up there in the sky where there's nothing to get in your way."

"Gosh, Eddie, will you take me for a ride sometime?"

"Kiddo, I'll take you for all the rides you want."

"Oh, I can hardly wait!"

"Then we'll do it soon, but right now we'd better start talking to the guys around here before they disappear for lunch. Stay right there. I'll come around and help you down."

By the time I got around to the port side of the Bristol, Clara was already standing on the hangar floor, running her fingertips over the smooth dope finish on the wing. With an air of pride, she said, "I got down all by myself, Eddie, and I didn't poke any holes in your wing, either."

Twenty-Eight

11:30 A.M. – Wednesday – September 22, 1926
DeMille Field, #2 – Los Angeles

I switched off the hangar lights and locked the door. When I turned, Clara was no longer standing next to me. She had walked about fifteen feet toward the front corner of the hangar to watch a Curtiss JN-6 biplane take off.

I watched the takeoff over Clara's shoulder, and said, "Now there's a real old-timer. She's called a Jenny and Curtiss has been building them since the beginning of the war."

"Well, she sure is pokey compared to the airplane that took off just before her."

"You're right. Jennies aren't very powerful, but they are easy to fly and quite forgiving of the kinds of mistakes cadet pilots make. That's why the military uses them for training beginning fliers. In fact, the first ship I ever flew was a Jenny."

When the Jenny finally lifted itself off the runway and began its leisurely climb away from the field, Clara turned and said, "Explain something to me, Eddie."

"Okay, if I can."

"How come you talk about airplanes like they're women, calling them 'she' and 'her'?"

"That's a good question. We all do it and I never really thought why, but I suppose it's because fliers have a special relationship with their airplanes. Sometimes we love them and sometimes we hate them, but either way, our lives depend on them and . . . well, life just wouldn't be nearly as much fun without our ships."

Clara seemed to consider that for a moment, then she said, "Well, that's all fine and good, but I'll bet your life would be a lot more fun right now without one particular woman. I haven't brought much fun into your life."

I smiled and gave her a wink. "Oh, I wouldn't say that. Heck, the fun with this particular woman is just getting started."

She gave me one of her coy looks and said, "I'm glad you feel that way."

"I do, indeed. Now, let's get to talking with some of these guys. We have to be very careful, though. I told you fliers keep track of each other, and seeing me here with a woman is going to start tongues wagging. And if someone recognizes you, it will be all over town before dark."

"Wouldn't it be better if I waited for you in the car like at the dealership yesterday?"

"Yes, that would be the safest thing to do, but . . . ."

"Don't worry, darling, it won't bother me like it did. I can do it."

Reluctantly, I said, "Okay," and we walked over to the Cadillac, where I said, "Remember, lock both doors and start the engine. I don't think anyone will bother you, but if you see anything at all that doesn't look right, pull around the front of my hangar and start honking the horn. I won't be far away. Oh, and if you have to do that, watch out for taxiing ships."

As Clara climbed into the Caddy, I gave her the keys and she gave me a kiss on the cheek. "Don't worry, Eddie. I'll do it just like you said."

I set off on a casual stroll and the first fellow I spotted was the guy who keeps his ship in the hangar two down from mine. We chatted for a few minutes before I brought up Blaylock's name. He knew the name, but that was it.

My next conversation was with a flier who gives sightseeing flights over the city. He, too, knew Blaylock's name, plus that Blaylock was a stunt pilot, but like the first fellow, he knew nothing more about him.

A few hangars further along I ran into the mechanic who takes care of my ship. He was tightening the bolts on an engine shroud when I walked up and he said, "Hiya, Mister Markham. No problems with the Bristol I hope?"

"None at all, Jack. You have her running like a fine watch."

"Good, that's what I like to hear."

"Say, Jack, I'm looking for a guy and I think you might know him. His name is Billy Blaylock."

Jack's smile faded. "Yeah, I know Blaylock."

"Can you tell me where he hangs out?"

"Yeah, he flies out of Burdette where most of them movie pilots are based. Do you mind me askin' why you're lookin' for him?"

I had an answer ready because I thought somebody might ask that question. "Well, he signed on to fly stunts for a film I'm working on, but he hasn't shown up for a few days."

Jack's response told me I had picked the right explanation. "That sounds like Blaylock, all right. Most of them movie pilots are right guys, but Blaylock's nothin' but a bum. He stiffed me for a hundred-dollar repair job a while back, so I ain't got no use for him."

"Sorry to hear that, Jack. When I find him I'll remind him that he ought to pay your bill."

"Thanks, but it prob'ly won't do no good. I hear those guys make good money, but he sure as hell don't never have any of it when it's time to pay his bills."

I spent another moment or two commiserating with Jack, and then I thanked him and headed back toward my hangar. I had gotten lucky on my third try and I now knew where to find Billy Blaylock. It was now time to take a peek inside the fox's den.

Clara saw me coming and unlocked the driver-side door. As she slid over and I climbed behind the steering wheel, she said, "You weren't gone long. Did you have any luck?"

"Yes, ma'am. I hit the jackpot on my third try. According to Jack, the mechanic who does the repairs and maintenance on my ship, Billy Blaylock flies out of Burdette field, which is down in Inglewood, about ten miles away."

"Good work! Are you going to tell Colonel Smythe that Blaylock is the killer now?"

"I'm going to call Smythe, all right, but to find out what he's turned up through his investigation. I want to have a little more solid proof before I tell him about Blaylock."

Suddenly there was a nervous tone in Clara's voice. "What kind of proof, Eddie?"

"Short of finding Blaylock and getting a confession out of him, the next best thing would be finding the ship he used to strafe us in Texas. If he's got the ship stashed somewhere and we can find it, it's proof beyond any doubt that he's the killer."

"Eddie, I'm gettin' scared again. Can't you just let Colonel Smythe find the proof?"

"That would be risky. Do you remember how we figured Blaylock knew where we would be yesterday?"

"Yes. You think he found out from somebody at March field."

"Right, and if I tell Smythe Blaylock is the killer, the same thing could happen again—somebody might alert Blaylock that we're onto him and he'd skedaddle before anyone caught up with him."

Clara seemed to think about that for a long moment before she said, "I guess you're right, but this is all very scary and I don't like it."

"I know, kiddo. I'm not happy about it either. We'll just take this slow and easy. I know a fellow at Burdette—the guy who sold me my Bristol—and he's in the business of restoring old airplanes. I'll bet he knows Blaylock's ship and there's a good chance he'll know where Blaylock keeps it. We'll take this that far and then decide what to do next."

"Okay, Eddie. I'll try not to be a fraidy-cat again."

The most direct route from DeMille Field to Burdette Air Port is east on Wilshire to south on Western Avenue to Ninety-Fourth Street in Inglewood. The drive took about half an hour, which put us at Burdette smack dab in the middle of lunch hour.

Hoping that Fred Lewis brought his lunch to work instead of going out to eat, I pulled up in front the Lewis Aircraft Services hangar in the southeast corner of the field near the Burdette Air Port office. Since the Cadillac was in plain view from the inside of the hangar, Clara again waited for me with the doors locked.

Fred Lewis is a bear of a man with broad shoulders, a topnotch of curly black hair, and a dour expression that belies a great sense of humor. Walking through the hangar doors, I spotted two fellows sitting at a workbench at the rear of the large open space. As my eyes became accustomed to the hangar's dark interior, I recognized the hulking frame of Fred Lewis. He was just unwrapping a sandwich from a black lunch pail on the workbench.

Fred recognized me. Putting his sandwich down, he wiped his big paw on his coveralls and shook my hand. "Hiya, Eddie, how's the world treatin' you?"

Shaking the massive hand he stuck out at me, I said, "Mighty fine, Fred. You?"

With a slightly lopsided smile, he said, "Can't complain. Wouldn't do no good if I did."

I chuckled. "Listen, Fred, I want to ask you about something, but I see you're having lunch. I can come back after a while . . . ."

"No reason to do that if you don't mind me eatin' my sandwich while we talk."

The fellow sitting next to Fred at the workbench was a young man who looked barely old enough to be out of high school. He figured to be a kid who was learning the aircraft mechanic's trade from a master.

At a glance from Fred, the kid jumped up from his stool and

grabbed the paper sack that presumably held the rest of his lunch. He said, "I'll go finish my lunch outside," and trotted off toward the open hangar doors.

Watching the young man leave, Fred said, "There goes one smart kid. One day he'll make a real fine wrench yanker. Now, whatcha want to talk about, Eddie?"

"It's a who, not a what. Do you know a stunt flier named Billy Blaylock?"

Like the mechanic at DeMille Field, Fred's expression turned sour, as if he'd just bitten into something in his sandwich that didn't taste good. "Yeah, I know the kid. I did some work on one of his ships a while back. What do you want to know about him?"

"Well, for starters, why the sour expression when I said his name?"

"Blaylock is a punk, plain and simple—thinks he knows it all, but doesn't have the sense God gave a rock."

"I'm beginning to get the idea Mister Blaylock isn't the most popular flier around."

"Then you're gettin' the right idea. None of the Black Cats will have anything to do with him 'cuz the kid is just plain reckless in the air, and he don't give a damn about anyone but himself."

The Black Cats is an exclusive organization made up of the best stunt pilots in the business. They do most of the movie flying in southern California, plus they perform at air shows and other events. The Black Cats were based at Burdette and their opinion, if Fred had it right, of Billy Blaylock told me a lot.

"You said you worked on one of his ships?"

"Yeah, a real oddball that was—an experimental pursuit ship Curtiss was trying to sell to the Air Corps, but for once the Army had enough sense to walk away from it before the dang thing killed a bunch of their pilots."

My interest level in what Fred was telling me jumped several notches. "That bad? What was wrong with it?"

Fred made weighing gestures with his hands. "It was all out of balance. Curtiss stuffed one of their big twelve-cylinder motors into a ship with stubby wings and a dinky tail to cut down on drag and weight. It went like a bat out of hell in straight and level flight, but the minute a flier tried to do any serious maneuvering, the thing wanted to fall out of the sky. I heard they lost two of the prototypes because of that instability."

"And this guy, Blaylock, can handle it?"

"Yeah, I gotta give him that much. Flyin' that dang thing is like ridin' a bucking bronco—ya never know what it's was going to do next, but he manages to stay ahead of it. How, I'll never know."

"So when you worked on his Curtiss were you able to improve its manners at all?"

He shook his head. "Didn't even try. All he wanted was a paint job—wanted to look like the American pursuits they flew in the war. He drew up the paint scheme he wanted with color pencils, but he couldn't even do that right.

"He got the colors of the roundels backwards, but by the time we got to that point I was so tired of fussin' with him, I just painted it the way he drew it. I figure it serves him right for bein' a know-it-all."

I grinned at that. "Tell me, did that ship have armament?"

"Not when we painted it, but the gun mounts and prop synchronizing gears were still there under the engine cowling, so all you'd have to do is dig up a couple of surplus machine guns, bolt 'em in, and rig the firing cables. Nothin' to it."

"Does Blaylock keep that Curtiss here on the field?"

"Used to. 'Bout a month ago he pulled up stakes and shipped both planes out of here."

That was not the answer I wanted to hear. "Any idea where he went?"

"Someone said he moved out to Brackett."

"Out by La Verne?"

"Yup, that's what I heard. Don't know if it's true or not." Then Fred gave me a suspicious look and said, "Eddie, how come you're askin' so many questions about this Blaylock kid?"

"Well, it's kind of complicated, but the gist of the story is he signed on as a stunt pilot for a Lasky-Paramount film I'm involved with, and while we were down shooting location scenes in San Antonio, he disappeared. I'm just trying to find out what happened to him."

Fred gave me a nod and a look that said he knew there was more to it. "Well, that's most of what I know about him. Guess I'd better be gettin' back to work."

He stood and I said, "One more question. You said he shipped both planes out of here. What's he flying besides the Curtiss?"

"He's got one those civilian versions of the PT-One that Ryan builds. He uses that one for gettin' around to save wear and tear on the Curtiss. His Ryan is easy to reco'nize 'cuz the wings are painted bright orange with a couple of wide black stripes. "

Offering my hand, I said, "Okay, Fred. Thanks for all your help."

We shook and he said, "No problem, Eddie. Glad if I helped

you out. Say, how's that Bristol flyin'?"

"Like an angel."

On that note I gave Fred a salute and left the hangar. Back in the Cadillac, I said, "Well, that was useful, but not as useful as I hoped. Blaylock kept his ships here up until a month ago, and then he moved them to an airfield out between Pasadena and San Berdoo. At least that's what Fred heard.

"He also told me some things about the ships Blaylock owns. One of them exactly fits the description of the pursuit ship that strafed us in Texas right down to the incorrect colors on the roundels."

"I guess that proves it was him, doesn't it?"

"It will as soon as I see the ship for myself."

Sounding disappointed, she said, "Okay, then I guess we're going out to this air field where he's supposed to be?"

"Probably, but not today. I'm going to stop for some gas and call Smythe to see what his investigators have found out. After that maybe we ought to get some lunch and figure out where we're going to stay tonight." Stifling a yawn, I added, "I could use a nap."

On our way into Burdette Field we'd passed a Richfield service station where Western crossed Manchester Avenue. I pulled in and, after the attendant filled the Caddy's tank and checked all the vital fluids, I parked next to a public telephone alongside the station office.

"Okay, kiddo, wish me luck. Maybe Smythe will have some news for us."

"I hope so. Good luck, Eddie."

I dropped a nickel in the slot and dialed O for operator. When she came on the line I said I wanted to make a collect person-to-person call to Colonel Efram Smythe at March Army Air Corps field. I didn't know if Smythe would accept the charges, but I was getting a little tired of single-handedly supporting the American Telephone and Telegraph Company.

While I was waiting for the connection to be made, I glanced at my wristwatch. It was a few minutes after one-thirty. I hoped Smythe was back from lunch.

Smythe was not only in his office, but he was feeling generous, too. When the call finally got to his desk, Smythe told the operator he would accept the charges. He even sounded almost cheerful when the operator told us to go ahead and he said, "Hello, Markham."

"Hello, Colonel. I'm calling to see if the investigators you sent to Rimrock airfield turned up anything."

"They did. I believe we now know exactly how the poisoned coffee got aboard our transport."

"I'm all ears."

"Do you remember the little lodge across the highway from the Rimrock airfield?"

"I sure do."

"Well, the first part of the story comes from the cook who works in the lodge's restaurant. He told us a young fellow showed up Saturday morning saying he had just landed at the airfield and needed to earn some money for food and fuel for his ship. The cook was short-handed because one of his waitresses was sick, so he took pity on the kid and put him to work clearing tables and washing dishes. He worked all day Saturday and showed up again for work on Sunday morning.

"Now, the rest of the story comes from the waitress who worked Sunday morning. She told us two army pilots—presumably Captain Miller and Lieutenant Jones—came in for breakfast early and they had the thermos bottle with them. While they were having breakfast, they asked the waitress to fill the thermos bottle with coffee. She was busy with customers, so she told the young man to take care of it.

"He did, and then a short time later, the young man mysteriously disappeared. Since he was the only one who handled the thermos bottle, we can conclude he's our killer."

Smiling to myself, I said, "Did you get a description of the young man?"

There was a short pause before Smythe said, "Yes, I have it right here. Both the cook and the waitress described him as young, not much more than twenty, and thin with blonde hair that need cutting, and blue eyes. Does that fit anyone you know?"

I turned and made a thumbs-up gesture toward Clara. "Yes, Colonel Smythe, it does. We encountered a fellow fitting that description yesterday afternoon. He was following us in a Chevrolet sedan, and when I tried to lose him on a winding mountain road, he opened fire on us with a pistol.

"He came within inches of putting a bullet in Miss Bow's head through the back window of our car, but before he could get more shots off, he lost control of his car and crashed into a tree at the side of the road. I kept going and, by the time the cops got there, he was gone, too. You can read about that part of it in this morning's *L.A. Times*."

Smythe was quiet for a moment and I thought he might be

making notes again. Finally, he said, "Do you think it was wise not to wait for the police?"

"I didn't know if the driver was injured or not, but I wasn't going to risk hanging around and letting him get another shot at Miss Bow. Remember, Colonel, my first priority is Miss Bow's safety."

"I understand, Markham. Under the circumstances I probably would have done the same thing."

"There's one more thing about the incident you should know."

"What is that?"

"It has to do with how the killer found us. I'm pretty sure he found us when we were at Glendale Air Terminal, and the only person who knew we'd be there is you. That suggests to me that someone in your organization is passing information to whoever is behind all of this."

Smythe was quiet for a long moment. Then he said, "As much as I hate to think one of my people would do such a thing, I must admit what you said suggests the same thing to me. I'll definitely look into it."

"Thanks, Colonel. That's all I've got for the moment, but before I hang up, do you have anything new from Camp Stanley and Kelly Field yet?"

"Not yet. The investigators didn't take off from Rimrock until a little while ago because a thunderstorm delayed them on the ground. They should get into Kelly tonight. I've intentionally kept their arrival quiet in the hope a surprise visit might catch someone off guard."

"Forgive me for asking, Colonel, but how much authority do your investigators really have?"

"Plenty. They're carrying teletyped orders directly from the Commanding General, Army Air Corps Western Division Headquarters, the Presidio, San Francisco. Those orders instruct all Army personnel to cooperate to the fullest extent with any requests made by the investigators."

Impressed, I said, "That ought to do it."

"Yes, it should."

"Okay, Colonel, thanks for the information."

"You're welcome. Stay in touch. And, Markham?"

"Yes?"

"Good luck."

"Thanks, Colonel."

Leaving the booth I took a good look around, but saw no one who appeared to be paying the slightest attention to us. As I slid behind the steering wheel, Clara said, "Good news?"

Starting the engine, I said, "Yes, very good news."

"Tell me."

Pulling back into the northbound lane of Western, I said, "Colonel Smythe's investigators have figured out how and when the coffee was poisoned."

"Really? How?"

I recited Smythe's report on what his investigators learned at Rimrock, concluding with, "Best of all, the descriptions of the young man given by the waitress and cook fit Blaylock to a T. That reminds me, do you happen to remember what color his eyes are?"

She only had to think about that for a moment. "Blue. I remember that clearly because his eyes were the first thing I noticed about him. They were a striking shade of pale blue."

"That also fits with the descriptions."

From the corner of my eye I saw Clara shiver. That was understandable. She had eaten lunch and, remembering how she had behaved that day in my drawing room, perhaps more with the man who was trying to kill her. That would make anyone shiver.

Getting back to my conversation with Smythe, I said, "In exchange for that information I told him what happened to us yesterday afternoon, and even though we didn't get a clear look at him, I fibbed a little and told Smythe the guy who shot at us fit the description of the young man who poisoned the coffee in Rimrock."

Clara said, "That wasn't a very big fib."

"No, it wasn't, and it ties the incidents together for Smythe. I also told him how we think Blaylock found us yesterday, although I didn't use his name."

"What did the colonel think about that?"

"As you would expect, he wasn't happy about the idea that he has a spy in his midst, but he did promise to look into it."

"Do you think he really will?"

"Yes, I'm sure he will. Disloyalty is something military guys like Smythe take very seriously."

"I should certainly think they would. Did the colonel have any other good news?"

"No, that was pretty much it. His investigators were delayed by a storm in Rimrock, so they won't get into San Antonio until . . . ." Suddenly the faint alarm bells I had been hearing since Alice read me Charlie Barton's wire went up to full volume.

Slapping the palm of my hand against the Caddy's steering wheel, I said, "Damn it! That's it!"

Clara jumped a little. "What's it, Eddie?"

"Something's been nagging at the back of my mind ever since Alice read me Charlie Barton's wire this morning. I just realized what it is."

Fear was back in Clara's voice. "What, Eddie? What's the matter?"

"What's the matter is that my guess about why Charlie wants to talk to us so urgently tonight is completely wrong."

Sounding puzzled, Clara said, "I don't get it."

"Do you remember I thought Wellman sent Barton out here because he's between a rock and a hard place? Because the Army is putting pressure on him to spill the beans Lasky doesn't want spilled?"

"Yes. Now you don't think that's the reason Charlie wants to meet us?"

"It can't be. I should have realized that the Army investigators couldn't have gotten to San Antonio by the time Barton sent that wire yesterday afternoon. In fact, Smythe said they won't get there until tonight. What's more, Smythe told me he's kept their arrival a secret, so Wellman has no idea the Army is about to kick down his door and demand that he tell them about the attack on us in the French village."

"Okay, so Charlie wants to talk to us about something else. Is that a big deal?"

My mind was racing through other reasons Barton might want to see us and I did not like one of those possibilities. "It could be. When I talked to Bill from Pasadena the other day, he said Lasky was very upset about not knowing where you are. And I'm sure the story about the Army looking for us that appeared with your photo in the *Times* yesterday morning upset him even more.

"I'm wondering if Lasky ordered Barton to set up a meeting with us so his security goons can grab you and put you someplace where Lasky can control the situation and keep you under wraps."

"Oh, no! We can't let that happen, Eddie!"

"No, we can't, especially when I'm pretty darn sure someone at Lasky-Paramount is involved in this right up to their eyebrows."

Twenty-Nine

2:00 P.M. – Wednesday – September 22, 1926
Western Avenue – Los Angeles

As we rolled past the empty fields and occasional light industrial buildings along Western Avenue between Inglewood and downtown, I nervously watched the rearview mirror for invisible followers and willed my mind to concentrate on what we should do about Charlie Barton. Maybe it was lack of sleep or it could have been my mental state, but whatever it was, my brain just kept going around in circles without even coming close to an answer.

Clara's mind must have been thinking about Barton also because she eventually asked the same question I was pondering. "Eddie, what are we going to do about Charlie Barton?"

Hoping she was having better luck at finding an answer than I was, I said, "I'm not sure, Clara. What do you think?"

Clara was obviously thinking more clearly than I because she had reduced the elements of the issue down to their simplest terms. "Well, it seems to me we only have two choices. We either meet Charlie or we don't. And, if you think there's a good reason to meet him, maybe you could set up something like you did when we met Colonel Smythe at that airfield, where we could watch for a trap before we actually show up."

"Yeah, but that didn't work out too well."

"I guess it didn't, if that's where Blaylock found us."

"That has to be where he found us. What makes me angry is that he must have been behind us when we went to the bank and to the Don Lee dealership and to the car rental agency and I never saw him."

"That's because you didn't know what to look for. Once that kid told you what kind of a car he was driving, you spotted him outside the hotel right away."

"Yes, I spotted him right after he had us trapped."

"But you lost him just like you said you would."

"It was too close. Do you realize that if you had moved a split second later when I told you to duck, you'd be dead right now?"

"Yes, and if you had moved a split second later when you pulled me out of the way in Texas I would be dead right now, or if you hadn't realized something was wrong with the pilots and figured out how to land that Army ship, we'd both be dead right now. For cryin' out loud, Eddie, you saved my life three times in less than a week! What more do you want?"

"I suppose, but . . . . "

"But nothing! You did all that and there's no two ways about it. Something's just got you down in the dumps right now. I understand that, but you've got to snap out of it, Eddie. I need you!"

It was the vehemence of her tone as much as Clara's words that startled me. "You're right. Maybe I'm just tired, but I can't get my mind to work right."

"Okay, I'll help you. Like you keep telling me, we'll get through this together. Now, is there any good reason why you need to meet with Barton?'

"No, I suppose not. I'd just like to know what he's got on his mind and find out if I'm right about why he wants to meet us."

"Okay. How about this? Suppose we decide not to meet him, but you call him like he asked and tell him he has to talk to you about whatever is so darned important on the telephone?"

I thought about Clara's idea. It made perfect sense. "Yes, that would work and it's a much less risky way to handle the situation."

"Good, then we won't meet him. That's one question answered. Let's try another one. Where are we going to stay tonight?"

"Well, when I was thinking we were going to meet Charlie, I had it in mind that we would stay on Ventura Boulevard in Toluca or Laurelwood. That's Route 101 and there are several motor hotels out there. Since we aren't meeting him, it doesn't make any sense to stay so close to where he apparently wants us to be. About the only requirement I can think of is that we should stay in the northern part of the county so when we call Charlie it won't have to be a long-distance call."

Clara seemed to be thinking that over. Then she said, "Could we stay in Hollywood? There are lots of hotels there."

"I'm not certain Hollywood is our best choice. Except for the flophouses between Gower and Western, most of the hotels are ritzy places with restaurants like the Dining Room of the Stars at the Hollywood Hotel. As you pointed out a while back, staying in one of those places increases the odds of you being recognized by somebody who knows you.

"Also, I'm not too hot on the idea of staying in a hotel where we could end up stuck in a room several floors up, which would put us a long way from the car in the event we needed to leave in a hurry."

"Okay," Clara said thoughtfully, "How about somewhere toward the coast on Santa Monica Boulevard? I think there are some auto courts out there."

I gave that some thought and it made sense. "That's a very good idea. There are a few tourist motor hotels on Santa Monica Boulevard between Hollywood and Beverly Hills. "

"All right, Santa Monica Boulevard it is. See, Eddie, we make a good team!"

Clara was right and she had just taught me a good lesson. Up until now I had made all the decisions, and that had been a mistake. She had a lot more savvy than most people, me included, gave her credit for. I vowed then and there to include her in figuring out our moves from that point on. Besides, it was her life we were protecting and she deserved some say in how we protected it.

"You're right, honey. We are a good team."

She leaned over and gave me a kiss on the cheek. "Okay, that's two questions down. For the next one, how about lunch? I'm gettin' pretty hungry. Is there a sandwich place or a delicatessen where we could pick something up to eat when we get a room?"

I have no idea how she did it, but Clara had charmed my brain into cooperating again. I knew just the place to get the sandwiches she wanted. "Yes, there are a couple of sandwich joints on Jefferson across from the University of Southern California. They cater to the student lunch crowd and they're only a couple of blocks out of our way."

Clara sounded justifiably pleased with herself. "Good! It'll be like a picnic! That's three good answers we've come up with."

"Kiddo, I'm sorry I was down in the dumps. I'm probably just tired. I think I'll do better if I can get a few hours of rest."

"I think you will, too, and I know how we can get you that rest. After we get a room and have our little picnic, you go to bed and sleep until it's time to call Charlie Barton. While you sleep, I'll stand guard. If I see any danger around, I'll wake you up right away. Do we have a deal?"

Clara stuck her hand out and I shook it. "Yeah, kiddo, we've got a deal."

I turned right on Jefferson, and two blocks later parked at the curb in front of Rick's Sandwich Shop. Rick's made up their sandwiches early in the day, wrapped them in wax paper, and laid them out in trays with neatly hand-printed cards identifying the kind of sandwich on each tray.

Clara took the lead, saying, "What kind of sandwiches do you like?"

I scanned the cards and said, "I'm hungry, I'll have a roast beef with cheddar cheese and a bologna."

She picked up my sandwiches, plus a chicken salad sandwich for herself. Then she went over to where cookies were displayed on a platter. "You like oatmeal cookies with raisins?"

I was getting a kick out watching her pick out the menu for our picnic. "Sure, oatmeal cookies are always good."

She told the woman behind the counter we would have two oatmeal cookies with raisins and two sugar cookies. Clara also picked out two shiny red apples and added them to our lunch. Then she walked over to a soft drink cooler and lifted the lid.

"Come over here and pick out what you want to drink."

I looked at the variety of bottles standing up to their necks in cold water and grabbed a Nehi grape soda. Clara picked out a Nehi root beer, and with the items for our picnic lunch selected, the woman behind the counter rang them up on her cash register. The sandwiches and apples were a nickel each and the cookies were three-cents apiece. Adding in our two soft drinks for ten cents, plus two-cents for the bottle deposits, our lunch came to a grand total of forty-nine cents.

The woman counted out my change from a dollar bill, loaded our purchases into a brown paper sack, and we were back in the Cadillac. The entire process had taken less than five minutes.

I turned right on Vermont Avenue and went around the block to get us back to Western. From there it was only about four miles to Santa Monica Boulevard, where I turned left in the direction of Beverly Hills.

We were in an unincorporated area of the county that was mostly farmland, but according to recent newspaper articles, that would soon change because in a few months Santa Monica Boulevard was slated to become the western-most leg of a new transcontinental highway. The highway, to be called U.S. Route 66, was to begin in Chicago and end in Santa Monica.

Besides going right through Hollywood, Route 66 will also pass through Beverly Hills, a planned all-white community established by a land development company right after the turn of the century. Beverly Hills had become a decidedly upper class area populated be some of Los Angeles' wealthiest people, including motion picture celebrities such as Mary Pickford and Douglas Fairbanks, Will Rogers, and Valentino.

Owing largely to the community's prosperous residents, the downtown district of Beverly Hills was becoming known for its exclusive and fashionable shops. We were only a few blocks from that ritzy shopping area when I spotted a motor hotel called the Rancho Rodeo Motor Lodge ahead on our right.

I pulled to the shoulder of the road and pointed to the sign. "What do you think, kiddo?"

"It looks swell to me. Who are we going to be at the Rancho Rodeo Motor Lodge?"

"I thought I would just use Jerome Miller again."

Putting on her mischievous grin, Clara said, "Okay, then I'm changing my name. I am now Eloise Miller of the Santa Barbara Millers."

Returning her grin, I said, "I'm sure mom would be honored."

Rather than a court layout of individual cottages, the Rancho Rodeo was a single structure built in an L shape. The long stem of the L paralleled Santa Monica Boulevard and consisted of ten rooms. The short stem stuck out toward the street on our left and housed the office. The open space between the L and the road was a graveled parking area, except for a large garden area at the end opposite the office. The garden consisted of a lawn, colorful flowers, a few short palm trees, and some brightly painted garden furniture, all enclosed by a white rail fence.

I parked the Cadillac in front of the office where it could be seen through the windows. This I did to assure the proprietor of the Rancho Rodeo that we were of sufficient means to be worthy of accommodations in their classy establishment.

As I walked in, a middle-aged Henna redhead in a Mexican style blouse decorated with colorful stitching stood up from a desk behind the registration counter and said, "Good afternoon, sir. Do you wish accommodations?"

"Yes, we need a room for two people and we'll be staying one night."

"Then you're in luck. We have one vacancy and it's our largest and finest room overlooking our beautiful garden. It rents for seven dollars per night. Will that meet your requirements?"

I told her it would, and while I entered my fraudulent information in a ritzy leather-bound registration book, she informed me that complimentary coffee and doughnuts were served in the office from six a.m. to nine. Hot cocoa was offered from seven to nine in the evenings.

When I had finished writing, I began counting out seven dollars from my billfold, but she stopped me. "Oh, no, sir. You can settle your account when you check out tomorrow. Check out time, by the way, is noon."

Thinking that it was rather novel to be so trusted by an innkeeper, I accepted the key she handed me. The key ring was also equipped with a brass oval tag that was engraved with the Rancho Rodeo's name and the number ten.

I parked the Cadillac next to the "beautiful garden" and we wasted no time in unloading our bags from the trunk. That chore completed, Clara went to work laying out our picnic on a table next to a large window overlooking the garden and I surveyed our accommodations.

The room really was quite spacious. The walls were painted a sort of sandy pink that went nicely with the burgundy bedspread, curtains, and upholstery on a pair of comfortable-looking arm chairs against the common wall we shared with the room next door. The headboard of the bed was against the opposite wall, which had no window looking out on the vacant lot next door.

Two doors at the back of the room opened onto a large bathroom with a combination tub/shower and a built-in closet. Looking around the room, I noticed an unusual feature, a stylish, compact Atwater-Kent radio set resting atop a small table between the armchairs, evidence that the proprietor of the Rancho Rodeo Motor Lodge spared no expense in providing the latest in luxuries for their guests. I did note, however, that the device was securely bolted to the top of the table on which it sat.

Clara noticed me looking at the radio. "Isn't that swell? We have a radio! Do you think you could find us some nice music to go with our lunch?"

I said, "Will do," and turned the knob labeled "On-Off/Volume." After waiting for the set to warm up, it rewarded my efforts by playing an Al Jolson recording of a song with rather silly lyrics called *Pasadena*.

Clara exclaimed, "Wonderful! And our picnic is all ready."

Sitting at the table, I surveyed the spread of sandwiches, apples, cookies and drinks all neatly arranged on paper napkins. "You set a mighty fine picnic table, ma'am."

"Thank you, sir. It's not as elegant as it might be, but who cares? I'm hungry!"

Without further ado, we enthusiastically dug into our late lunch. After wolfing down two sandwiches and an apple, all washed down with my grape soda, I decided to save my cookies for later.

When we had finished, Clara said, "Okay, Eddie, turn off the radio and get into that bed."

I did as instructed, hanging my jacket in the closet, laying out my trousers on one of the armchairs, and setting the Colt on the nightstand. Once I was stretched out on the bed, Clara sat beside me.

"I'm going to read my book while I keep watch. When should I wake you up?"

With eyelids that were already drooping, I said, "About six."

"Okay, darling. Sweet dreams."

I slept like a log and woke up to find Clara sitting on the edge of the bed again. She was gently shaking my shoulder, and when my eyes opened, she gave me a sweet kiss and said, "Wake up, Eddie. It's six o'clock and I love you!"

Smiling up at her, I said, "Mmm, I can't think of a nicer way to wake up."

Her mischievous grin instantly appeared. "Well, I can."

"Stop teasing, you vixen, and let me up so I can splash some water in my face and get my eyes open."

By six-twenty I was awake, dressed, and locking the door to room ten as we left to call Charlie Barton. I turned left out of the Rancho Rodeo parking lot onto Santa Monica Boulevard. Clara, probably wondering why I had not turned right toward the downtown area of Beverly Hills, asked, "Where are we going to make the telephone call?"

"Hollywood. Even though we're making a local call and I don't think anyone can easily find out where it originated, I'll feel a little safer calling from somewhere other than where we're spending the night."

"You're right, it's better to play it safe."

The traffic on Santa Monica was heavier than it had been during the afternoon—probably people making their way home from work—and the sun had already set, so all I could see in the rearview mirror were headlights. Again playing it safe, I turned left on La Cienega and cut up to Sunset Boulevard, watching the mirror to see if any of those headlights followed us. None did.

I turned right when we got to Sunset and continued east about six blocks to a good-sized grocery market on the southwest corner of Sunset and Havenhurst. I picked the spot because the market stayed open late and had a well-lit, paved parking area with a public telephone on its west side. There was an empty parking place next to the booth and I pulled into it.

"Okay, kiddo, here we go."

"Should I wait in the car while you make the telephone call?"

"If you want, but I'd rather have you come along so you can at least hear my side of the conversation."

Clara sounded pleased. "Oh, I'd much rather come with you."

"Then let's go."

I stepped into the booth and fished around in my jacket pocket for the receipt from The Tides Inn on which I had jotted Charlie Barton's home telephone number. A little more pocket fishing turned up a nickel. With Clara standing close by, I dropped the nickel in the slot and dialed Barton's number. According to my wristwatch, it was precisely six-forty-five.

Barton answered on the second ring and I said, "Hello, Charlie, Eddie Markham here."

He sounded happy to hear my voice. "Hi, Eddie. I was hoping it was you. I was afraid you hadn't gotten my wire."

"I got it. What's cooking?"

"Can you come over to my place? I need to discuss some things with you."

"No, Charlie, I can't come over to your place."

There was surprise in his voice. "Why not? Is something wrong?"

"There's plenty wrong. Clara is still very much in danger and I'm not taking her any place we might be expected to show up."

"Has something else happened?"

"Yes. Another attempt on her life was made yesterday afternoon."

Now he sounded shocked. "Oh, no. What happened?"

"I noticed a car following us, and when I tried to lose him, the guy started shooting at us. He got off a lucky shot that missed Clara by a fraction of an inch. It was a damned close call."

Out of the corner of my eye I saw Clara shiver. I reached down and took her hand as Charlie said, "Oh, God! Is she okay?"

"Physically, Clara's fine. Emotionally, she's pretty upset over all of this so you can probably understand why we're being extra cautious." Clara gave my hand a squeeze.

"Yes, of course, but we need to talk."

"We're talking right now, Charlie. Tell me what you need to tell me."

Barton hesitated for a long moment. "Okay, Eddie. I guess the first thing is that Bill Wellman is very worried. He expected to hear from you again."

"Tell Wellman I've been a little busy. What else?"

"The big problem is Jesse Lasky. He's furious and he wants his star back."

"Lasky can just sit and stew for all I care. He had a chance to prevent all this by letting Wellman call in the authorities last Friday, but Lasky was more concerned about bad publicity than he was about his star. It's a little late to be changing his tune now."

I was getting a little hot under the collar, and from the tone of his voice, so was Barton. "Letting Lasky sit and stew, as you put it, is easier said than done. He's trying to put the blame for Clara being missing on Bill and me, and he's making things pretty tough on us."

"Is anybody shooting at you?"

"Well, no, but . . . ."

"Then you don't know what tough is, pal."

Barton paused for another moment and I guessed he might be counting to ten. Finally, he said, "Eddie, you're right, of course, but one of the reasons Lasky called me back to L.A. was to try and convince you to hand Clara over to him and his security people. I don't suppose there's any chance of you agreeing to do that is there?"

"That's not my decision to make, Charlie. It's entirely up to Clara and she's vehement about having nothing to do with Lasky until this mess is cleared up."

"Oh, come on, Eddie. You're running the show; she'll do what you tell her to do."

"That's hogwash, Charlie. Here, I'm going to put Clara on and you can ask her yourself."

Before Barton could say anything, I put my hand over the telephone mouthpiece and said, "Clara, Charlie seems to think that not going to Lasky for protection is my idea, not yours. He wants to hear it from you."

To call Clara's expression angry was an understatement. She said, "Let me in there, Eddie, I'll let him hear it from me all right!"

Clara and I traded places and she said into the telephone mouthpiece, "Charlie, you can tell Jesse Lasky to go straight to hell, and this ain't Eddie talkin' now, it's me."

What came next was a long pause during which, I surmised Barton tried to pitch Clara on how concerned Lasky was for her wellbeing, because when she spoke again, she said, "That's a bunch of hogwash and you know it, Charlie. Lasky doesn't give a damn about me; all he cares about is getting rich off of Clara Bow. And I can tell you he ain't gonna be doin' that much longer, either! Now, here's Eddie. I'm through talking to you."

As Clara and I traded places again, I gave her a wink and she gave me a guess-I-told-him look. Into the telephone mouthpiece, I said, "I'm back, Charlie. Are you satisfied now?"

Barton sighed audibly, and sounding as if a ton of cow manure had just landed on him, he said, "Yeah, Eddie. Lasky will be hopping mad, but at least I can tell him I got it straight from Clara."

"Fine. Do you have anything else for me?"

After a short pause, he said, "No, I guess that's it."

"Okay, I have a couple of questions for you. Has anything unusual happened in San Antonio during the past few days?"

He paused again, as if thinking, before saying, "No, not that I can think of."

"How about anyone missing from the cast or crew?"

"I can't think of anyone . . . no, there is something. That stunt pilot Schulberg was so hot on flew the coop. The last time anyone saw him was early Friday morning. I guess he got cold feet or somebody gave him a better offer. I'm glad we don't really need him."

I gave Clara a nod and asked Barton my second question. "Speaking of Schulberg, what's he saying about all this?"

"He hasn't said a word that I know of. Lasky's been doing all the hollering. Maybe Schulberg is showing some good sense for a change by keeping his yap shut."

"Okay, last question: When are you going back to Texas?"

Sounding miserable, Barton said, "If I still have a job, I'm scheduled to fly back on Friday."

"All right, Charlie. That's all I wanted to know. If you need to reach me, leave a message with my secretary. And, just to be clear, she doesn't know where we are either, but I check in with her from time to time."

"Okay. Look, Eddie, I'm really sorry you and Clara are being put through the wringer like this. If I can do anything to help, just say the word."

"I will, Charlie. Goodnight."

I dropped the receiver back on its hook without waiting for a response from Barton. "Okay, kiddo, let's skedaddle."

Thirty

7:00 P.M. – Wednesday – September 22, 1926
Santa Monica Boulevard – Hollywood

I followed a random and meandering path back to Santa Monica Boulevard, keeping a sharp eye on the rearview mirror for anyone else following the same random path. The only things I saw in the glass were empty streets and the light from an occasional streetlamp refracted by the spider web of cracks in our back window.

After a while Clara said, "What do you think, Eddie? Was Charlie trying to lure us into a trap or were we worried about nothing?"

"Well, Barton admitted he came out here from Texas on orders from Lasky to try and convince us you'd be better off under his protection, so it seems to me if Lasky went to the expense of flying Charlie out here, he'd be likely to cover his bet with some sort of plan to catch up with us in case Barton failed.

"But if Lasky had a scheme cooking, I don't think Barton knew about it. Charlie invited us to his house, and I bet Lasky had someone watching the place in case we showed up there, or maybe to follow Barton if he left to meet us somewhere else."

Clara said, "Then we did the right thing by not meeting Charlie?"

"I'm certain of it."

"Did he say anything else that I missed?"

"Only that Billy Blaylock has been among the missing in San Antonio since last Friday morning, but we already knew that."

When we finally meandered back to Santa Monica Boulevard, I turned west, toward Beverly Hills, and Clara said, "Where are we headed now?"

"I'm not sure. Are you getting hungry?"

"Yes, a little."

"Okay, we'll see what kind of food they serve in Beverly Hills. If you don't mind, though, I'd like to get a peek at the Rancho Rodeo just to be sure there aren't any surprises waiting for us there."

"Okay. What are we gonna do tomorrow?"

"We need to talk about that. I've got a couple of ideas we can discuss."

"Eddie, I get the feeling you're going out of your way to include me in making choices, and I think that's really swell of you, but you don't have to do that. I have complete faith in you. If I didn't, I wouldn't be here."

"I appreciate that, Clara, but I realized this afternoon that I've been making a big mistake by not talking things through with you before making decisions. From now on, we're making those decisions together. Like you said, we're a pretty good team."

Clara was quiet for a while as if she was deep in thought. Finally, she said, "Darling, I think I said some things this afternoon I shouldn't have said. I was trying to snap you out of the funk you were in, and as usual, I overdid it. I never meant to make you think I don't trust you or anything at all like that."

"I don't think that, but what you said made me think of some other things. For example, I think you are a whole lot smarter than I thought you were before we got to know each other. I also like the way you think. My head gets all cluttered up with stuff that doesn't really matter. You have a way of going straight to the heart of an issue, and that makes matters a lot clearer when a decision needs to be made. I'd be a fool not to take advantage of that kind of intelligence."

"Gosh, Eddie, do you really think I'm smart? Nobody ever said that to me before!"

"I don't think it, I know it. I also think you sometimes go out of your way to hide how smart you are. I'm not sure why you do that, except maybe because you have the idea men prefer dumb women."

"Don't they?"

"I can't speak for all men, but for me, I don't have much use for dumb people, male or female. I much prefer being around intelligent people who think for themselves, especially when it comes to the woman with whom I would like to spend the rest of my life."

"Eddie, do you really, truly think I'm smart enough to be that woman?"

"I really, truly do. You like to learn, you catch on quick, and you have a kind of natural savvy that makes you see things differently than others. The fact that you're very likely the cutest, sexiest woman in the world is just a bonus—a very pleasant bonus, but not an essential one."

She was quiet again for quite a while, and then I heard what sounded like a sob. I looked over and saw that Clara's face was buried in her hands and she was crying like a baby. I put a hand on her shoulder and said, "Honey? What's the matter? What did I say to upset you?"

Clara wiped her eyes with the backs of her hands, sniffed, and said, "You only said the words—the exact words—I've always dreamed a man would say to me someday, but I never really believed that dream would ever come true."

"Well, I meant what I said, but I didn't mean to . . . ."

"Eddie, I don't mean to be so emotional, but sometimes I feel like I'm living in that dream—that none of this is really happening and I'm gonna wake up and find out I just dreamed you, that you aren't real. Sometimes that scares the hell out of me."

"Well, kiddo, that's only fair."

Startled, she said, "What do you mean it's only fair?"

"Sometimes I have to pinch myself to be sure I'm not the one who's dreaming. I mean you could probably have any leading man in Hollywood, or any man anywhere for that matter, so why me? Then I wonder if all this isn't just some attachment you formed because I happened to be in the right place at the right time to save your life—that you've fallen in love with me out of gratitude and nothing else."

Suddenly Clara sounded very sincere and serious. "Eddie, a minute ago you said I was smart. I am. I'm smart enough to learn the difference between real honest love and other kinds of . . . of attachments. Sure, I'm grateful to you for saving my life and protecting me, but that's only a small part of what I feel for you, and I can prove it."

That surprised me. "You can?"

"I can. Think back to that production meeting in the old barn when we first met. Do you remember that?"

"Sure. You kept looking at me while Wellman was up there talking. I thought maybe I reminded you of someone."

"You did. You reminded me of someone I met in my dreams. I'm trying to say I could tell even before we ever met that there was something different . . . something really special about you. That's why I came over to meet you after the meeting. And do you remember when I came to your drawing room on the train?"

"Oh, yes. I'm not likely to forget that."

"Well, I wish you would. It was rotten of me, but I came there to test you."

Another surprise. "Test me? What do you mean by that?"

Her voice took on a tone of sadness and maybe regret. "I mean I was strongly attracted to you and I wanted to find out if you were really a different kind of man, or if you were just like all the rest. Oh, don't worry, I never would have really jumped in bed with you, but if you had been willing, I'd have known you were just another guy who wanted to screw me because I have a nice face and I can act sexy."

"So, I take it I passed your test?"

"Oh, yes, but when you rejected my . . . my advances so strongly, I was actually hurt. You passed my test with flying colors, but then I was afraid you really didn't like me. It took me a while to realize it was the other Clara Bow you didn't like, which meant you might like the real me. I decided right then and there, long before you saved my life in Texas, that I was going to find a way for you meet the woman I really am under all that hogwash I dish out for the fans. I just never expected the chance to do that would come along the way it did."

It was my turn to be quiet while I thought things through. Clara had just explained two events that had been nagging at the back of my mind ever since our relationship changed, and I did not doubt the truth of her explanation about the drawing room scene in the slightest. It was exactly the sort of crazy scheme one of her movie characters might have thought up.

My lack of a prompt response to her confession seemed to be worrying Clara. In a very small voice, she said, "Eddie, maybe I shoulda kept my mouth shut about that stuff, but I wanted to prove what I said—that I was attracted to you long before you saved my life. I hope you aren't mad at me. Are you?"

"Kiddo, you're right, that was a rotten thing to do and I'm darn close to being furious with you for playing that kind of dirty trick on me, but I think I understand why you thought it was necessary, and I can't be mad at you for that. I just hope you won't feel you need to do something like that again."

"Oh, you don't have to worry about that. I may not know all there is to know about you yet, but I'm pretty impressed with what I've learned so far—impressed enough to know I'd really like to be that woman you want to spend the rest of your life with."

Near the end of our conversation we passed the Rancho Rodeo.

I drove right by because I did not want to be too obvious about taking a look at what was going on there. A ways beyond the motor hotel I made a U-turn and drove back to park on the opposite side of Santa Monica Boulevard.

As I studied the automobiles in the parking area, Clara asked, "Does it look okay, Eddie?"

"I think so. There are only nine cars in the lot. One of them is parked in front of the office, so it might belong to whoever is working at the registration desk. Each of the remaining cars is parked in front of a room, which leaves two empty slots, ours and the one for room number seven."

While we were sitting there at the side of the road, a man came out of number five and walked to the office. He returned a few moments later carrying a cup of something, probably complimentary hot cocoa. After the fellow closed his room door nothing else moved at the Rancho Rodeo for at least ten minutes.

"Okay, I think we're all right. We'll check everything again before we pull in after dinner. Let's go find something good to eat."

I made another U-turn and drove into Beverly Hills proper. The business district is mostly to the south of Santa Monica Boulevard. To the north were the gently curving streets of Beverly Hills' ritzy residential areas. I turned south on Rodeo Drive—well, it actually angles to the southeast—and headed toward Wilshire Boulevard, which runs through the heart of what passes for downtown Beverly Hills.

There was only one long block of Rodeo Drive between Santa Monica Boulevard and Wilshire, and just as we reached the end of that block I saw a sign on the right advertising Momma Luca's Italian Ristorante.

"How do you feel about Italian food, kiddo?"

Enthusiastically, Clara said, "I love spaghetti and meatballs!"

"Okay, we'll give Momma Luca a try."

The restaurant's building was a large residence that had been converted into an eatery. As we walked into what was probably a foyer in the original scheme of things, an older fellow in a well-worn tuxedo jacket welcomed us to Momma Luca's and showed us to a small, intimate table for two in a dining room I guessed had once been the parlor. We were partially hidden from view by one of several large potted plants that served as both decoration and room dividers.

The maitre d' seated Clara and left a pair of leather-bound menus on the table. He told us that our waiter would be along momentarally. I looked at Clara over a typically Italian red and white checkerboard tablecloth and a romantic candle stuck artistically into a squat wine bottle so the melted wax dribbled down onto the glass. The candle's soft light did wonderful things to her eyes and complexion, giving them a glowing radience that would have made a beautiful painting.

She caught me staring at her. "Whatcha thinkin', Eddie?"

I reached across the table and she put her hand in mine. "I'm thinking what a lovely portrait you make in the candlelight."

Clara Bow, a woman who must have heard such complements hundreds of times, actually blushed. She squeezed my hand and said, "Even with a big wad of gauze stuck to my face?"

"Even so."

With a loving smile, Clara said, "Thank you, Eddie. I hope you still think thoughts like that when I'm old and gray."

"The glow I'm seeing comes from within you. It will always be there."

Our little romantic interlude was interrupted by a young fellow with facial features identical to those of the maitre d', which made me think Mamma Luca's was a family business. He said, "Good evening, folks. What can I bring you to drink?"

I said, "What do you have?"

"We have coffee, tea and a selection of Italian soft drinks."

When I continued to look at him without saying anything, the young man gave me the universal waiter's wink of the times and added, "I believe I also saw a bottle of grape juice that looks a great deal like a fine imported Italian Chianti, but of course cannot be because wine cannot be served to our customers."

I gave Clara a glance and she was wearing her sly grin. She gave me a small nod and I said, "Then we'll each have a glass of grape juice."

"Yes, sir. I'll bring that immediately."

Opening the menu before me, I said, "Well, let's see what kind of spaghetti and meatballs this law-abiding restaurant offers."

Looking down the bill o' fare, I found a variety of pastas, including Clara's favorite. When I looked up again, I saw that Clara had not opened her menu and was still looking at me. I said, "I hope you haven't lost your appetite. They've got some pretty tasty sounding stuff in here."

Clara smiled her soft smile that melted my heart every time I saw it. "You choose for both of us, Eddie. I just want to enjoy being here with you."

I winked. "All right, kiddo, I hope you were serious about liking spaghetti and meatballs, 'cuz that's what we're going to have."

"Spaghetti and meatballs sound wonderful."

When our waiter returned with two large wine glasses filled to the brim with what tasted a lot more like a good quality Chianti than grape juice, I told him we would both have Spaghetti Bolognese dinners with meatballs. He said, "Our dinners come with a cup of Minestrone soup and a small green salad with Italian-style dressing. Will that be acceptable?"

"That sounds just fine."

While we drank our Chianti and waited for the Minestrone to arrive, I said, "Since you've been kind enough to explain some things to me tonight, perhaps you will answer one more question for me."

Clara grinned. "You want to know what I'm doing saying I love you when I'm supposed to be engaged to Victor Fleming, don't you?"

"Very good mind reading, kiddo. Yes, since I'm not in the habit of going around falling in love with engaged or married women, I do wonder about that small detail."

Putting on a serious, concerned expression, she said, "Well, I hope you aren't in the habit of going around falling in love with any women, engaged or not."

"I am not."

"Well, put your mind at ease. Victor and I are just good friends. The engagement was a gimmick thought up by Lasky's publicity department. Victor is directing my next movie, the one I'm scheduled to make after *Wings*, and since we've been seen together, somebody came up with the bright idea that having us be in a torrid romance would help sell the picture.

"Victor and I started seeing each other in sort of a romantic way, but it wasn't long before we both realized that wasn't going to work. But we really like each other as friends, and Victor has done a lot to help me. He introduced me to his agent and a lawyer he uses to negotiate contracts. They were the ones who got me my new contract with Lasky—one that makes the studio pay me what I'm worth to them and cuts B. P. out of the picture."

"I see. So I needn't worry about Fleming socking me in the jaw when he finds out what's been going on behind his back?"

Clara snickered. "Victor wouldn't hurt a fly, especially for that reason. In fact, I'm sure he will approve of you whole-heartedly. He really does care about me and wants me to be happy just like I want him to be happy, and when I tell him how happy you make me, he'll probably shake your hand."

As we enjoyed an excellent Italian dinner, the conversation drifted off to the sorts of subjects couples getting to know one another talk about—subjects like where we would like to go on a vacation and what kinds of music we like. It was quite enjoyable to be normal for a short time.

By nine o'clock we were back in room ten at the Rancho Rodeo Motor Lodge with the radio softly playing romantic orchestra music while we nibbled on cookies and each other for dessert. When the latter activity threatened to eliminate any possibility of planning the next day's activities, I said, "Okay, kiddo, we'd better slow down and think about what we're going to do tomorrow."

Clara frowned and glared at me. "Boy, you sure know how to ruin a mood. I certainly hope you won't be like this when nobody's trying to kill us."

"Trust me, you don't need to worry about that."

She put on a petulant face and said, "I hope not. All this fooling around without . . . well, it's making me crazy. And it's not good for my complexion either."

"You're complexion is lovely, kiddo, just like the rest of you. I'm only trying to keep you that way."

Clara sighed. "I know, I know. You said you had a couple of ideas about what we need to do tomorrow. Tell me."

"I think the first thing is to find out if Blaylock's ships, especially the Curtiss he used to strafe us, are really at Brackett Field. If they are, we can let Smythe deal with Blaylock."

Frowning again, Clara said, "After we've been trying so hard to hide from him, going right where he is supposed to be seems awfully foolish."

"It might be, but I think I know how we can do it without Blaylock even knowing we're there. How would you like to go for an airplane ride tomorrow?"

She brightened. "Really? In your airplane?"

"Yes. We can fly over to Brackett, and we might be able to spot Blaylock's ships from the air without even landing. If not, we can land, taxi around the field, and maybe find them that way. Then we head straight for home."

The idea of going for an airplane ride had Clara's spirits soaring again. "Swell! It'll be fun!"

"Another thing I think we need to do after we locate Blaylock's ships is get some help finding out who Blaylock is working for."

"Won't the Army do that?"

I nodded. "They'll try, but it might take them a while. If we can find out for ourselves, we'll know who we have to watch out for after Blaylock is out of circulation."

Clara looked puzzled. "Who can we trust to help us do that?"

"I know a fellow who is a detective sergeant with the Los Angeles Police Department. I interviewed him a while back to get background for a novel, and we've become pretty good friends since. He's as straight as an arrow and a darn good cop. I'm pretty sure he'll help us without making things worse than they already are."

Dubiously, she said, "A cop, huh? They've never been my favorite kind of people, but if you trust him, I guess it's okay."

"Okay, then we have a plan. Now it's your turn to get some sleep while I stand watch."

"Okay, Eddie, but I sure wish you were coming to bed with me. I sleep a lot better with you next to me."

Recalling her bad nightmares Tuesday night at The Tides Inn, I said, "Tell you what, you hit the sack and I'll turn off the lights so it looks like we've retired for the night. If everything stays quiet for a while, I'll come to bed, too. Deal?"

She nodded. "Okay, deal."

When Clara slid between the sheets in a pretty blue nightgown, I kissed her goodnight. She looked up at me and whispered, "Goodnight, darling. Thank you for being so wonderful."

I said, "I don't know if I'm wonderful or not, but if I am, it's because you make me that way."

After turning off the radio and the lights, I settled into a chair at the table with Wellman's Colt close at hand. With the exception of an occasional automobile passing on Santa Monica Boulevard, everything was quiet and peaceful. Even Clara seemed to be sleeping better, although I did hear her moan softly a time or two.

By the time the hands on my wristwatch pointed to eleven-thirty, I decided it was safe to turn in. Moving the Colt to the nightstand on what had become my side of whatever bed we were sleeping in, I stripped down and slipped into bed next to Clara.

She snuggled against me almost immediately and I put my arm around her waist. I shifted my head on the pillow to keep her hair from tickling my nose and tried my darnedest to think about anything but the soft, warm woman pressed against my body.

Thirty-One

By seven I had showered, shaved and dressed for the day. I then sat on the edge of the bed and gently woke Clara.

Her eyes popped open wide and clear. With a smile, she said, "G'mornin', darlin'."

"Good morning, kiddo. How did you sleep?"

"I slept just like I want to sleep every night for the rest of my life, cuddled up next to the man who loves me. How 'bout you?"

"Well, once I got positioned so your hair didn't tickle my nose, I slept great."

Clara giggled. "I could get one of those night caps like they wore back in Victorian days."

"Oh, I think we can manage without going to that extreme. I'm going to take a look around outside and bring us back some coffee from the office."

"Okay, while you do that, I'll get myself up and moving."

I kissed her on the cheek and stepped outside. Everything looked perfectly normal, so I locked the door and strolled down to the office. There I poured coffee into two cardboard cups and doctored Clara's with cream and sugar. I set the cups on a chrome-plated tray, added two tasty-looking raised, glazed doughnuts, and returned to our room.

Clara was still in the shower, so I opened the drapes a little and sat at the table to watch the beginning of a glorious, sunny day. The flowers blooming in the garden were a dazzling palette of red, orange, yellow, and white. This was going to be a great day for flying.

Almost as if Clara was reading my mind, she stepped out of the bathroom and said, "Eddie, is this outfit okay to go flying in?"

She was wearing her peach-colored dress with the built-in scarf collar, a lovely outfit, but not very practical for flying. Having anticipated that problem, I had a solution in mind. "Well, kiddo, you might want to wear a pair of flats instead of those heels to make climbing in and out of the ship a little easier."

"Okay, I'll change my shoes. Anything else?"

"Yes, dresses and airplanes don't mix well, so we're going to make a stop on the way to the field and get you some flying togs."

"Really? Wow, this is fun!"

I refrained from comment because I did not want to put a damper on her enthusiasm. The flying togs I had in mind were probably quite different from what she was imagining.

After changing into her flats, Clara came over to the table and exclaimed, "Oh, doughnuts!"

"Yup, nothin' but the best for guests of the Rancho Rodeo Motor Lodge."

She opened the drapes a little father so she could see the garden from her chair and said, "Speaking of which, where are we staying tonight?"

"This place seems decent. How 'bout spending another night here?"

"Sounds okay to me."

We sat there for a while enjoying our coffee and doughnuts until about eight-thirty, when I said, "Okay, kiddo, it's time for us to head for the field."

"All right. Give me just a minute to put a fresh bandage on."

While she performed that chore, I walked to the office and informed the Henna redhead that we enjoyed their hospitality so much we wanted to stay until Friday, she seemed genuinely pleased. When I got back to room number ten, Clara was already to go. She even had my overnight case next to the door.

Turning left out of the Rancho Rodeo, I drove east on Santa Monica to La Cienega, where I turned right. Two blocks later I turned right again, this time onto Pico Boulevard. Just before we got to Robertson Boulevard, I pulled to the curb in front of an establishment called Workmen's Clothing.

Clara took one look at the decidedly blue collar emporium and her jaw dropped. "You're kidding, right? This isn't where we're getting my flying clothes?"

"It sure is."

She looked at me and shook her head in something like disbelief. "Holy cow, Eddie! First you have me shopping for old

271

lady dresses at Penney's and now here of all places?"

"Relax, kiddo. This is the fastest solution to the problem. Besides, nobody's going to see you."

"You're going to see me!"

"True, but I already know what you look like when you're all dolled up."

Sounding resigned to a fate worse than death, Clara said, "Well, I have to admit that having you in my life will certainly cut down on my clothing expenses."

"Just one of the many benefits of being . . . of hanging around with Eddie Markham."

Clara grinned broadly. "You almost slipped and said it, didn't you?"

"I almost said what?"

"Missus Eddie Markham, that's what."

Feeling my face heat up, I said, "Maybe. Come on; let's get this done so we can get into the air."

She leaned over and gave me a kiss on the cheek. "You're funny, Eddie. That's another reason I love you so darn much."

Inside Workmen's Clothes Clara drew admiring glances from a couple of fellows who were shopping for boots and cotton work shirts as I steered her over to the coverall department. I took the smallest pair I could find on the rack and held them up to Clara so I could see how they would fit.

Looking thoroughly disgusted by the prospect of wearing such a garment, she said, "I suppose you want me to try them on, too."

"Nope, they're the smallest size on the rack, so they'll have to do. The legs and sleeves are too long, but we can roll them up and you'll be fine."

She mumbled, "That's a matter of opinion," and followed me to the checkout counter where I paid a grand total of two dollars and fifty cents for the coveralls.

Ten minutes later I pulled up alongside my rental hangar at DeMille Number Two. When we were in with the small door closed and locked behind us, I said, "Okay, kiddo, you can change into your new duds while I make sure the Bristol is ready to go flying."

Being a good sport, Clara went over to a corner of the hangar and got busy changing into her coveralls. Starting at the tail, I got busy giving my trusty ship a thorough inspection. I had not taken her up in few weeks, so I wanted to be absolutely sure she was still in tiptop shape.

From the rudder fin I worked my way forward, moving control

surfaces and checking bracing wires for tautness. I measured the fuel in the tank to be sure it was full and lifted the engine shroud to check the Rolls-Royce engine's oil level and the radiator coolant. I examined the wooden prop for any signs of a fracture, and finally, I checked the condition of the tires. Everything was exactly as it was supposed to be.

As I finished inspecting the Bristol, I noticed Clara standing nearby in her oversized coveralls watching me intently. I smiled and she said, "Eddie, if you laugh, so help me, I'll conk you with a wrench!"

She had rolled the pants cuffs up a good six inches to keep from tripping over them and the sleeves were similarly adjusted. America's most popular motion picture star was a sight to behold, but I stifled my grin and said, "You look fine, kiddo. Now you can climb up into the rear cockpit like I showed you while I lock your dress away in the Cadillac. The hangar door will be open while we're gone, and we don't want anyone walking off with your new dress."

"You're darn right we don't! Then I'd be stuck in this fetching outfit all day!"

With a grin I couldn't stifle, I said, "Heaven forbid! Oh, and give me your handbag, too. You won't be needing it."

When I returned from the Cadillac, Clara was sitting in the rear cockpit looking quite pleased with herself for getting there without poking any holes in the wing fabric. I grabbed a cloth drawstring sack from its nail on the hangar wall and climbed up onto the wing.

"How's it feel, kiddo? You all comfy?"

Glancing around her new and somewhat cramped environment, she said, "This is swell!"

"Good, then you're ready for your next lesson in the fine points of flying."

I balanced the cloth sack on the narrow section of fuselage between the two cockpits, loosened the drawstring, and drew out a leather helmet with rubber hoses attached to the earpieces on the sides of the helmet. From there the two hoses were combined into one with a metal Y connector something like a doctor's stethoscope.

Holding the helmet up, I said, "This is your flying helmet and the hoses are part of what's called a Gosport tube. The Gosport tube lets us talk back and forth while we're flying."

"Nifty!"

"The end of the hose from your helmet screws onto a fitting

over here." I leaned over and screwed the hose onto a matching fitting on the starboard side of the cockpit. "This hose runs forward and ends in a speaking tube in the front cockpit like this one. I held up a funnel-shaped metal tube attached to a second rubber hose.

"This hose also goes up to the front cockpit and attaches to my helmet. When you want to say something to me, you talk into this and I'll hear what you're saying through the earpieces in my helmet. And when I want to say something to you, I'll talk into the speaking tube in the front cockpit and you'll hear it through your earpieces."

Examining the leather helmet I handed her, Clara said, "Gosh, this is a swell gadget!"

"Well, it looks a little crude, but it works surprisingly well. It was invented by a British flying instructor so he could talk to his students while he was giving them lessons in the air. Go ahead and slip the helmet on."

Without the slightest hint that she was concerned about how it was going to mess up her hairdo, Clara pulled the helmet on. Like the coveralls, it was a little large, but I managed to take up the slack by tightening the chin strap.

Speaking louder because the helmet earpieces now covered her ears, I said, "There ya go, kiddo. Is that too tight?"

"No, it's fine."

"Good. Now we can try on your goggles."

I reached down into the bottom of the cloth sack and pulled out a pair of glass flying goggles. After slipping them over her helmet, I tightened the head strap securely so the goggles would stay in place."

"How's that?"

"Swell! I feel just like an aviator!"

"You look like one, too. A very cute aviator, I might add."

Clara smiled, apparently no longer concerned about the less than glamorous, oversized coveralls I made her wear. I said, "Okay, there's one more thing we need to do, and that's fasten your safety belt. You'll find the metal ends of the belt on each side of your seat."

She fished around on the floorboard and came up with both halves of the belt. I leaned in and snapped the belt ends together and pulled the long end tight around her waist. "There, is that too tight?"

"It's a little snug, but I guess that's better than being too loose."

"Yes, I don't want you bailing out on me!"

Clara leaned forward and gave me a kiss on the cheek. "I wouldn't think of doing such a thing!"

Straightening, I said, "Okay, now I'm going to raise the hangar door and find someone to help us prop the engine. Will you be okay by yourself for a couple of minutes?"

"I'm fine, Eddie, all ready to go!"

I climbed down from the wing and pulled the chain that raised the big metal door at the front of the hangar. When it was fully raised and the pull-chain was locked so the door wouldn't come back down, I stepped out into the bright sunshine and looked around for someone to prop the engine.

Propping an aircraft engine is a tricky operation because, if not done right, a fellow could easily lose an arm. It's happened more than once, so I not only needed to find someone who could spare a minute, but someone who knew how to pull the prop through correctly.

Fortunately, I didn't have to look any further than the hangar next to mine. The fellow who kept his ship there—a chap by the name of Marty—was doing some maintenance on his Kinner Airster, an awkward looking little biplane that flew surprisingly well and was built right over at the Kinner hangar in Glendale.

I walked into his hangar and said, "Hiya, Marty."

"Hi, Eddie. What's up?'

"I'm taking the Bristol up for a little hop and I was wondering if you would mind propping it for me."

"Heck, no, Eddie. I'll be glad to. Just let me wipe this here oil off my hands."

As we walked back to my hangar, I said, "I haven't flown her in a few weeks, so she might take a couple of pulls."

"Don't worry; we'll get her a goin'. Where you headed?"

"Oh, just takin' a young lady friend of mine up to see what flying is like."

As I climbed up to the front cockpit, taking the Gosport bag with me, Marty said hello to Clara. Disguised as she was in helmet and goggles, I wasn't too worried about him recognizing who he was speaking to.

"Hello, young lady. This your first flight in an air-o-plane?"

I was attaching the front cockpit Gosport tube and I noticed Clara pause for a moment, probably cautioning herself against mentioning her recent flight in a three-engined Army transport ship.

"Yes, and I'm very excited. This is going to be fun!"

Marty laughed at her enthusiasm. "Sure it's gonna to be fun, young lady, but you watch out. Once you been up, you're gonna be hooked and you'll wanna be flying all the time."

I heard Clara giggle and say, "That might not be so bad."

I fastened my safety belt and felt Bill Wellman's Colt pistol poke me in the back. The Bristol's seats are made of wicker and have no padding, which made the Colt even more uncomfortable than usual. Deciding I was not going to fly with the damned thing stabbing me in the back, I surreptitiously moved it from the waistband of my trousers to my right jacket pocket. My lower spine immediately thanked me.

Interrupting the conversation between Marty and Clara, I tossed the empty Gosport bag down and said, "Marty, please throw this over there against the hangar so it won't get blown away by the prop wash."

"Sure thing, Eddie."

While he did that, I pulled my helmet over my head and slipped my goggles on. Then Marty walked around to the front of the ship and hollered, "You ready for me to give her a whirl?"

"Yup, all set. Switch off."

That meant the engine ignition switch was in the off position so it wouldn't accidentally start while Marty rotated the propeller to spread some oil in the cylinders and position the prop to be pulled. When he completed that chore, Marty backed away from the prop and yelled, "Switch on!"

I turned the ignition switch to the run position, advanced the throttle, and yelled, "Contact!"

Starting a few feet to the starboard side of the nose, Marty took a brisk step forward, reached up with both hands to grab the prop, and then swung it down in a clockwise direction as he continued moving toward the port side of the ship, thus positioning himself well beyond the reach of the prop.

As I expected, the Roll-Royce engine let out a couple of sputtering coughs and the prop snapped to a stop. I turned the ignition switch back to the off position and yelled, "Switch off!"

Marty rotated the prop and stepped back into his starting position. "Switch on!"

I turned the ignition switch back to the run position. "Contact!"

Marty swung the prop again and this time the Rolls coughed several times, caught, and roared to life. I pulled the throttle back to its idle position and turned around to see how Clara was responding to the racket of 275 horsepower. I need not have worried. She was grinning from ear-to-ear and nearly jumping up down with excitement. I gave her a thumbs-up and she gave it right back to me.

Marty moved around to a spot just behind the port wing and picked up the rope attached to the chock blocks in front of and behind the tire. The chocks kept the Bristol from being pulled forward by the prop until I was ready for it to do so. I pointed toward the rope in his hand and gave him a positive nod.

Marty pulled the rope, the chocks slid away, and the Bristol began slowly rolling forward. After throwing Marty a salute of thanks, I got my feet on the rudder pedals and gently advanced the throttle. The Bristol responded by rolling a little faster.

Once clear of the hangar, I advanced the throttle more and pushed down on the left rudder pedal, which caused the ship to swing its nose to the left. Another hundred feet or so of taxiing brought us to the south end of the runway. On days when there was little or no wind to speak of, the standard departure was to the north.

I took a good, long look to the south, making sure no ships were approaching to land, and then advanced the throttle wide open and applied pressure on the right rudder pedal to counteract the ship's natural tendency to turn left during the takeoff run. The Roll-Royce's song rose to a high pitch and the Bristol jumped forward. She was as anxious as I was to get airborne!

Rolling along the smooth dirt runway, the ship accelerated quickly and before we were even a third the way down the strip, the Bristol began to feel lighter. I gently pushed forward on the stick to lift the tail skid off the ground. Just as we reached the midpoint of the runway I felt the Bristol's weight transfer from the wheels to the wings. We had reached takeoff speed. I eased back on the stick and we were airborne.

The Bristol was now in her element and she climbed like a homesick angel. Holding a heading of due north, I picked up the Gosport speaking tube and said, "Hey, kiddo, how are you doing back there?"

It took Clara a moment to get her speaking tube off the hook, but when she did, I heard, "Wonderful! This is absolutely wonderful, Eddie!"

"It is," I yelled back, "And now you understand why I gladly put so much money into this old gal!"

Clara's voice sounded tinny coming through the Gosport tube, but her words were very clear. "I sure do!"

"Okay, we're just about a thousand feet above the ground now. I'm going to turn to the right. That will point us toward Brackett Field, and if you look to the left after I turn, you'll see the

Hollywoodland sign on Mount Lee."

"I'll look for it!"

Replacing the speaking tube on its hook, I took another good look around. We were in an area surrounded by several small airports, so I was keeping my eyes open for other ships that might be around us as I put the ship into a gentle right turn. The last thing I wanted to do was scare Clara by making steep turns.

Since I was flying in my own backyard, so to speak, I did not need an aeronautical chart to know that Brackett Field was just a little north of due east so I kept an eye on the compass located at the top center of the instrument panel and rolled the Bristol's wings level on a heading of eight-seven degrees. That would take us close to Brackett and I could use landmarks on the ground to locate the field when we got close.

Next I glanced at the black face of the altimeter mounted directly below the compass. Altimeters have two hands, just like a clock. The short hand points to the ship's altitude in thousands of feet and the long hand registers the altitude in hundreds of feet. So when the short hand was almost to the white numeral "2" and the long hand indicated between seven and eight hundred feet, I gradually pulled the throttle back to the engine's cruising speed. The Bristol responded in a very ladylike manner by gently lowering her nose into level flight. We were flying at an altitude of two thousand feet.

A quick look at the airspeed indicator to the right of the altimeter told me we were cruising along at ninety miles per hour. I estimated that Brackett was about thirty-four or thirty-five miles from DeMille Number Two, which figured out to a flight time of a little less than twenty-five minutes. We had left the ground at seven minutes past ten, so unless my navigation was not as good as I thought it was, we would be circling over Brackett Airfield by ten-thirty.

After a quick look at the engine instruments—there are only two, coolant temperature and oil pressure—and seeing their needles pointing exactly where they were supposed to be pointing, I took a look around outside the cockpit, and spoke into the Gosport tube.

"Clara, do you see the Hollywoodland sign?"

"Yes, it's a little behind us now."

"Well, if you look along the ground between us and the sign you'll see a large green area."

It only took a moment for her to spot the landmark. "Yes. I see it. What is it, a park?"

"It's Hollywood Memorial Cemetery, and if you look along the edge of the green area closest to us, you'll see Lasky's new studio."

The Los Angeles basin, of which Hollywood is a part, is a naturally hazy area, so landmarks are sometimes hard to pick out from more than a thousand feet up, but Clara had good eyes. She shouted excitedly, "Yes, Eddie, I can see it!"

"Good! Now, if you look straight down, you can see the eastern part of downtown Los Angeles, and up ahead you can see the Los Angeles River. We'll be flying over it in just a couple of minutes."

"Oh, Eddie, this is so swell! You can see everything from up here. There's the river!"

I think I was having nearly as much fun pointing out landmarks as she was looking at them. "That green area of mountains between the Hollywoodland sign and the river is Griffith Park, and when we cross the river, the city you can see due north is Glendale."

On a day like this one when there is very little wind, the Bristol will hold a course pretty well on its own, but I kept an eye on the compass just to make sure I did not get so busy playing tour guide that I let us wander off course. The compass still indicated eighty-seven degrees, just as if it was nailed to that heading.

I also kept watching for other aircraft, and a couple of times I spotted another ship scooting along below us. There was not, however, much traffic up where we were. Most of the local fliers stayed down around a thousand feet.

Then, when we had been airborne for about thirteen minutes, I spotted another landmark I thought would interest Clara. Holding the voice tube to my mouth again, I said, "If you look ahead and just a little to the right you'll see a town with a big water tank just this side of it. Can you see it?"

It only took Clara a moment to spot the town and its water tank. "Yes, I see the town. What is it?"

"The name is painted on the water tank. See if you can read it."

The letters were curved around the tank, so she could not see the entire name, but she figured it out. "El Mon . . . El Monte. That's where Ruth is!"

"That's right. Give her a wave as we fly over."

"Oh, quit kiddin' me, Eddie. She couldn't see me waving way up here."

"You're probably right, kiddo, but you never know." I was tempted to turn around and see if Clara waved, but we were getting close to our destination and it was time to look for landmarks to help locate the airfield. I said, "Okay, Clara, we're almost there, so I need to pay attention to business."

"Okay, Eddie. I'm havin' fun lookin' at stuff even if I don't know what I'm lookin' at."

I could not help but smile. This was one of the things about Clara I loved the most. When something caught her interest, she was like a kid with a new toy—no phony sophistication from her, no sir.

Scanning the ground ahead, I got a surprise. My navigation estimates were a lot better than I had any right to expect. I remembered from past trips out this way that there was an area of low hills surrounding a small lake just west of the field. Those low hills were directly ahead of us.

A moment later I saw the field. Brackett had one runway that ran very close to due east and west. A windsock atop a building to the left of the runway showed that the wind here was a good deal stronger and was coming out of the east.

That meant that if I had intended to land, I was in the perfect position to make a straight-in landing from the west. But landing was my alternate plan. My primary plan was to circle the field from our two-thousand foot altitude and see what I could see. I made a slight turn to the right and held that course until I was abeam the field, then I turned into a slow easy circle to the left.

Most of the airfield businesses and hangars were clustered at the northwest corner of the field, so I concentrated on studying that area and immediately spotted what looked like a Ryan PT-1 that matched the description Fred Lewis gave me of Blaylock's second ship. The instant I saw it I realized I had seen the ship somewhere before, but I could not think of where. At the moment, however, that was not important. What was important was that the Ryan was parked alongside a single-ship hangar something like the one I rent. That hangar was a likely place to look for Blaylock's Curtiss.

As we came around to the south side of the field again I could see that the big door of the hangar was open, but I could not see what, if anything, was inside because of the deep shadows in the hangar. The only way I was going to see inside that hangar was by landing. So be it.

I rolled out of the circle and pointed the Bristol's nose south, and began descending. Holding the Gosport's voice tube up to my mouth I let Clara in on what I was up to.

"I spotted Blaylock's second ship down there next to a hangar that's probably where he keeps the Curtiss we're looking for. I can't see in the hangar because it's too dark, so I'm going to touch down and take a look from the runway."

A good deal of Clara's earlier enthusiasm was gone from her voice when she said, "Okay, Eddie, if you think that's what we have to do."

"Don't worry, kiddo, we won't even stop. We'll just take a quick look and be gone."

I leveled off at five hundred feet, which was the typical pattern altitude for most small airports, and turned back toward the field. With my head on a swivel, I watched for other traffic in the landing pattern. Seeing none, I turned west, parallel to the runway and began descending to land.

A ways beyond the west end of the strip I made a right turn which was soon followed by another right turn that lined us up with the runway. I throttled back and let the Bristol's nose sink a little sooner than I normally would because I wanted to set her down right at the very end of the strip. That way we would be on the ground as we rolled past what I suspected was Blaylock's hangar, and I could get a look inside and take off again with out having to taxi around on the field.

A few feet above the end of the runway I pulled the throttle off and let her sink to the dirt strip. The Bristol landed lightly on her wheels and I turned to look through the open door of the hangar as we rolled past.

It was a quick look, but it told me everything I wanted to know and then some. The Curtiss was in there all right. I could tell by the odd configuration of its radiator hanging down below the engine shroud. I also saw something else that raised my pulse rate a couple of notches. The Curtiss' prop was turning and the ship was rolling out of the hangar.

Thirty-Two

I shoved the throttle wide open and, within two hundred feet, the Bristol's tires were clear of the Brackett Airfield runway. I held the stick back for the best rate of climb she would give me and we headed skyward. To anyone watching our quick departure would simply look like a student practicing touch-and-go landings.

As the altimeter's long needle approached seven hundred feet, I pushed her nose down and the Bristol began to accelerate. Just beyond the end of the runway, I put the ship into a tight left bank and held the turn through one-hundred-eighty degrees so we were heading back to the west and parallel to the runway.

Looking down at the airfield as we flew past I saw Blaylock's Curtiss sitting in the takeoff position at the west end of the runway while he waited for another ship to land. Was he going up in the Curtiss because he had seen us circling the field or was it just a coincidence that had him taking the ship up at that exact moment? I supposed it could have been the latter, but that was more wishful thinking than any belief I had in coincidences.

With the airfield falling away behind us, I said into the Gosport speaking tube, "Clara look back at the field and watch the ship that's just taking off. Tell me where he goes."

"Okay, Eddie. Is something wrong?"

"Maybe. That's Blaylock's Curtiss on the runway and I don't know if he saw us circling the field or if it's just a coincidence he's taking his ship up right now."

After a long moment, Clara said, "He's just leaving the ground now."

"Okay, let me know which way he turns."

We were heading back in the general direction of Los Angeles, but I wasn't paying much attention to navigation. All I wanted at the moment was put as much distance between us and Billy Blaylock as possible. I would figure out where we were going when I knew where he was going.

Clara provided the answer to that question a moment later. "Eddie, he's turning the same way you turned, like maybe he's following us."

So much for coincidence. "Okay, thanks, Clara. Keep watching him and let me know if he starts catching up with us."

"I will, Eddie."

I was trying to think about what to do next, but all the possibilities swirling around in my head were making it tough to concentrate. Then, suddenly, as if a switch was turned, my mind shifted gears and I was back over France flying my Spad pursuit ship. In those days I had a precise thought process I used for making quick combat decisions like I needed right now.

The first step was to quickly compare the enemy's advantages to my own. In Blaylock's case, his first advantage was speed. The Curtiss was at least sixty miles per hour faster than my Bristol. His second advantage was firepower. In Texas he strafed us with a pair of thirty calibre machine guns, and I had to assume they were still in their mounts under the Curtiss' engine shroud. Blaylock's third advantage was his flying skill. I already knew he was a hell of a pilot.

The list of our advantages was shorter. The Bristol was designed for close aerial combat, so the engineers had given it all the maneuverability they could. I knew she could make tighter turns and steeper ascents and descents than the Curtiss. The only other advantage I could put on my side of the ledger was my own flying skill. I was a hell of a pilot, too, or at least the Army had once thought so. I had a feeling we were about to find out if that was still true.

What about Blaylock's disadvantages? Fred Lewis told me the experimental Curtiss was extremely unstable, especially during maneuvers. Okay, Markham, how do you turn that disadvantage into your advantage?

Through my helmet earpieces I heard Clara say, "He's still a long ways back, but he's definitely catching up."

"Okay, keep watching him."

Still trying to think of how I could turn Blaylock's unstable ship into my advantage, I took stock of the ground terrain around us. The way ahead and to the south was wide open. The way to the north was blocked by the lofty San Gabriel Mountain range four or five miles off our starboard wing . . . . the mountains! That was the answer.

The air around mountains is almost always turbulent because the natural air flow is disturbed, especially when there was some wind aloft like we had today. If I could lure Blaylock in close to the mountains, the turbulent air currents combined with his ship's inherent instability would bounce him around enough to make accurate shooting nearly impossible. The Bristol would be bounced around, too, but it could take that sort of turbulence in stride.

I angled our course to the northwest and grabbed the speaking tube. "Clara, the ride is going to get a little bumpy in a few minutes, but don't let it scare you. It won't hurt us."

The tone of Clara's voice now had a note of panic in it, but she was doing her best to be a brave trooper. "Okay. I'll try not to be scared. He's still back there and getting closer every minute."

Trying to interject something positive into the situation, I said, "Good. That's exactly what I want him to do."

She made no reply and I watched the mountains getting bigger and bigger as we got closer and closer. At a distance of a mile I felt the first turbulence. I held my course. A thousand feet from the mountainside I could clearly make out individual rocks and trees and the ride was getting a lot rougher. Still I held my course.

When we were a little less than five hundred feet from the mountains I banked left to begin following the natural terrain. We were bouncing around quit a lot, sometimes bumping up or down as much as twenty or thirty feet.

Clara yelled into my helmet earpieces. "Eddie, I think he's shooting at us!"

I risked a quick look back and saw the twinkle of muzzle flashes through the arc of the Curtiss' prop. That sight added one more advantage to my side of the equation. Blaylock was still well beyond the effective range of his guns, so shooting at us now was something any experienced pursuit pilot would know was just a waste of ammunition.

That made me realize Blaylock was too young to have served in the war. He had no actual combat experience. I, on the other hand, had logged many, many combat missions, and that experience came with a bag of tricks the kid chasing us was lacking.

I had my hands full keeping the bouncing Bristol pointed where I wanted it to go, but I grabbed the Gosport speaking tube just long enough to yell, "Clara you can stop watching him now. Lean over and get as low in the cockpit as you can. Don't unfasten your safety belt; just keep your head down."

Clara's voice was shaky, but she was doing her best to sound brave. "Okay, Eddie, I will."

There wasn't much in the way of protection between the rear cockpit and the Bristol's tail, but the fuselage frame and bracing might be enough to stop a lucky shot. It was not much, but it was all we had.

We hit a pretty solid bounce that dropped the Bristol at least thirty feet, and I risked another look back. Blaylock had closed the gap enough that he was now within gun range. It was time to pull something out of my bag of tricks.

I pushed down hard on the left rudder pedal, causing the Bristol to yaw and skid to the left. A second later I heard a "thwat" sound from somewhere to the right. A quick glance in that direction showed me a tiny flap of wing covering fluttering in the wind out near the end of the lower wing. It marked the spot where one of Blaylock's bullets had hit us.

Guessing he would expect me to use the same trick again, but back to the right, I romped down on the left rudder pedal again and took a quick look back over my shoulder. The Curtiss was bouncing around like a rubber ball back there as he tried to get us back into his sights.

I repeated the skid maneuver once more to the right and decided it was time to pull a new trick out of the bag. The one I had in mind was a doozy. A Boche pilot had once pulled it on me and it worked so well he darn near got away with it.

First, I pulled Wellman's Colt out of my jacket pocket and stuffed it between the seat and my left thigh where it would be handy. Then I pulled the throttle all the way off and eased the stick back. The Bristol dropped fifty feet like an express elevator and hung on the edge of a stall as the airspeed bled off. I added just enough throttle to hold the Bristol in that attitude and grabbed the Colt, releasing its safety with my thumb.

The original idea of the maneuver was to cause the pursuing pilot to over-fly your ship, thus putting him directly in front of your guns. In this situation, though, the only gun I had was the Colt and using it would be tricky.

To have any chance of hitting the Curtiss, I needed to keep the Bristol's nose up, and while bouncing around in the turbulence, aim through the narrow vertical gap between the top of the propeller arc and the bottom of the upper wing. From where I was sitting that gap looked damned small and, if my aim got too low, I would hit our prop, which could mean disaster. Worse, the chances of my actually hitting the Curtiss, let alone causing any serious damage, were small. I had to give it a try, though, because if I could just get one round into Blaylock's ship, it might give him cause to back off a little and offer us a better chance of escaping in one piece.

Two or three seconds after I put my plan into action Blaylock was less than thirty feet above our upper wing. Resting my hand on the top of the windscreen, I pointed the Colt through the gap and pulled the trigger. I kept on pulling the trigger until the pistol's breech locked open, indicating that I had fired all eight rounds. It all happened very quickly—no more than a dozen seconds from start to finish.

I dropped the now worthless pistol to the cockpit floorboard, where it rattled around with the spent brass shells it had just ejected, and lowered the Bristol's nose as I shoved the throttle wide open again. Then I put the ship into a steeply banked, tight left turn. My plan now was to retrace our route back to Brackett while taking advantage of the Bristol's maneuverability by twisting and turning to keep Blaylock off our tail. If I could get us back on the ground at the airfield, Blaylock would have to call off his pursuit.

When the turn brought us back to an easterly heading, I took a look over my shoulder, expecting to see the Curtiss making the same turn I had just made. But he wasn't. For some inexplicable reason, Blaylock was headed off to the southwest and the Curtiss was sinking like a stone.

I looked forward to be sure I wasn't flying us into the mountainside, then took another quick look back to make sure I had really seen what I thought I saw. I had, and this time I also saw a thin stream of gray smoke blowing back from under the Curtiss' engine.

Son of a gun! One of the Colt's slugs had actually hit something vital, causing Blaylock's engine to seize up, and he was dead-sticking for an emergency landing somewhere. I quickly turned back to the right, intending to follow the Curtiss down. This time I was going to be damned sure of what happened to Blaylock.

When I was more or less following the same course and rate of descent as the Curtiss, I grabbed the Gosport speaking tube and yelled, "Clara, are you okay?"

A moment later her shaky voice sounded in my helmet earpieces. "Yes, I'm okay."

"Good. You can sit up again. Blaylock's done."

Sounding both surprised and relieved, she said, "What happened, Eddie?"

"I tried an old war maneuver and it worked. I shot out something vital in his ship with Wellman's Colt pistol. Blaylock is on his way down to an emergency landing."

Dropping the Gosport speaking tube, I concentrated on Blaylock and quickly saw what he intended to do. He was trying to line his ship up with a dirt farm road that ran east and west along the south edge of a citrus orchard. It was a lousy place to make a dead stick landing because the wind was blowing across the road from the north, and even though the wind was light here, barely more than a breeze, it was going to make an already unstable ship even harder to land. Regardless, he had picked his spot and now he was committed to it.

As we drew closer to the Curtiss, I saw something I had not been able to see when the ship was behind us. The pilot was not wearing a helmet and his mop of blonde hair was now clearly visible, removing any doubt that it was Blaylock in the cockpit.

I leveled off between two and three hundred feet and circled to watch his landing. The Curtiss was wobbling badly, but Blaylock was still keeping it pretty well lined up with the dirt road and I found myself actually rooting for a fellow pilot in a sticky situation.

His wheels touched almost exactly in the center of the road, but he came down too hard and the ship bounced half a dozen feet back into the air. In the same instant the Curtiss jumped to the right as if shoved by a gust of wind.

Blaylock made a valiant effort to get his ship lined up with the road again, but there was nothing he or any other pilot could have done to correct the Curtiss' course at that point. The starboard landing wheel came down hard in a drainage ditch along the right side of the road and dug in, causing the ship to pivot violently to the right and driving its nose into the far side of the ditch with such force that the impact collapsed the starboard wing assembly. Then everything stopped and nothing moved down there but a growing plume of gray-black smoking coming from under the Curtiss' bent engine shroud.

As my circle brought us around to the east side of the wreckage, I clearly saw Blaylock slumped over the starboard side of the cockpit. He was making no effort to climb out of the Curtiss. Having seen similar scenes play out many times in France, I knew what was inevitably going to happen in the next few seconds, and there was absolutely nothing I could do about it.

We were coming around the south side of the wreckage when the aviation fuel leaking from the ruptured fuel tank finally reached the hot engine and the Curtiss exploded into a huge ball of flame so intense I thought I could feel the heat from it clear up where we were. When we got back around to the east again I caught another glimpse of Blaylock's body through the thickening black smoke cloud and bright orange flames. He was suffering the same fate as the rest of his ship.

Clara's voice came shakily through my earpieces. "God, Eddie, is he still in there?"

I raised the Gosport speaking tube to my mouth and told her what was more wishful thinking than fact. "Yes, but I'm sure he was killed outright in the crash. Blaylock was already dead before the flames got to him."

At that moment a movement to the southwest caught my eye. It was a cloud of dust being raised by a farm truck racing along a road that intersected the one on which Blaylock had crashed. I decided to get us the heck out of there before the driver of the truck got close enough for a good look at the Bristol.

I continued circling until we were pointed east, at which point opened the throttle to gain some speed and rolled the wings level. We skimmed along over the farms just above the tree tops for a mile or so before I turned to the south and began climbing. When we reached two thousand feet, I made a slow turn to the right, pointing us in the general direction of Los Angeles and DeMille Number Two.

We touched down on the runway at eleven-twenty-two. We had been in the air exactly one hour and fifteen minutes. It seemed a good deal longer.

Under normal circumstances I would have parked the Bristol outside my hangar and recruited some help to push her back into the hangar tail-first, but these were far from normal circumstances. Instead, I pointed the Bristol's nose into the hangar and gave the throttle just enough of a blip to roll her through the open hangar door and cut the ignition switch.

Before she coasted to a stop I had my helmet, goggles, and safety belt off and was climbing out onto the port wing. I looked at Clara. Her head was down and for one very scary moment I thought she might be hurt, but as I leaned over the rear cockpit, she raised her head and looked at me.

I said, "Come on, honey, let's get your gear off and get you down on the ground."

We removed her helmet and goggles before I unfastened her

safety belt and helped Clara out onto the wing. From there I jumped to the hangar floor and lifted her down from the wing.

Clara collapsed into my arms and began crying. Amidst sobs that shook her body, she said, "Oh, Eddie, it was just awful! It was horrible!"

I didn't know if she was referring to our close call in the air or to the sight of Blaylock's body in the blazing wreckage of his ship, but it didn't really matter. I just held Clara close and let her cry. After standing there like that for several minutes, her sobs subsided a little and I backed her up to lean against the trailing edge of the lower port wing.

When I started to move away, Clara grabbed my arm just as she had done after Blaylock damn near killed her in Texas. I said, "I'm only going over to lower the hangar door before one of my neighbors stops by for a friendly chat. I'll be right back."

She released my arm and I trotted over to lower the door. After it was down and I had slid home the bolts that locked the door in place, I went back to Clara. She looked at me with wet cheeks and I put my hands on her shoulders. "Honey, listen to me for a second. I know it was horrible, but it's all over now and Billy Blaylock will never try to hurt you again."

Clara nodded and whispered, "I know."

"Good. Now do you feel up to changing back into your dress so we can get out of here?"

She nodded again and in a slightly louder voice said, "Yes."

"Okay, kiddo, you wait right here and I'll bring in your dress and your bag."

Clara put a hand on my arm, but did not grab me this time. She just said, "Please hurry, Eddie, I really need you close."

I was gone less than a minute, and when I returned with her dress and handbag, Clara was standing up and wiping her cheeks with one drooping arm of her coveralls. I laid her dress and bag on the wing and gave her a gentle kiss. Her lips felt soft against mine and the kiss lasted longer than I had meant it to.

When our lips parted, Clara gave me a small smile. "You'd better let me get changed or we'll never get out of here."

She began stripping off the oversized coveralls right there next to the wing, and while she did that, I picked up the cloth Gosport bag from where Marty had tossed it when we left. After disconnecting the Gosport hoses in the rear cockpit and stuffing Clara's helmet and goggles back into the bag, I repeated the process in the front cockpit, but instead of dropping my goggles into the bag, I hung them from the throttle knob where they were usually kept. While I was up there, I fished Bill Wellman's Colt out from where it was laying under the seat among the spent shell casings and dropped the pistol into my jacket pocket.

I returned the Gosport bag to its nail and chocked the port tire just for safety's sake. Then I walked around to the starboard wing and inspected the bullet holes Blaylock had put there. There were two of them and it appeared as if both bullets had passed right through the wing without damaging anything but the fabric.

I gave the Bristol an affectionate pat on the wing and quietly said, "Sorry you were wounded, old gal, but the damage isn't bad, so you'll be as good as new once we get the holes patched." I looked up at her proud nose, gave her wing another pat, adding, "You did everything I asked of you today without a word of complaint. Thanks, old gal."

I heard Clara clear her throat and I turned around. She was standing back by the Bristol's tail. With a smile, she said, "Are you ready to go or would you two like to be alone for a while?"

Smiling back, I said, "Miss Bristol here deserves a little praise. She got us safely through a real bad situation today."

With her coveralls folded over her arm, Clara joined me and ran her fingertips over the torn wing fabric. "Yeah, Miss Bristol, even if you are the 'other woman,' I'm sorry you got shot. Thanks for keeping us safe."

"You know, kiddo, you just made a friend for life."

Grinning a little now, Clara asked, "You think she'll take me up for another ride someday?"

"Any time you want. We'll hang your snazzy flying suit on that nail over there so it'll be all ready to go."

"Okay, but we're only keeping it as a souvenir. The next time we go up I'm gonna be properly dressed so Miss Bristol won't be ashamed to be seen with me."

Once we had locked the small hangar door behind us and climbed aboard the Cadillac, Clara leaned over and raised herself up off the seat for a minute so she could see her face in the rearview mirror. "Eddie, would it be all right if we went back to the hotel for a few minutes? I'm a real mess. I'd like to wash my face and put myself back together before we go anywhere else."

Resisting the temptation to tell Clara she looked damned good to me just the way she was, I said, "Sure, kiddo we can do that. We're not far from the Rancho Rodeo, so it'll only take a few minutes to get there."

Later, as I turned west onto Santa Monica Boulevard, Clara thought of something else she wanted to say. "Eddie, I know you're gonna tell me I don't need to apologize, but I have to say this: I'm sorry for being such a cry baby. I was scared to death, and when it was all over, I just fell apart. I tried not to, but . . . ."

"Listen, kiddo, I've seen big, brave pursuit pilots climb out of the cockpit with tears in their eyes after a tough mission like we just flew, so don't feel bad. Besides, you came through when I needed your help up there, and being brave when the going gets tough is all that counts."

Clara put her hand on my right knee and squeezed. "It means an awful lot to hear you say that, darling."

Thirty-Three

Pulling into the Rancho Rodeo's parking area I noticed the wooden housekeeping cart out in front of room number five, so I was not surprised when we walked into our room and found that it had not been made up yet. It did not matter in the slightest.

Clara made a beeline for the bathroom. I sat at the table and listened to water running in the bathroom sink while my nerves settled. It had been the same for me during the war. The dangers I faced during fierce combat seldom sank into my brain until well after the mission ended. That is when I got the jitters.

Forcing my mind not to dwell on events that might easily have ended quite differently, I placed Bill Wellman's Colt on the table and began disassembling it. I had no proper cleaning tools at hand, but I did the best I could with paper napkins left over from our doughnut breakfast and my pencil for a ramrod. A firearm that had just helped save our lives deserved better.

The cleaning chore done, I reloaded the magazine with seven fresh rounds from the box of ammo Wellman gave me with the pistol. Then I worked the slide to move one round from the magazine to the chamber, removed the magazine, and inserted one more fresh round for a total of eight in the pistol.

I had just clicked the magazine back into the Colt's grip when Clara came out of the bathroom. She looked fresh as a daisy, but her expression was solemn. I watched her sit wearily on the end of the bed and asked, "How are you doing, kiddo?"

"Okay I guess, but my legs are still shaky."

Sitting next to her, I said, "So are mine. The shakes are a normal reaction. They go away after a while."

Clara leaned her head against my chest and I held her. After a minute or two, she looked up at me. "Eddie, is it really over?"

"Yes, at least the immediate danger is over. There's no guarantee whoever hired Blaylock to kill you won't send someone else to take his place, but I think we have a little breathing room before that happens. We can use that time to good advantage by trying to find out who's behind all this. My cop friend can help us with that. He knows how to find out such things."

"Then we should probably get a move on because I could use some lunch." Then, with a small smile, she added, "All this being brave business makes a person hungry."

"It does," I agreed. "How do you feel about Mexican food? I know a swell little tamale joint up on the strip."

"That sounds swell."

With the Colt once again poking me in the small of the back and my ever-present overnight case stashed behind the Cadillac's seat, we headed east on Santa Monica Boulevard. I cut up to Sunset on La Cienega and a few blocks later we pulled to the shoulder in front of El Cantina del Sol.

The Cantina is a dinky little eight-table joint with colorful Mexican serapes on the walls and aromas from a small kitchen out back that always made my mouth water. A radio in one corner of the room belted out spirited Mexican tunes, creating a lively, festive mood among the mostly Spanish-speaking lunch crowd. It was the sort of place you see in motion pictures where a beautiful senorita with dark flashing eyes leaps upon a table and dances to entertain the admiring vaqueros from a nearby rancho.

It pleased me that Clara was quite taken with the joint and was soon smiling and tapping her toes to the music. The Cantina was just the ticket to raise one's spirits.

Knowing that I had been there many times before, Clara asked me to choose our lunches. I told Dolores, the young senorita serving us, that we would have the chicken tamales accompanied by rice and beans.

The Cantina del Sol's tamales are huge, but Clara managed to put the whole thing away along with most of her rice and black beans. She hadn't been kidding when she said she was hungry.

Done with lunch, I paid the bill, left a generous tip on the table for Dolores, and steered Clara to a public telephone on the wall of a narrow hallway that led to the Cantina's back door. I pushed a nickel in the slot and dialed a number from memory.

My call was answered immediately by the officer manning the telephones. "Sixth precinct, Patrolman Wallace speaking."

I said, "Detective Sergeant Mackie, please."

"Okay, stay on the line a minute while I find him."

While I waited, I leaned down and gave Clara a kiss on the cheek. She looped her arm through mine and a strong male voice with more than a hint of Scot in it said, "Homicide, Detective Sergeant Mackie here."

"Hello, C. K. This is Eddie Markham."

"Eddie! It's good to hear your voice. How has the world been treatin' ya, lad?"

"Not so good at the moment, C. K. I'm afraid I've gotten myself into a bit of a jam."

"Well now, that will never do. How can I be of help?"

"I could really use some off-the-record advice on how to handle a bad situation."

"Of course. I can make some time for you this afternoon. Ah . . . I take it this is something you'd prefer not to discuss over the telephone or here at the precinct?"

"You take it right, C. K."

"Very well, then, do you know the picnic ground at the east end of Mulholland dam?"

"I do."

"Supposing I meet you there in half an hour."

"See you there."

As I pointed the Cadillac east on Sunset Boulevard, Clara said, "You called him Seekay? That's a strange name."

"Those are his first and middle initials, C and K. I believe the C stands for Chester, but everyone just calls him C. K."

"Oh. And what are you going to tell him?"

"I think we should tell him the whole story from start to finish, including the parts we didn't tell Smythe. If C. K. is going to help us find out who hired Blaylock, we've got to take him completely into our confidence."

In a skeptical tone of voice, she said, "I suppose you're right, but are you sure we can trust him? They say there are a lot of crooked cops in the Los Angeles Police Department."

"That's true, but if there is only one honest cop in the department, it would be C. K. I think you'll agree with me when you meet him."

I turned left off of Sunset onto Cahuenga Boulevard and, just past Franklin, I turned right and we began winding our way up through the hills above Hollywood. Clara asked, "Where on earth are we meeting this C. K.?"

"Up at Lake Hollywood. Ever been there?"

"Gosh, I didn't even know Hollywood had a lake."

"Actually, it didn't until a couple of years ago when they built the Mulholland Dam to make a reservoir. It's actually quite pretty up there, lots of trees and a couple of picnic grounds. C. K. could tell we wanted to discuss something privately, so he picked Lake Hollywood because it will be deserted on a weekday afternoon."

When we finally arrived at the picnic ground just east of the dam, there were no other cars around. I parked the Caddy near a wooden picnic table and we made ourselves comfortable. It was an easy scene in which to be comfortable under a blue sky with a few puffy white clouds, surrounded by shady oak trees, and serenaded by cheerful Meadowlarks going about their business in a field across the road. The air smelled fresh and sweet with no trace of the exhaust fumes that poison the air in town.

Five minutes later I heard a vehicle coming up the road. It turned out to be Mackie's official LAPD Dodge Brothers Roadster. He parked it alongside the Cadillac and strolled over to our table.

Detective Sergeant C. K. Mackie would be hard to miss even in a crowd. Barrel-chested and broad-shouldered, he stood over six feet in height with a ruddy complexion, graying hair and a carefully trimmed mustache. C. K.'s LAPD uniform was sharply pressed and his demeanor was all business, but if you looked closely at his cool gray eyes, you might see a twinkle, hinting at a sense of humor that lurked beneath his no nonsense appearance.

I stood and we shook hands. Mackie said, "Good to see you again, Eddie, and who might this pretty young lassie be?"

There was no doubt in my mind that C. K. knew exactly who the pretty young lassie with me was. As a detective sergeant at the Hollywood precinct, he had encountered most of the area's motion picture celebrities, many of them under less than ideal circumstances. Still, I humored him with a formal introduction. "C. K. meet Miss Clara Bow. Clara, this is my good friend, Detective Sergeant C. K. Mackie."

C. K. bowed slightly from the waist and said, "Good afternoon, Miss Bow. I'm honored to meet you."

Clara smiled up at him. "And I'm pleased to meet you, C. K. Eddie has been saying some very nice things about you."

C. K.'s gray eyes twinkled. "You should not be believin' everything the lad tells ya. He has been known to exaggerate from time to time. For example, he's told me he finds himself in a jam, yet I cannot for the life of me imagine how that could be with such a lovely lassie at his side."

Clearly charmed by Mackie, Clara said, "That's nice of you to say, C. K., but I'm afraid I am actually the cause of the trouble we're in."

Seating himself across the picnic table from us, C. K. said, "Well, then, we will just have to get the both of you out of that trouble. Why don't you tell me all about it?"

I said, "We'll do that, C. K., but make yourself comfortable because it's a long story that begins a couple of weeks ago when one of Jesse Lasky's motion picture directors, William Wellman, asked me to serve as a consultant on the production of a motion picture about the Great War. We were both pursuit pilots during the war and first met in France."

As I related the events of the past two weeks, C. K. removed a small notebook from his uniform jacket and began writing in it. From time to time, he interrupted my narrative with a question to clarify some point or other. In all, my telling of the story took about forty-five minutes. When I concluded our tale with the account of that morning's aerial encounter with Blaylock, the sergeant closed his notebook and shook his head. I could not tell whether that response was one of disbelief or amazement or both.

"Eddie, that's quite a yarn, and if I did not know you so well as I do, I would be thinking you made it up out of that fertile writer's imagination of yours. But, going by Miss Bow's expressions as you told your story, I cannot doubt a word of it.

"Now, before we go any further, I must remind you that I am a sworn police officer, and as such, if I have knowledge of a crime that has been committed, I'm obligated to act on that knowledge. From what you've just told me, it appears you may be technically guilty of a crime or two. For that reason, I am going to consider what you've told me as hypothetical—a story you might be considering for one of your novels. Are we clear on that?"

Nodding, I said, "Yes, C. K., we're clear."

"Good. Now what questions do you want to ask me about this hypothetical situation?"

I went straight to the heart of the matter. "Since we can think of no possible personal reason this fellow, Blaylock, could have had for wanting Clara dead, we've come to the conclusion he was working for someone else—someone who would benefit from her death. The question is, who? Until we have an answer to that question, Clara is still in danger."

C. K. leaned forward, resting his arms on the picnic table, and said, "Miss Bow, I am not particularly a fan of motion pictures, and if my dear wife didn't occasionally insist on me taking her to see a picture show, it is most likely I would never set foot in a theater. This being the case, the fact that I recognized you right away would seem to indicate that you are a celebrity of some renown, and it is my experience that one does not reach such heights of celebrity without stepping on some toes along the way, thus creating enemies who are jealous of your success. Now, whose toes might you have stepped on?"

Clara shook her head. "Nobody's, at least nobody who would want to hurt me. I've thought about this a lot, and I just can't think of anyone who hates me that much or who would make money or anything if something happened to me."

Mackie nodded thoughtfully. "All right, Miss Bow, let's look at this another way. For the past several weeks we have been investigating the death of another young motion picture actress. She was also quite valuable to her employer, and yet it was her employer whom we arrested and charged with her murder. While his motive for killing still isn't entire clear to me, it would seem that this actress had decided to leave the studio before the completion of her contract, and that, along with a substantial life insurance policy, resulted in her death. Perhaps you knew this young woman. Her name was Lillian Lawrence. She worked for Western National Studios."

"I didn't know her personally, but I know who she was, and her situation was nothing like mine. I just signed a brand new contract with my studio for more money and everything. Lasky-Paramount would lose a fortune if I . . . if something happened to me."

I interrupted to bring up a point that needed to be made. "Despite that, C. K., I strongly suspect someone at the studio is involved in this somehow because Blaylock had information about Clara that could only have come from somebody high up in the studio, and there is someone in such a position whose toes Clara has stepped on."

Opening his notebook, Mackie said, "And who might that be?"

"A fellow named B. P. Schulberg. He's the one who brought Clara out to Hollywood to make pictures in the first place and he made a good deal of money exploiting her while he paid Clara a miniscule wage. Also, Clara is the only reason Schulberg is on the gravy train with Paramount. Lasky hired him because he owned Clara's contract."

C. K. looked up from his notebook. "And how has Miss Bow stepped on this fellow's toes?"

"Her new contract is with Lasky-Paramount directly, which cuts Schulberg out of the picture entirely. Rumor has it that his days at the studio are numbered because he no longer controls Clara and Lasky has little use for him otherwise."

Mackie turned to Clara. "What about that, Miss Bow? Is this fellow mad enough to want revenge?"

Clara looked at me for a moment, and then turned to Mackie. "I'm sure B. P. is upset with me, but I can't imagine him having the nerve to kill anyone."

I added, "There is some agreement with Clara on that score, C. K. As it was put to me by another Lasky employee, Schulberg is a conniver, not a killer. Still, I'd bet money he's involved somehow."

Mackie closed his book again and said, "Okay, here's how I think we might best proceed with getting to the bottom of all this. I'll spend what's left of today and tomorrow morning talking with some people of my acquaintance who are in the know about the, shall we say, unseemly side of the motion picture business. Perhaps they'll provide some information that will help us get a handle on who might be behind the attempts on Miss Bow's life.

"I suggest we meet here again tomorrow around noon." With a smile, C. K. added, "Bring your lunch and we'll make a picnic of it. No sense letting all of this beautiful scenery go to waste."

"Okay, C. K., but I do have another question or two about what we should be doing in the meantime."

With a slight smile, Mackie said, "Might you be wondering what you should do concerning the United States Army's interest in all this?"

"That's certainly one of my questions. Would it be wise to call Colonel Smythe and let him in on who killed his pilot and that the killer is, himself, now dead?"

"No, Laddie, I don't believe I would do that for the simple reason that it would implicate you in Blaylock's death, and we don't need to add that to your worries."

That didn't seem right to me. "But," I protested, "I acted in self-defense this morning. Blaylock was trying to shoot us out of the air!"

"Indeed he was, but tell me this: Is there any way on God's green earth anyone will be able to know from the wreckage that the crash was anything but an unfortunate flying accident?"

"Well, no, probably not, but . . . ."

"The Army is perfectly capable of figuring all this out for itself, especially since you filled them in on enough of the story to point them in the right direction. By this time they've probably already identified this Blaylock chap as their killer. Eventually, they will find out that it was his flying machine that crashed out there in the orange orchard, or whatever it was, and since there is no one left alive to prosecute for the murder of their pilot, some reports will be typed and that will be the end of it. Justice has been served.

"Now, if you go sticking your nose into the Army's efficient and thorough investigation with some story about how you singlehandedly shot this scalawag out of the sky with your trusty shootin' iron, that will require more reports to be typed, more hearings to be held, and in general, a nice tidy investigation will get all mucked up with a bunch of unnecessary details. You follow me, Laddie?"

I saw Clara grinning out of the corner of my eye. "Yes, I guess so, but what about Blaylock wrecking his car in Laurel Canyon?"

Mackie shook his head. "What about it? Some fellow, probably under the influence of illegal alcohol, lost control of his car and crashed it into a tree. It happens all the time, and since no witnesses have come forward to say otherwise, that's all there is to it."

"And the missing license plates and registration information? Won't that raise suspicion?"

"Not much. It probably just means the car was stolen. The boys in our traffic division are certainly not overworked, so this will keep them busy earning their pay for a while. You'll actually be performing a public service by staying out of the matter. Wouldn't you agree, Miss Bow?"

Grinning broadly and nodding her head vigorously, Clara said, "Oh, yes, Sergeant Mackie. I certainly agree."

I sighed. "All right, you two have me outnumbered."

Clara leaned over and put her arm around my shoulder. "That's right, darling. Remember, you asked C. K. for his advice, and since he's been kind enough to give it to you, it's only smart to do as he suggests."

Mackie winked at Clara and said, "So, Laddie, if you're quite through asking superfluous questions, I'll get to work so as to have some news for you tomorrow."

C. K. walked over to the Cadillac with us, and as I opened the passenger door for Clara, he said, "Now, Markham, I'm counting on you to continue taking good care of this young lady so I can persuade her to autograph a photo of herself for Missus Mackie, thus adding significantly to my husbandly stature at home."

Standing on the Caddy's running board, Clara leaned over and planted a kiss on the sergeant's cheek. "C. K., I will not only sign a photograph for Missus Mackie, I will happily hand deliver it!"

I walked to Mackie's roadster with him and said, "C. K., I want you to know how much I appreciate your help. I'm in way over my head with all of this."

"I wouldn't say that. It seems as if you've handled several very bad situations quite admirably. I would say, however, it's high time somebody chipped in and gave you a hand. I'm glad you decided to call me."

"Thanks, C. K."

Then, with a twinkle in his eye, the sergeant said, "And I don't suppose it has escaped your notice that Miss Bow is quite smitten with you."

"Is it that obvious?"

"Perhaps not to others, but I'm paid to notice such things. The way that young woman looks at you leaves little doubt that, unless you take precautions, she'll have you dressed up in a monkey suit and walking down the aisle of a church before you know what's happened."

I simply smiled at Mackie and he said, "Yes, that is equally apparent to me."

Thirty-Four

As I started the Cadillac's engine, Clara blurted, "I like him!"

"I thought you would. C. K. is a charmer, but don't be taken in by his beguiling ways. He's in the acting business just like you. As a detective, C. K. uses all manner of tricks to put suspects and witnesses at ease so they'll open up and tell him things they wouldn't say otherwise. He's very good at it."

"I can see that, but I don't care. He's a lovely man and I like him."

"I do, too."

After winding our way down from the Hollywood Hills, I turned right on Franklin and zig-zagged through Hollywood's business district to Santa Monica Boulevard. As I turned right toward Beverly Hills, Clara said, "Eddie, I hate to bring this up, but we have another pressing problem to solve."

I tensed, wondering what new crisis she had thought of. "What problem?"

She must have sensed my tension because she said, "Relax, darling, I was making a little joke. I'm out of clean clothes to wear and was going to ask if we could find a laundry place to get our stuff washed and cleaned. Get it? Cleaners . . . pressing problem."

I smiled. "Yeah, I get it. Sorry. After the day we've had, the mere idea of another crisis gets my blood pressure up."

With an apologetic tone in her voice, Clara said, "I guess I shouldn't be joking about problems, but C. K. made me feel so much better about everything, I'm almost giddy with relief."

"That's all right. Even though things are looking up, I don't want to get complacent just yet. In answer to your question, though, I'm in the same boat about clothes, so let's load up our laundry and find a cleaning establishment. I'll ask at the hotel office. They'll know where we can take our stuff."

The time was about three-thirty when we pulled up in front of room number ten at the Rancho Rodeo Motor Lodge. Inside, we each collected and bundled our dirty laundry. Then we loaded the bundles into the Cadillac's trunk and drove over to the office.

Miss Henna Redhead was behind the counter and eagerly recommended a place called Singer's Cleaners and Dryers that offered overnight service. Singer's, she explained, was just off Santa Monica Boulevard on Cañon Drive.

We located the place without difficulty and left nearly our entire wardrobes to be cleaned and pressed. The jolly, roly-poly woman behind the counter cheerfully informed us that everything would be sparkling clean and ready to pick-up by ten Friday morning.

That chore completed, we strolled across Cañon drive to the Pacific Electric Railroad depot and I used one of their public telephone booths to call my office. It was a few minutes past four o'clock. Elsie answered on the first ring.

"Edward Markham's office."

"Hi, Elsie. Anything for me today?"

"Yes, Mister Markham, I have three telephone messages for you. That Charles Barton called at one-thirty this afternoon and asked me to tell you he is leaving for San Antonio in the morning, but you can reach him at his home telephone number tonight if you need to. He said you had the telephone number."

"Yeah, that's the number you found for me yesterday. Who else called?"

"The other two messages are from Mister Jesse Lasky at Lasky-Paramount Studios."

I looked over at Clara standing three or four feet from the booth. She was watching me and my expression must have told her something was up because she quickly stepped over to the booth's open door and whispered the words, "What's wrong?"

I held up my hand and said to Elsie, "Oh? What did he want?"

"Well, the first message was actually from his secretary. She called a few minutes after nine this morning and said Mister Lasky wanted to speak with you. When I told her you were out, she gave me Mister Lasky's telephone number and asked that you call him as soon as possible.

"The second call came in at one-fifteen this afternoon and it was Mister Lasky himself on the line. He said it was extremely urgent that he speak to you. When I told him you weren't in the office, he said to have you call him at his home tonight if you didn't get back before five o'clock. Do you want the numbers?"

"Yes, hang on while I find something to write on."

I fished around in my jacket pockets and came up with the same Tides Inn receipt on which I had written Charlie Barton's home number. I handed it to Clara along with my pencil and whispered, "Write down the numbers I'm going to give you."

She nodded and I said, "Okay, Elsie, what's the studio number?"

"It's Hollywood 0112."

I repeated the number and Clara wrote it down. "All right, got that. What's Lasky's home number?"

"That one is a Beverly Hills exchange, Bradshaw 8491."

After repeating that number for Clara, I said, "Okay, Elsie. Thanks. Anything else?"

"No. I sent off the letter to New York about the manuscript, but otherwise, nothing."

"Okay, hopefully I'll see you Monday morning. If that doesn't work out, I'll call and let you know."

Elsie sounded decidedly displeased on hearing the possibility that I might not be in on Monday. She simply said, "Yes, Mister Markham. Goodbye."

I dropped the receiver back onto its hook and looked at Clara. She looked worried. "Mister Lasky called you? What does he want?"

"He left two messages. Both just said he wants me call. Elsie said the messages sounded urgent."

"Oh. Are you going to call him?"

Looking out at the automobile traffic passing the busy intersection, the uneasy feeling I had been feeling for most of a week came rushing back. We were standing in plain view of the cars going by in the same damned small town in which Lasky lived.

"Not right now. We need to talk about that, but first, we need to get out here. Did you know Lasky lives right here in Beverly Hills?"

She stared at me in surprise. "Oh, God, that's right. He does. I'd forgotten . . . ."

"Come on, kiddo, let's get back to the Rancho Rodeo before Lasky pulls up to the curb and offers us a ride in his damned limousine."

I parked in the space next to room ten and opened the

passenger door for Clara. As she stepped down out of the Cadillac, I handed her the room key and suggested she get in out of sight while I grabbed my overnight case and locked the car.

When I walked into our room, Clara was sitting with her elbows on the table and her face in her hands. I locked the door and sat next to her.

"What's bothering you, kiddo?"

Without looking up she said, "I feel awful, Eddie. I should have remembered Mister Lasky had a place here. I've been to parties at his house, for heaven's sake!"

I put a hand on her arm. "That's nothing to be concerned about. I don't think any harm has been done, and we'll just move to another place tomorrow."

She looked up with wet eyes. "I know, but . . . . Eddie, I don't know how much longer I can do this. I feel like I'm falling apart!"

Gently using my fingertip to brush away a tear that was rolling down her cheek, I said, "Honey, you won't have to do this much longer. We're on the home stretch now. With C. K.'s help we'll get the answers we need to make all this go away."

Clara took my hand in hers. "Yes, but what about Mister Lasky's telephone calls? What are we going to do about that?"

"Okay, let's talk about that. What do you think we should do?"

She frowned and shook her head. "I honestly don't know. What do you think he wants?"

"Well, Charlie no doubt told Lasky he wasn't able to convince us we should let the studio protect you, so my guess is Lasky's calls to me are a last ditch effort to make us change our minds. Does that make sense?"

"I suppose so. Mister Lasky is used to getting his way about everything, so we've probably made him very angry."

"That's what I'm thinking. Our refusal to cooperate may now be as much a matter of pride to him as it is a matter of your safety."

Clara nodded. "I think that's right."

"Then, as far as I'm concerned, Jesse Lasky's hurt feelings are the least of our worries right now, so my inclination is to do nothing about his telephone calls, at least until after we talk with C. K. tomorrow. We can always reconsider what to do about Lasky then. Does that make sense to you?"

She nodded again. "Yes, Eddie, that makes sense."

"Okay, then . . . ."

Clara interrupted with a question that took me by surprise, but told me a lot about her state of mind. "Eddie, will you come to bed with me tonight? I mean instead of staying up and standing guard until after I'm asleep?"

Her expression told me how I needed to answer that question. "Yes. I don't think we're in any immediate danger right now, so . . . ."

Clara brightened a little. "Thank you, darling. I really need to be close to you tonight. My knees are still wobbly from this morning."

I smiled. "Mine, too, kiddo."

She managed a small smile in return. "Oh, they are not. You just said that to make me feel better. You're not afraid of anything."

Wishing that were true, I made a joke of it. "That's me, known as 'Fearless Eddie' far and wide."

"Go ahead and kid all you want, but I know it's true. And while we're on the subject, thank you for bringing us back safely this morning." Then, after a pause, Clara said, "I know this will sound strange, but in an odd way, I'm grateful that all this is happening."

She was right, it was a strange thing for her to say. "I see. You're enjoying all this fun, are you?"

Clara scowled at me. "That's not what I mean and you know it."

"Okay, what do you mean?"

"I mean if none of this had happened, we might not have fallen in love and we wouldn't be together now. Having you love and care for me is worth everything we've been through and more. You've shown me who you really are in ways most women never get to see in their men."

I was embarrassed and I am certain it showed. Trying to get myself down off of the pedestal she seemed determined to put me on, I said, "Well, I did promise Wellman and Fleming I would see that you got back safely from Texas, and . . . ."

Clara stared me straight in the eye. "Is that all it was? Really?"

"Well, no, not . . . ."

"Eddie, you could have walked away and left me to Lasky's people the minute we got back to Los Angeles. That's all you promised to do, but you didn't walk away. You stood by me and risked your own life doing it. That's a hell of a lot more than just keeping a promise. Now, if I'm wrong, you tell me. Go ahead, tell me I'm wrong."

I sighed. "No, Clara you aren't wrong. I just don't want you to build me up into something more than I am. I'm no hero, I'm just a guy who loves you, and I figure if you love someone, they come before anything or anyone else."

Clara's eyes were moist again, but her tone of voice was vehement. "That's exactly what I'm talking about! Your idea of what love means is a whole lot different from any other man I ever met, and you've proven over and over that you really believe what you say. That, darling, is what makes you so special and makes me love you in ways I only dreamed about before we met. Do you understand that, Eddie? Do you?"

"Yes, honey, I understand."

The tears in her eyes started to flow and she squeezed my hand tight. "Doggone it, Eddie, sometimes you are the most hard-headed man in the whole world. You said once I could choose any guy I wanted. I don't think I'm that big of a deal, but if you think I am, just remember, I choose you, nobody else, just you. Now, damn it, hold me!"

We both stood and I tried to let go of her hand so I could put my arms around her, but she stopped me. "No, not here."

With that, Clara led me over to the bed, kicked off her shoes, and stretched out. Then looking up at me with the softness of love filling those big brown eyes, she said, "Now hold me."

Thirty-Five

By quarter past eleven Friday morning, we had breakfasted on coffee and doughnuts, picked up our cleaning at Singer's, packed our bags, and checked out of the Rancho Rodeo Motor Lodge. Our next stop was Greenblatt's Delicatessen to pick up a couple of sandwiches for our lunch meeting with C. K. Mackie.

I had just turned left on La Cienega to cut up to Sunset when Clara said, "Eddie, could we stop at a drug store later? I used the last of the gauze this morning and I've only got a little adhesive tape left."

"Sure. How do the wounds look? Are they healing okay?"

Clara reached up and touched the patch of gauze on her cheek. "I think so. The scabs are starting to loosen up. I could probably do without the bandage, but it looks pretty horrible."

At Greenblatt's we ordered sandwiches—a corned beef on rye for me and a Swiss cheese on pumpernickel for Clara—along with a pair of bright red apples, two sodas, and a couple of Baby Ruth candy bars for something sweet. As our sandwiches were being made, I glanced over to the table at which Bill Wellman and I sat during the lunch meeting that was the first link in a chain of horrifying and surreal scenes in which Clara and I had found ourselves battling the demons of a nightmarish netherworld. It took a moment for my mind to grasp the fact that only two weeks and a day had passed since that meeting. To my memory it seemed a moment in the dim past.

When we arrived at the Mulholland Dam picnic ground, Mackie's Dodge roadster was already parked near the same wooden trestle table we occupied the day before. I noted with some curiosity that the detective sergeant was dressed in a civilian suit instead of his customary dark blue uniform. Clara noticed the same thing, and as we approached the table, she said, "My goodness, C. K., don't we look dapper today."

Standing, C. K. said, "Why thank you, Miss Bow, and may I add that you are looking quite lovely yourself."

Smiling her most beguiling smile, Clara replied, "Thank you, sir. But, please, won't you call me Clara?"

"I would consider it a privilege to call you Clara." Then, as we sat at the table, C. K. said, "Hello, Eddie, I trust you spent a quiet evening?"

"We did, C. K. Nary a single bad guy appeared all night."

"Glad to hear that, Laddie."

"How about you, C. K.?"

"I spent most of the time since we last saw each other playing a game of connect the dots."

Clara put on her puzzled look. "Connect the dots? I don't know what that is."

C. K. explained. "It's a kiddies' pencil and paper puzzle of the sort the *Times* prints in the funnies section of their Sunday edition. The puzzle consists of random appearing dots which, when correctly connected by pencil lines make a cute drawing of a bunny or doggy or some such critter."

She nodded. "Oh, yes. I've seen those."

Mackie continued, "I fear, however, that the picture created in my puzzle is far from cute. In fact, Lassie, you may find some of what I've learned in the past twenty-four hours quite upsetting."

With apprehension in both her tone and expression, Clara asked, "What did you learn, C. K.?"

"I began the puzzle with a list the names you gave me yesterday—mainly Lasky, Schulberg and Blaylock. From there I set out to draw lines of connection between those names, as well as a few new names that came up during the conversations I had with the folks I mentioned yesterday."

Opening his lunch pail and pulling out a sandwich wrapped in wax paper, C. K. continued. "Besides the obvious connections between the various people who work for Lasky, the first interesting connection I uncovered was between this fellow, Schulberg, and Joe Ardizzone, better known as "Iron Man" by his associates."

I tensed at hearing Ardizzone's name, but it meant nothing to Clara. With a frown, she said, "Who's he?"

Looking her straight in the eye, C. K. said, "Iron Man Joe

happens to be the boss of Los Angeles' most powerful crime family. Those are the people behind the rackets—prostitution, rum running, gambling, and that sort of thing."

Clara paled. "B. P. is involved with gangsters?"

"I'm afraid so, Lass. The connection is a little vague, but my informant claims your Mister Schulberg was on the receiving end of some substantial loans—loans that were not meant to be repaid in legal tender."

I chimed in to clarify what Mackie was telling us. "He means Schulberg was paid by the mob for some service or other he performed for them."

Swallowing a bite of his sandwich, C. K. said, "Exactly right, but that's where the vagueness enters the story. My informant didn't know what services Schulberg was expected to provide in exchange for the money, but he was of the opinion that it had something to do with Schulberg's involvement in the motion picture business."

She said nothing, but Clara's expression of disbelief made it clear that this was all news to her. It was also news she found shocking.

As I opened our paper sack from Greenblatt's and placed Clara's sandwich on the table in front of her, Mackie went on with his findings. "The next connection I discovered was also with Ardizzone, along with his right-hand man, Frank Dragna. They, I discovered, are connected to the flier who died yesterday, William 'Billy' Blaylock.

"It seems Blaylock, Ardizzone and Dragna go back a few years during which the mob paid Blaylock a good deal of money on a regular basis for, shall we say, importing certain items of contraband from Mexico. In other words, Blaylock has been flying booze, drugs, and who knows what else across the border in his airplane. The fellow I spoke with said, Blaylock has made a small fortune in this endeavor."

I had been munching away at my corned beef on rye as Mackie spoke, but Clara's sandwich still lay unopened on the table. When C. K. paused to take another bite of his sandwich, I said, "I can't say that I'm surprised at hearing Blaylock was connected with the mob. He spent a good deal of money on the two ships he owned, and it was more than one is likely to make flying movie stunts. Now we know where that money came from."

C. K. nodded. "Yes, Laddie, that would likely be the explanation." Then, turning to Clara, he said, "Lass, I'm sad to say you may find the next connecting line I made even more upsetting."

Clara looked up at Mackie with an expression of dread. "What is it?"

"Well, Clara, there is no easy way to put this, so I'll just say it straight out. I found there is also a connection between Iron Man Joe and one Robert Bow."

Her jaw dropped. "My father?"

"Yes, Lass. The sad truth of the matter is that your father is into the mob for a substantial sum—debts incurred as a result of loans and gambling losses."

For a brief moment Clara seemed to be at a loss for words. When she found them, she said, "I don't understand. I've given him a house and a great deal of money. How could he be in debt to the mob?"

C. K. looked genuinely sorry for Clara. "I can't give you all the details because I don't have them, but my impression of the situation is that your father has a taste for living the high life, as well as a fondness for games of chance and betting on horses.

"If it's any consolation, this is not the first instance I've seen where new-found wealth has led the family member of a motion picture actor astray. It's generally a case of folks who have long dreamed of high living suddenly finding themselves with the means by which to fulfill their dreams. Spending seems to become an addiction for them and they spend more and more until they find themselves in trouble."

Clara, staring vacantly at something only she could see, slowly nodded her head as if in acknowledgement that the situation Mackie described fit her father. Then she looked up at C. K. and simply asked, "How much?"

"Twenty thousand dollars."

Clara covered her face with her hands and, leaning forward, rested her elbows on the table. I put a comforting arm around her and she leaned her head against my shoulder. Looking across at C. K., I raised my eyebrows in a questioning expression. He gave me the answer to my silent question in the form of a small nod, and I knew Clara had not yet heard the worst of the news.

C. K. took a deep breath in preparation for delivering that news. "Clara I'm truly sorry to be the bearer of such sad tidings, but the information I just gave you was confirmed independently by two sources, so I must believe it."

Taking a deep breath of her own, Clara raised her head from my shoulder and looked at Mackie. "It's not your fault, C. K. Ever since my father came here from Brooklyn he's been throwing money around just like you said. They pay me a lot, so I wasn't worried about it. I didn't realize how bad the situation was."

Mackie said, "That's usually the way it happens. Now, Clara, I must ask you a personal question."

"What?"

"Do you have a will?"

She frowned, puzzled by Mackie's question. Softly she said, "Yes."

"And should you pass on, who would inherit your estate?"

"My . . . father."

I could almost see the thought process going on her mind before Clara jerked her head up. "Oh, God! My own father is trying to kill me, just like my mother did!"

The part about her mother was a surprise, apparently part of the childhood she didn't want to talk about. Whatever that story might be, Clara had reached the breaking point. She burst into tears and buried her face against my shoulder. I held her tighter, wishing I could take away her pain.

Thankfully, C. K. knew how to do that. "Now, now, Lass, let's not be quite so hasty to jump to conclusions. Quite honestly, I don't believe your father has any knowledge of, or involvement in, the attempts on your life. Let me tell you a little about how this sort of thing works with the mob."

On hearing Mackie say he didn't think Robert Bow was in on the scheme to kill her, Clara dried her eyes with my handkerchief and looked at him across the table.

"You see," C. K. began, "The mob is really quite benevolent when it comes to letting folks run up debts, especially people who have collateral. In this instance, your prominence and assumed wealth were the collateral.

"But there is a limit to their benevolence, and when that limit is reached, they demand payment of the debt or else. If payment isn't made, they increase the pressure, making threats of dire consequences. If payment of the debt still isn't forthcoming, they usually take matters into their own hands.

"In your father's case, I think the first thing Frank Dragna—he typically handles debt collection—would have done is call B. P. Schulberg to find out what's what. Now, Clara, supposing Dragna asked this fellow Schulberg if you could be made to pay your father's debt, what do you think he would have said?"

Clara seemed to think about the question for a moment before saying, "I guess B. P. would have said no because he knew I was determined to stop my father from spending my money. That's one of the reasons I bought father his own house, and when I did that, I made it clear to everyone at the studio who might have loaned father money that I was no longer going to pay his bills."

C. K. nodded. "And when was this, Clara?"

"I'm not sure of the exact date, but I bought the house for him about two months ago, so around then sometime. I know what I did sounds heartless, cutting off my own father like that, but when I negotiated my new contract with Lasky, I made sure father was included. He gets one hundred dollars a week for doing almost nothing. I thought that with no rent to pay, he could live on that much." In a tone of voice that was full of disappointment she added, "I guess I was wrong."

"From what I've learned, that timing fits with what happened next. Now, let me ask you something else. Does Mister Schulberg know the terms of your will?"

Softly, as if she no longer had the energy to speak in a normal tone, Clara said, "Yes, I guess so. He sent me to his lawyer to make the will. And there's another thing. B. P. insisted that I should have life insurance. He called it an investment. So I bought a fifty thousand dollar policy from some insurance man who is a friend of B. P.'s."

C. K.'s expression was grim. "And your father is the beneficiary of that policy?"

Clara simply nodded and Mackie said, "I'm afraid that just added more fuel to the fire. So, if we assume Schulberg told Dragna he didn't think you would voluntarily pay your father's debt, which he no doubt did, Dragna would have asked more questions about such matters as your will and life insurance.

"By this time, I imagine Schulberg was growing rather nervous. Based on his previous dealings with the mob, he could surmise the reason for Dragna's questions, but that he did nothing about it and continued to cooperate is strong evidence of the hold the mob has on him.

"To make a long story short, Dragna would have gone back to Iron Man Joe with what he learned from Schulberg and a decision would have been made. Apparently, that decision was to kill you so your father would inherit your estate and collect the life insurance, making it possible for him to pay his debt.

"Ardizzone or Dragna then called Blaylock with instructions to cause your death and make it look like an accident. Blaylock would have been given information provided by Schulberg on where you were and what you were doing so he could plan your demise.

"Now, if the first attempt on your life—the one in Texas—had been successful, it might have been explained as some sort of a mix-up in which Blaylock thought he was supposed to fly in and shoot up the village. If the Army ship had crashed and nobody thought to check for poison, it also might be considered an accident. However, in both incidents, Eddie, here, threw a monkey wrench into Blaylock's plans, causing them to fail.

"As you can probably guess, the mob takes a dim view of failure, so Blaylock would have been getting panicky by the time he found you in Los Angeles Tuesday afternoon. That would explain why he shot at you in Laurel Canyon. At that point he probably didn't care whether your death looked like an accident or not. He would have been far more worried about what the mob would do to him if he let you escape again.

"Now, mind you, Lass, most of this speculation on my part, and what actually happened might be a little different than what I just described, but if I were a betting man, I would wager mightily that my version isn't far off the truth."

Clara was staring vacantly in the direction of her uneaten Swiss cheese sandwich on the table. To my eyes, she looked as if she had reached the saturation point—that she had heard all the bad news she could take.

I looked across the table at Mackie, watching him take a bite of a cookie from his lunch pail and wash it down with coffee from a thermos bottle. He had said all he was going to say without further prompting. Knowing, C. K., however, I was fairly certain he would not have gone to all the effort of finding out what was going on without also giving serious consideration to how the situation could be resolved. I took it upon myself to ask the question he was waiting for.

"All right, C. K., you've given us the bad news, now please tell us how we get out of this mess."

Mackie took a moment to organize his thoughts. Clara looked up at him with what I thought might be a somewhat hopeful expression.

"Well, Laddie, we have three choices, but none of them are particularly appealing. The first is to see that charges are brought against Ardizzone, et al for murdering the Army pilot and attempted murder charges for trying to kill Miss Bow. At first glance this may seem to be the proper and correct way to proceed, and in a just world it would be. Unfortunately, the world we live in is far from just.

"With that fellow, Blaylock, dead we have no witnesses who can testify about what happened except Schulberg, and it's a certainty that he would not be a cooperative witness. What's worse is that Iron Man Joe and his cronies are in solidly with the Los Angeles district attorney, Asa Keyes. Even if we had enough evidence to prove Ardizzone's guilt, Keyes would either find a way to avoid prosecuting or he would intentionally lose the case.

"That leaves the Army. The government could prosecute Ardizzone, but they're in the same boat as Keyes with regard to the lack of solid evidence. It can be proven beyond a reasonable doubt that Blaylock killed their pilot, but that's as far as it goes. So the first of your choices is very unlikely to result in a satisfactory resolution to the situation. Do you understand that?"

I said, "Yes, I can see that seeking a legal remedy is pointless. What's our second course of action?"

"It's a relatively simple solution. Clara, here, simply goes to an attorney and makes a new will that leaves her estate to someone other than her father, and she replaces him as the beneficiary of her life insurance policy. Once Ardizzone and Dragna know about the changes, there is no longer any benefit to them in killing Clara.

"Again, this appears to be a good solution to the problem, but when you consider the options left to the mob when the will and insurance have been changed, it no longer looks so good. Iron Man Joe is not going to throw up his hands and say, 'Gosh, I guess we're out twenty Gs.'"

I asked, "What do you think they would do in that situation?"

C. K. pursed his lips for a moment as if in thought, then said, "Most likely Joe would send a couple of boys after Mister Bow and he would be held for ransom. They would figure that, despite Clara's unwillingness to pay her father's bills voluntarily, she would come across with the money to keep him alive."

"And if she didn't pay up?"

Without hesitation, C. K. said, "They would kill Mister Bow as an object lesson to anyone else who thought they could cross the mob and get away with it. In fact, they might well kill him even if Clara paid the ransom, just to tie up any loose ends that might come back to haunt them later."

Shaking her head vigorously, Clara said, "No! No matter what he's done, he's still my father. I don't want anything like that to happen to him."

Mackie nodded. "I was sure you wouldn't, so that leaves choice number three, which is the least appealing at first glance, but is the solution most likely to bring an end to this situation without anyone else being killed."

With what sounded to me like defeat in her voice, Clara said, "What is it?"

"Well, Lass, if you have the twenty thousand, it is simply to pay the mob their money. I know it means giving in to the scoundrels, but it is the only thing that will assure everyone's safety. Could you put your hands on that much cash?"

Clara nodded. "Yes, it would wipe out most of my savings, but I have it."

"And are you willing to pay that stiff a price to make all this go away?"

She nodded again. "Yes. I don't want to die, I don't want my father to be killed, and most of all, I don't want put Eddie through any more of this. He's risked his life four times to save mine. That's enough."

I thought of several things to say, but kept my mouth shut and let C. K. do the talking. He said, "Okay, then, that's what we'll do. How quickly can you get the money?"

Clara shrugged her shoulders. "I don't know much about banks, but I guess I could go in and withdraw it right now."

Mackie looked thoughtful for a moment before saying, "Okay, that's step one. The next problem is getting word to Ardizzone that we want to deal with him, and step three is actually delivering the money.

"I have a telephone number I'm fairly certain will get to Iron Man Joe, but making the call would be up to you, Eddie. Are you willing . . . ."

"Of course, I am, C. K. Let's go make the call."

"Okay, but first let's get our ducks all nicely in a row. The plan I think makes the most sense is to start by going to Clara's bank and withdrawing the money. Next, Eddie calls and sets up a meeting for later this afternoon or this evening. Then we take Clara somewhere safe—I think Missus Mackie would be quite willing to entertain Miss Clara Bow for a while—while we make the payoff."

I looked at C. K. "You're going with me to deliver the money?"

"Yes, if you want me to. That's why I wore this monkey suit today. Mister Ardizzone would not take kindly to you showing up with a policeman in tow. Also, I can't afford to be seen actually meeting with Iron Man Joe, but I can certainly be nearby in case something goes wrong."

"Thanks, C. K. That's above and beyond the call of duty."

With a grin and a twinkle in his eye, Mackie said, "L.A.'s finest at your service." Then he turned to Clara. "One more thing, Lass. I think it would be a wise idea to make the changes in your will and insurance policy we discussed even though you're paying the mob their money. That way Eddie can tell Joe that trying this sort of stunt in the future will get them nowhere. It's not much, but knowing this twenty Gs is all they're ever going to get out of you will probably result in no further credit being extended to your father, and that would go along way toward putting an end to his extravagances."

Nodding, Clara said, "Yes, that would be a very good thing to do. And thank you, C. K. I don't know what would have happened to us if you hadn't stepped in to help. I just hope this will really be the end of it."

C. K. gave Clara a fatherly smile. "I think it will be, Lass. Then you and this young fellow here can go about your business, which unless I am sorely mistaken, will include matrimony in the foreseeable future."

I'm not sure, but I thought Clara blushed. I'm sure I did.

Thirty-Six

1:15 P.M. – Friday – September 24, 1926
Lake Hollywood – Hollywood

Clara did her banking at the main branch of the Citizens National Bank downtown on Spring Street and we agreed that Mackie would follow us there. I found it comforting to look in my review mirror and see a friend back there for a change.

Clara appeared to be lost in thought as we rolled through Hollywood on Sunset toward downtown L.A. That was not surprising. She had received a great deal of disturbing news in the past hour and no doubt needed time to absorb it all. We were nearly to Spring Street when Clara finally said, "Eddie, we didn't get a chance to talk this over. Do you think we're doing the right thing?"

"In the first place, this is your decision to make, and in the second place, I don't think there's much to discuss. While it irks me no end to see those scoundrels get away with murder and collect their money, too, paying them off appears to be the only way we can put an end to this."

Clara did not sound convinced of that. "Do you think it will really work, that those men will leave us alone after we pay them the money?"

I had been pondering the same question and I gave Clara the only answer I had. "When it comes to dealing with men like these, I don't think there are any guarantees, but I trust Mackie's judgment, so that's where I have to put my faith."

"I trust him, too. Everything he said makes sense."

The main branch of the Citizens National Bank is located in a substantial twelve-story building on the northwest corner of Spring and Fifth Streets. I turned right on Fifth and found a place to park. Mackie drove past us and pulled into another vacant spot further down the block.

We met just inside the building's lobby and C. K. said, "I'll wait out here while you conduct your business, Clara. Then we'll use one of these public telephones to call Ardizzone."

Inside, the bank was a typically ornate, high-ceilinged space where even the smallest sounds reverberated between the marble floor and polished granite walls. Clara walked directly over to a low railing, beyond which were several mahogany desks, mostly occupied by earnest looking young men speaking into telephones.

A woman promptly stepped up to the other side of the railing and asked if she could help us. Clara told her we wanted to speak with Mister Brian Cavanaugh. The woman walked briskly past the desks to a door with the words "Branch Manager" imprinted on its frosted glass window. She knocked, went in, and came back out a moment later to escort us into Cavanaugh's office.

Brian Cavanaugh was a stocky fellow in a handsomely tailored blue surge suit. His hair was graying and his voice was welcoming as he said, "Good afternoon, Miss Bow. Please have a seat and tell me how we can help you."

Clara and I sat and she proceeded to tell Cavanaugh she was there to withdraw twenty thousand dollars in cash from her savings account. On hearing that news, the branch manager looked less welcoming. Bankers much prefer substantial amounts of money flowing into their vaults rather than flowing out of them.

He glanced nervously at me and then back at Clara. "Ah, certainly, Miss Bow. I trust you aren't withdrawing the funds because you are in any way dissatisfied with our service."

Clara said she was delighted with their service and the funds were needed to conduct some personal business. After hemming and hawing for a moment or two, Cavanaugh told us it would take several minutes to retrieve the money from their vault. Then he prepared a withdrawal slip and presented it to Clara for her signature. She signed the slip and Cavanaugh walked out into the main area of the bank.

Cavanaugh's several minutes turned out to be about fifteen, and when he returned, he was accompanied by a uniformed bank guard carrying a small metal box by its handle. The guard set the box on Cavanaugh's desk and waited while the branch manager opened the box and checked its contents. Then Cavanaugh dismissed the guard and withdrew two neat stacks of one hundred dollar bills, each banded with a brown paper strap upon which was printed "$10,000."

He set the stacks on his desk and laid a withdrawal receipt in front of Clara with a fountain pen. I found myself a little disappointed at how insignificant the two stacks of bills looked. It seemed to me a sum of money that great should be more impressive.

Cavanaugh asked Clara if she would like a manila envelope in which to carry the money and she said she would. Two minutes later I followed Clara out of the branch manager's office with the simple nine-by-twelve envelope in my hand. The guard was waiting for us outside Cavanaugh's office and walked along behind us until we stepped out into the building lobby where C. K. was waiting for us.

C. K. glanced at the package in my hand, nodded, and said, "Okay, let's see if we can reach Ardizzone on the telephone."

We stepped to the telephone booth closest to the rear of the lobby and Mackie handed me a folded slip of paper. I handed him the manila envelope to hold while I unfolded the note. The only thing on it was a hand-printed telephone number—TR 6491.

Mackie said, "Getting Joe on the line will take a little doing. I suggest you tell whoever answers the call your name and that you are calling for Miss Clara Bow. If they ask the nature of your business, I would simply say you are calling to arrange the payment of Robert Bow's debt. If Ardizzone is in, that should get him to the telephone.

"What you say to him is up to you, but I recommend keeping your story simple. Say only what you think needs to be said to set up a meeting, and make sure you allow us enough time before the meeting to take Clara back to my home in Hollywood. That's about all I can tell you, except to sound confident. Good luck."

I looked at Clara before stepping into the booth. She looked as nervous as I felt, but she managed to give me a small smile.

Leaving the booth door open so Clara and C. K. could hear my end of the conversation, I deposited a nickel and dialed the number. After the third ring a gruff-sounding male voice said, "Yeah?"

I said, "My name is Markham. I want to talk to Joe Ardizzone on behalf of Miss Clara Bow."

"Yeah? Well, I'll see if Mister Ardizzone wants to talk to you."

The line was quiet for a while, although I could hear a muffled conversation in the background. Then the gruff-sounding guy came back and said, "Mister Ardizzone says what do you want to talk to him about?"

"Tell him Miss Bow wants to make arrangements to pay the

money her father owes him."

After a few moments a different voice, one with some kind of European accent, said, "Yeah, this is Ardizzone. Who the hell are you and what do ya want?"

"My name's Markham and I've got twenty grand here that Miss Clara Bow says belongs to you. She told me to make sure you get it."

Iron Man Joe was naturally suspicious of strangers bearing gifts. He said, "Oh yeah? So how come this dame suddenly gets so generous?"

Several possible answers to his question occurred to me. I picked the one I thought Ardizzone would best relate to. "Probably because she's gettin' annoyed by the ignorant morons you keep sending to kill her. I put the last one, that idiot Blaylock, in the ground and I'll happily put the next guy you send in the same place unless you'd like to get your money and put an end to this nonsense once and for all."

I glanced at C. K. He raised his eyebrows in surprise, but he also had a hint of a smile on his face. From the sound of Iron Man Joe's voice, he wasn't smiling. "Oh, tough guy, huh? Okay, pal, here's what you do. You bring the money to . . . ."

"Not so fast, Joe. There are a couple of strings tied to this money. You agree to 'em or no soap."

"What kinda strings?"

"First, you call your boys off and leave Miss Bow alone, and second, you don't take any more markers from her old man, in fact you don't even let him into any of your joints. If those conditions are Jake with you, you get the cash."

Ardizzone was quiet for a long time and I was beginning to think I might have overplayed my hand when he finally said, "Okay, pal, if you're on the level, you got a deal. Meet me in thirty minutes behind the warehouse at Olympic and Santa Fe. But I'm warnin' you, if you're pullin' some kind of stunt, you and the dame are fish food."

"Make it three-thirty. It'll take me that long to get there from where I am."

Iron Man Joe agreed to that and I dropped the telephone receiver on its hook. Mackie said, "What's the word?"

"Three-thirty behind the warehouse at Olympic and Santa Fe."

C. K. returned the manila envelope to me and said, "We'd better get a move on. My house is on La Mirada at Van Ness."

This time I followed C. K. instead of the other way around. He cut down to Wilshire Boulevard and followed it more or less north to Santa Monica Boulevard, which he took west as far as Van Ness. We only traveled north on Van Ness for a short distance before C. K. pulled to the curb alongside a well-kept bungalow with colorful flowers growing in beds beyond a neatly trimmed lawn. A pleasant-looking woman in a pale blue housedress was watering one of the beds with a sprinkling can.

I pulled up behind Mackie's Dodge and he walked back to open the Cadillac's passenger door for Clara. As he did so, C. K. said, "Eddie, sit tight, this will only take a moment."

Mackie took Clara's hand to help her down from the car and she turned to me. "Please be careful, Eddie, and hurry back."

"Will do, kiddo. You just relax and I'll be back before you know I'm gone."

Clara nodded, but her big brown eyes were full of concern. When C. K. had introduced Clara to his wife, he returned to the Caddy's driver-side door. "Slide over, Laddie. This will look better if appears that I'm just your driver."

I slid over to the passenger side of the seat and held the twenty-grand manila envelope in my lap. C. K. climbed in behind the steering wheel and we began retracing the route we had just followed from downtown.

As he drove, C. K. briefed me on what he expected to find when we got to the meeting. "I don't mind telling you, Eddie, you made me a little nervous when you were talking to Joe on the telephone, but you must have said the right things or we'd be dead in the water. Just don't go too far with the tough guy act. Okay?"

"Okay, C. K."

"Now, are you still carrying that forty-five pistol?"

"Yeah, I've got it."

"I'm going to suggest you leave it with me in the car. That way if they pat you down, you'll be clean, and God forbid, if there's any shooting to be done, I'll do it in the name of the law."

Almost gratefully, I pulled the Colt out of the waistband of my slacks and set it on the seat between us. "There's one round in the chamber and seven in the magazine. The damned thing kicks like a mule."

Mackie glanced at the pistol on the seat. "Yeah, I know, Laddie. It's a mighty poor choice of a weapon. That's why I brought my service revolver along.

"Now, when we get there, Joe will have at least two of his boys with him, but you'll only see one, his driver. The other one or ones will be out of sight, probably up on the roof of the warehouse watching you over the sights of a rifle.

"I'll wait for you in the car. They'll be there when we arrive and I'll park so I can cover you through the side window here. I don't think Joe or any of his boys know me on sight, but there's no sense takin' any chances on that score.

"When we stop, you get out and meet Joe halfway between the cars. He'll want to check the money, and once that's done, it should be the end of it. Just try not to let 'em see you sweat. These guys are like a pack of dogs, they can sense fear. Any questions, Laddie?"

"No, C. K. I think I've got the picture."

As we turned onto Olympic, I noticed C. K. reach up and pull his fedora down a little lower on his forehead. Then, as we turned into the warehouse yard at Santa Fe, he said, "Good luck."

The scene was almost exactly as C. K. said it would be. There was a big dark blue four-door Packard parked all by itself behind the warehouse. A man I presumed was Joe Ardizzone climbed out of the backseat as we pulled up. A second fellow—a small guy with a big bulge under his jacket—was standing next to the Packard's passenger-side back door. Together, the two of them walked to a point about halfway between the two cars and waited.

I stepped out of the Cadillac and walked over to meet them. When I got there, Joe said, "You Markham?"

"Yup, that's me."

"Who's your pal in the car there?"

"Just a friend with a strong interest in my welfare."

He stared at Mackie for what seemed like a long time. Finally, he pointed to the manila envelope in my hand and said, "That the dough?"

"Yup, that's it."

To his driver, Joe said, "Take a look, Jimmy. Make sure it's all there."

Jimmy took a step toward me and held out his hand, looking me square in the eye as he did so. I handed him the envelope and he stepped back to tear it open.

While Jimmy was counting the hundred dollar bills, Ardizzone said, "Just who the hell are you, Markham?"

"Just a friend of Miss Bow's. I take care of little chores for her when something needs doing."

Joe continued to stare at me with his best menacing expression. I kept my face as blank as I could while the sweat ran down the small of my back and C. K.'s words rang in my ears, "Don't let 'em see you sweat."

Just as I was figuring that Ardizzone's driver must be using all his fingers and toes to count the money, he said, "It's all here, boss."

Joe didn't take his eyes off me. "Okay, Markham, you can tell the dame I agree to the strings she put on that cash. And when Iron Man Joe gives his word, that's just like money in the bank, if you get my meaning."

I nodded and Joe stuck his hand out to shake. I looked down at his hand like it was the last thing in the world I wanted to touch.

Joe chuckled. "I know we ain't the best of pals, Markham, but I suggest you shake my hand on this, 'cuz if you don't you could have a fatal accident before you get back to your car."

The light dawned. "I see," I said, "Shaking hands is the 'okay' signal to your guy with the rifle up on top of the warehouse."

As we shook, Ardizzone said, "You catch on quick, Markham. I like that in a guy"

Resisting the temptation to tell him I really did not much care what he liked or did not like, I simply nodded. With that, Joe and Jimmy turned around and walked back to the big Packard. I stood there for a few seconds watching them, and then I turned and walked as casually as I could manage on slightly wobbly legs back to C. K. in the Caddy.

As I climbed in, the Packard roared off, spewing gravel from its rear tires as it fought for traction. C. K. said, "Well done, Laddie. Did he tell you he accepted the conditions you put on the money?"

"He did. Said his word was like money in the bank."

"Strange as it may seem, Eddie, he was being straight with you. Even among thieves, a man's word is his bond. You and Clara are in the clear as far as Joe Ardizzone is concerned, although, I'd suggest being cautious for another day or two so he'll have time to call off anyone else he's set on your trail."

I nodded, but something about my expression made C. K. look at me with concern. "You okay, Laddie?"

"Yeah, C. K. I'm just swell. Let's get the hell out of here and go someplace where the air doesn't stink."

Half an hour later C. K., Clara and I were standing in Mackie's front yard where the air was filled with floral scents. It was a definite improvement.

C. K. said, "Clara, you can be quite proud of your young man here. He walked into the lion's den cool as could be and had the lion practically eating out of his hand."

Clara had her arm looped through mine and she pulled me a little closer. "That's the kind of guy Eddie is, C. K. He keeps doing that sort of thing without any hesitation. I don't mind telling you, it's one of the reasons I love him so much."

Mackie chuckled and I blushed. "Eddie's a good one, all right, Clara. You'll get no argument from me on that score." Then to me, C. K. said, "You two go off and relax for the weekend, then, if you don't mind, Laddie, check in with me Monday morning, just in case I catch wind of anything you should know."

"I don't mind at all, C. K. I guess you already know how grateful we are to you for stepping in and helping us, but I'll say it straight out. Thanks, C. K. I don't know how much longer we could have kept going without you."

I felt Clara nod her head and with a broad smile and a twinkle, Mackie said, "Anytime, Laddie. That's what policeman friends are for."

As I pulled away from the curb in front of Mackie's bungalow, I had no idea where I was going next, so I drove back to Santa Monica Boulevard and pulled into a parking lot between a drugstore and a small grocery.

On the way, Clara told me about Helen Mackie. "She's just exactly the sort of wife you would expect C. K. to have—kind and generous and friendly. She kept me so occupied I lost track of the time. It was almost like you said; you were back before I hardly knew you were gone."

She paused for a long moment as if she expected me to say something. When I could not think of anything to say, Clara said, "Eddie, darling, was it awful?"

"No, it wasn't awful. I'm just glad it's over."

"Is it, Eddie? Is it really all over?"

"Ardizzone gave me his word on the conditions we put on the money, and C. K. says his word is good, so yes, it's over. C. K. did say we should keep our heads down for another day or two just to be on the safe side. And, of course, we still have Lasky to deal with."

Clara looked up at the drug store. "Eddie, there's a pay telephone over there. Let's go call Mister Lasky right now and get that over with, too."

Not particularly looking forward to the chore, I said, "Okay. I guess we might as well. He'll want to talk directly to you, though. Are you up to that?"

"You bet I am."

"All right. When you talk to Lasky, tell him you'll be in late Monday morning."

"Late Monday morning?"

"Yeah. I'll tell you why when we're done."

I stepped into the telephone booth and looked at the loose change from my pocket. I did not have a nickel. "Clara, do you have a nickel?"

"I'm sure I do." She fished around in her handbag and came up with a nickel, which I dropped into the slot. I dialed Lasky's private number and a woman answered. "Mister Jesse Lasky's office. Who's calling please?"

"Eddie Markham calling for Lasky."

She recognized my name immediately. "Oh, yes, Mister Markham. Mister Lasky has been expecting your call. One moment, please."

No more than five seconds later Jesse Lasky, himself was hollering in my ear. "Markham, where the hell are you and what have you done with my actress?"

"Where the hell we are is none of your damned business. As for Clara, she's standing right here and she's got something to tell you."

After trading places with me, Clara said, "Hello, Mister Lasky, this is Clara."

She looked at me wide-eyed and held the receiver away from her ear. I could hear Lasky haranguing at her from two feet away. Clara calmly waited for him to finish yelling, and then she said, "Mister Lasky, I will be in your office at ten o'clock Monday morning. We have some things to talk over and . . . ."

The hollering started all over again and I made a gesture to change places again. When I was in back in the booth I did some hollering of my own. "Lasky, shut up! You're damned lucky I haven't had you thrown in jail, and I'm warning you, if I see anyone who even remotely looks like a Lasky employee between now and Monday morning, I'll shoot him dead on the spot. You hear me?"

I cannot say whether it was my comment about having him thrown in jail or my threat to shoot any of his employees I saw, but something caused him to simmer down. That seemed to be a clue about how to handle the guy, but I was not in the mood to think about what it meant. He said, "Okay, Markham, you don't need to be shooting anyone. Just be sure she's here Monday morning."

"We'll both be there, Lasky."

I never heard what he had to say to that because I dropped the receiver into its hook and ended the call. When I looked at Clara, her eyes were wide with surprise.

"Eddie! Nobody talks to Mister Lasky like that!"

"I do when the situation warrants it. Now, let's go into this drugstore and get the gauze and adhesive tape you need for your cheek."

Our shopping chores completed, I turned west on Santa Monica Boulevard and Clara said, "Eddie, you said you would tell me why we're not going back to the studio until late Monday morning."

Looking over at her, I smiled a genuine smile and it felt like something I hadn't done in a long time. "Kiddo, I thought we might take a drive up to the Casa del Pacifico for the weekend and, maybe on Sunday, we can go on up to Santa Barbara for the day so you and my folks can get acquainted. That is, assuming you'd like to do that."

Sliding across the seat to plant a kiss on my cheek, she said, "Eddie, really?"

"Yeah, but only if you want . . . ."

In her excited little girl voice, Clara said, "Oh, yes! Yes! I want that more than anything!"

"Then hang on, kiddo. Next stop Ventura."

Actually, our next stop turned out to be a Gilmore gasoline station in Thousand Oaks, where I stopped to fill the tank and make a long distance call to the Casa del Pacifico Motor Inn. I recognized Ambrose DeBoyce's voice immediately when he said, "Good afternoon, this is the Casa del Pacifico Motor Inn."

"Hello, Mister DeBoyce, this is Eddie Markham calling, although the last time we spoke, you knew me as Allan Wilkinson."

"Oh, yes, Mister Wilkinson. How can I help you?"

"Well, Mister DeBoyce, I'm pleased to say that the difficulties we were experiencing during our last visit have been resolved, and we would like very much to pay a return visit to your fine motor inn."

DeBoyce said, "We would be honored to have you and . . . your lovely wife back. When will you be arriving?"

"We're in Thousand Oaks right now and we plan on driving straight up there, so we should be there in about an hour. Tell me, Mister DeBoyce, would cottage number nine be available by any chance?"

"It surely is, Mister Wilkinson. How long will you be with us?"

"We'll be checking out early Monday morning."

"That will be just fine. Oh, and Mister Wilkinson, I'm certainly happy to hear those difficulties you mentioned have been satisfactorily resolved. Missus DeBoyce will be relieved when I tell her that news."

Thirty-Seven

7:00 P.M. – Friday – September 24, 1926
U.S. Highway 101 – Ventura

It was a few minutes after seven o'clock by the time we reached the outskirts of Ventura and my stomach was grumbling. I figured if I was hungry, Clara had to be starving, since she had not eaten any of her lunch.

"Hey, kiddo, you gettin' hungry? You should be. All you've eaten today is a doughnut."

"Oh, Helen gave me a heavenly slice of homemade apple pie while we were waiting for you and C. K., but I am a little hungry."

"It seems to me I remember passing a Chinese take-out joint on Thompson Boulevard the last time we drove this route. How 'bout we stop and pick up something to eat in our room?"

"That sounds good, unless there's a chop suey place around."

I glanced over at Clara and she was grinning at me. "You and your chop suey!"

My memory of the Chinese take-out place proved accurate, and I pulled to the curb in front of the Hong Kong Takee Out. We ordered cartons of chicken chow mein and sweet and sour pork—seemingly enough to feed a small army—and I paid the tab of a buck-twenty-five.

At twenty-five minutes past seven I stepped into the Casa del Pacifico's office and received a warm greeting from Ambrose DeBoyce. "Mister Wilkinson, welcome back to the Casa del Pacifico Motor Inn!"

"Thank you, Mister DeBoyce. You have no idea how happy we are to be back."

"Well," he said with a smile, "Your cottage is ready, all we need to do is get you and Missus Wilkinson registered." He stopped, appeared to think for a moment, and then said, "There is one thing, though. I certainly recognized the young woman with whom you are traveling, and if you want to refer to her as your wife, that's fine with me, however, when it comes to the official registration book, I'm afraid we must be a little more . . . shall we say, truthful, than we were last time. Can I persuade you to register under your real name? Mister and Missus will be fine, you needn't include Miss Bow's name."

"Sure, Mister DeBoyce. There is no longer any reason for secrecy as far as I'm concerned. As for the 'Missus' part, I'm taking steps to make that truthful, too. "

DeBoyce proved himself a devout romantic by beaming at me and saying, "Oh, that's wonderful! We could tell the two of you were very much in love when you were here before. Missus DeBoyce will be very excited to hear the news!"

Smiling, I held my hands up in a 'slow down' gesture. "Please, don't tell her quite yet. I'm planning something for tomorrow night and I'm hoping to keep it a surprise, which reminds me, can you recommend a good, quality jeweler in town?"

He could and did, writing the name Krause Jewelers and their address on a slip of paper, which I carefully folded and slipped into my billfold. I also asked DeBoyce if he would mind making a six o'clock dinner reservation at the Pierpont Inn for us. He said he would be delighted to do so.

Then I signed the register and paid for our three nights' lodging. I actually got a little thrill out writing, Mister & Missus Edward Markham, Los Angeles, California.

Ten minutes later I had unloaded our bags from the Cadillac and locked it, and Clara had laid out our dinner on the table by the big window. I pulled the window curtain open a little wider and turned out all the lamps in the room except for the one over the dressing table so we could enjoy the twinkling carpet of lights below us.

As I joined Clara at the table, she said, "I'm afraid we don't have any plates or anything to eat off of, so we'll just have to eat out of the cartons and share."

"I think we can work that out."

Clara grinned her version of a silly grin at me. "I didn't know if you were worried about catching my cooties."

"They haven't done me any harm so far, so I'm willing take the risk."

"I guess compared to all the other risks you've taken for me, this one is pretty tame."

Digging in with our chopsticks, we traded the cardboard cartons back and forth until we were both full, after which we just sat holding hands and enjoying the view. It was then that I remembered how I had signed the registration book.

"Oh, I meant to tell you that Mister DeBoyce insisted I register using my real name this time."

Clara beamed. "So I'm missus Eddie Markham now? I kinda like the sound of that."

"I do, too, but I'm afraid DeBoyce knows who you really are. He said I didn't need to write your name in the register, but I think he wanted me to know he was wise to us."

She frowned. "I hope he isn't upset with us."

"Not at all. He seemed quite friendly and understanding about it all."

We sat for a few minutes just watching the lights twinkle, then Clara surprised me with a comment that seemed to come out of the blue.

"Eddie, I don't know how to cook."

Even in the darkened room I could see that her expression was quite serious. Wondering what prompted the comment, I asked, "Oh? Is cooking something that interests you?"

"Yes, a lot. Helen Mackie is a wonderful cook, and I want to be just like Helen—taking care of a home, doing the laundry, cooking delicious meals, and maybe even raising a couple of kids. That's something Helen never got to do."

The sincerity in her tone of voice was matched by her expression. I said, "Sounds like you've given the subject a lot of thought, but wouldn't all that be hard to do with your acting career?"

She looked at me with eyes that had never seemed more sincere. "Darling, I only wanted to be an actress because it was something I could do that would get me away from . . . from a bad life. The money and all the rest of it don't mean anything to me. I've already made up my mind about all that. That's why I want to meet Mister Lasky Monday. I'm gonna tell him I'm through after the next picture. He won't like it, but I don't really care what he likes anymore.

"Being a wife and mother is a dream I've had all my life—a dream I didn't think would ever come true until now."

"I see. Well, kiddo, we'll just have to see what we can do about turning that dream into a reality."

Her hand tightened around mine. "Really, Eddie? Do you think we could really do that?"

"I'm pretty sure we can kiddo. Just bear with me a little longer; I've got an idea or two on that subject."

She grinned at me. "And you're not gonna tell me what those ideas are?"

I grinned back. "Not tonight, but soon, very soon."

Clara put on a pouty face and said, "Well, phooey. You're no fun. I guess I might as well go to bed."

When I heard water running in the bathroom sink, I walked over to the dressing table where Clara had left her jewelry. I took the note DeBoyce had given me with the name of the jewelry store out of my wallet and picked up the diamond solitaire ring Clara had been wearing as an engagement ring for the sake of appearances since we stopped for dinner in Santa Paula Sunday night. I placed the ring on the note paper and used my pencil to trace a circle the same size as its inner circumference. Then I put the paper back in my billfold and congratulated myself on what a clever fellow I was.

Clara walked out of the bathroom a few moments later in a sheer white nightgown that ended about mid-thigh and left no doubt as to what charms it was not concealing. She put her arms around my neck and pulled my face down to hers for a kiss. It was a hell of a kiss—one that left me a little breathless.

"Hurry to bed, darling."

After getting ready for bed and placing Wellman's Colt on the nightstand—more out of habit that out of any real sense of need—I slid between the sheets. Propping myself up on my left elbow, I put my right hand around Clara's waist and kissed her.

I had merely intended to kiss her goodnight, but the kiss quickly escalated into something else entirely—a sharing of passion that left us both breathless. Within seconds, Clara pulled my face to hers again and said only, "More."

This time Clara threw me a curve. Placing her left hand over my right, she pushed my hand up from her waist to her breast and pressed my fingers into the firm flesh there. The extent of her desire was readily apparent, and my own arousal became equally apparent.

A hundred thoughts swarmed around my mind, but one flashed brighter than all the others: Clara and I had shared a bed for the past five nights and managed to avoid doing what she had once referred to as "anything we have to be ashamed of later." Was now the time to retreat from that lofty moral ground? The answer to that was no, and I knew it.

Gently sliding my hand back down to her waist, I ended the

kiss. She opened her eyes and looked up at me, asking an unspoken question. I was not sure how to answer that question, even if could have found my voice to speak an answer.

There was no need, though. She answered her own question. I felt the tension leave Clara's body as she relaxed. "I'm sorry, darling. That was wicked of me. I just love you so damned much and I want . . . I want . . . ."

Giving her as tender and non-passionate a kiss on the lips as I could manage to shush her, I whispered, "I know, Clara, and you know I feel the same. Just trust me a little longer. It will be soon, very soon."

"Eddie, darling, I intend to trust you for the rest of my life."

I rolled onto my back and she slid close, resting her head on my chest. That's how we went to sleep, or at least she went to sleep. It took me a while longer to reach that state. One part of my mind was intent on convincing another part that such high-toned ethics and Victorian morality were severely outdated.

7:00 A.M. – Saturday – September 25, 1926
Casa del Pacifico Motor Inn – Ventura

Clara was still sleeping when I returned from the bathroom after bathing and shaving, so I quietly slipped out of our cottage to procure some badly needed coffee. When I returned with the tray carrying two cups, the bed was empty and sounds of running bathwater, accompanied by wisps of steam, were escaping from under the bathroom door.

I opened the blinds covering our big window and sat at the table to enjoy my coffee and the dawning of a new day—a day I hoped Clara and I would remember for the rest of our lives. Clara showed up about fifteen minutes later wearing a white silk slip. She sat next to me at the table and picked up her cup.

She smiled at me and said, "Good morning, darling. I must say you're looking exceptionally chipper today."

"And with good reasons," I said as I leaned over to steal a quick kiss from the most famous lips in America.

Clara cocked her head to one side as she often did to express puzzlement. "Oh? Would you care to tell me what those good reasons might be?"

"You mean besides spending the day with the sexiest, cutest and most desirable woman I have ever known or imagined knowing?"

She put on her wide-eyed look of surprise expression. "My

goodness!" Then she added a coy little grin and said, "Yes, darling, in addition to all of that."

"I was thinking we could enjoy a relaxing day topped off with dinner at the Pierpont Inn tonight."

Clara's grin widened. "That would be lovely, Eddie. Now I feel just as chipper as you look. See what happens when you share your innermost thoughts with me? What else do you have planned for us today?"

"Well . . . ah . . . I thought we might make some telephone calls."

In a playful tone of voice, she said, "And to whom do you think we should make these telephone calls?"

"It seems like a good idea to let my folks know we plan to pay them a visit tomorrow. Then, I thought you might like to chat with Ruth—you know, to tell her the coast is clear and all."

She leaned her elbows on the table, rested her chin on her folded hands, and put on a wise expression. "Eddie, you might as well know right now that I can always tell when you're keeping secrets from me. You're up to something, and you'd best tell me what it is before you get yourself into trouble, mister."

My gaze had wandered to Clara's bare shoulders, covered only by the thin white straps of her slip, and lower to the fullness of her barely concealed breasts. Clara thunked me on the forehead with an index finger then pointed to her face. "And keep your eyes up here, not down there!"

Feeling properly chastised, I put on a guilty expression. "Gosh, I can't get away with anything, can I?"

"You certainly can't, so you might as well just fess up. What's going on in that sneaky mind of yours?"

"Nope, you will just have to wait and see what happens."

Clara pouted. "Well, pooh on you." Then switching to a haughty expression, she added, "Besides, I already know what you're up to."

"Then we'll just have to see if you're right or not."

Glancing at my wristwatch, I saw that the day was progressing rapidly. It was already nine o'clock. I said, "In half an hour I'm going out to take care of a small errand, so I suggest you make yourself decent in case you have any visitors while I'm gone."

I thought I saw an instant of concern pass over Clara's face, but she quickly covered it up with an I-don't-care expression. "Go ahead, desert me. See if I care. Maybe some handsome fellow who doesn't keep secrets will show up and sweep me off my feet. That would teach you a lesson!"

I agreed that it certainly would and took another swallow of now tepid coffee. Clara set to the chore of putting on her skirt-sweater outfit with a bright pink blouse.

About nine-forty she accompanied me out of cottage number nine and, while I started the Cadillac, Clara walked over to the office for a second cup of coffee. As I left the Casa del Pacifico, she was sitting at one of the tables outside the office with her book and coffee. She gave me a wave and a smile to let me know that she was not holding a grudge about my secret-keeping.

Krause Jewelers was located on the northeast corner of Main and Oak Streets. As I pulled to the curb in front of the store, I saw a tall, slender, distinguished-looking gentleman unlock the front door and turn over a small cardboard sign in the window so that it now read "Open" instead of "Closed."

I entered the store and, from behind a glass counter where he was arranging a display, the distinguished-looking fellow said, "Good morning, sir. How can we help you this morning?"

"Good morning. I am in need of a wedding set and Ambrose DeBoyce at the Casa del Pacifico Motor Inn recommended your shop as being the best place to find what I'm looking for."

"Oh, yes, Mister DeBoyce is one of our valued customers." He offered his hand and said, "I'm the owner, Edgar Krause."

I shook his hand and said, "Edward Markham. Pleased to meet you, Mister Krause."

"Likewise. Might I presume that, because you know Ambrose from the Casa del Pacifico, that you are visiting our fair city rather than a local resident?"

"You may. I live in Los Angeles and I came up for a weekend vacation."

"Wonderful! Welcome to Ventura!"

"Thank you, Mister Krause."

"Now, I believe you said you were interested in a wedding set—engagement and wedding rings?"

"That's correct. I'm looking for something nice, but not pretentious, if that helps any."

Krause nodded knowingly. "Then your timing couldn't be better. The current trend is moving away from the more elaborate multi-stone styles of the past few years to simpler settings designed to show off a larger, single diamond to its best advantage, and we have just received an assortment of the newer styles. May I inquire as to the price range you would prefer?"

Remembering the additional amount I had withdrawn from my bank on the day we purchased the Cadillac—ten one-hundred-dollar bills now carefully tucked into my billfold—I said, "I was hoping to find something around one thousand dollars."

Krause's eyebrows went up slightly at the mention of a grand. "I see. Then you are looking for something of the finest quality."

"Yes, Mister Krause, this is one time when only the best will do."

He explained that, since he had just opened for the day, he had not yet removed the more exclusive pieces from the safe, but it would only take a few moments for him to assemble a collection of the most recent styles for my consideration. While he went off to fetch the rings, I looked around the store. Display cases were lined up along three of the four walls, with a fourth case containing what I took to be mostly costume jewelry occupying a space in the middle of the room. The display case across the rear of the store was lower than the others so customers could sit in chairs and make their selections in comfort.

The store's decor was mostly pale pink and beige, with dark maroon accents on the crown moldings and ceiling pillars. It was all very tasteful and understated, a rather surprising combination in a tourist town that would be full of vacationing families during the summer.

I turned to take a seat at the low display counter across the back of the room and felt Bill Wellman's forty-five give me a poke. I could only imagine what Mister Krause would think if he knew I was carrying the pistol. Hopefully, it would not choose the wrong moment to slip from the waistband of my trousers.

Edgar Krause returned from the backroom of his shop carrying a small silver tray with a black velvet insert that held two rows of six wedding sets tucked into slots in the material. He set the tray down on the low counter in front of me and said, "Take a few moments to look them over, Mister Markham. See if one doesn't strike you as just the right design."

I slowly moved my gaze over the glittering array of facets among shining gold and platinum settings. When I got to the row closest to me, my eyes came to rest on a delicate and unique setting that immediately made me think of Clara. Pointing, I said, "May I take a closer look at that set?"

Krause said, "Certainly," as he moved the wedding band and engagement ring to the front of the tray.

A gold crown-shaped setting was perched atop the engagement ring with something like a buttress on each side. Two tiny circles of gold filled the openings created by the buttresses on each side of the mounting. The upper edges of the ring were engraved with a delicate art deco design. But the most beautiful part of the engagement ring was the diamond. It glittered with a radiance that nearly took my breath away.

The wedding band was by comparison quite simple. The top surface of the band was smooth, polished gold while the edges were engraved with the same delicate deco pattern as the engagement ring.

After I had stared at the set for a few moments, Edgar Krause said, "You have excellent taste, Mister Markham. The diamond is what we commonly refer to as a European cut and weighs two-point-five carets. The rings are pure ninety-nine percent fine twenty-four karat gold. All of the engraving was done by hand. Would you care to take a look through the loupe?"

I said I would, although I doubted that my limited expertise would give me much appreciation of what I saw. Holding the loupe to my right eye, I slowly turned the engagement ring around in my other hand. The precision was amazing in something so tiny. I might not be a jewelry expert, but I recognized quality when I see it.

Returning the loupe and the ring to Krause's tray, I said, "It looks beautifully made. What is the price of this set?"

Krause noted some pencil figures on a tiny cardboard tag attached to each of the rings by a short string. Jotting the figures on a pad of paper, he made some calculations and said, "The total for the set, including a lovely presentation box is one-thousand-and-seven-dollars."

"Well, Mister Krause, you just sold an engagement set."

Edgar was obviously pleased. "Wonderful, Mister Markham. Now what about the sizing of the rings? Do you know the lady's ring size?"

I had been so enthralled by the beauty of the rings, I had completely forgotten about the matter of sizing. I showed Krause the slip of paper on which I had drawn the circle from Clara's ring. "This is the inside circumference of a ring she currently wears on her left ring finger."

Krause took the slip of paper and compared my circle to the inside diameter of the two rings. "It looks as if we're in luck, Mister Markham. The circle appears to be an exact match to the rings, which are a size six. Of course, we'll be happy to make any necessary adjustments in size, but the rings should fit quite adequately until then."

"Terrific."

He removed a dark maroon presentation box from a drawer on

his side of the counter. When Krause opened the box, I saw a gold "K-J" monogram on the white silk under the lid. He carefully slipped the two rings into the slots provided for them and held the box up for my examination. It looked pretty swell to me and I said so.

"Very well, Mister Markham, I will prepare the bill of sale. How do you plan to pay for the set?"

"In cash."

Krause's eyebrows went up again on hearing that piece of news. Thinking he might be concerned about whether I actually had that much cash with me, I removed the folded stack of one-hundred-dollar bills, along with a five and two ones from my billfold. Setting the cash on the counter in front of Krause, I said, "There you are, one-thousand and seven dollars."

By eleven, or a few minutes after, I was back in the Cadillac with the precious dark maroon box safely tucked away in my overnight case behind the seat. As I drove back to the Casa del Pacifico, my mind replayed for the umpteenth time the events that had led me to this point just hours from asking Clara Bow to become my wife.

It is quite true that those events spanned only two weeks' time, and to someone who saw only the calendar it would surely seem as if Clara and I were rushing into something. The truth of the matter, though, was that during the last nine days of those two weeks we had been through pure hell—a horrifying nightmare of events that forced us into an intimacy of a sort few experience. And during those nine days we had come to know each other to a far greater extent than most couples achieve in months or even years.

That was how I became intimately acquainted with the real Clara—an intelligent, thoughtful and loving woman who needed me in her life as much as I needed her in mine. More than once during the past nine days we had come within a hair's breadth of losing those lives, a truth that gave me absolute confidence in our ability to survive anything the future might hold in store for us. Few marriages, I would wager, are built upon such a rugged foundation of faith and assurance.

Thirty-Eight

Clara was still sitting in front of the office when I got back to the Casa del Pacifico, but she had abandoned her book and appeared to be enjoying the view through the court's entrance. When she saw the Caddy, however, she jumped up and gave me an enthusiastic wave. By the time I had parked, she was waiting for me at our cottage door.

"Welcome home, Eddie. I missed you!"

Hugging her, I said, "Good. That means you're hooked."

She grinned broadly. "I guess I am. Do you know that, besides the time you and C. K. were gone yesterday, this is the first time in a week we've been apart for more than a few minutes?" Then, switching to her coy expression, Clara asked, "Did you get your 'errand' run okay?"

"Yup, all done."

"Good, then you can buy me lunch before I pass out from hunger."

"All right, kiddo, what kind of food are you in the mood for?"

Going back to her grin, Clara said, "The kind we eat!"

"Then I know just the place."

The restaurant I had in mind was one I had passed earlier on my way to Krause Jewelers. In fact, it was in the same block as Krause's shop. The eatery, known as El Patio Restaurant, was located at the center of a small two-story shopping court built in the style of a quaint Spanish village.

Following a muy delicioso lunch of chicken enchiladas, we strolled south on Main Street, looking at the shops and businesses in the heart of downtown Ventura. I chose south as our direction, because I did not want to take a chance on Clara noticing Krause's and wanting to go in for a look-see.

Leaving the downtown area, I drove south on California Street and continued to the point where it dead-ended at the beach in front of a large three-story block-shaped building that turned out to be the Ventura Bathhouse and Auditorium. The parking area in front of the bathhouse was crowded, as was the beach beyond it. Still, the sunshine and salt air were too inviting not to take at least a short stroll, so Clara kicked off her shoes and off we went traipsing through the sand.

Looking out at the happy beach-goers, who were engaged in all manner of activities, from sunbathing to picnicking to tossing beach balls around, Clara said, "Gosh, I haven't been to a beach in years. As a kid I used to go to Brighton Beach in Brooklyn with my first boyfriend, but this is much nicer—all clean and pretty."

"Even with all these people?"

"Sure! Beaches are supposed to be full of people having fun. What else are they good for?"

I chuckled at her perspective on beaches. "I guess you're right, kiddo. I just never thought of it in quite that way."

"See, mister? You stick with me and you'll learn all kinds of stuff."

After about fifteen minutes, I stopped and balancing first on one leg and then the other, I dumped the accumulation of sand from my shoes and said, "What do you say we turn around and head back to that bath house where we parked the car? I saw some public telephones in front of the place and we still need to make our calls."

Clara thought that was a good idea, so we turned around and retraced our steps. About halfway back we met a young couple walking arm and arm in the opposite direction. I noticed that the woman, an attractive redhead who wore her hair in the same style as Clara, was staring intently at us, or more accurately, she was staring at Clara.

I saw the woman say something to her young man, and then as we came abreast of them, she turned toward us and to Clara said, "Excuse me ma'am, but aren't you Clara Bow, the movie actress?"

Clara glanced at me and I nodded, indicating that I didn't see any harm in her answering the woman's question. She smiled and said, "Yes, that's me."

The young woman and her beau both got excited expressions on their faces and the boy said, "Gosh, Miss Bow, we love your movies!"

The girl added, "Yes! We think you're just the cat's whiskers!"

Clara grinned back at them and said, "Thanks, kids. I'm always glad to meet fans."

Gushing, the girl said, "Oh, you're so nice! I'm Lizzy and this is my boyfriend Walter. Could we please have your autograph?"

"Sure, kids. What would you like me sign?"

Walter patted his pockets and came up with a color picture postcard showing an aerial view of Ventura. "Here, we got this to send to friends back home in Fresno, but we can get another. This is way more important!"

Lizzy said, "I have something to write with." She dug around in her handbag and found a dark blue Sheaffer fountain pen.

As Clara wrote a short note on the back of the postcard, Lizzy looked at me. "Hi, mister. Are you anybody?"

I couldn't help laughing and she turned beet red. "Oh, I'm sorry, mister. I didn't mean . . . ."

"That's okay, Lizzy, and to answer your question, no, I'm nobody famous."

At that moment Clara finished writing and said, "Don't let him fool you, kids. This is the author, Eddie Markham."

Lizzy said, "Wow, an author? Could we please have your autograph, too, Mister Markham?"

Clara grinned at me as she handed over the postcard and fountain pen. I looked at what she had written. In a neat hand, the note said, "To my very special friends, Lizzy and Walter- Have fun at the beach! Love always, Clara Bow."

Below that I scrawled, "Lizzy and Walter- Best wishes, E. J. Markham." As I wrote, Lizzy said, "When we get back home I'm going to the library and check out one of your books!"

I handed the postcard and fountain pen back to Lizzy, and Walter looked over her shoulder as they read what we had written. Walter said, "That's great! We met that actor, Douglas Fairbanks once, but he wasn't nearly as nice as you!"

Clara laughed. "Next time I see Doug, I'll tell him he should be nicer to his fans. Now, kids, if you'll excuse us, we have to be going."

Lizzy said, "Oh, sure. We don't want to keep you, Miss Bow. Thanks for talking to us and for the autograph and for being so nice!"

As we resumed our walk, Clara said, "I'm awfully sorry, Eddie. Sometimes that happens and I really hate to be mean to my fans."

"Don't worry about it, kiddo. Who knows, maybe I gained a new fan myself today."

The public telephones at the Ventura Bathhouse were located under an arched arcade that ran across the front of the building. I picked one and dialed O for the operator. When she answered, I explained that I was out of town and needed to make some long distance telephone calls, but had no change. I asked if it would be possible to bill the calls to my home telephone number in Los Angeles. The operator said she would be happy to do that, so I gave her my home number and then the first number I wished to call in Santa Barbara, California.

Millie picked up the telephone on the second ring and I said, "Hi, sis, its Eddie."

Sounding pleased to hear my voice, Millie said, "Hiya, big brother. Whatcha know?"

It was our standard telephone opening. My next line was, "Not much, sis."

She giggled and I said, "I'm calling because I'd like to stop by for a visit tomorrow and I wanted to see if you and the folks will be home."

"Gee, that sounds swell. It's been ages since you were here. I'll be home for sure. Let me ask mom if she and dad have plans. Hang on."

I heard a clunk and pictured her setting the handset on the small telephone table in the hall. A moment later she was back. "Eddie, mom and dad are going to church in the morning, but they're always home by eleven. Is that okay?"

"Sure, sis, that will work out just fine."

"Mom also said you should stay for Sunday dinner. She said about three o'clock."

"Tell mom I'd like that, but ask her to set two extra places instead of just one because I'm bringing someone with me to meet you all."

Millie had a suspicious note in her voice when she asked, "Male or female?"

I chuckled. "Female, sis."

"Oh? Could it be that my big brother is finally going to get me a sister-in-law?"

Clara was standing just outside the booth listening to my end of the conversation. She looked a little nervous. I gave her a wink and said, "That's a distinct possibility, sis."

"Well, aren't you the sly one? Tell me, who is this mystery woman with whom my big brother is so smitten?"

"Nope, sis, you'll just have to wait until tomorrow and be surprised, and believe me, you're gonna be surprised."

"Oh, Eddie, you're mean!"

"Heck, sis, you've known that all along. Tell mom and dad we'll get there around noon. See ya tomorrow."

I depressed the receiver hook to break the connection and signal the operator. To Clara I said, "All set, kiddo. They're expecting us for Sunday dinner. That okay with you?"

Clara's face lit up like a little girl. "Oh, that's swell, Eddie. I can't wait!"

I told the operator the next call I wanted to make was person-to-person to William Wellman at the Saint Anthony Hotel in San Antonio, Texas. While she was making the connection I glanced at my watch. It was almost two, which made it four o'clock in Texas. Hopefully, Bill was in his room or someplace in the hotel where he could be paged.

Wellman answered the telephone in his room and I said, "Hello, Bill, Eddie Markham here."

"It's about time I heard from you, you louse. Where the hell are you?"

"We're near Los Angeles. I was just calling to tell you Clara's in the clear now. Nobody is trying to kill her anymore."

"Well, that's good news. What the hell has been going on?"

I gave Wellman a condensed version of the story right up to and including what C. K. Mackie found out and the payoff to Ardizzone. When I finished, he said, "You're kiddin' me. It was the mob tryin' to kill Clara to collect twenty grand from her old man?"

"That's about the size of it."

"I guess that's not so surprising. We all know Clara's a hell raisin' slut. This just means she comes by it . . . ."

I saw red. "Wellman you don't know what the hell you're talking about, so shut your filthy mouth!"

Clara was standing a few feet away watching the beach, but when she heard that, she jerked her head around and looked at me in wide-eyed surprise. She started to say something, but closed her mouth and just stared at me.

"And another thing, Wellman, if I ever hear you talking like that again or treating Clara with anything but respect, you'll answer to me, and I guarantee you'll regret it!"

"Eddie, calm down for cryin' out loud. I was just . . . ."

"We're done, Bill. You owe me for twelve days. You can subtract the expense money you gave me if you think that's fair, but I'll expect a check by the end of next week. And you can send someone over to my office to pick up your Colt anytime after

Monday."

Wellman started to say something, but I broke the connection then clicked the receiver hook a couple of times to signal the operator one more time. While I was waiting, I said to Clara, "I'm calling Ruth's sister so you can tell her the good news that it's safe to come home. That okay?"

Clara still had a stunned look on her face. "Yes, but . . . ."

"Don't worry about Wellman."

The operator came back on the line and I gave her Esther Jackson's number in El Monte. When the call started ringing, Clara and I changed places and I walked across the covered arcade to look out at the ocean. I hoped it would have a calming effect. I had already upset Clara on a day I wanted to be perfect.

Clara and Ruth talked for quite a while. When their conversation finally ended, she came over and put her arm through mine. "Eddie, are you all right? What happened to get you so upset? I've never seen you like that."

I managed a small smile. "And, hopefully, you never will again. Wellman just made a snide remark I didn't care for and I told him so. Now, tell me how Ruth took the good news."

"She sounded really happy. I told her we would arrange to come out and pick her up, but she said she had promised to show her family my house, so they're all going to take a Sunday drive up there tomorrow.

"Ruth said she would get the house all ready for me, but I told her I wasn't exactly sure when I'd be back. Probably Monday night."

Half an hour later we were back at the Casa del Pacifico with Clara sitting in one of the armchairs reading and me at the desk bringing my journal up to date. That done, I walked over to the bed and sat next to Clara's chair.

She looked up with concern. "Eddie, darling, are you sure you're okay?"

"I'm fine now, honey. I'm sorry I got so angry, and that you had to hear what I told Wellman. I didn't mean to upset you. How 'bout we just put it behind us and get back to having a nice day?"

Clara nodded. "I just want you to understand that I know what kinds of things people like Bill Wellman say about me, and I can't really blame them because of the way the studio publicity people make me look.

"The thing is, I really don't care what Wellman or any of those jerks think about me, but the fact that you called him on whatever he said means everything to me. I'm not upset with you. You just proved all over again how much you love me. I could never be upset about that."

A few minutes before five Clara announced it was time to get ready for our night on the town and disappeared into the bathroom to do whatever women do to get ready for a night on the town. For me, the process was much simpler. I donned my freshly pressed brown suit, a clean white shirt, and a pale blue tie. The last steps in the getting ready process were slipping the dark maroon ring box into my jacket pocket and returning Wellman's pistol to my waistband for hopefully one of the last times.

When Clara returned, she was wearing the same Kelly green dress she had worn during our first trip to the Pierpont Inn. Standing in front of the dressing table mirror, she noticed my reflection watching her.

Clara turned around and gave me a happy smile. "What do you think, darling? Am I fit to be seen in public?"

"Kiddo, you're stunning. I guarantee every man in the room will be jealous of me tonight."

"Thank you for saying that, but I don't care what every man in the room thinks. I only care what you think."

"I think I'm the luckiest man in the world. You look fabulous."

While you would not expect it from a woman who is used to public adoration, Clara was actually blushing when she said, "All right, mister, let's go have some fun."

With her arm in mine, we walked into the lobby of the Pierpont Inn a few minutes before six. The same fellow was holding forth behind the maitre d's podium, but his welcome was something of a surprise.

"Good evening, Mister Markham. You're table is all ready. Please follow me."

As we followed him into the dining room, I wondered how he knew who I was on sight. The only thing I could figure was that Ambrose DeBoyce had given us a little build up when he made the reservation.

When maitre d' seated us at the very same table next to the window and adjacent to the dance floor, I got the feeling whatever build-up DeBoyce had given us wasn't so little. As our host placed our menus on the table, he said, "Isaac will be with you in just a moment. Enjoy your evening at the Pierpont Inn, Mister Markham."

Aside from there being quite a few more people in the dining room than on our last visit, the place looked exactly the same, right down to the sign on the grand piano informing us that The

Clippers would be playing for our listening and dancing pleasure. Outside our window, the cloudbank out over the ocean told me another glorious sunset was about to begin. I wondered how DeBoyce had arranged that trick.

Isaac, resplendent in his red vest, arrived at our table, saying, "Good evening, Mister Markham. Welcome back. Would you like to begin with Planter's Punch and, perhaps, our fresh crab cocktail?"

I glanced at Clara and she gave me a small nod. I said, "Isaac, that sounds like a wonderful way to begin the festivities."

"Very well, sir. I'll be back in just a minute with your drinks."

"Thank you, Isaac."

Clara reached across the table and took my hand. "Eddie, these people are treating us like royalty. It's just like at one of those fancy places in Hollywood."

"I think we have Ambrose DeBoyce to thank for that. I asked him to make this reservation for us and I suspect he did a little more than that."

Isaac returned to our table with two Planters Punches in tall goblets. They had a cheerful pinkish-orange glow about them that mirrored the colorful sunset beginning outside our window. As he set the glasses down, Isaac said, "Your crab cocktails will be along shortly."

"There's no hurry, Isaac. The night is young and we have all the time in the world."

He nodded politely and said, "Yes, sir."

As Isaac headed back toward the kitchen, I raised my glass and said, "Here's to a wonderful evening in the company of the loveliest and most delightful woman I have ever known. May this night bring with it memories we will cherish for a lifetime."

We clinked glasses, tasted our drinks, and Clara said, "You know, Eddie, that's almost exactly the same beautiful toast you made when we were here before, except you added the part about cherished memories this time. That makes it even more beautiful."

The sun chose that exact moment to begin it's descent behind the clouds, making the sunset erupt into a glorious display of reds, oranges and purples. Clara noticed the change and, staring out at the magnificent spectacle, she gasped, "Oh, look, darling. It's even more beautiful than the last sunset we saw here!"

I stared out at the magnificent colors for a moment, and then looked back at Clara. Her face was aglow with the amazing light coming through the window. If I had not already been head over heels in love with her, the wide-eyed, almost childlike wonder in her expression would have done the trick right then and there.

Clara noticed me staring at her and cocked her head to one side as if curious about what I found so interesting about her. I said, "You are absolutely radiant in this light. If such a thing is possible, it makes you even more beautiful."

With eyes full of love, she said, "Oh, Eddie, I hope you never get tired of looking at me the way you are right now. It makes me feel so special I could burst with joy."

Since I could not think of an intelligent reply, I just smiled and we went back to watching the sunset. Just as the vivid colors faded into darkness, Isaac arrived with our crab cocktails. After placing them before us, he said, "If you haven't decided on what to have for dinner yet, our chef has prepared a special entree' tonight that isn't on the menu, lobster ravioli in a tomato cream sauce with sautéed vegetables. It's one of his specialties."

I looked at Clara and said, "Lobster ravioli sounds interesting. What do you think?"

"It sounds wonderful to me. Let's try it."

The crab cocktails, Lobster ravioli, and a dessert of Italian pear spice cake made for a festive and delicious meal that fit the occasion perfectly. Then, just as a busboy cleared our table, The Clippers announced their presence and started things off with a romantic medley of popular ballads. A moment later, Isaac returned with another Planters Punch for Clara and coffee for me.

As he turned to leave our table, I said, "Isaac, we might step outside for a breath of fresh air, but we'll be back."

Clara gave me her cocked to one side look of curiosity, and Isaac said, "Certainly, sir. If you would like to take a stroll on the veranda, you can step out through that door in the corner beyond the dance floor."

Standing, I said, "How 'bout it, kiddo, feel like a little fresh air?"

Her curious look changed to a small smile that made me think Clara had a pretty good idea of what was coming. "That would be nice, Eddie."

The Pierpont Inn's veranda extended the full length of the dining room and overlooked the beach. Two large lights on the roof over our heads illuminated the breakers as they rolled up onto the sand, making them stand out in sharp contrast to the dark sea beyond.

About halfway down the veranda, next to a wooden bench between two of the dining room windows, Clara stopped and pointed. "Oh, look, darling! Those little glowing sea creatures are putting on another show for us! Isn't it beautiful?"

I looked where she was pointing and, sure enough, the dark areas between breakers were glowing with blue-green phosphorescence. "It is beautiful. Let's sit and watch for a bit."

Without the sun's warming effect, the air was cooling rapidly. I decided it would be a good idea to pop the question before it got too chilly to stay outside.

We sat close together on the bench and I took Clara's hands in mine. "Clara, I have something important I'd like to discuss with you."

I was certain from the tiny smile playing at the corners of her lips that she knew what I wanted to discuss. I had also noticed earlier that the rings she had been wearing on her left hand were now on her right hand. There was no fooling this girl.

Looking into her eyes, I said, "A few days ago you told me about a dream—a dream of sailing away to a place where people live in homey cottages with beautiful gardens and big back yards where kids could have fun and grow up being loved my their parents. Do you remember telling me about that?"

Clara nodded. "Yes, darling, I remember. It's a dream I've had for as long as I can remember."

"Well, I think it's a wonderful dream and nothing would make me happier than making that dream come true for the woman I love with all my heart. Clara, would you do me the honor of becoming my wife and helping me make that dream come true for both of us?"

With tears welling up in her soft brown eyes, Clara said, "Oh, yes, Eddie! Yes! Yes! Yes! There's nothing I want more in the whole world!"

Removing the dark maroon box from my jacket pocket, I said, "Then here's a little something to make it official."

I opened the box, removed the engagement ring, and slipped it on the ring finger of her left hand. It fit perfectly. Clara held her hand up to look at the ring and gasped. "Oh, Eddie, it's the most beautiful ring I've ever seen! It's stunning!"

Taking my future wife in my arms, I kissed her tenderly on the lips. I cannot remember a time in my life when I felt more joy in my heart than I did at that moment.

When we returned to our table in the dining room, The Clippers announced they were taking a short break. I seated Clara and walked over to the piano player, to whom I made a request. He nodded and promised to fill the request as soon as they started their next set of songs.

Clara and I spent the next fifteen minutes or so lost in each other. It pleased me more than I can say to see a contentment on her on her face I had never seen there before. If I had harbored any doubts at all about asking Clara to become my wife, her expression sent them scurrying like wispy clouds on a warm fall day.

When The Clippers returned, the piano player announced, "We're going to play a very special request now dedicated to a couple who only minutes ago became engaged right here at the Pierpont Inn. For Clara and Eddie, here is the beautiful Gershwin ballad, *Someone to Watch Over me.*"

The band began its introduction to the song and I stood, offering Clara my hand. She smiled a warm smile and we walked onto the dance floor. As we danced, she looked up and said, "Eddie, I feel almost like I'm dreaming, but if I am, please don't wake me because this is the most wonderful dream I've ever had."

Thirty-Nine

Noon – Sunday – September 26, 1926
Jerome & Eloise Markham Residence – Santa Barbara

The trees lining Chapala Street were bigger now, but otherwise, the three-story Victorian at 1632 looked just like it had when my folks moved there soon after my twelfth birthday. The house sat well back from the street behind a stone and wood fence. A narrow driveway ran along the right side of the house past bay windows at the front corner and off the dining room. The front porch and entry were on the left side of the house below a peek-roofed balcony outside the master bedroom. A tall, ornate brick chimney rose above the living room on the right side of the house.

Dark brown trim outlined the windows and eaves against a fresh coat of tan paint. A dormer-style window under another peaked roof off the third-floor bedroom was centered at the front of the house. This had been my personal and private window on the world during my teenage years.

During the hour-long drive up U.S. Highway 101 from Ventura, Clara had been unusually quiet. I thought I knew the reason, but I asked just to be sure. "Why so glum, kiddo?"

"I'm not glum, darling. I'm just a little nervous about meeting your family."

Even though I suspected that was the reason for her quiet mood, I still found it surprising that a woman who was used to performing on a film stage in front of an entire motion picture crew would be upset at the prospect of meeting three everyday people. The only explanation I could think of was that acting was just her job, whereas meeting my family was an event of deep personal importance to her.

Trying to put her mind at ease, I said, "Like I told you before, honey, they're going to love you just as I do. There's nothing to be nervous about."

"But they're so educated. I've never spent much time around such sophisticated people. I'm afraid I won't know how to act."

"Kiddo, just because you don't have a lot of book learning doesn't mean you aren't smart. You are. Just try to relax and be yourself. Besides, they'll probably be just as much in awe of meeting you as you are of meeting them."

"That's part of the problem. Supposing they have the same opinion of me that people like Bill Wellman have? They'll think you've taken up with some sort of wild floozy."

I almost laughed at her choice of words. "Clara, I doubt very much that my folks and Millie have any such opinions, and even if they did, spending ten minutes with you would be enough to convince them that you aren't at all that sort of person. Trust me about this. You'll see I'm right."

Pulling into the driveway, I had the distinct feeling my earlier pep talk had done little to alleviate Clara's fears. As I opened the passenger-side door of the Cadillac for her, I noticed her looking up at the somewhat imposing house with something like dread on her face.

By the time we reached the porch, Millie was already standing in the doorway. She ran out to give me a welcoming hug. "Eddie! It's so good to see you, big brother!"

Her enthusiasm darn near knocked us both off the porch, and as she hugged me, I felt her body stiffen a little. Into my ear she whispered, "Oh my gosh! Is that who I think it is?"

Disentangling myself from her overwhelming welcome, I grinned and said, "It might just be. Millie, meet Clara. Clara, this crazy woman is my little sister, Millie."

Millie ran over and eagerly shook Clara's hand. "Wow, Miss Bow, this is a real treat! I'm so excited to meet you!"

Smiling in a way that told me Millie's welcome was bolstering her confidence, Clara said, "I'm excited to meet you, too, Millie. Eddie has told me so many wonderful things about you."

My little sister gave me a suspicious look. "He has? Well, that has to be a first! Come on in and meet the rest of the family."

She took Clara by the hand and walked into the house, leaving me out on the porch like the forgotten man. I followed them into the foyer where Millie introduced Clara to dad. Mom and I exchanged hugs and she said, "Eddie, it's so good to have you home for a visit. We don't get to see you nearly often enough these days."

Dad gave Clara a slight bow from the waist and said, "Hello, Miss Bow. It is indeed a pleasure to make your acquaintance."

Millie then introduced Clara to mom. Mom's reply was more reserved, but still welcoming. "Good afternoon, Miss Bow. It's very nice of you to come all this way to visit us."

Smiling in obvious appreciation of the warm reception, Clara said, "Thank you all for making me feel so welcome, but please, won't you just call me Clara?"

Mom seemed to be warming up to Clara already. She said, "All right, Clara, come into the living room and make yourself to home."

Millie chimed in, "Yes, Clara, the living room is right over here," and trotted Clara out of the foyer. Mom followed along, leaving dad and me alone for the moment. Dad offered his hand, saying, "Welcome home, son."

I shook my father's hand, returning his warm, firm grip. "Thanks, dad. It's good to be here."

Never one to beat around the bush, dad said, "Now, before we go into the living room, help me understand the situation here. Millie said she thought the friend you were bringing to meet us might be your intended, and I could not help noticing a rather nice engagement ring on Miss Bow's hand. Was Millie's assessment accurate?"

"In a nutshell, yes, she gave you the straight story."

"Then congratulations, son. If I seem a little surprised by this turn of events, it is only because I was not aware that you were seeing anyone, as they say, 'seriously.'"

"I know this all seems rather sudden and I'm anxious to tell you about what's happened during that past few weeks leading up to our engagement, but it's a rather long and complicated story, so I hope you won't mind waiting until a little later to hear it."

"Not at all, son. All things in good time. Now, shall we see what the womenfolk are up to?"

In the parlor, Clara was sitting at one end of the tufted leather chesterfield with Millie at the other end and mom sitting across the coffee table from them in her favorite Morris chair. Mom was saying, ". . . it's quite an old house. We moved here in nineteen-ten, but the house was built before that. By the time we came here the house had been wired for electricity, but many other things have been modernized since then."

Seeing dad and me walk in, mom said, "Jerome, what year was this house built? Do you recall?"

Dad said, "Yes, dear. The house was constructed in eighteen-ninety-four."

In typical Victorian fashion, hand-carved woodwork was everywhere throughout the house, such as the ornate stair railings and newel posts, window and door frames, built-in shelves and cabinets, and the fireplace mantel. Clara seemed to find this elaborate woodwork enchanting.

"All of the detail work is beautiful, and you've taken such good care of it. It's like living in a fairytale home. I just love it!"

Mom said, "Thank you, Clara. We are rather proud of it, especially since newer homes are not nearly as nicely finished." Standing, she added, "Now, I must tend to dinner. Perhaps Millie and Eddie will take you on a tour of the house."

Clara nodded enthusiastically, and Millie said, "Sure! Come on, Clara, I'll show you around this museum."

I suspected Millie's enthusiastic invitation had more to do with getting her future sister-in-law all to herself than it did with the house. I hoped she would not put Clara on the spot with personal questions about how we met and such.

With Clara and Millie off on the grand tour, dad and I were once again left to our own devices. Dad suggested we make ourselves comfortable in his study.

The house was built with five bedrooms, two on the third floor, two on the second floor, and one on the ground floor. It was in this ground floor bedroom that dad created his study. The room was finished in dark wood paneling between built-in bookshelves that held a small library of books on the law and other subjects dad found interesting. Most of the highly polished hardwood floor was covered by an authentic Persian carpet in shades of gold and dark red.

The room was furnished with a large mahogany desk and tufted leather desk chair, in front of which there were two armchairs upholstered in dark red leather to match the carpet. It was in these two chairs that dad and I made ourselves comfortable.

Dad said, "Son, as you might imagine, you peaked my curiosity when you described the story of your engagement to that charming young woman as 'complicated.' If you are in a mood to tell me that tale now, I would enjoy hearing it."

"Sure, dad. I'd be happy to. I first met Clara only two weeks ago when I accepted a temporary consulting position offered me by a fellow flier I met in France during the war. His name is William Wellman and he directs motion pictures for the Lasky film company. Wellman was undertaking the production of a major motion picture about pursuit pilots during the war, and because of my wartime experiences, he thought I was someone on whom he could rely to help guarantee the accuracy of the scenes he would be filming."

I went on to describe the pertinent events of the past two weeks, from the strafing incident in Texas to delivering the money owed by Clara's father to mob boss, Joseph Ardizzone. I concluded the story by saying, "So even though Clara and I met only two weeks or so ago, we have been in each other's company almost continuously since that time, and have came to know each other better than most couples do in months of courting and what on the surface may appear to be a very short courtship is actually an extremely intense period of acquaintance."

Dad nodded. "And from your description, son, a rather intimate one, as well."

Feeling a little defensive, I said, "Yes, an intimate one as well, but given the circumstances, avoiding that intimacy would have put Clara at great risk. I can assure you, dad, we did nothing during that time that I would be ashamed to tell you."

"I believe I know you and your principles well enough to accept that without reservation, son, although I'm not sure others would be so inclined. That, however, is neither here nor there.

"As for the rest of your story, it seems we are quite fortunate to have you and Clara with us today. You took some rather great risks, although I would have been more surprised had you done otherwise."

"I take no great pride in any part of it. I simply did what I had to do."

Dad looked thoughtful for a long moment. "Edward, I do not intend to meddle in your affairs, but as your father, I must ask if you have considered the possibility that Miss Bow's feelings for you might be more out of gratitude than love."

"Yes, dad, I've given that possibility a good deal of thought, and it has been the subject of our conversations on more than one occasion. Clara readily admits to feeling grateful, but she has also proven that her interest in me precedes the first attempt on her life in Texas. Moreover, she has discussed in considerable detail her feelings for me.

"From childhood on, Clara's life has been difficult. It is only through determination and persistence that she achieved success, and yet Clara is abandoning her acting career for marriage and parenthood. That she is committed to doing so is ample proof of her desire to build a new life with me."

I have never been able to completely read dad's feelings. He is adept at keeping a courtroom face that masks his thoughts, so I had no clear indication of his thoughts on the matters we were discussing. I could only hope he understood the situation.

"Edward, I have one other concern relative to Clara. That her father became indebted to the underworld is not a positive sign. That connection has already brought you into contact with some undesirable people. I would hope that the future holds no further such entanglements."

"It won't, dad. Clara and her father are quite different people. She realizes he is largely responsible for much of her unpleasant childhood and that his only interest in her now is as a meal ticket. While in some ways it is a shame, she has broken all of her connections with him and is determined that he will no longer be part of her life. It saddens me that she doesn't have the benefit of a loving family, but I have hopes that you and mom and Millie may someday fill that void in her life."

Dad appeared to consider that idea for a moment. "Well, Edward, it seems to me you have entered into this relationship with as much thought and deliberation as the circumstances allow. While I cannot say I have no reservations in the matter, I will say I have confidence in you. For that reason I offer my congratulations and best wishes for the success of your union."

"Thank you, dad. I think you know your blessing means a great deal to me."

Apparently confident that he had performed his fatherly duties, dad suggested we join the rest of the family before they came looking for us. We found mom, Millie and Clara in the kitchen, where Clara had donned an apron and was receiving instruction from mom on how to remove the meat from the cooked chicken.

When she saw us, Clara gave me a big, bright smile. "Eddie, this is grand! I'm learning all kinds of cooking tips from your mom."

Stepping between mom and Clara, I put an arm around each of them and said, "Good! You couldn't have a better teacher in the art of cooking. Mom's Sunday dinners are known far and wide."

Mom laughed and said, "Oh, go on with you, Eddie. Besides, it's high time we started churning the ice cream for dessert. Why don't you and Millie take Clara out and show her how that's done. The mixture is in the icebox and ready to go."

With astonishment Clara said, "You make your own ice cream?"

Grinning a sly grin, Millie said, "You bet we do, and it's the best you ever tasted. We'll even let you turn the churn."

Giving Millie a look of mock reproach, I said, "We'll all take a turn at the cranking, especially you, Millie. It's one of your greatest skills."

Millie stuck her tongue out at me, removed the galvanized cylinder of ice cream mix from the ice box, and marched out through the backdoor. Clara and I followed her to the garage where a fresh block of ice sat in a tin tub next to the ancient ice cream churn over which I labored many hours as a kid.

Picking up a hammer from the workbench, I began breaking up ice while Millie instructed Clara on how the mixing cylinder fit into the churn. When I had created enough ice chips to get the churning started, I showed Clara how to fill the churn around the cylinder with alternating layers of rock salt and ice.

"Clara, the rock salt helps keep the ice in the churn cold while the paddles inside the cylinder mix up the ingredients—milk, cream, sugar, eggs, and fruit or flavoring—and keep them in contact with the metal cylinder walls, which gets freezing cold from the ice."

"Gosh, that looks complicated!"

Millie replied, "Oh, he's just making it sound that way so you'll think he's smart. It's really very simple."

Clamping the cranking mechanism to the top of the churn, I gestured toward the crank and said, "Okay, Miss Know-It-All, show us how simple it is."

Millie began turning the crank and said, "Okay, watch and be amazed!"

While I returned to the chore of ice chipping, Millie and Clara took turns at the crank. During the next forty-five minutes we regularly added more ice and rock salt to the churn, and the crank grew harder and harder to turn.

Millie explained, "The crank gets harder to turn as the mixture in the cylinder gets colder. The harder it is to turn the crank, the closer we are to having ice cream."

I watched Clara as we worked, and I could tell from her expressions that she was thoroughly enjoying the ice cream making process. She reminded me of my excitement during my first turns at the crank as a boy. The almost childlike amazement Clara experienced over something as simple as making ice cream was one of her most endearing charms. To my way of thinking, the current societal trend toward 'sophistication' was vastly over rated.

At three o'clock we were all seated around the dining room table and, after dad said grace, we dug into mom's delicious chicken and dumplings. I always enjoy Sunday dinners with my family, but seeing Clara at the table added a special warmth to the occasion.

Part of that feeling grew out of the family conversation about day-to-day subjects that had no great significance beyond the dinner table, but nonetheless drew us together. That Clara was welcomed into that conversation by the rest of my family gave me a sense of joyous wellbeing. This, I thought, is how life is supposed to be.

Dessert was an especially enjoyable experience because it consisted of mom's wonderful peach cobbler topped with the ice cream Millie, Clara and I had churned. When dinner was done and we had all shared in the chore of clearing the table, mom insisted that we leave the dishwashing for later and retire to the parlor where we could be comfortable.

Once everyone was seated, I stood and said, "Mom, dad, Millie, I have an announcement to make."

Teasing, Millie said, "Well, it's about time!"

That got a chuckle out of everyone and put me at ease. Even though they all knew what was coming, I had their rapt attention. "Last night was a very special occasion; for it was last night that I asked Clara to become my wife and she made me the happiest man on earth by accepting my proposal."

Dad said, "Well, congratulations, Clara and Edward! This calls for a toast."

While dad poured dollops of his favorite brandy into snifters and mom looked a little wistful, Millie launched a barrage of questions. "When is the wedding? Where are you going to have it? Are you going to stay in Los Angeles after you're married?"

Father put an end to the questions by raising his glass. "Here's to the marriage of Clara and Edward. May their new little family be equally blessed with the love and happiness my dear Eloise and I have shared these many years."

Forty

9:00 A.M. – Monday – September 27, 1926
Office of Jesse Lasky, Paramount Studios, Hollywood

Plain, soft features behind a pair of round wire-frame spectacles gave Jesse Lasky more the appearance of a bookkeeper than one of Hollywood's first motion picture tycoons. There was a predatory glint in Lasky's eyes, though, that made it clear this man was no bookkeeper.

When Clara and I arrived for her ten o'clock meeting with him, Lasky was holding court in what I thought might be temporary quarters on the ground floor of the new administration building alongside the studio gate at Marathon and Bronson. As a general rule tycoons prefer their offices up high so they can better survey their domains.

Upon spotting Clara, Lasky jumped up and rushed to embrace her. "Clara, darling, it's so good to see you. You had us all terribly worried."

Shrugging out of the hug Lasky was trying to give her, Clara said, "Yeah, I could tell how worried you were." Lasky was making a point of ignoring me, but Clara put an end to that. "Mister Lasky, I think you already know Mister Edward Markham."

Lasky glared at me. "Yes. Mister Markham and I spoke via the telephone just the other day. Now, let's get down to business. Take a seat . . . both of you."

The last part of his comment seemed to be Lasky's concession to the fact that he was stuck with me whether I was welcome or not. While Clara and I sat in a pair of comfortable leather guest chairs, Lasky sat at his desk and held up a sheet of paper. "This is a long-term pre-production schedule for your next four films, beginning with that Elinor Glyn project, IT, after you finish . . . ."

Clara interrupted. "Well, you can toss that schedule in the rubbish because after I finish *Wings*, I'll make one more picture for you, then I'm through with acting."

If that pronouncement surprised Lasky, it didn't show. As if he was addressing a child, Lasky said, "No, no, Clara, darling, that isn't how it works. We have a contract. You cannot just stop whenever you want."

Clara said nothing. She simply turned her head and looked at me. That was my cue. Looking the man straight in the eye, I said, "Lasky, four attempts to kill Clara were made during the past few days and all of them were planned and carried out by Paramount employees and the Los Angeles mob. I've kept a very complete journal with documentation to back it all up. Unless we get some cooperation from you in this matter, your goose is cooked."

Lasky gave me a look that was somewhere between a sneer and a grin. "You're bluffing, Markham. If you had that kind of evidence you would have handed it over to the police by now. You've got nothing."

I smiled back at him. "You're right, Lasky. I've got little that would convince a courtroom jury, but the court of public opinion is another matter. I occasionally write feature articles for the Hearst newspapers, and I'm wondering what their readers would think about a studio with mob connections that would attempt to murder one of its most popular actors. That's just exactly the kind of story Hearst thrives on."

"That's blackmail, Markham!"

"Right again. And we haven't even mentioned the U. S. Army's investigation when they connect Billy Blaylock with Paramount, which I can make happen with a single telephone call. Like I said, your goose is cooked, Lasky."

The conversation from that point on isn't worth repeating. Lasky didn't like it, but he ultimately decided releasing Clara from her contract was the least costly way out of the jam B. P. Schulberg had created for him. After a letter to that effect was dictated and signed, Clara and I drove up to my place in Silver Lake.

10:45 A.M. – Monday – September 27, 1926
Edward Markham Residence, Silver Lake District

Built three years ago on a hillside within walking distance of the Silver Lake reservoir for which the area is named, my little Spanish bungalow has only two bedrooms and less than 900 square feet—a fact which requires that I keep things neat and tidy.

Clara was fascinated by all the custom cabinets and other built-in spaces I had installed to store things out of sight and out of the way. It's a cozy place for one, but would be crowded for two, and it certainly wouldn't do as a place to raise kids.

Outside, the bungalow was surrounded by a high hedge with front and rear gates. Because of the hillside location, the garage and my office were located under the house. There were also decks off the back of the house on both levels with a wooden staircase connecting the two. We sat on the upper deck enjoying the view of the hills behind the bungalow and we made plans.

First, we discussed our wedding. Clara was of a mind to keep the ceremony simple and homey, which suited me just fine. She even had a location in mind. "Do you think your mother and father would let us have the ceremony and reception in their home?"

"I'll ask, but I'm pretty sure nothing would please mom more, and Millie will be overjoyed."

"Oh good!"

Then Clara looked thoughtful for quite a while before saying, "Eddie, I don't know much about planning weddings, but I think the bride's father is supposed to walk her down the aisle, and I don't want my father anywhere near my wedding. Would it be all right to ask C. K to do it?"

Her question took me by surprise at first, but after thinking about it for a while, the idea made perfect sense. C. K. and Helen Mackie impressed Clara as the ideal married couple—the kind of people she would pick for parents if she had that choice. And because they have no children of their own, C. K. might get a kick out of walking an "adopted" daughter down the aisle.

"He might even put on a civilian monkey suit, as he calls them, for the occasion."

Clara's face lit up. "Do you really think he would do it?"

Nodding, I said, "You made quite an impression on C. K. because you aren't at all what he expected from dealing with motion picture people in the past, and he puts a lot of faith in his impressions of people. Oh, he'll grumble about getting gussied up, but C. K. will march you down the aisle with pride."

During the next few weeks we spent as much time as we could together with a schedule by which Clara stayed at her place during the week when they were shooting scenes for Wings and stayed with me in Silver Lake on the weekends she didn't have to work.

While she was busy acting, I dove into the rewrites for my new book. It was a busy time, but a happy one. Clara was getting a big kick out of making plans for the occasion. Among the other decisions made was the date—Saturday, October 30—the pastor who would perform the ceremony, and the flavor of the cake— white cake with strawberry frosting.

Then there was the question of our honeymoon. We only had a few days free before Clara would have to get back to the studio, so I suggested a trip to Santa Catalina Island just off the southern California coast. It was the closest place I knew where you could go for a few days and feel a million miles away. And since days were typically clear and sunny this time of the year, I suggested we fly over in the Bristol. We devised a plan whereby Clara would take the train to Santa Barbara with most of our luggage Friday morning and I would fly the Bristol up after a meeting scheduled for Friday afternoon. That would allow us to take off for Catalina right after the reception on Saturday and spend a little more time on the island.

We also made weekend trips up to Santa Barbara for the purposes of obtaining a marriage license and working out details for the ceremonies with my folks. In truth, dad and I were mostly observers on these occasions.

3:00 P.M. – Friday – October 29, 1926
Edward Markham Residence, Silver Lake District

The big weekend finally arrived, and as I dressed for work, I hummed a song that was on my mind the day it all began: Once again I was "Sitting on top of the world, just rolling along. Just rolling along."

THE END

Afterword

In an item dated November 1, 1926, the *Examiner's* Thomas Wodehouse reported, *"The last known sighting of missing aviator and author Edward Markham was about three P.M. last Friday afternoon. Reportedly, he was departing DeMille airfield in Los Angeles for a trip to Santa Barbara in his two-passenger biplane."*

The next time anyone saw Eddie Markham he was still in the wreckage of his Bristol on a hillside southeast of Santa Barbara. When search parties found the ship, Markham was dead, having succumbed to injuries sustained in the crash.

According to weather reports for Friday, October 29, 1926, an unusually large and heavy layer of marine fog came ashore along the Ventura-Santa Barbara coast late that afternoon. Accident investigators speculated that, despite being an experienced pilot, Markham flew into the fog, miscalculated his position, and descended into the hillside.

Clara and the Markham family finally learned of Eddie's fate late Saturday afternoon at the Markham residence which was decorated for a much happier occasion. Clara's reaction and the events of the next few weeks were described by Millie in her letter to a cousin.

Dear Cousin Emma,

I hope you can forgive me for taking so long to bring you up to date on things here. As you can no doubt imagine, losing Eddie comes as a terrific shock to all of us.

Of the family, Miss Bow (Clara) had the most profound response to the news. She was sitting on the chesterfield in our parlor, and when the sheriff's deputy told us they had found

Eddie, Clara turned white as a sheet, started to stand, and fainted dead away to the floor.

We sent for the family doctor, who upon examining Clara, admitted her to a small private clinic nearby and ordered peace and quiet for treatment of shock. Clara spent five days at the clinic and I visited her every day. Most of that time was spent with me chatting about anything cheerful I could think of while Clara stared out across the ocean outside her window. On one particularly clear day we could see the channel islands from her room, and when she noticed them, Clara pointed and said, "He was going to take me there . . . across the ocean to a wonderful place . . . ."

I don't know what she was thinking or exactly what Eddie had told her, but whatever promise he made was obviously very important to her. I tell you, Emma, there must be nothing finer than to be loved as much as Clara and Eddie loved each other. I could see it in their eyes when they were together and in Clara's eyes as she sat there missing him.

We held the services for Eddie on Friday and Clara sat with us in the funeral chapel's family room. Afterwards, Clara gave each of us a warm hug, as if she was holding onto the only family she would ever have. Maybe that's how she saw us, but despite our efforts, mom and I could not convince Clara to stay longer.

Saturday morning my folks said goodbye to Clara at the house and I took her to the Southern Pacific station. Standing on the platform outside her train window, I watched large tears fill her big brown eyes and roll down her cheeks. Then, as the train began to move, Clara touched the glass with a finger in the same way she had pointed toward a magical island where my brother promised her they would live a wonderful life together.

Those who have read a fair and objective Clara Bow biography, like David Stenn's *Clara Bow ~ Runnin' Wild*, know she never got to that magical island, instead spending her final years as a recluse in a Culver City rental cottage. Would her life have been different if that fogbank had not come ashore when it did in 1926? After getting to know Eddie's Clara, I like to think so.

Could it all have happened just as Edward Markham described it? Again, I like to think so, but before you make up your mind, take a look at the postcard below. It was found in a Visalia, California antiquarian bookstore by a collector who recognized Eddie Markham's name. The back is severely damaged, but . . . .

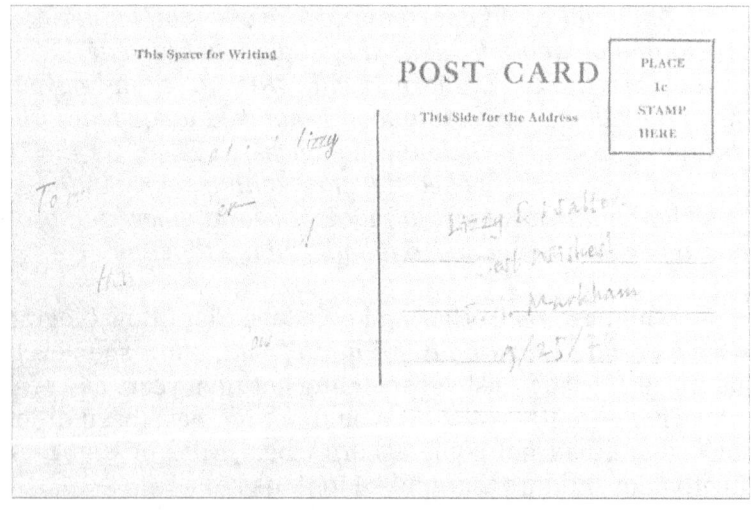

SOMEONE TO WATCH OVER ME

Ira Gershwin   George Gershwin

There's a somebody I'm longing to see.
I hope that he turns out to be
Someone to watch over me.

I'm a little lamb who's lost in the wood.
I know I could always be good
To one who'll watch over me.

Although he may not be the man some girls think of
As handsome, to my heart he carries the key.

Won't you tell him all my love I will save.
I'd be his slave. Oh, how I crave
Someone to watch over me.

Meet H. P. Oliver

H. P. Oliver began his career with a degree in journalism from San Jose State University and spent the next twenty-some years writing award-winning entertainment and educational media. Now he applies his creativity and imagination to writing historical mysteries.

About mystery writing, Oliver says, "To be truly engrossing, a mystery needs a little meat on its bones—something more than just figuring out who done the evil deed. Taking a story back in time or even basing it on actual historical events is a great way to endow a good yarn with even more color and depth. Historical periods and locations give the writer an opportunity to take most readers where they've never been before."

H. P. Oliver lives in northern California and spends much of his time working on projects throughout the western states. In addition to his love of history, Oliver's interests range from vintage film to restoring classic cars.

For information about H. P. Oliver's books, including synopses, previews, video trailers, and purchase links, visit his fan site at www.HPOliver.com, where you will also find illustrated history articles and other fascinating features. Plan to stay a while!

Books By H. P. Oliver

CLASSIC MYSTERIES IN HISTORY

THE TRUTH BE TOLD
(E-book)

AND THE ANGELS SING
(E-book)

SILENTS!
(E-book & Paper)

GOODNIGHT, SAN FRANCISCO
(E-book & Paper)

WINGING IT
(E-book & Paper)

JOHNNY SPICER CAPERS

JOHNNY SPICER: THE FIRST CAPERS
(E-book)

PACIFICA
(E-book & Paper)

REVOLVER
(E-book & Paper)

TEMBO
(E-book & Paper)